Pawsitively Cursed

A Witch of Edgehill Mystery

Book Two

MELISSA ERIN JACKSON

Ringtai
PRESS

Ebook ISBN: 978-1-7324134-5-0
Paperback ISBN: 978-1-7324134-7-4

Front cover design by Maggie Hall.
Stock art via Designed by Freepik, iStockPhoto, Shutterstock.
Family tree designed by Drew Clark.
Interior design and ebook formatting by Michelle Raymond.
Paperback design and formatting by Clark Kenyon.

First published in 2019 by Ringtail Press.
www.melissajacksonbooks.com

To my favorite branches of my family tree: Mom,
Corey, and Sam

Previously, in Pawsitively Poisonous …

Edgehill, Oregon is home to a large population of friendly stray cats, the annual Here and Meow Festival, and Amber Blackwood, resident witch. Except no one in town knows that the curious items in her shop, The Quirky Whisker, are more than just clever toys and organic tinctures—they're crafted with magic.

Descended from two families of witches, Amber and her estranged cousin, Edgar, are Edgehill's only magical residents. When Amber and her sister Willow were teenagers, their parents died in a mysterious house fire. The tragedy was declared an accident, but Amber suspects her parents may have been murdered, victims of a fire set intentionally by a member of the cursed Penhallow witch clan.

Now an adult, Amber is comfortable in her routine life— that is, until the arrival of the town's new police chief. Even three years later, Chief Owen Brown is as suspicious of her as he was from day one. Amber knows he's unaware that she's a witch, but he clearly senses something … *different* about her.

So, when Melanie Cole, Amber's closest friend in Edgehill, is found poisoned with a vial of Amber's sleep tonic clutched in her hand, the chief is quick to suspect Amber. Soon, however, it's revealed the vial contained nothing but natural sleep remedies.

As the case proves more and more difficult for the chief to solve, especially once Amber's name is crossed off the short suspect list, the pair fall into an uneasy alliance. The chief is feeling the pressure to solve the homicide of one of Edgehill's beloved residents, and Amber is desperate to figure out who might be trying to frame her. The alliance, in part, is based on the chief's belief that Amber's odd behavior, and her tendency to know things she shouldn't, is due to psychic abilities. Amber allows the misconception, as it gives her closer access to information that will help her find Melanie's killer.

Digging into Melanie's past reveals she was having an affair with long-term Edgehill resident Derrick Sadler. A chance encounter between Amber and Derrick's daughter, Sydney, a child prodigy in fashion design, reveals that Whitney, Derrick's wife, lied about her alibi the day of Melanie's death. Whitney knew about the affair, giving her both motive and opportunity.

Thanks in part to Amber's sleuthing, the chief is able to apprehend Whitney. Finally, Amber thinks she and the chief might have something close to a friendship forming. But late one night, a few weeks later, Amber uses a flashy spell in her shop, and the chief witnesses it while standing out on the sidewalk. His wide-eyed expression tells her he saw it all. He hurries away, now knowing Amber's biggest secret.

CHAPTER 1

"Get back here!" Amber called, crawling on hands and knees after the toy lion that bucked and thrashed under her coffee table like an agitated bull. Every time she reached for it, the little thing jumped away from her on its tiny beige plastic paws. Amber wasn't quite sure what the little creature was up to—it seemed possessed, if she was quite honest with herself—but whatever it was, it couldn't be good.

Amber's specialty was using her magic to animate plastic toys she then sold in her shop below. But every once in a while—like now—one of the toys took on a personality of its own. And it was rarely a pleasant personality.

A low, guttural growl reverberated next to her, and she turned to see her cat, Tom, watching the flailing toy with unmitigated alarm, his pupils blown wide.

At the sound of Tom's distaste of the situation, the lion stilled, halting its little plastic meltdown, and focused its attention squarely on Tom.

Oh no. "Tom Cat," she said, voice low and even, "don't run. If you run, it'll chase you."

The tiny lion adjusted its posture, its feet solidly on the ground in a wide stance, threw its head back and roared. The sound was loud enough that Amber felt a slight vibration in the floorboards beneath her hands, but it wasn't a display she would have labeled terrifying or even awe-inspiring. Tom, however, arched his back, tail puffed out, and hissed with a ferocity that even made Amber flinch.

Tom took off in the other direction, nails scrabbling on the wooden floor as he struggled to find purchase to aid in his escape. He didn't have far to run in Amber's tiny studio apartment. The lion gave chase. The thing was surprisingly fast—a little *too* fast. Amber lunged for it as it went tearing past her, but her hands met only air.

"Hold still, Tom!" she called as she hopped to her feet, not sure where the cat was now. Another roar sounded from beneath the bed, followed by Tom hissing and spitting in response. The dust ruffle flapped as Tom went sprinting from his usual safe space, the tiny lion hot on his tail.

Amber scurried after them, yelling at the lion to stop and for Tom to calm down. They ran under the dining room table, wooden table and chair legs smacking together like discordant wind chimes. Amber darted around one side of the table, then the other, hardly able to keep up. The lion was no bigger than a cell phone and its teeth were made of plastic—they couldn't do that much damage. But she couldn't very well explain that to Tom.

Alley sat on the kitchen counter, keeping a reasonable distance while she watched with mild concern, her tail wrapped around her paws.

"Are you going to help your brother?" Amber asked.

Alley squinted her eyes closed.

Amber dropped to her knees again, just in time to see

the lion lunge for Tom's tail and chomp down on the tip of it. Tom screeched like he was being skinned alive, then bolted out from under the table, the horrible lion holding onto the end of Tom's tail even as the cat bucked and flailed, trying to dislodge it.

This was even worse than the time Scarlet the dragon had come to life, and then released a ball of flame that melted her own body just before that same flame set the curtains on fire. The dragon had terrified Tom, but hadn't gone after him directly, at least.

This lion had pegged Tom as his next meal and wasn't letting up.

Finally thinking to use her magic, Amber focused on her magic thrumming beneath her skin like a dull electric current and willed a burst of it outward. She imagined it like wisps of swirling blue smoke, even though her magic was invisible even to her. She pictured it forming two hands that scooped up either creature, and just like that, the pair was quickly lifted from the ground just before Tom attempted to seek safety under the bed again. The lack of gravity's pull startled both animals enough that Amber was able to run over and grab Tom. She tucked him under one arm and used her free hand to detach the crazed lion. Once her focus shifted, the spell was broken, and the lion was newly possessed by the desire to rend flesh from bones.

Amber extracted the lion—a tuft of white-and-orange fur clutched in its tiny jaws—then tossed Tom onto the bed. He hit the fluffy comforter with all four paws, hissed once more for good measure, and zipped to the floor and underneath the bed.

3

The lion wiggled frantically in Amber's grasp, all the while attempting to spit out the fur so its mouth was free to attack her cat. It clearly had no desire to go after her despite the grip she had on it; it only had beady little eyes for Tom. The thing was surprisingly hard to hold onto, keeping her so focused on not dropping it—this one had taken a lot of work to craft—that her mind was unable to conjure up a helpful spell.

Her magic still thrashed beneath her skin, though. It always got riled up in highly emotional situations.

Amber yelped and let out a string of colorful curses as the lion sank its fangs into her thumb. It didn't break skin, but the teeth clamped down on her nail so hard, her vision swam for a moment. Without thinking, she shook out her hand, desperate to knock the thing loose, and it went flying off her finger. Some of her pent-up magic was involuntarily released at the same time, causing a gust of wind to help free her of the tiny beast. The lion smacked into a wall with such force, it shattered on impact into several large shards of painted plastic.

Amber groaned loudly and tipped her head back to stare at the ceiling. Her thumb throbbed in time with her racing heart. Her magic had calmed down, at least.

She didn't need this. Not today.

The lion had been a special request from a woman who was throwing a circus-themed birthday party for her six-year-old son.

Next week.

She really needed to perfect the design soon. What would happen if the same thing happened at a party full of little kids? She supposed the children might get a kick out of it, but she couldn't imagine the parents would once the toy started biting people. No one in town knew that Amber's infamous toys were animated by magic; they all thought she was merely an engineering genius.

Amber walked over to the small pile of lion pieces. A few of the plastic bits were reduced to tiny shards. And one of the delicate plastic discs she'd infused with a movement spell had snapped clean in half.

Why hadn't she kept her wits about her so she could perform a deactivation spell?

Now she'd need to start over.

She glanced about her studio apartment and winced at the mess. Plastic pieces lay in heaps on her dining table. Boxes of completed cats sat in a corner, set aside for the Here and Meow Festival. A series of half-crafted animals littered her coffee table along with sheets of paper covered in scrawled spells. Most of the words were scratched out, marking them as defective. Her personal grimoire lay open next to an eyeless flamingo.

The toys had completely taken over her apartment.

She had more room to work downstairs in her shop—plus it would give Tom a break—but ever since Chief Owen Brown had seen her using her magic two weeks ago, she'd been too anxious to use said magic where she might be caught in the act. She and the chief had worked together to solve the murder of Amber's friend Melanie Cole; Amber and the chief had finally started to form something close to a friendship. But that had all fallen apart now. She suspected her anxiety over the whole thing was making her magic glitch.

She'd replayed the scene countless times over the past two weeks—the way he'd been standing outside the Quirky Whisker, eyes wide, just moments after she'd used her magic to float an ill-behaved toy cat back to a table. How he'd hurried away.

She hadn't seen or heard from him since, but she could only guess what he was thinking. He'd known for a while that something about her was off. He'd linked her to dozens of odd incidents around town but hadn't been able come up with an explanation. When he'd nervously posed the possibility that she was psychic, she hadn't corrected him. She'd needed his help to solve the mystery of her friend Melanie's death; he could have thought whatever he wanted.

Once he had something concrete to hold onto—an explanation for her odd behavior and even odder store—he'd started to treat her better. But now? Would the no-nonsense police chief be able to swallow the "I'm a witch" pill as easily as he'd accepted her supposed psychic ability?

There was precedence for police working with psychics. Witchcraft, however, was meant for the pages of fantasy novels, not real life.

She sighed to herself. Getting the lion finished was what was important here. Not what the chief thought of her. The townsfolk hadn't shown up wielding pitchforks and torches, so she had to assume he was keeping his discovery to himself. Assuming he even had a word for this discovery. The Edgehill rumor mill would have been working overtime if news got out that odd Amber Blackwood was a witch.

At the very least, Amber could paint the plastic pieces

needed for the new lion toy—she couldn't get in trouble doing that.

But first …

Lying on her stomach, Amber lifted the dust ruffle to peek underneath. "Come on out, Tom," she cooed, reaching an arm out toward him.

He scooted back so he was just out of range of her fingertips.

"I'm sorry," she said. "I really am."

The orange-and-white tabby remained unconvinced.

Amber sighed. She'd already fed him and Alley breakfast, but she knew food was the only way to get back into his good graces. She got to her feet. "Fine. You win."

She walked the few feet to the cats' little nook and grabbed a bag of treats. Giving it a crinkle, she looked over her shoulder to see a pink nose peeking out from underneath the dust ruffle.

Alley lay curled on the bench seat now, but a black ear swiveled in the direction of the crinkling. Though Alley hadn't lifted a paw to aid her brother during his time of torment, she would no doubt happily gobble down treats she hadn't earned.

Once Amber opened the bag, Tom scurried out of his hiding place and sat obediently in front of his bowl. A pink tongue snaked out in anticipation. Amber wondered if Tom had been a dog in a past life.

She plinked three treats into either bowl and Tom dove for them. Alley soundlessly hopped to the floor to eat hers before Tom did. After he'd licked the bowl clean, he stood and rubbed against Amber's ankles, purr cranked up to level ten. All was forgiven.

Now to work on this dang lion toy …

Collecting her supplies in a tote bag, she called a good-bye to her cats and made her way down the stairs from her apartment to the shop below. The store wasn't due to open for another half hour, so she would have some quiet to herself to get the painting done.

Though the Here and Meow Festival wasn't until May—three months from now—Edgehill was experiencing a rare uptick in winter tourists. Posters advertising a trial run of the junior fashion show were plastered all over town. The adult fashion show had been a staple of the festival for years, but this year, there would be a junior version as well. The trial run for the juniors was scheduled for later in the month. Amber didn't have the faintest clue why people were so invested in the event, but she was glad the young designers were getting recognition for their talent. Amber wondered how Sydney Sadler, a participant in the show, was faring in the wake of her mother's arrest. Sydney's mother, Whitney Sadler, had teamed up with another Edgehill resident, Susie Paulson, to discreetly poison Melanie. While Susie had only wanted to make Melanie sick so Susie could take Melanie's position as the head of the Here and Meow Festival, Whitney had wanted Melanie gone for good.

Amber hoped the looming fashion show was keeping Sydney busy and distracted.

Personally, Amber was being kept busy by the stack of animated toy orders waiting for her. Willow, her younger sister, was due to join her in a month or so to help—it couldn't happen soon enough. Amber needed all the extra help she could get.

Once downstairs, Amber turned on the hot plate in her little cooking alcove so she could make herself a cup of her signature hot chocolate. Then she laid out her supplies on the worn wooden counter that ran along the back of the shop, the wall of dried herbs, teas, and tinctures stored behind labeled drawers taking up the space behind her.

Fifteen minutes later, mug of steaming chocolate nearby, Amber was absorbed in the task of painting the lion's long, thin tail. The creature was a jumble of white pieces at the moment; she always made extra parts just in case. A small pile of miniature talons here, the curved haunch of a leg there. The round, pale face of the lion stared at nothing from its place on the countertop, its eyes two small, empty holes.

Amber had just brushed on the last touch of muted yellow onto the elongated, oval-shaped tip of the tail when she heard the unmistakable click of her front door unlocking.

She froze, paintbrush gripped in one hand, eyes wide. No one in town had keys to her shop. Had the chief decided he could no longer allow a witch in his town and had come to cart her away?

The rational part of her mind told her that if he really *had* come after her with that pitchfork-wielding mob, they would kick the door in, not quietly pick the lock.

She glanced up just as the door swung open. The person who walked through was not the six-foot-tall police chief, but a much smaller older woman.

Amber grinned. "Aunt Gretchen!"

CHAPTER 2

Amber carefully placed her painting supplies on the counter and then hurried around it and toward her aunt standing in the middle of the Quirky Whisker. She stood at five and a half feet, and had lost some weight since Amber had seen her nearly a year ago. Her aunt lived in Portland, Oregon now. Her brown hair was liberally streaked with gray—had she stopped dying it?—and her complexion was a bit pale. But her grin matched Amber's.

When she pulled her aunt into a tight hug, the gesture was returned with a laugh.

"Easy now," Aunt Gretchen said, chuckling as she patted Amber's back, her head just below Amber's chin. "I'm an old lady with fragile bones."

"Pah!" said Amber, pulling away but holding onto the woman's arms. "Not that I'm not happy to see you, but what are you doing here? The Here and Meow is still months away."

"Oh, I know," she said, "but Willow will be here soon, won't she? I was anxious to see my girls before things got too hectic here."

Too hectic? Aunt Gretchen always showed up during the *peak* of the festival, never before. She said she preferred it that way. So why was she here three months early?

10

Amber squinted at her aunt. Gretchen had never been a huge fan of traveling, which she did less and less of as she got older. "Spill. I have ways of making you talk if you won't do so willingly."

Gretchen's mouth quirked up, though Amber wasn't sure why. It hadn't been an idle threat. "I've missed you, my sweet girl," she said, patting Amber's cheek with her cool hand.

Amber's eyes narrowed further.

With a sigh, Gretchen said, "I haven't been feeling well lately and I wanted the comfort of my family. Is that sufficient?"

Something twinged in Amber's chest. "Oh no. What's wrong? You shouldn't be traveling if you're not feeling well. I would have come to you. Do you want to come upstairs? I can make you some tea, or—"

Gretchen huffed and Amber snapped her mouth shut. "That right there is why I didn't mention anything sooner. You're such a worrier! If I'd told you I felt ill, you would have dropped everything to come see me. I don't want to upend your life."

"You upended yours when Mom and Dad died," Amber said. "Coming to look after you is the least I could do. Chicken soup, tinctures—"

Gretchen wrinkled her nose. "Your tinctures were always rather … questionable."

Amber gasped. "They're not *all* bad."

Though if Amber was being honest with herself, especially in the wake of Melanie's death, she wondered if she should not only throw out her current supply of tinctures but stop trying to make them altogether. Most of what Amber knew of magic had been self-taught. There had been much trial and error over the years—often more error than trial.

She and Willow had never received the full witch education from their parents that they'd been promised once they graduated high school. But their parents had died before that happened.

Their grimoires had gone up in smoke with the rest of their house, further distancing Amber from her witch heritage. When it came to her magic, she always felt as if she was floundering in the dark. She didn't have Willow's knack for glamour spells. She wasn't a skilled kitchen witch like her aunt. Gretchen claimed her own talents didn't stretch beyond herbs and tinctures—so if Amber and Willow wanted to test their magic beyond that, they'd be on their own.

Amber's best spells, as far as she could tell, were the ones that came from contact with a person or object. She needed connection, something that tied her to her subject. Tinctures and potions were always a step away. And, when Amber used them, something often backfired.

Perhaps crafting her animated toys was as far as Amber's magic would ever take her. She grimaced slightly as she thought about the possessed lion incident. Not every witch could be a master at the craft, just as every person couldn't be a master musician.

The reality of it still stung.

"If it makes you feel any better," Gretchen said, clearly reading the distress on Amber's face, "Annabelle was rather awful at tinctures too."

Amber stilled.

Annabelle.

Amber and Willow's mother. Gretchen spoke so little of her deceased brother and sister-in-law that sometimes Amber wondered if the woman had entirely purged them from her memory.

"Is that right?" Amber asked, trying to keep her tone light and nonchalant. Whenever Gretchen *did* speak of Amber's parents, Amber feared she'd say the wrong thing and Gretchen would clam up again.

"Oh, yes," Gretchen said, a small wistful smile on her face. "Annabelle tried as she might to be a kitchen witch like her mother, but it never seemed to work out for her. Once, when she was a young girl, she crafted a sleep tonic for Miles—your grandfather—since he'd been complaining about terrible nightmares. She wanted it to be a surprise though, sure she'd be able to prove to everyone once and for all that she was just as good at tinctures as her mother. So, one night, she slipped the tonic into Miles' nightly glass of milk."

Amber, mouth slightly agape, softly asked, "And did it work?"

"Like a charm!" Gretchen said.

Amber grinned.

"Problem was, he didn't wake for three days!"

"Oh my God!"

"Mmhmm. Poor Annabelle was too scared to tell anyone what she'd done and kept quiet for nearly a full day, terrified she'd killed her own father. Your grandmother Ivy found her hiding in a closet in the attic and soon figured out what had happened."

Amber winced. "Was he okay?"

"Oh, sure. Eventually," Gretchen said. "It became a running joke in the family that one could never leave an unattended drink lying around, or else Belle would slip something into it to make you sleep for a week. Your father loved that story. She made the mistake of sharing it with him when they first started dating. He told that story to everyone he could."

Amber frowned, wondering why *she'd* never heard it. But her parents had been so close-lipped about their magic for most of Amber's life. Willow and Amber grew up knowing they were witches, and knowing their parents were, but it was to always, always be a secret.

Amber knew they'd moved to Edgehill when she was very young specifically because it was a town *not* inhabited by other witches. They'd moved several times before Edgehill became their permanent home. They wanted a normal life, they said. For themselves *and* their daughters.

The only family Amber had met, aside from Aunt Gretchen on the Blackwood side of the family, had been Uncle Raphael and his son Edgar—the Henbanes. They'd moved to Edgehill when Amber was twelve. Amber remembered her mother being furious that her older, estranged brother had put down roots in the same, remote town as she had. Amber hadn't seen her uncle and cousin much, even though they'd both lived in Edgehill for years. They'd moved to the outskirts shortly after Edgar's mom, Kathleen, passed away. Even at twelve, Amber had worried about the two grieving men alone in their house out in the middle of nowhere.

She'd wanted to get to know her uncle and cousin. Two

more witches to share experiences with, especially with Edgar, who was only a few years older than she was. She'd wondered, if she could only find a way to his house, if he could teach her about her magic. Willow had so obviously taken after the Blackwood side of the family. Maybe Amber was more like a Henbane—like her mother, uncle, and cousin.

Any time Amber or her sister had tried to ask more about their powers, their parents would say they needed to wait until they were eighteen. Once they were adults, they'd promised, the girls would truly learn what it meant to be witches.

Then their parents had died, taking their secrets with them. Uncle Raphael abruptly moved away. Edgar suffered a psychotic break.

A frown tugged at the corners of Amber's mouth. "I wish we'd had more time with them."

Gretchen sighed. "I know, dear. Me too."

A somber quiet settled over them. Amber wondered if Gretchen was lost in her own memories of Annabelle and Theodore Blackwood.

Amber, deep in her gut, believed something sinister had happened the night her parents died. It hadn't been started by an electrical glitch, no matter what the firefighters said. How had two able-bodied, healthy adults not smelled the smoke? What little had been found of their remains had been located mostly in their beds. Had they lain side by side, sleeping peacefully while their house went up in flames around them?

Amber didn't buy it.

"Maybe they had a nightcap or two since you girls were having a sleepover at your friend's house and they slept more soundly

than usual," a neighbor had offered to a sobbing Amber as she stood outside the blackened remains of her house.

Willow had sunk to the sidewalk beside Amber then, her back to their home, staring off into space.

Fire trucks had lined Ocicat Lane, red lights bouncing off the walls of nearby houses, all left untouched by the fire. None of the neighbors had heard or seen anything unusual, though a few claimed the flames had burned blue. But none could say when the fire started. No one had noticed anything was wrong until it was too late to save the house or her parents.

Nothing about it had felt right to Amber. Not then, and not now.

"You have that look on your face again, little mouse," Aunt Gretchen said now.

Amber pulled herself out of her thoughts. "What look?"

"That look that means you're thinking about things that will never bring you any peace."

"Don't you wonder what happened that night?"

Something flashed across her aunt's face. Anger, maybe. Then it was gone. "Why don't you help me find a place to stay, hmm?"

Subject change, as usual. "You don't want to stay here?"

"You live in a shoebox."

"It's quaint!"

"It's tiny," she said. "A tiny apartment for my little mouse. Go on. Find me a suitable place. The Manx, maybe? Something with a king-size bed and a bathtub with power jets."

Amber tried not to let her disappointment show. She should have known better, though. Aunt Gretchen didn't talk about that night. Amber had tried countless times in the days and months after the fire, when her aunt had swooped in from Portland to become the new guardian for the Blackwood girls. Amber had poked and prodded at Gretchen's defenses, hoping the woman would crack under pressure. Amber had been sure Gretchen knew more about the fire than she let on. They would get into horrific screaming matches about it—potted plants and chairs and knickknacks tossed around the room by unseen hands as Amber's magic rebelled right along with her.

"Get out of that head of yours," said Aunt Gretchen from off to Amber's right.

She snapped out of her memories once again to find her aunt had moved to the other end of the store and now stood at the base of the stairs, holding firm to the straps of her overnight bag. Amber figured she had ten minutes tops to get her aunt situated upstairs before she would need to open the store. She'd have to call the Manx on her lunch break.

Amber hurried over to her waiting aunt, taking her bag from her. "How long are you here for?"

"Time will tell."

After a long pause, Amber staring down her nose at her aunt, she said, "Are you sure you're all right? You look a little rundown and pale."

"You have the bedside manner of a rotting toadstool," she said, huffing. "I'm here for family. That's all."

When they were halfway up the stairs, Gretchen said, "Speaking of, when you have some free time, maybe we should pay Edgar a visit."

Amber nearly missed the next step and had to place a

steadying hand on the wall beside her to keep herself from stumbling. Then she stopped altogether, continuing to watch the slowly ascending figure of her aunt. "Why?"

"I'm here for family, remember? He's family, too. Even if only by marriage."

Amber hadn't seen Edgar in years. After the fire, he'd told anyone who would listen that they hadn't burned in their beds while they slept, but that they'd been trapped inside.

She'd often wondered if "trapped" hadn't meant that they'd been stuck under the debris of a collapsed roof, or that objects had obstructed their paths to doors or windows or hallways, but that some*one* had trapped them inside. Amber's gut had always told her another witch was behind it. Someone from her parents' past, maybe. Someone tied to the reason why a family of four witches purposefully ended up in a town devoid of magic.

A Penhallow, her gut said. *Only a Penhallow would do something so terrible.*

She'd tried to ask Edgar about it. Every time she mentioned the clan of cursed witches, his eyes had grown wide with fear. Though many things could do that to him back then.

And, a month later, Edgar completely recanted his story and checked himself into a mental hospital in Belhaven. Once he returned to Edgehill, Amber had tried to keep in contact with him, but he became a recluse who refused visitors. After being shut out time and again, she'd given up.

As much as Amber believed Edgar had been of sound mind when he first made his claims about the suspicious circumstances of her parents' death, Aunt Gretchen had been adamant that Edgar was "off his nut." The screaming matches that resulted in flying pots and books often centered around the fact that Amber thought people should take Edgar seriously, while Gretchen wholeheartedly disagreed. Her aunt had said he was a bad influence and that he was filling Amber's heart and mind with false hope.

So why did she suddenly want to see someone she so thoroughly dismissed years ago?

Once Amber reached her studio and had set Aunt Gretchen's bag on the bed, she found her aunt standing by the window, arms wrapped around herself. Amber instinctively knew her aunt was staring out into the distance at the half-finished building that had once been the Blackwood family home. Gretchen had started the slow restoration process a year or so after the fire, but the project had been abandoned after Willow had been accepted into a design program in Portland.

Willow had left for college. Gretchen left to resume her life in a bigger city not so haunted by ghosts. And Amber had stayed behind.

Amber sidled up next to her aunt now.

"Aunt Gretchen?" Amber said softly, gaze focused on the distant strip of Ocicat Lane. "Please tell me what's going on. Why are you here now when you hate to travel? Why do you suddenly want to see Edgar?"

Her aunt took a long, shuddering breath. "There's no easy way to say this, little mouse, so I'll just come out with it. The Penhallows have resurfaced, and I believe they're heading for Edgehill. I believe they're heading for *you*."

19

CHAPTER 3

"*What*?" Amber asked, whirling to face her aunt. "What do you mean they're coming for me?"

Aunt Gretchen turned toward Amber and grasped her hands. "Oh, my sweet girl ..."

"Aunt Gretchen, please tell me what's going on. You're starting to scare me."

The Penhallows, a witch clan family burdened with cursed magic, had often been the bogeymen in her nightmares—the people she could blame for her parents' death. Rumor had it that the family had gone underground after the Blackwood parents died. She hadn't heard so much as a whisper about them in fourteen years.

With a sigh, Gretchen said, "Every night since the death of your parents, I've taken a tincture to grant me a window into your and Willow's futures." Before Amber could voice the flurry of questions that Gretchen clearly saw forming in Amber's mind, the woman soldiered on. "I'm not a clairvoyant. I cannot see very far into the future, nor do these visions come to me with crystal clarity."

Amber hesitated. "How does it work?"

"I take a bit of it with my evening tea, and if there's a looming threat on the horizon, it will manifest in my dreams,"

Aunt Gretchen said, letting Amber's hands go. "Remember when Willow just started dating that rat Jeffrey Sanders?"

Amber cocked her head. "Her old boss who ended up getting arrested for money laundering?"

Aunt Gretchen nodded. "Mmhmm. And you remember where she was when that arrest happened?"

Amber blinked several times in rapid succession, wracking her memory. "She went to see *you* because you fell and injured your hip."

"Did I though?" Gretchen smiled.

"You sneaky witch," Amber said, laughing. "What else?"

Gretchen laughed too. "I made up an excuse to keep you girls home one day during high school when there was an outbreak of norovirus."

With a gasp of sudden realization, Amber said, "That was the weekend you took us to the beach! You let us cut school on a Friday. I just thought you wanted to get us away from everything for a few days."

"I did," she said. "But I also wanted to protect you from contracting a nasty bug."

Amber was suddenly sixteen again, waking up to the horrible news that her house had caught fire with her parents inside. She recalled the ashen face of Alice's mother when she hurried into Alice's bedroom where she, Amber, Willow, and Julie had been fast asleep in their sleeping bags on Alice's floor.

Had Gretchen seen *that* event coming?

"No," Gretchen said, and Amber wondered if perhaps her aunt was clairvoyant after all. "I know that look, little mouse.

I didn't start taking the tinctures until *after* Belle and Theo died. I was just as shocked by it as you were."

Amber sighed, her mind circling back to where this conversation had started. "So … you're saying you dreamed the Penhallows are coming for me?"

"*A* Penhallow. Singular," said Gretchen. "They've been keeping a low profile for years, but they appear to be resurfacing. A friend of mine in Maine said a Penhallow was detected there recently. They leave behind a trace—a signature—if they use their twisted magic. You can almost touch it. When you walk into the dregs of it, it's as if you've stepped into a giant cobweb. It clings to you.

"As for *your* Penhallow, I don't know his or her name, or what they look like. I just know a Penhallow is bringing their cursed magic to Edgehill, and they have you in their sights."

Amber didn't understand.

"Why me?" she asked, trying her best not to let her panic rise from the hollow pit of her stomach and choke her. "I'm … not exactly a skilled witch. I'm a screwup at best; amoral at worst. Don't the Penhallows only try to siphon powers from the most powerful?"

Gretchen frowned, her dark brows knitted together, and her mouth pulled into a tight line. If Amber didn't know her no-nonsense aunt any better, she would have thought the woman was going to burst into tears. Something twinged in her chest again; Amber worried she'd somehow just said something horribly offensive to her aunt without meaning to.

"Aunt Gretchen, I—" Amber swallowed. "What did I say? I didn't mean—"

"Oh, my sweet girl," she said, placing a hand on Amber's cheek, just as she had downstairs. "I fear this is all my fault."

Movement down on the street below caught Amber's eye, and she glanced out the window just as the door to Purrfectly Scrumptious opened and out sauntered Savannah the Maine coon. If Betty Harris was opening her doors, it meant it was opening time for Amber as well. Tourists were already milling around Russian Blue Avenue, peering in shop windows and cooing at the town's plethora of friendly street cats. A pair of giggling girls bent down to pet Savannah, who had rather dramatically flopped onto her back on the sidewalk so passersby would have better access to her furry belly.

"We'll talk later, little mouse," Gretchen said, pulling Amber's attention back to her aunt. "I'll take a nap while you open up shop. I'm exhausted."

Aunt Gretchen *did* seem even paler now than she had when she'd arrived. How sick *was* she?

"Go," her aunt said. "Stop looking at me as if I already have a foot in the grave. Out you go!" She waved her hands at Amber as if she were a pesky fly.

Amber laughed. "All right, all right! I'm going. If you need anything, just—"

"Bye, little mouse."

Shaking her head and smiling to herself, Amber hurried for the steps and into the shop below.

The morning was busy, the tinkling bell above her door

sounding several times an hour. When managing the shop by herself truly became unmanageable in the months before the Here and Meow, she often hired a couple of teenagers to help with customers and to man the register.

Now, as Amber clicked the lock shut on her front door and flipped her open sign over, she let out a weary sigh. Would checking in with Lily and Daisy Bowen this week be too premature? The real tourist influx was at least a month away, but this junior fashion show was proving to be more popular than Amber would have guessed.

But before she even considered calling the Bowens, she needed to make arrangements for her aunt and grab something to eat.

After a quick check upstairs, she found her aunt fast asleep on the comforter, mouth agape, and a curled-up dozing cat on either side of her. Smiling to herself, she quietly made her way back downstairs, grabbed her purse, locked up, and stepped out onto Russian Blue Avenue.

The Manx Hotel was only a few doors down from her favorite sandwich shop, The Catty Melt. It was a quick ten-minute drive to the hotel from her shop. Evidence of the Here and Meow's impending arrival could be seen not just in the new flood of wandering tourists, but in the mailboxes topped with cat ears, posters advertising sign-ups for the 5k run, and the banner for the festival itself stretched wide across the major intersection of Catnip and Scritch Boulevards.

A familiar pang in her chest reminded her that her friend Melanie wouldn't get to see what all her hard work on the festival would look like this year. She told herself to call Kimberly

Jones, the new Here and Meow Festival director, soon to see how she was faring in her new role.

The Manx was the ritziest hotel in Edgehill. It looked more like a sprawling Victorian-era mansion than a glamorous high-rise in a big city, though. The building was a soft brown with striking black accents. Elegant black cat statues were scattered around the property. Several were perched on the corners of the roofs, watching passersby like silently judging gargoyles.

Amber walked up to the low, black fence that circled the property, and swung open the gate on silent hinges. A black cat statue sat at the top of the short flight of stairs. When Amber reached the top, however, the cat statue mewed, its tongue a bright flash of pink.

"Well, hello," Amber said, slightly startled.

The cat stood and immediately trotted to the black front door, then glanced over its shoulder as if to say, "Welcome to the Manx Hotel. Please follow me." An oval-shaped window rested in the center of the door. Cats had been etched into the glass—a tumbled mass of paws, whiskers, and pointed ears.

Amber grabbed hold of the thick, clear doorknob and turned. The door had only been opened a sliver before the black cat slunk through and disappeared inside.

The lobby was a wide, open space, the walls and floor made of a rich, dark wood. A wide staircase rose up behind the C-shaped registration desk sitting squarely in the middle of the room. An open doorway sat on either side of Amber, leading into what looked like lounging areas. Amber thought she heard the faint sound of voices—she couldn't be sure if they belonged to guests or a TV kept at low volume.

A woman, who Amber was almost sure had been in Willow's graduating class, stood at the desk, a phone pressed to her ear. She looked up at Amber and smiled, holding up a single finger before she offered the person on the other end of the line a few noises of understanding. Wedging the phone between her ear and shoulder, she turned to the computer—Amber could only see part of the monitor's back peeking above the lip of the desk—and clacked away on a keyboard.

Amber glanced around the lobby again, waiting for the woman to get off the phone. A burst of laughter sounded from the open room to her right. Masculine laughter. Curious, Amber walked to the doorway and peeked in.

The lounge area had a couch and several recliners arranged in a loose half-moon shape, all facing a flat-screen TV on a dark wood stand. The screen was dark. Three men sat in the chairs, talking and laughing. Well, one man talked, animatedly gesticulating as he told what looked to be a very involved story.

"And then he said, 'Not with a raccoon in your shorts!'"

The men burst into howling laughter again.

Amber smiled at the sound of it. And then she recognized one of the men as Connor Declan, the reporter from the *Edgehill Gazette*. She could honestly say she had never seen him look as happy as he did then, laughing with his friends. He seemed younger somehow, his eyes brighter. As if he sensed her, his gaze swiveled in her direction.

"Hey, Amber!" He waved.

She knew, instantly, that Connor Declan was a bit inebriated. She grinned. "Hey, Connor."

One of the men sat in an armchair closest to the door and

turned in his seat to look at her. All three were handsome, well-put-together guys. Amber wondered if they were old college buddies.

"Well, hel-lo," the guy said, doing his best to cock an eyebrow at her with the swagger of a seafaring pirate, but he mostly looked like he was suffering an unfortunate facial tick.

"Introduce us to your friend, you fiend!" the man sitting next to Connor said. He slapped the back of his hand against Connor's chest for added emphasis.

"Ow!" Connor said, swatting his friend's hand away. "Guys, this is Amber Blackwood."

"Oooh," the pirate said, nodding. "You're Willow's hot older sister, huh? Man. I had it bad for you in high school."

Amber had no recollection of who this guy was. And she was also sure now that they were *all* drunk. At noon. On a weekday. "So what's the occasion for this … celebration?"

The guy sitting next to Connor wrapped an arm around Connor's neck and yanked him to his chest, while roughly scrubbing his hand through Connor's hair. Connor laughed and squirmed, trying to break free. His friend, over Connor's loud pleas to unhand him, said, "It's this knucklehead's birthday! Well, it's tomorrow. We started partying a little early."

"I can see that," Amber said with a laugh.

The pirate was still turned in his armchair, an elbow resting on the back, his face in his hand. "Since tomorrow is Saturday, we're going to *really* celebrate tonight." He gasped, and Amber wasn't sure if he'd just accidentally swallowed a fly or if he'd suddenly learned the meaning of life. With both hands gripping the back of the chair now, he stared wide-eyed at Amber. "We're going to Just Kitten later." He snorted. "Just Kitten! I just got it! It's a comedy club, and 'just kitten' is like … it's like a cat … but a small cat! A kitten! Like kidding, but with tiny paws." He chuckled softly to himself, muttering the name over and over to himself.

Connor slowly shook his head, then said, "We might need to force him to take a nap soon."

"Just kitten!" the pirate said, wiping his eyes.

"Probably a good idea," Amber said, smiling.

"Excuse me, Amber?" came a female voice behind her.

She turned to see the receptionist standing behind her, a bright smile on her face. "Oh, hi. I'll be right there."

The woman nodded and headed back for the desk. Amber returned her attention to the men and said, "Well, happy birthday, Connor. I hope you guys have a great weekend."

Connor, finally unhanded by his friend, flushed a little. Amber wasn't sure if it was due to the headlock, the alcohol, or something else. "Thanks!" He looked like he wanted to say something else, but the energy in the room slowly grew awkward, so Amber waved again and backed out of the room.

A chorus of high-pitched "*Happy birthday, Connor!*" erupted from the room, followed by another upswell of laughter. She shook her head slightly, amused.

When Amber reached the desk, the smiling blonde leaned toward her, shot a quick glance toward the room the men were cackling in, and then turned back to Amber before saying, "They've been like that since ten this morning."

"Did all of them go to Edgehill High?" Amber asked, trusting her gut that the receptionist had gone to high school there, too. The tag pinned to her crisp, black button-up said her name was Carrie.

"Definitely not. Only Connor and Wesley."

Ambers eyes widened. "That's not Wesley *Young* is it?"

Carrie grinned. "Yep."

Amber glanced toward the open doorway for a moment, then back at the receptionist. "Who would have thought that acne-covered, scrawny Wesley Young would turn into *that*?"

"Right?" She grinned. "Willow would pass out in a dead faint if she saw him. He followed her around like a lost puppy all through high school."

Amber remembered that all too well. One Halloween morning, they'd walked out the front door of their house to head for school and found Wesley Young standing in the middle of their street, a giant sign held above his head that said, "Willow, you're the bee's knees. Will you go to the Halloween dance with me?" A yellow felt band was wrapped around his head long-ways, floppy pink petals radiating out from it. Willow was so embarrassed, she let out a semi-hysterical shriek, ducked her head, and dove into the backseat of the car waiting at the curb.

His petals seemed to wilt as he realized his plan to woo Willow hadn't worked. As Amber tried to come up with words of encouragement for the boy, he dropped the sign in the middle of the street and sprinted down Ocicat Lane, the petals flapping around his face.

"Anyway," Carrie said now. "What can I help you with today?"

"My aunt is in town for a while and wanted me to check if you have anything available."

"Oh, tell Gretchen I say hi!" Carrie said, attention focused on her computer. A few clacks of her keys. "How long is she in town?"

"I'm not sure, honestly."

"Hmm." A few more clacks. "We've got something open for this weekend only, then we're booked up for *weeks* after that. People are coming in from all over to see the fashion show."

Amber's mind flashed to young Sydney Sadler again.

"Well, really, I think people are coming in from all over to see if the Olaf Betzen rumors are true," Carrie said. "He's usually so secretive about where he's going, you know?"

Amber did not know. "Yeah totally," she said, hoping her accompanying laugh wasn't too fake. "So, uh, let's go ahead and book this weekend. We'll figure out the rest later." Amber knew neither she nor her aunt could afford to stay in a place this swanky for too long anyway.

"You got it," Carrie said.

Amber paid for three nights and snagged a set of keys.

She had just turned to leave, when she came up short. Connor Declan stood behind her. "Geez, Connor!"

"Sorry," he said, laughing nervously. She could smell the alcohol on him. It wasn't overwhelming, but it clung to him all the same. "I uh ..." He rubbed the back of his neck. "So ... uh ... after the comedy show, we're going to meet up at the Sippin' Siamese. Would you like to join us? We're probably going to play pool and be generally obnoxious. If you have other plans or that doesn't sound like something you'd wanna do, or if you—"

He'd grown increasingly redder as he talked, so she hurriedly cut him off with a "What time?"

"Oh! I … uh … eight?"

"Sounds great. See you then."

"Yeah?"

She was almost positive this was a terrible idea. Dating non-witches was just … not something she did anymore. But Connor looked so hopeful. Plus, she couldn't shut the guy down on his birthday, could she? "Yeah."

He grinned. "Awesome! I mean, cool. Yeah, I'll—we'll—see you then."

She nodded and watched him walk away. Just as he reached the doorway to the lounge, Wesley poked his head around the corner, startling Connor, as he said, "*Awesome! I mean, cool!*"

Sometimes Amber felt as if she'd never escape high school.

Still, she found herself smiling as she stepped out of the Manx Hotel. She hadn't really been out with friends since Melanie died. Melanie had been the one to push Amber out of her comfort zone more and more. Tried to get her to meet more people. She could almost hear Melanie's voice in her head as Amber made her way down the steps: "He's cute. You're cute. Let yourself have some fun."

Okay, Melanie, she said to herself, nodding slightly. *Maybe I will.*

CHAPTER 4

When Amber returned to the Quirky Whisker half an hour later—a pair of wrapped-up turkey-on-rye sandwiches in her purse—she didn't expect to see her aunt in the shop. She also didn't expect her aunt to have company. Gretchen stood in front of the counter, talking animatedly to someone standing on the other side, his or her arms resting on the worn wood. Amber could only make out a bent elbow and fair skin.

Letting herself in, Amber tried to keep her annoyance in check. Annoyance that stemmed from how quickly Amber had turned back into a curmudgeonly thirty-year-old who preferred the company of her cats over people. The logical part of her brain told her she was still grieving Melanie; it had been less than two months since she had died. It had taken Melanie a while to pull cautious Amber out of her shell, and now that Melanie was gone, Amber was retreating again. It was easier to keep to herself. You couldn't be left behind if there wasn't anyone to leave you in the first place.

My, she was in a morbid mood all of a sudden.

Amber knew she wasn't being fair. Gretchen had lived in Edgehill for quite a few years; it wouldn't be unreasonable for her to still have acquaintances here—though she'd never mentioned any.

The tinkling of the bell above the door gave away her arrival, and Gretchen and her guest turned toward the sound.

"Hey, big sis," Willow said, smiling from her spot behind the counter.

Amber let out a squeak of surprise. No matter how far into her shell Amber went, there was always room for Willow and Aunt Gretchen.

"How am I this lucky to have you both here so soon?" she asked, hurrying over to greet her sister.

They met halfway in a hug. Willow, though younger, was a smidge taller than Amber. As always, she smelled of lavender and soap. Amber wondered if somehow her mother had known Willow was going to grow up to be a tall, thin woman with long limbs and hair. Willowy was the perfect description for her. Her brown hair was in two French braids now, the ends reaching her waist. Amber was several inches shorter, and average in every way when compared to her sister.

When they pulled apart, Willow's bright green eyes almost seemed to twinkle. It was no wonder all the boys in high school had fallen all over themselves around her. Amber felt bad for all the Wesley Youngs of the world. There was something almost ethereal about Willow. And she was clueless about it half the time.

"Well," said Willow, draping her long arm around Amber's neck and swiveling them both to face Gretchen, "I wouldn't have been here this soon had it not been for our lovely aunt leaving me a *very* cryptic message the other night saying it was imperative—her word, not mine—that I get to Edgehill immediately and that I shouldn't tell you because you'd worry."

Amber squinted at her aunt.

"What?" she asked innocently. "You would have called me with a million questions if Willow let the cat out of the bag too early."

She wasn't wrong, but Amber wondered when she'd become a worried mother hen.

"Plus!" said Willow. "I heard a rumor that *Olaf Betzen* is going to be at the fashion show at the end of the month. Like I'd miss that! Why didn't you tell me?"

Amber still had absolutely no clue who Olaf Betzen was.

Upon seeing Amber's blank look, Willow gasped, putting a hand to her chest. "You know … the host of *Ramp It Up*?"

Amber blinked at her.

"*Ramp It Up* is only the *biggest* fashion reality TV show in the world. And has been for ages," Willow said. "The junior edition of the show only started a year ago, but it looks like it'll be even more popular than the adult one. Olaf hosts both. He's supposedly here to see the show since they've started casting for season three already."

Amber blinked again. "How did anyone from the show even find out about it?"

"Letty's Instagram feed, obviously," Willow said. "Angora Threads has over three hundred thousand followers."

Angora Threads was a local custom clothing shop run by Letty Rodriquez. She was also heading the internship for the junior designers who would participate in the fashion show later in the month. Amber shot a helpless look at Gretchen.

Her aunt laughed softly. "We really need to get you out of the house more, dear. Even *I* knew that."

Amber harrumphed. "Did you just get here?" she asked Willow, steering them away from the topic of her abysmal lack of knowledge about pop culture.

"Mmhmm. Ten minutes before you did." Willow sniffed the air like a bloodhound. "You've been to the Catty Melt. Turkey on rye?" She quickly unslung her arm from around Amber and scurried to her other side, attempting to pilfer one of said sandwiches straight out of the purse still on Amber's shoulder.

Amber swatted at her and quickly sidestepped her. She rounded the side of the counter, putting a barrier between herself and her family. "I didn't get you one!"

"Rude," Willow said, arms crossed, though she was smiling slightly. When the three of them were together, Amber and Willow often found themselves squabbling like children again. "So what's the deal?" she asked her aunt, her tone light. "What was so imperative?"

Dropping her bag onto the countertop, Amber matched Willow's stance, then focused her attention on Gretchen. "You want to tell her or should I?"

Sighing, Gretchen told Willow the same thing she'd told Amber that morning: the Penhallows had resurfaced and they had Amber in their sights. Willow paled further and further the more Gretchen talked. Then she followed up with all the same questions, namely, "Why Amber?" and "Why now?"

Their aunt still didn't have an answer for them. They went over and around the same small pieces of information, but Amber felt no more enlightened now than she had twenty minutes before.

It wasn't long before the shop needed to be open again.

Willow helped Gretchen collect her things—and Gretchen's sandwich, which Amber suspected Willow would eat in its entirety before Gretchen got a chance—and escorted their aunt to the Manx, the hotel key shoved into Willow's pocket now.

Amber did her best to scarf her sandwich down before she had to unlock the door for the customers milling around Russian Blue Avenue. The influx of tourists made more sense now, at least. They were here because of this Olaf Betzen character, more than being supporters of young creative talents.

Willow was back within half an hour and joined Amber in the familiar steady rhythm of running the shop. Whether it was sisterly intuition, familial magic intuition, or some combination of the two, when they were together, they often were able to sense the other's needs without speaking much at all.

The sound of Willow's infectious, tinkling laugh rang throughout the afternoon, bringing a smile to Amber's face every time. Between being quite busy with tending to customers and Willow's calming presence, she was able to keep worrying thoughts about the Penhallows and her parents' deaths out of her head.

Henrietta Bishop, with her wild mop of red hair, was their last visitor of the day, hurrying in to buy her weekly batch of sleepy tea just before closing. She and Willow squealed when they saw each other and were still deep in conversation well after Amber flipped the open sign over.

As they talked, Amber tidied up the store. Her curmudgeonly side assured her that Willow and Henrietta were doing just fine without her; her well-adjusted side told her it was terribly rude not to at least say hi. The curmudgeon in her won out.

A group of young boys had made a mess of the toy display in one corner. Plastic animals of all types and colors were strewn about the floor. As she righted them, placing bears, giraffes, and cows back on their feet, those worrying thoughts she'd been keeping at bay all day started to creep back in.

What could the Penhallows want with her? What was Gretchen keeping from them? Well, what *else* was she keeping from them? Amber knew in her gut that Gretchen was holding onto information about her parents' deaths. Were their deaths connected to the Penhallows? If so, why? Amber had never met—nor seen, as far as she knew—a Penhallow in her life.

"Earth to Amber!"

She startled, stumbling back a half step from her awkward squatting position on the floor. A tiny snap sounded from under her foot. Glancing down, she saw that she'd accidently broken the horn off a unicorn's head under the weight of her heel. "Oh, dang it," she muttered, picking the creature up. She stood, holding the body in one hand and the severed, twisted white horn between two fingers of the other.

"Sorry!" Willow reached forward and waved a hand over the creature. Instantly, the horn disappeared from Amber's fingers and refastened itself to the unicorn's forehead. "Good as new!"

Eyes wide, Amber glanced around her sister to make sure Henrietta—or anyone outside—hadn't seen Willow's display of magic.

Willow rolled her eyes and laughed softly. "Don't worry.

Henrietta left over ten minutes ago. She said goodbye, but you were too deep in la-la land to hear her."

Amber frowned. "Be careful about your magic," she whisper-hissed, gaze flicking out onto the currently deserted Russian Blue Avenue. "There are more people around right now and we can't afford—"

Willow sighed dramatically, then abruptly turned away from Amber, walking further into the store. "What's with you? You're even more tightly wound than usual."

Amber clenched her jaw. She placed the unicorn back onto its shelf to keep herself from crushing the toy in her fist. "You mean other than the fact that my closest friend here died almost two months ago?"

Willow frowned. "I didn't mean … I know—"

"And did you miss the whole 'the Penhallows are after me' thing? Aunt Gretchen wouldn't have come all the way here—and lure *you* here, I might add—if she didn't think it was important. So, yeah, I'm worried."

Willow folded her arms and bit her lip. She looked around the store, an odd, distant look on her face. It took her a while to finally look Amber in the eye. When she spoke, her voice was soft. "So you don't think she's just overreacting?"

So Willow *was* worried. Amber realized that while Willow's flitting about and bubbly laughter had been keeping Amber grounded all day, it had been a defense mechanism for Willow. What one could see on the outside with Willow didn't always match the inside.

"Gretchen doesn't overreact," Amber said, most of the bite in her tone gone now.

"I know." Her sister sighed, then started to fuss with the ends of one of her braids. It was a nervous tick she'd had for as long as Amber could remember. "Do you think this is about Mom and Dad?"

Amber's shoulders sagged, her chest aching at how much her sister sounded like a scared fourteen-year-old again, not a woman of twenty-eight. "I don't know, Will. Instinct says yes, but it's been fourteen years since they died. Since anyone has even *seen* a Penhallow. Gretchen says the witch—whoever he or she is—is going to be a threat *eventually*. It's on the horizon. We still have time."

Willow closed the short distance between them and took her sister's hands in hers. "I won't survive it if something happens to you."

Amber pulled her sister into a hug, and Willow rested her chin on Amber's shoulder. "Nothing will happen to me, okay? We'll figure it out. We always do."

Willow nodded, her chin still on Amber's shoulder.

After a few long moments of this, Amber knew it was her turn to lighten the mood, to pull Willow out of her silent brooding. "Oh, hey, remember Connor Declan?"

Willow pulled away to look Amber in the eye, then hiked a brow. "This is the second time you've mentioned him in only a couple months. Are you finally giving up your ridiculous ban on non-witch men?"

Amber flushed slightly, unable to stop it.

"Oh my God! Are you … are you *hooking up* with him? Is the drought over? Did Connor Declan clear the cobwebs out of your lady cave? It must not be that great if you're still *this* stressed out …"

"Willow!"

Her tinkling laugh made Amber laugh too.

"No, you pervert!" Amber said. "Nothing like that. But I did run into him today. It's his birthday tomorrow so he's partying it up with a couple friends. He invited me to meet him tonight at the Sippin' Siamese. Want to come?"

"Yes!" she said, eyes alight. "Why didn't you tell me this sooner? What am I going to wear? I haven't been to the Sippin' Siamese in ages." Willow smiled wistfully. "I went to so many open mic nights there. Kissed so many boys in dark corners of that bar …"

Then she darted away and toward the stairs leading up to the studio apartment.

"Wesley Young is going too." Then Amber winced.

Willow whirled around. "*No.*"

"He's hot now."

"No way."

"Yes way."

"I am intrigued. I hope he's not in costume this time." Then Willow grinned. "Hurry up, dear sister. We only have three hours to make you presentable."

Amber's hair was pulled back in a loose ponytail, as usual. She looked down at her maroon top, black slacks, and black flats. "What's wrong with what I'm wearing?"

Willow wrinkled her nose. "It's cute you think I'd let you go out to meet a hot, eligible man while wearing—" she gestured vaguely in Amber's direction, "*that.*"

Amber frowned.

"Now get your butt up here! I may be a witch, but even *my* powers are limited. Time is of the essence!"

Amber grumbled to herself as she followed the tinkling sound of her sister's laughter up the stairs.

At half past seven, Amber was showered, had allowed Willow to French braid her mass of wavy brown hair, and had applied a fresh layer of eye makeup and mascara. Normally she went with just lip gloss and called it a day. Her brown eyes looked big and innocent thanks to Willow's insistence on green eye shadow. Her soft pink gloss had been replaced by a swipe of red lipstick.

Amber didn't own very many dresses but had a favorite little black one she wore for nearly all special occasions. Willow, however, kept glamouring the dress into a red just as vibrant as Amber's lipstick.

"Willow!" Amber would protest, then painstakingly work her way through a spell to turn it to its original color. With a flick of Willow's wrist, it would shift back to red.

This happened three times before Willow retreated into the bathroom. "If you change it back to black one more time, I'm adding a plunging neckline."

Amber walked over to stand in the doorway of the bathroom, watching as Willow's hair cycled through a series of magically crafted hairstyles: stick-straight, swooped up in a messy-chic bun, down around her shoulders in loose ringlets, then shrunk up into tight corkscrews. It happened so quickly, it was as if she were swiping through the styles on her phone. Amber willed herself not to be jealous.

"It's so ... revealing," Amber protested, holding her hands out to either side as she looked down at herself. She was almost certain the dress got a little tighter every time Willow shifted the color. At least it hadn't gotten any shorter; it still hit her at mid-thigh, and the sleeves still came to her elbows.

Willow turned her attention away from her reflection—her hair currently sporting blonde highlights that hadn't been there a second ago—to give Amber a quick scan. "You look amazing. You *want* Connor to come unglued when he sees you. That's the whole point of dresses like that."

Amber honestly wasn't sure that it *was* what she wanted. He was two years younger than her, after all. But was that really that big of a deal? Was she coming up with excuses because she was scared to date again?

And even because he was, as Kimberly Jones said, "a tall, *tall* drink of water," Amber really didn't know him that well. Up until this afternoon, she hadn't even been sure he'd been remotely interested in her. Unlike Jack Terrence from the Purrcolate coffee shop who had been shamelessly flirting with her for years and had even asked her out once.

Anxiety had caused her to shoot him down.

"You wouldn't have said yes if you didn't like him, Amber," Willow said now, swiping mascara onto her lashes, her mouth stretched wide—it seemed impossible to apply mascara without making that face.

Amber thought of how flustered Connor had been when

he'd asked her out earlier. She'd never seen him flustered before. She'd also never seen him tipsy before.

Willow laughed. "You *do* like him. It's written all over that face of yours."

Allowing a soft smile, Amber said, "I think he's cute."

"Good enough for me." Willow gave herself a once-over, smoothing out her dress, hers a deep green. Unlike Amber's nearly skin-tight dress, Willow's flared out wide from her thin waist. Her hair was clipped half up and styled in thick waves that came to her midback.

Connor wouldn't give Amber a second look once Willow breezed into the room.

After they'd put in a quick call to their aunt to make sure she didn't need anything, the pair headed out for the Sippin' Siamese.

Edgehill was positioned between Marbleglen to the north and Belhaven to the south. The Sippin' Siamese, a small hole-in-the-wall, was just on the border between Edgehill and Belhaven, in what most people considered the shadier part of town. Several businesses had folded over the last several years and had never been taken over by new owners. Houses were more rundown, and lawns were surrounded by sagging chain-link fences.

But the Sippin' Siamese was always packed. They had the best beer on tap in all of Edgehill, local bands from the surrounding towns played there most weekend nights, and the food was greasy and incredible. At least, it had been the last time Amber visited the place with Melanie a couple years ago, just a few weeks after Melanie first moved to town.

The bar sat on a street with an empty field on one side, and a row of businesses on the other. Willow pulled into a gravel lot a few doors down from the bar, and Amber did her best to scoot out of the car without having a wardrobe malfunction. Thankfully, Willow hadn't put up a fuss when Amber pulled on her low kitten heels; Willow, being so tall, was often forced to wear flats so she wouldn't intimidate men more than she already did. Despite the chilly February evening, they left their jackets in the car—it would be too hot inside to wear them, and there would be nowhere to keep them once they took them off.

They walked up the sidewalk, the empty field to their right left giving off a mildly creepy vibe in the waning light. Amber imagined a cursed Penhallow witch lurking out there in the shadows behind an overgrown bush, watching and waiting for the perfect opportunity to strike.

Stop being paranoid, Amber! she chastised herself.

Once they passed a boarded-up diner and a tattoo parlor—open only by appointment—Amber could hear music. The glow from inside cast large boxes of yellow onto the sidewalk. From the sound of it, it was country night. Not her favorite.

The Sippin' Siamese was a squat wooden building with an attached open patio. Several people were outside, smoking, drinking, and laughing. The sign for the bar rested on top of a long wooden pole. In the middle of the rectangular glowing sign, a svelte, human-like Siamese cat sat in a black wrought-iron chair, thin legs crossed, a martini glass hoisted in the air. It winked one blue eye. The name of the bar was written in swirling cursive below the seductive-looking cat.

A wooden kiosk stood just outside the front doors, a rotund, balding man sitting behind it. He'd been engrossed with his phone screen until they were standing right in front of him. He glanced up, opened his mouth, then immediately shut it. His gaze shifted from Amber to Willow and back again.

"Well, if it's isn't the Blackwood sisters," he managed. "I haven't seen you here in ages, Willow!"

"Hey, Jake," Willow said, moving around the kiosk to give Jake a side hug and an air kiss.

He looked ready to pass out, face flushed. "You girls go on inside," he said. "Cover's on me."

"You're a doll," Willow said.

Jake blushed further.

Willow pulled the door open and music tumbled out at three times the volume. People milled about near the doorway, forming a semi-circle around the karaoke area where a girl belted out a song Amber had never heard before. When she hit a particularly long, high note, the crowd around her cheered and whistled their approval.

Amber and Willow squeezed past the small herd of people near the door, only to get crushed in a mass crowding around the bar. Amber suspected nearly half of the patrons were tourists. She tried to push her way through people, saying "excuse me" often, but was having a hard time being heard over the din of music and shouts and laughter. Willow was several people ahead of Amber and suddenly let out an excited squeal. She and a blonde woman pulled each other into a tight hug, then they backed away long enough to flail and jump around. The woman then pulled Willow farther into the room, presumably to where her friends were.

Amber felt impossibly out of place now. What did she think, strolling into a bar in this insanely tight red dress with her red lipstick and no clue what she was doing here? Her ethereal, social butterfly of a sister belonged here. Amber belonged at home with her cats.

She realized then she didn't have Connor's number, so she wasn't sure how to find him in this crowd. Not that he'd be able to hear his phone. What if they weren't even here? Or running late?

Pull it together, she told herself. *You're a grown woman. You can handle this.*

"Excuse me," she said, louder now, and started to push her way through the crowd, black clutch purse held firmly in her hand. She hoped she wouldn't step on anyone's toes. Something brushed against her backside and she really hoped someone hadn't purposely tried to grope her.

Just beyond this room was a second. That one had an additional bar, a dance floor, and a few pool tables. Willow reached the second door then and turned to wave a long arm in the air to get Amber's attention. Willow only had enough time to point at the door, then to the dance floor, before the blonde had dragged her into the next room. Amber followed, desperate to get out of this smaller, stuffier room, hung heavy with the smell of old beer and warm bodies.

The music was even louder when she made it into the

larger section of the bar, but it was significantly less crowded and much cooler. She spotted Willow out on the crowded dance floor, holding the hand of the very clearly drunk blonde woman. A railing ran along the edge of the dance floor on all sides, with entry points at the corners. Amber found an empty spot along one of the nearby railings. The group of forty or so people on the floor were line dancing. Willow was in the middle and, surprisingly, knew the dance; she tried to coach her newly found friend through the steps. The friend often turned the wrong way, bumping into Willow or the man next to her. Willow and the woman were all smiles though, heads thrown back in laughter as they tried to keep up with the crowd dancing in unison around them.

When that song ended and the DJ announced which dance was up next, there were several moments of mild pandemonium as some people ran off the floor and others hurried on to get a good spot. Willow and her friend stayed put. Willow scanned the crowd until she located Amber, and then gave her an enthusiastic wave. Amber smiled, waving back. She felt like a chaperone at a high school function.

As the new dance started, Amber looked around, hoping for some sign of Connor or his friends.

With her head turned to the right, someone said in her left ear, "You look incredible."

She turned in the direction, but the person was on her right now. He lightly touched her elbow. "I thought this outing would be a bust, but you just made my night."

Her stomach gave a little flip at the sound of his voice, and she turned back to her right. The flutter she felt unnerved her, if only because she'd never reacted this way to him before. She realized rather suddenly that she was very glad to see him. She grinned up at him. "Hi, Jack."

CHAPTER 5

Jack Terrence, the owner of Purrcolate, smiled wide. "Hi, Amber."

"Is Larry here?" she asked, looking around for his brother. It was a bit odd to see one without the other.

"Nope, just me. Flying solo."

Amber cocked a brow at him. "Come here often?"

He shrugged. "Sort of. I don't think I've ever seen you here before."

"It's been a while," she said. "I'm not much of a … drinker. Or a dancer." *Or a socializer*, she wanted to add.

"Yeah. This doesn't really seem like it's your scene. Not that I know what your scene is, really," he added quickly. "I haven't lived here long enough to even know what my *own* scene is. Other than hanging out at bars by myself, I guess. I think I like this place because I went to a line dancing bar back in Seattle when I lived there. Larry and me. Did you know we came from Seattle? I'm guessing everyone knows that." He coughed, then idly scratched at his freshly shaved face.

Sometime during his rambling, she'd propped an elbow up on the railing, placed her chin on her fist, and watched him, quite amused.

"I don't know why I can't seem to stop talking. I swear I'm

49

not drunk. And I don't come here to just leer at women either. I promise," he said. "Okay. Well. I'm going to go fling myself into the nearest river now. Have a nice night."

Amber laughed when he actually made to leave, and she placed a hand on his arm to stop him. "Don't go. My sister has abandoned me and you're the first friendly face I've seen." When a slightly wounded expression flashed across his features for a split second, she internally winced. "Not that I only want you to stay for that reason. I mean, I was happy to see you regardless of the fact that your face is friendly."

It was Jack's turn to laugh. A sudden silence fell between them, but they didn't break eye contact. The DJ announced the next dance—"Tush Push"—which elicited a wave of excited cheers from the crowd.

"Do you want to head out to the patio?" Jack asked. "It's … quieter out there. I mean, if you were interested in talking. But if you wanted to dance …?"

"Horrible dancer," she said.

"You can be a horrible dancer and still be a pretty decent line dancer."

She looked over just as Willow and the drunken blonde bumped into each other, the blonde turning in the wrong direction once again.

"The patio sounds great," Amber said.

She tried to get Willow's attention, but her sister was too consumed in the dance to notice. Jack jerked his head toward the patio door; she followed him, passing two pool tables with games currently in play. Someone took a starting shot and the cue ball *clacked* against the solid and striped balls positioned in a neat triangle in the middle of the table. A group of very young-looking guys set up another table to play beer pong. Who knew a place in Edgehill could be this lively?

The cool night air was a welcome relief when she stepped out onto the patio after Jack. The crowd here had thinned a little, so Amber and Jack were able to snag a small table in one of the corners closest to the sidewalk. A waist-high black iron fence enclosed the patio area. She did her best to ignore the dark, still field across the street.

Jack sat with his back facing the sidewalk and smiled nervously at her. Then he glanced away. He wore a dark blue button-up shirt and jeans and ran his hands up and down his thighs now. She wasn't sure if his palms were clammy and he was trying to rectify that, or if it was an anxious tick, because now that they were sitting across from each other, clearly neither one had a clue what to say.

Aside from idle pleasantries and flirtatious banter exchanged while she placed an order for coffee and one of Jack's famous blueberry scones at Purrcolate, they really hadn't talked about anything of substance. He'd flirted and chatted amicably with her every time she walked in. Sometimes he seemed like he was about to ask her out again, but she'd always cut off the conversation or found an excuse to leave when things headed that direction.

No non-witch men for her. Not after Max.

Though she hadn't bothered with witch men in a long time either. Granted, pickings were non-existent in a place like Edgehill.

She had a sneaking suspicion that she would rather like

Jack if she let herself get to know him. Every time he saw her—and his face lit up like he'd just witnessed a miracle—her first instinct was to run in the other direction. Connor was handsome and seemed to be interested in her, but he didn't fill her with quite the same level of inner panic the way Jack Terrence did.

Amber tightly held her small black clutch in her lap. She needed to be at home with Alley and Tom. It was safer there.

"Oh, uh … did you want anything to drink?" Jack asked now, pulling her out of her mini meltdown. He shot a thumb toward the door that led back into the noisy bar.

"Oh, I'm okay, thanks." Though she felt parched the instant she said no. Would it be weird to suddenly change her mind?

He nodded absently.

They'd gone from being unable to shut up to being unable to talk at all. Should she ask him about his brother? About how business was going?

She glanced toward the field on the opposite side of the street. Dark trees and shrubs surrounded by shadows. She wasn't sure why the "maybe there's a Penhallow lurking in there" thought was hanging on for dear life, but it was.

"You okay?" Jack asked.

She refocused on him, only to have movement on the sidewalk near the kiosk catch her eye. Glancing around Jack, she saw Connor Declan and his two friends had arrived. It would be rude to not flag them down, right? Would it be ruder to leave Jack to go talk to Connor?

When she glanced back at Jack, she'd caught him gazing at her. His expression softened. There was no doubt that there was a torrent of things he wanted to say to her. She very much suspected he felt the same panic she did.

"Umm … some people I was meeting just got here."

Jack visibly deflated.

"I'll be right back. Promise! I just wanted to let them know where to find my sister."

Jack's expression made Amber worry that the second her back was turned, he would launch over the railing surrounding the patio and go sprinting off into the dark.

"Don't move!" she said, playfully wagging a finger at him.

He nodded, his gaze raking over her for a second as she stood up in her ridiculous red dress, but then he quickly looked away.

"Hey, Connor!" Amber called out, walking to the other end of the patio. The kiosk sat in the space made between the patio's fence and the side of the Sippin' Siamese's front room. From here, Amber could see the same woman who had been belting a power ballad was still at it. The guys were fumbling in their back pockets for their wallets to pay the cover charge to get in. They all wore jeans and plaid shirts. Wesley Young sported a cowboy hat.

Connor looked over and his eyes widened. "Hey to you, too. Wow, you look amazing."

Amber looked down helplessly at herself again. "Wasn't my idea."

"Va-va-*voom*!" Wesley said, walking up behind Connor to sling an arm over his shoulder. He gave Amber a once over. "You're a fox, you know that?"

He was clearly very drunk again. Still?

"A foxy, foxy fox."

Amber angled a raised eyebrow at Connor.

"There might have been a bit of pregame happening before we left," Connor said. "And it may be my birthday, but I'm pretty sure I'll be designated driver because these two are out of control."

Wesley, though he still had an arm around Connor, kept trying to talk to his friend behind them, who had a phone pressed to his ear.

"Hey, Wesley?"

He whirled forward at the sound of Amber's voice. It took a second for his eyes to stop swimming long enough to focus on her. He smirked. "Yes, Foxy?"

"Willow's here."

Eyes wide, he stood straight as a board. Then he bent toward her at an angle so severe, it caused Connor to stumble a step forward and Amber a step back, even though they were still separated by the low fence. In a whisper that was so loud that Amber had to fight a laugh, he said, "She's inside right *now*?"

"Sure is."

He stood straight again, released Connor, and used both hands to adjust his cowboy hat. "I'm ready."

Then, without further explanation, Wesley marched for the front door, pulled it open, and deftly sauntered inside. Jake, who was manning the kiosk, called after him, but Wesley Young was on a mission.

Connor tipped his head back to the sky before looking

back at Amber and saying, "I'll go keep an eye on him. He's such a mess. I'll see you in there?"

"Yeah," she said, then waved at the other guy as he paid the cover for them all and followed Connor inside.

Jack was still sitting awkwardly at the table when she returned and sat across from him. "Do you need to …?" He shot a thumb in the direction of the bar again.

"All good." She needed to get the pained look off his face. "So what made you move to Edgehill of all places when you'd been in a city as exciting as Seattle?"

He seemed to sag with relief at the question. "Larry came here on a whim almost ten years ago. He really fell in love with the place and would come back every year for the Here and Meow. Cut to a couple years later, and I had just finished culinary school and was really itching to start a bakery. Most restaurants fail in their first year, but in a place as expensive as Seattle? I didn't think I could compete. Larry, on the other hand, had always wanted to open an internet café.

"One night, we were out drinking with some friends and someone drunkenly said Larry and I should combine our two passions and open a place together. Larry dragged me to the Here and Meow that year—kicking and screaming—five years ago. Love at first sight, me and this town. Within a year of that trip, we'd cut the ribbon at Purrcolate."

Amber couldn't help but smile as he talked. She loved Edgehill and was always delighted when she met someone who'd been ensnared by the place's charm. It was what had initially bonded Amber and Melanie.

"You said your sister is in town?" Jack asked, a bit more

relaxed now. The smattering of freckles across his nose was muted in the soft light here on the patio. "Willow, right?"

Amber nodded, telling him about Willow and their aunt. She skirted around the topic of her parents and the fire. She knew he knew about their deaths—everyone in Edgehill did—and was grateful when he made no attempt to ask about them.

She eyed the field again, picturing a Penhallow sizing her up from the safety of the dark field. But Aunt Gretchen had said the Penhallow threat was coming, not already here. Likely she was worrying prematurely.

"Do you see something over there?" Jack asked.

Amber flushed a little. "No, sorry."

She asked him about culinary school to get the conversation back on track. As much as she enjoyed talking to him—both joking and laughing more the longer they talked—she suddenly found herself distracted by yet something else. Instead of the field across the street, now it was the shift in energy on the patio. A person picked up his phone, looked at Amber, then nudged his companion to show him something on his screen. Someone got a call. And then another. Small rectangles of blue light sprouted up around the patio, one by one, like fireflies flicking to life at dusk. Then Amber's phone buzzed in her clutch. Jack pulled his phone out of his pocket.

Before she could voice her confusion, the patio door burst open and Willow stood there, breathing hard, eyes wild. Amber was on her feet before she realized it.

"What?" Amber asked, her stomach in knots. "What happened?"

Willow hurried to her. "Someone was just found dead at

the Manx Hotel. A town-wide text just went out. I … I don't know details, but … it's an older woman and—"

Amber didn't hear what else her sister said. She was already running.

It wasn't until Amber was halfway down the sidewalk, the country music a mere hum in the distance now, that she remembered she hadn't driven here. There were no car keys in her clutch.

"Amber! Wait up!" It was Jack.

She slowed and turned to him. "Where's Willow? I have to make sure my aunt is okay." She heard the mounting panic in her own voice.

"Connor's with her. We're meeting them in front. C'mon."

Amber's mind was such a buzz of nerves, she didn't protest when Jack grabbed her hand and pulled her after him, jogging to the gravel lot. He opened the door to his little four-door black sedan—not out of some act of chivalry, she thought, but because she likely looked like she was going to pass out—and then deftly maneuvered his car out of the tight space and out onto the road.

By the time they pulled up in front of the Sippin' Siamese, Connor and Willow were waiting. Connor ran around the back to get in behind Jack, and Willow climbed in behind Amber. Willow didn't say anything, just squeezed Amber's shoulder.

Her aunt hadn't been feeling well. Amber thought about how pale the woman had been when she first arrived. Had she been sicker than she let on? Amber had been out at a bar when her aunt was ill and alone in an impersonal hotel room. If something had happened to her, Amber knew she'd never forgive herself.

The drive to the Manx Hotel was only twenty minutes, but it felt like half a lifetime. Amber was too nervous to check her phone, but Willow informed her every few minutes that she still didn't know any details.

When Jack turned onto Calico Boulevard, the hotel just a block away, the flash of red and blue lights sent Amber's heart into her throat. For a moment, she was back on that sidewalk outside her burned home, emergency lights bouncing off the walls, the smell of charred wood heavy in the air.

"Oh God."

She startled when Jack lightly patted her leg. His hand was there, then gone. She supposed her muttered plea hadn't just been in her head.

An ambulance sat outside the Manx as well, the doors thrown open. There wasn't a stretcher inside, just bright yellow-white light and shelving covered in medical equipment. The second Jack pulled to the curb a few doors down, Amber and Willow were out of the car and jogging up the sidewalk. Willow slipped her hand into Amber's. They were sixteen and fourteen again.

People stood around in front of the hotel, some wrapped in blankets, some in robes and slippers. No one fell to their knees at the sight of the Blackwood sisters and apologized for their loss when the pair moved past them and up the steps to the front door. But, Amber guessed, most people staying at the Manx wouldn't be locals. These people didn't know them.

Unlike the somber scene outside, the lobby buzzed with nervous energy. A cluster of hotel staff in crisp black outfits huddled together on one side of the lobby. Amber didn't see Carrie among them. One of the staff members stood apart from the group, giving his account to a uniformed police officer. Amber could only see the man's back, but if she had to guess, she'd say it was Garcia, one of the officers she'd met briefly a few weeks ago when Whitney Sadler was apprehended. Amber wondered if the cut on his arm inflected by a kitchen-knife-wielding Whitney had scarred.

The realization that Chief Owen Brown would more than likely be here turned Amber's stomach inside out.

Guests stood in clusters around the lobby.

"What do we do, just run upstairs?" Willow hissed at Amber.

Just then, a tall, lanky figure started to make his way down the wide staircase directly behind the reception desk. Amber recognized him instantly—Carl, Edgehill's newest and youngest addition to the force. He was a sweet guy, but very green. And a bit like an overly excited puppy.

"C'mon," Amber said, pulling Willow behind her.

They rounded the desk, then hurried up the steps. They met Carl halfway.

"Whoa there," Carl said, hands out. His face lit up a second later. "Amber! Hi." His attention swiveled to Willow. "Well, *hello.*"

Amber fought an eye roll. "Can we go up, Carl? Do you know if my aunt is okay?"

"Your aunt?" He frowned. "I'm so sorry, ladies, but I can't let you up there. He made that real clear. 'Carl,' he said, 'don't let anyone up here. I mean it. It's an active crime scene.'" He chewed on the inside of his cheek. Softly, he said, "I'm real sorry. If you wait in the lobby, I'll have Chief Brown come talk to you right away."

This couldn't be happening. A *crime* scene?

Willow's grip on Amber's hand clenched so hard, Amber yelped. When she turned to her sister, her lips were moving quickly, though no sound came out. A spell. What on *earth* was she doing? Was she really going to use her magic in a hotel full of people? In a hotel where Owen Brown was surely just a few hundred feet away?

The same Owen Brown who, two weeks ago, had seen Amber use her magic. He knew her secret. It had been a long, long time since a human knew her secret. Her palms sweated.

Carl let out a muted grunt. Amber's attention snapped back to him. His eyes had glazed over. Then, without a word, he started down the steps again as if he didn't see them. Amber and Willow quickly let go of each other's hands so Carl had an unobstructed path down the stairs. He slowly trudged forward like an unseeing zombie.

"What did you do to him?" Amber hissed after he'd made it to the bottom of the steps, turning her attention back to her sister.

But Willow was nearly to the top of the staircase. Amber scrambled to catch up with her.

"Simple manipulation spell," Willow said, large brown eyes scanning the three hallways—one to either side of them, and one straight ahead. "He currently thinks he's sleepwalking through his apartment. He'll snap out of it when he makes it outside and will be *quite* confused, so I suggest we hurry."

Amber blew out a breath, a headache forming.

"This way," Willow said, turning right.

They had just reached the open door of Room 18, Aunt Gretchen's room, when Amber heard Chief Owen Brown's voice. "There's nothing we can do for her now. We should get a hold of the coroner as soon as possible. I don't have the faintest clue what killed her."

Willow let out a strained whimper.

Amber swayed and grabbed the doorjamb to keep herself on her feet. "Aunt Gretchen?" she choked out, running into the room. To hell with Chief Brown and what he thought of her. This was her *family*.

But no sooner had she bolted into the room, she came up short, breath whooshing out of her. Not because of what she saw, but what she felt. The air was thick in this room. It felt sticky almost, like walking into a wall made of spiderwebs.

The second the comparison came into her mind, she remembered something her aunt had told her earlier that day. That you could feel when a Penhallow had used their twisted, cursed magic. Amber felt the sticky remnants of it now.

Had a Penhallow come to Edgehill just as Aunt Gretchen had warned her? But she'd said the witch had been coming for *Amber*. Had her intel been wrong?

In the space between the window and bed, Amber's gaze

snagged on something on the floor. A pair of feet in sensible black shoes, toes turned out so that the inner ankles rested on the plush beige carpet. That's all she could see—a pair of lifeless feet.

A massive wall of man stepped into her path and she sucked in another breath as she looked up into Chief Brown's irate face. "I can't imagine what you're doing here, Miss Blackwood. That fool boy Carl wasn't supposed to let anyone up here."

"This is my aunt's room," she managed, feeling more than a little annoyed that her voice cracked on the last word.

The reality of the situation seemed to dawn on him then and the creases in his forehead smoothed out. "Oh, Amber, I thought you knew …"

It was true then. Willow let out a pained sob somewhere behind the chief. Was this really happening to them again?

"Can I at least see her?" Tears welled in her eyes.

Chief Brown gently grabbed Amber by the arms before she managed to make it past him.

"Let me go!"

"Amber!" he said, shaking her slightly. "It's not her! It's not your aunt. It's a maid. She was in here to bring your aunt extra towels. We don't know where your aunt is. I'm sorry. I … I thought you were with her and knew it wasn't her."

Amber sagged against him. "Oh, thank God." Then she pulled away when it dawned on her that she just callously said she was glad someone else had died instead of her aunt. "I didn't mean … I just …"

"It's fine," he said. "But this is still a crime scene, and I need you out of here."

"Right. Of course," she said. "I'm sorry for barging in here."

A look she couldn't describe passed across his face. Was he remembering what he saw? Her using magic to stop an object in midair?

"What in the blue blazes is going on here?"

Amber suddenly felt light as a feather, and she grinned at the chief, unable to help herself. She peered around his frame and spotted her aunt in the doorway, a bag of food in her grasp from a nearby Chinese take-out place. Willow squealed and threw her arms around her, almost knocking the woman off her feet.

When Amber's gaze met her aunt's, she willed her to know what she was thinking. *You were right.*

Aunt Gretchen's expression hardened, one that confirmed what Amber already knew.

A Penhallow was in Edgehill.

CHAPTER 6

Though Aunt Gretchen offered a very compelling argument about why she should be allowed to take her suitcase with her, the chief told her that since the room was now an active crime scene, it meant her suitcase was an active piece of evidence until it was cleared. So, with only her bag of Chinese food in her possession, Aunt Gretchen followed Amber and Willow out of Room 18. The expression on Chief Brown's face told Amber she would be hearing from him one way or another, likely sooner rather than later.

An active crime scene. The phrase repeated in Amber's head like the chorus of an annoying pop song. An active crime scene.

It meant the maid hadn't suffered from some freak medical condition. It meant her death had been deemed suspicious. The non-witch Edgehill police force had no way of knowing about the sticky-magic residue left by the Penhallow. Amber had only seen the maid's lifeless feet, her inner ankles lying flat on the carpet. Whatever had happened to her resulted in her falling face-down. What had been done to her body?

Had what happened to her been meant for Gretchen? Wrong place, wrong time for the maid? Or a message?

I'm here. You're not safe.

"You're staying with me," Amber said, looping her arm through her aunt's as she steered them toward the stairs. "Because I'm assuming you won't go back to Portland."

"Absolutely not," her aunt said, only a slight waver to her voice. "Not now."

Once they made it down the stairs, Amber spotted both Connor and Jack waiting in the lobby, hands shoved into the pockets of their jeans, both looking ten shades of confused. They weren't speaking to one another, though their silence didn't seem tense.

Jack noticed her first and broke away from Connor to meet them halfway across the crowded lobby. He smiled warmly at her aunt. Amber wasn't sure if the two had ever met before this. "I'm so relieved to see you, Gretchen. You had us all worried. Is everything okay?" That second question was angled at Amber.

"I think so," Amber said, though the knot in her chest still hadn't unfurled. "It … it was a maid."

Jack winced. "Any idea what happened?"

"None," she said.

"You're that nice young man who makes those sinfully delicious scones," Aunt Gretchen said by way of greeting. It was also her superpower to be able to talk about anything *other* than the elephant in the room. Even if the elephant was bright pink, wearing a hat, and doing a jig.

"That's me," Jack said. "I don't know if we've ever formally met. I'm Jack Terrence." He held out his hand.

Aunt Gretchen shook it, then gently patted the back of it with her free hand. She looked over at Amber and winked. In a stage whisper, she added, "He's a cutie. I'll drink a tincture with his name on it tonight."

Amber knew her aunt was just trying to distract her, but she still couldn't help the flush of color that rose into her cheeks—a color that was no doubt the same shade as the dress she wore.

At the same time that Jack said, "A what?" Amber said, "Oh my God, please don't do this now."

Aunt Gretchen grinned, then quickly turned her attention to her left. "Willow, love, stop picking at my food."

"Sorry!" Willow said. Amber glanced over at her just as the tail end of an egg roll disappeared in her mouth. She licked her fingers.

Connor, shamefaced, held the Styrofoam container in his hands, the lid flipped open and resting against his chest. His open palms had been fashioned into a table to better aid in Willow's food thievery. He glanced at Gretchen. "I didn't know it was yours."

"Girl is a bottomless pit," Gretchen said.

Willow fastened the container's top and pulled the plastic bag up around it. She looked up at Connor, then away, taking the bag from him. "Sorry we ruined your birthday."

"Far from it," he said, smiling softly at her. "We spent many a night at the Sippin' Siamese in high school. It was like old times. Didn't realize how much I missed it until tonight."

"Underage drinking, Willow, really?" Aunt Gretchen chided, but there was no bite to her tone, implying she'd been well aware of Willow's many rebellious exploits in high school.

Amber watched as Willow and Connor fidgeted in front

of each other. She wondered how he was going to get back to his friends, assuming they were still at the bar.

"I can take you ladies home and then take Connor back to the Siamese …" Jack offered.

Everyone in their little group looked mildly disappointed with this suggestion, though it was the most logical one.

"Sounds good," Amber said, mustering up the best approximation of a smile as she could.

They all filed toward the Manx's front door. Amber, with Jack just behind her, had just reached the doorway when the sensation of someone watching her set the hair on the back of her neck on end. Was the witch still here? She glanced over her shoulder, scanning the crowd as if someone would be wearing a nametag that read, "Hi, I'm a Penhallow. I'm cursed and want you dead."

Her gaze snagged on Chief Brown standing in the middle of the staircase, currently giving a dressing down to Carl, who stood in front of him, head lowered. The chief looked up suddenly, his dark eyes narrowing when he spotted Amber. His lips pursed into a thin line.

She quickly broke eye contact and went out the door after her family.

Jack pulled in front of the Quirky Whisker ten minutes later. The inside of the store was dark, its knickknacks and oddities a series of smudgy shadows behind the glass. On the opposite side of the street, a faint glow of light shone in one of the back rooms of Purrfectly Scrumptious. She wondered if it was Betty Harris or her husband, Bobby, who was still there at this hour. She suspected it was Betty, and she pictured her bent over a freshly baked cake, applying an elaborate series of fondant layers. There would be flour splashed across her apron, and a smear of colored frosting on one of her dark cheeks.

Amber, Willow, and Gretchen had been squeezed into the back of Jack's car, Connor up front. Willow helped Gretchen, who seemed a little unsteady on her feet now, out of the car. Nerves? Shock? Was her illness, whatever it was, getting worse?

Amber had been sitting behind Jack and got out now, then stood awkwardly by his open window. She'd had fun with him on this not-date, however brief it might have been. "Thank you for dropping us off."

"Of course," he said, temple resting against the headrest as he looked up at her. "Let me know how she is in the morning."

She didn't have his number. She didn't have Connor's either, but at the moment, his attention seemed to be squarely focused on Willow and Gretchen. "I could call you, but ..."

Jack flushed. "Right. Uhh ..." He fumbled in his pockets to get his phone. Amber rattled off the numbers and he programmed her in, immediately calling her so she would have his number too.

She couldn't tell from here if Connor was bothered by any of this. Was *she* bothered by any of this? Was Jack? What in the world was happening tonight?

Rounding the front of the car, she waved at the two men. Connor had an elbow stuck out the window, and his gaze flicked between Amber and Willow several times, his mouth

68

drawn down in a slight frown. So perhaps he *did* feel as strange about this evening as she did.

"Have a nice night, guys," Amber said. "Thanks again. And happy birthday, Connor."

"Yes, happy birthday, Seven!" Willow said.

Eyes wide, he froze for a second. Then he laughed. "You weren't supposed to remember that!"

"I remember all," Willow said, tone ominous, followed by a wicked grin.

Connor laughed and shook his head. With another wave from both men, the car pulled away from the curb.

Aunt Gretchen looked from Amber to Willow and back again. "Which one of you likes the brown-haired nerdy one again?"

Amber groaned, fishing around in her clutch for the keys. "We have more important things to discuss."

After letting them in, Amber locked up behind her. She stared at the lock, thinking about how Aunt Gretchen had used her magic to unlock it. What would stop a Penhallow from doing the same? How much safer were they here than Gretchen had been at the Manx? At least there had been more people around there. They were nearly isolated here. Amber's hands shook and she balled them into fists. "Do you two think you could ward this place to kingdom come?"

Assuming, of course, that a Penhallow hadn't already been here. The only good thing about the use of their cursed magic was that it left a trace any one of them could feel. The Quirky Whisker, at least for now, felt untouched.

"I haven't needed to use one in quite some time, so I'm a

little rusty," Aunt Gretchen said. "But we can salt the entryways at the very least."

"I can layer an alarm of sorts on the doors and windows too," Willow said. "I have a tincture I was experimenting with when I needed proof that my roommate was eating my food in the middle of the night. Turns out she was a sleep-eater. Ate a whole box of cereal—dry—at three in the morning once."

Aunt Gretchen chuckled. "If we each add a strand or two of hair to it, we'll feel it if someone we haven't given permission to enters this place."

Amber was out of her depth here. She'd never attempted a protection spell. She'd never had a reason to even consider one. Nevertheless, she helped her aunt and sister collect the materials they needed to get started. She felt more like a lowly apprentice helping her masters work, than a witch worthy of all this fuss.

Could she even be sure that Aunt Gretchen's intel was correct? Was the Penhallow after her at all? Yet, she supposed, the Penhallow could have tracked Gretchen down in Portland if she truly had been the target. Was Amber in the Penhallow's sights as some kind of Darwinesque plot to take out the weakest link before working their way up the Blackwood chain? Was eliminating Amber only the beginning of their plan?

After Gretchen and Willow had secured the downstairs, they went up to the studio. The cats didn't act remotely freaked out, which was another sign to Amber that the Penhallow hadn't been here. Yet.

Aunt Gretchen salted windows, muttered protective spells, and created tinctures. They worked well together, her aunt and sister, using terms and mentioning ingredients Amber was unfamiliar with.

Within an hour, both Willow and Gretchen were changed— Willow magicked a pair of Amber's pajamas into something that would fit Gretchen comfortably—and passed out on the bed, the cats curled up between them.

Amber had insisted on the couch despite their protests, partly because she knew she wouldn't be able to sleep tonight. Not after a Penhallow had, presumably, tried to kill her aunt.

Slowly, she crept off the couch and padded to her window seat, peering out at her unfinished family home far out on the horizon. The burned areas had been removed, but the house had yet to be completed. A place where whatever knowledge she might have gained about the Penhallows had gone up in smoke. It wasn't as if she could pop over to the library and check out a stack of books on witch family legacies. Not accurate ones, anyway.

She tipped her head back to rest on the wall behind her, then gazed at her sleeping aunt and sister. Gretchen knew— had always known—more about the Penhallows, but she'd kept that information close to the vest. Amber had asked and asked, but was shut down time and again. Even now, Amber saw the hesitation in her aunt's eyes. Remembered how deftly the woman had steered clear of the subject as much as possible tonight.

The conversation Amber originally had with her aunt came back to her, and her attention snagged on the same thing it did the last ten times she'd replayed it in her head. *Maybe we should pay Edgar a visit.*

Why now?

There were too many unanswered questions. Her magic thrummed. It needed an outlet. She'd heard of restless leg syndrome—was there such a thing as restless magic syndrome?

She needed to get the heck out of her studio before her magic erupted and leveled the building.

With a final glance at her sleeping family, she silently climbed off the window seat, changed into jeans and a sweater, grabbed her shoes and purse, and made her way down the stairs in bare feet.

Her aunt wouldn't talk to her about her parents and the fire and the Penhallows? Fine.

She'd find answers herself.

CHAPTER 7

Amber had just reached the front door—shoes now on her feet and purse strapped over her shoulder—when someone behind her said, "And where are you going at this hour?"

She sighed and squeezed her eyes shut. No one could make her feel like a little girl again the way her aunt could. Dropping her hand from the doorknob, she turned around.

Aunt Gretchen stood at the base of the stairs, backlit by the warm yellow light cascading down the steps, casting her face in deep shadows. But Amber could have seen that furrowed brow and pinched mouth even with her eyes closed. Her aunt's arms were folded across her chest, one foot stuck out in front of her, ready to tap out a rhythm of disappointment if necessary.

"I need to find someone to talk to about all this, because *you* won't," Amber whisper-hissed, surprised by the venom in her own voice. "You've shut me down *every* time I try to talk to you about my parents or that night. Every. Single. Time. And now the Penhallows are apparently back here and they almost killed *you* this time. You might not be scared about that, but I am. Call me a worrier if you want to, but I'm not going to keep pretending like nothing is happening here."

Amber felt her magic's thrumming beneath her skin turn

73

to something closer to thrashing. Her aunt was the only person she'd ever met who could make her feel this frustrated. This boxed in. Her chest heaved and the hand not currently clutching her keys in a death grip opened and closed.

When a small display of ever-burning candles lifted from their nearby shelf—which Amber saw out of the corner of her eye, as she had yet to stop glaring at her aunt—Gretchen closed the distance between herself and Amber. She got into Amber's space, head tipped back to look her in the eye, and pointed a finger in her face. "Calm yourself. What have I always said? Be careful about your magic. What if someone sees you?"

It was almost the exact same thing Amber had said to Willow earlier. Be careful. Hide. Deny. And what had that denial gotten her? Chief Brown saw her magic anyway. Keeping their secret wasn't keeping her safe. If anything, it made her more *unsafe*. Because she felt wholly unequipped for all this—she didn't even know what "this" was.

"Who cares?" Amber snapped. "It's only a matter of time before the Penhallow comes back. I can't do anything but make really crappy tinctures and plastic toy animals that perform children's tricks. If a Penhallow comes after me, I'm a goner. So who cares who sees me? My days are numbered, right? So are yours. Just like Mom and Dad's were."

Amber had never gotten confirmation from her aunt that the Penhallows were responsible for her parents' death, but it never stopped her from asking. Even if the question had gone unanswered for fourteen years. She maintained her death glare at her aunt, putting her sixteen-year-old self to shame. Amber was older now, had run out of patience, and was scared half out of her mind. She wasn't going to back down now.

A few books and a marble cat statue rose into the air now too, hovering, waiting for the okay from Amber's magic to fly about the room. Amber felt like a coiled spring.

"You can do more than children's tricks. Much more."

Amber faltered for a moment, the floating objects wobbling in midair. It was the soft, almost sad tone her aunt had used that got to her. "What?"

Her aunt crossed her arms, breaking eye contact. "*This* is what you can do," she said, waving a hand at the hovering objects. "You have a strong affinity for the manipulation of matter—moving objects, changing the form of objects. And thanks to the Henbane part of you, you can also manipulate time."

Henbane. Her mother's maiden name.

With a dejected sigh, Gretchen added, "Just like your mother could."

Amber staggered back a step and the objects in question hit the ground, her anger drained out of her in an instant. The curving tail and one ear of the marble cat statue snapped off on impact. She groaned inwardly; that thing had been expensive.

Then her brain caught up. "Time?" Amber asked.

"Before that overactive mind of yours starts running through the possibilities … no you can't go back in time and stop your parents' deaths. But you *can* freeze time for short durations. You can even reverse it or speed it up. But, again, you're *not* a time traveler; you're quite limited in how far back you can go."

Amber blinked at her. Nothing in all Amber's years of self-taught magic had even *hinted* that she had magic strong enough or capable enough to manipulate something as complicated as time.

Clearly sensing Amber's bewilderment, Gretchen said, "While Willow's magic clearly comes from the Blackwood side, *your* magic favors your mother's. We Blackwoods are known for our tinctures and healing abilities—and that can mean healing a broken inanimate object, a broken bone, or a broken heart. The Henbanes, however, have always had an affinity for manipulation of matter and time. Belle saw it in you from a young age," Aunt Gretchen said. "And she did her best to squash it."

Amber shook her head, blinking quickly. She'd gone for so long without answers, and now she was drowning in them. "Why did she want to *squash* my powers? It's who I am."

"But it's not, little mouse. You've lived a full life without your powers. They don't define you. Your mother didn't want you to rely on your magic like a crutch."

A *full* life seemed like a stretch, but she kept that to herself. Amber felt like her life had been put on hold the moment her parents died. And her lack of knowledge about her history had been a big part of that. On some level, she'd never felt truly comfortable in her own skin—and neither had her magic.

Edgar was a Henbane. Did *he* know how to manipulate time?

"Why did she want to squash my powers?" Amber asked again.

After a few moments, her aunt sighed. "I don't know all the details of this myself—"

Amber cocked a brow.

Hands raised in innocence, Aunt Gretchen said, "Honestly. I'm in the dark about some of this, too … but your mother had a bit of a dark past. Rumor has it, when she was in her early twenties, she'd been involved with a Penhallow."

Amber's eyes widened. "Involved *how*?"

Gretchen shrugged. "I don't know. Some rumors implied it was merely her falling in with the wrong crowd, others imply it had been a romantic entanglement that went awry. Your mother didn't like talking about it. I'm not even sure how much your father knew."

Amber chewed on the inside of her cheek. "Was whatever happened back then the reason why they moved to Edgehill?"

"Yes," she said. "That much I do know, even if I don't know the details of why."

A bit desperately, Amber tried to ask the same question she'd been asking for years. "So it might have been a Penhallow who tracked her to Edgehill and then killed her and my father?"

Aunt Gretchen lowered her gaze to the dark floor beneath their feet. "I believe so, yes. I'm almost certain."

Amber felt tears prick her eyes and she had to walk away from her aunt. It felt as if something in her chest had cracked. Her aunt had *known*. Had known all this time that her parents had been *murdered*, that it hadn't been some freak electrical glitch. For fourteen years, she'd lied to Amber about it. Lied to her face, lied by omission—it didn't matter. Lying was lying.

She was family, the only close family Amber had left aside from Willow, and she'd lied to her. Repeatedly. About the one thing that had ever truly mattered to her. The thing that kept her feeling trapped in Edgehill. No matter how much she loved this town, the mystery of her parents' death kept her rooted here more than anything else.

Amber paced, head tipped back to the ceiling as she willed herself not to cry. She wasn't sure if she was more upset by the truth, or by the lies.

She stopped and rounded on Gretchen. The woman had the decency to look nervous. "Why didn't you tell me *any* of this sooner?"

"Your mother told me not to," she said. "Demanded it."

Amber was shocked into silence again.

Before Amber could get her jumbled thoughts in order, Gretchen spoke. "That tincture I take at night? The one that grants me foresight? Well, I used to make it for your mother. In the weeks before their deaths, she'd been plagued with nightmares of fire. She was sure it was a premonition, but there were so few details in the dreams, she didn't know if it was a premonition of something she could change, or merely a warning of something she couldn't escape. I gave her the tincture to help bring her clarity." After a pause, she said, "She'd even considered seeking out her brother's help. His late wife, your aunt Kathleen, had been a Caraway. Caraways often have an affinity for the sight; your mother thought he might have some advice about how to interpret her visions."

"Did she ever talk to him?" Amber asked.

"Not that I know of," she said. "Edgar, by all accounts,

had inherited a touch of the sight from his mother. But Belle never sought them out."

Amber could only guess as to why. What had caused the falling out in the first place?

"All your mother told me was that …" Her aunt's bottom lip shook, and her eyes misted over. Amber hadn't seen her aunt cry in almost fourteen years. It was as if she'd cried herself dry when Belle and Theo Blackwood died. "All she told me was that I had to make sure you girls were away from the house that night. She said the danger they faced could be dealt with, but she couldn't keep herself and your father safe while also worrying about you girls."

Magic hummed beneath Amber's skin again, but now it felt confused, bumping around haphazardly like a trapped insect. It wanted to lash out, but where? How could Amber so desperately want to pull her aunt into a tight hug and shove her away at the same time?

"We had a slumber party at Alice's that night," Amber said. "How did you have anything to do with that? You weren't even in Edgehill then …"

"I called Alice's mom and asked if she could keep you girls at the house overnight because your mother was planning a surprise for your father and needed you out of her hair," Gretchen said, threat of tears mostly gone now. "When she confirmed she would be home for the evening and would be able to look after you, I cast a memory-wipe spell so she wouldn't remember the last two minutes of our conversation, then I cast a spell for persuasion. I urged her to ask Alice to invite you girls over for a sleepover, since Alice would be leaving for summer camp soon and she should get some time in with friends before she left. I needed it to seem like the idea came from Alice and her mother. Within a day, the plans were in place and no one was the wiser but myself and Belle."

Amber felt her own bottom lip shake now, and briefly sunk her teeth in to still it. "Did my dad know this was happening? What the plan was?"

A tear ran down Gretchen's face, and she quickly swiped it away, sniffling hard. "I don't know. I want to hope so. I want to hope he knew what was coming and he chose to lay beside your mother and accept their fate. Especially if it meant keeping you two safe. But …"

The majority of her parents' remains had been found in their beds. Had they taken something to remain unconscious? Had they chosen to go out together, hands held tightly, as flames licked up the walls?

Yet, Edgar had said they'd been *trapped* inside. That they'd tried to get out and couldn't. Had he truly suffered a psychotic break and made all that up? Or had the break been caused by what he'd seen that night?

Either way, Gretchen had not only known, but she'd done nothing to save them. She'd known her mother had predicted there would be a fire, had predicted that she and Amber's father were in danger, and Gretchen hadn't intervened. If anything, Gretchen had helped it along by agreeing to get Amber and Willow out of the house.

Jaw clenched, Amber's attention snapped to her aunt. The woman looked broken, her shoulders slumped. But Amber found it hard to muster up any sympathy right now.

"Why didn't you stop her? Why didn't you help them?" Amber ground out.

Gretchen worked her jaw, eyes rimmed in silver. "You don't think I blame myself every day for what happened that night? Belle *told* me they'd be fine. She told me that I just needed to make sure you girls were somewhere else and that everything would be all right." She visibly swallowed. "I did what she asked—I kept you safe and I obeyed her wishes—but it meant that I lost my brother in the process. He'd been the glue that held our family together. Your grandparents—my parents—both passed a year after Theo. The grief was too much for them both. You and Willow never met them because Belle was so paranoid about keeping you isolated from anything or anyone related to magic. Why she let me into your lives when she shut out nearly everyone else, I'll never know. But I trusted her because Theo worshipped the ground your mother walked on. Theo didn't fall easily."

Amber didn't know what to say to any of this. Movement caught her eye toward the back of the store and she glanced over Gretchen's bent head to see Willow sitting at the base of the staircase, hand pressed to her mouth. The glint on her face from of the weak light illuminating the steps told Amber that her sister was crying. Amber wondered how long she'd been listening.

"I ..." Gretchen cleared her throat, her voice wavering, pulling Amber's attention back to her. "I love you girls as if you were my own. I loved your mother like a sister. But ... but I'm so, *so* angry with her for not giving me a choice. She'd made her decision based on information only she seemed to know, and it took my brother. It destroyed my parents. It destroyed both of you."

Amber was crying now. She wasn't sure when that had started.

"So, *no*, I don't enjoy discussing that night, Amber," Gretchen said now, some of her familiar steeliness returning. "It was the worst night of my life. But what happened, happened. Dwelling on the past won't change anything. They're gone and life goes on. It has to."

But that wasn't entirely true. The past—specifically Amber's mother's past—had crept back into Edgehill, leaving behind a cursed, sticky mess. It had killed an innocent woman who had nothing whatsoever to do with Amber and her twisted family tree.

"I can't be here," Amber said, voice far away and small.

"What?" Gretchen said, bewildered. "We don't know who or where the witch is. Don't leave now. It's not safe. Especially not at night. You just need some sleep and then we can discuss what to do next in the morning."

Amber took several steps back. "I just need some fresh air."

Before Gretchen or Willow—who was on her feet now—could say or do anything to stop her, she was out the door.

CHAPTER 8

Neither her sister nor her aunt chased her down. Amber guessed Gretchen had tried, and Willow had held her back. Willow would know that the harder someone pushed Amber, the more she pushed back. Her theory was confirmed when, several minutes later, a text message popped up on her cell phone, which was currently fastened to her dashboard. Her car was already well on its way to putting considerable distance between itself and the Quirky Whisker.

Amber's gaze quickly flicked to the message.

Text me every 10 minutes so I know you're okay. I'm scrying your location already. If you don't message me, I WILL find you and drag you back.

Amber had no idea where she was going. Her half-formed plan when she'd crept out of her studio with her shoes in hand like some rebellious teenager had flown out of her head when Aunt Gretchen had finally started talking. Amber thought about driving up Ocicat Lane to stare at the old house. Perhaps she could beg her mother's ghost to pay her a visit to explain what in the heck was going on. And why she'd kept so much from her and Willow.

What Amber truly wanted, though, was to go back to several hours ago when her biggest worry was whether or not her dress was too tight. Would her affinity for time-related spells let her do *that*?

Even her mind's voice sounded bitter right now.

Ten minutes later, she pulled into the half-full parking lot of Feral's Diner. Edgehill didn't have a 24-hour ... well, anything ... but the diner stayed open until midnight. It was well-lit and people milled around both inside and in the lot. Amber pulled into a spot near the back, with several empty spaces between her and the nearest car.

She texted Willow. I'm fine. You know where I am. I just need time.

Fair enough.

Relieved, Amber set her phone on the passenger seat. Mere moments later, her phone pinged again.

I still expect to hear from you in ten.

Amber sighed and slouched a little in her seat. She had no desire to go *into* the diner. She wasn't hungry and she didn't want to be around anyone, let alone the crowd of people inside.

Strangely enough, though, the longer she sat there, everything her aunt had told her spinning around in her head, the more she realized there was only one person she truly wanted to talk to right now.

She snatched up her phone again and dialed his number, hoping it wasn't too late and that he was somehow already settling in for the night. But, after an evening like tonight, she supposed he would be up for a while. Amber wedged a thumbnail between her teeth.

He answered on the second ring. "Hello, Miss Blackwood."

"Hi, chief."

"What can I do for you?" he asked, only slightly repressing a sigh, as if offering her assistance with anything, even if it *was* his job, pained him a little.

"What happened to that maid?" she asked, wasting no time. "I mean … how did she die?"

The pause on the other end lasted for several long seconds. "You know I can't tell you that."

"I think whoever did this meant to hurt my aunt," Amber said. "She won't be safe until whoever did this is caught." *And neither will I.*

"The entire Edgehill police force is working on it, Miss Blackwood." His tone was flat, even, and perfectly comforting. Amber hated it. "I understand why you're concerned—I would be too—but you have to trust that we're doing everything we can to find out who is responsible for this. We want him caught just as much as you do."

"Or her," Amber said, subtly reminding him that while he'd suspected Derrick Sadler of being Melanie Cole's murderer, they'd figured out with Amber's help that the killer had been Derrick's wife.

"Or her," he amended. "Was there anything else, Miss Blackwood? It's going to be a long night for me. We're only a couple hours into this thing."

As much as Amber had always dreaded her interactions with the chief in the past—thanks to his general distaste for her—this professional, officer-of-the-law tone was somehow more off-putting. She needed him to talk to her. They'd been developing some kind of a rapport a few weeks ago. It wasn't like they were ever going to be friends, but they'd been civil. He'd confided in her. She wanted that back.

"Are you really just going to pretend like nothing happened?" she asked.

It occurred to Amber then that she'd lost patience with merely sweeping things under the rug, and hoping everything would work itself out if you wore blinders for long enough. She knew now, more than she ever had before, that ignoring what was right in front of you was sure to come back to bite you in the butt later.

"I don't know what you mean, Miss Blackwood." But his voice had lowered a fraction, and then she heard a door open and close. In a tone a little sharper, he added, "This isn't a good time."

She imagined him closed off in that little closet-sized interrogation room, his back turned to the cameras that were wedged into two corners of the ceiling. On some level, she knew her anger and frustration with her aunt was being redirected at the chief, but she plowed ahead anyway. "I know more about this murder than you do."

He gave a short laugh of disbelief. "Didn't you *just* call here a second ago asking how the woman died? How can *you* know more than I do if you don't even know the cause of death?"

"I know *who*, not how."

He didn't respond. She pictured his blonde brows pulling together, his mind whirling. *Should I believe her?* his mind must be saying. *Should I even entertain the idea of listening to her when something about her is so monumentally* off *that I don't even have the proper words to label it?*

86

"Can you meet me down at the station in fifteen minutes?" he asked, irritation evident in his tone. Irritation at her or himself, she couldn't be sure.

"I can be there in ten." She disconnected before he could chastise her for potentially ignoring the speed limit.

She called her sister.

"Hello?" Willow whispered. She'd answered the call so quickly, Amber hadn't even heard it ring. "Are you okay?"

"I'm fine," she said. "I'm going to meet with Chief Brown now, though, so I don't want you to storm the place when I haven't sent a message every ten minutes."

"The same chief who saw you use your magic and has treated you like a leper ever since?" Willow was still whispering. Was she closed in the bathroom? Sitting on the steps leading up to the studio?

"Yep, that one," Amber said. "I need to fill out some paperwork to get Aunt Gretchen's luggage back."

The lie had come easy.

"I'm on your side, you know," Willow said. "It's you and me against the world, right? Don't shut me out now too."

Amber wasn't sure how Willow could always tell when she was lying. "I just need time to process this. It's been a rough night for me."

"They were my parents too."

Amber's eyes welled up. "I know, Will. I didn't mean—"

"We can talk about it in the morning," Willow said.

Before Amber could get out another half-formed apology, Willow had ended the call.

Sighing to herself, Amber pulled her purse onto her lap and

fumbled around inside until she successfully unzipped one of the inner pockets. There was only one item in this particular pocket: a small, rubber white cat. Her mother had given it to her when she was eight, and an orange one to Willow. With the tiny cat in hand—the tips of its ears smudged from spending most of its days in her purse—Amber placed it on the inner lip of the dashboard. The cat stood on all fours, a tiny smile on its face. "*What do you have planned for me now?*" its expression seemed to say.

Amber tossed her purse back onto the passenger seat and started the car. The dashboard lights flicked on, the muted green illuminating the grooves decorating the cat's body in a rough approximation of fur. The lines were barely visible now, though. The end of the cat's tail was missing.

While she drove, she cast the simplest glamour spell she knew. It was a rhyme her mother had taught Amber and Willow when they were very young, and their still-developing magic needed an outlet. It was one of the few spells her mother had taught them.

"*One by one, let's have some fun. Two by two, let's turn it blue.*"

The white cat's "fur" flipped to blue. Seconds later, it turned back. The spell was weak, but it had kept Amber and Willow busy for hours as children. They'd spent even longer penning other rhymes in hopes they could get their cats to turn something other than blue, but they'd never been able to. Amber wondered now if the little rubber cats had been enchanted by her mother to *only* turn blue.

It was the last thing Amber had left that had graced her mother's fingertips.

"One by one, let's have some fun. Two by two, let's turn it blue."

Over and over and over. From white to blue and back again.

The small bursts of magic helped ease some of the tension that had been mounting with every emotional interaction she'd had tonight. She needed to dispel some of it, like slowly letting the air out of a balloon, before she met with the chief. She couldn't imagine he'd be very forthcoming with information if she got so upset that all the furniture in the police station levitated on its own.

The small bursts also helped clear her mind enough to formulate a plan for this discussion with Chief Brown. She needed him to accept that she had information about this case that was literally impossible for him to understand without her knowledge—as limited as it might be—of magic and witches.

She just hoped she wouldn't actually have to levitate furniture in order to get him to believe her.

There was only one available spot in front of the station, and she angled her car into the diagonally aligned space, wedging herself between two cop cars. She plucked the rubber cat off her dashboard and slipped it back in her purse, zipping it safely inside.

After releasing a long, slow breath, she stepped out into the cool night air. The streetlights reflected off the dormant blocks of emergency lights lining the cop cars' hoods. It was quiet in this part of town in the late hours, even if other areas were currently teeming with Olaf Betzen-obsessed tourists. This area was populated by now-dark businesses and office buildings that were a flurry of activity during work hours. Now it felt like the dark streets of a ghost town.

Amber flicked a glance toward the *Edgehill Gazette* office a few doors down, and she wondered if Connor and his drunk buddies were still at the Sippin' Siamese. Had Jack stayed? Had he driven home after he dropped Connor off? Had he gone home with a nice girl who wasn't on a cursed witch's hit list?

Blowing out one more calming breath, Amber willed herself to concentrate. She could worry about men later. Well, there was *one* she had to concentrate on, but thankfully her entanglements with him weren't romantic.

There were only a few people in the lobby of the station. An aggrieved-looking woman sat between two teenage boys who had their arms crossed, mouths pulled down. They were slouched on either side of her on the sad-looking sofa. On the other side of the small waiting area in one of the mismatched plastic chairs sat a very drunk man who looked like he'd either taken a tumble down a hillside or gotten into a bar brawl—and lost. He hummed tunelessly to himself, eyes closed and head swaying to a song only he could hear. Occasionally he would burst into raucous laughter. His hands were folded neatly in his lap.

The woman sitting between the two boys—her sons, if Amber had to guess—kept shooting sidelong looks at the man whenever he erupted into unexplained chuckles.

Amber walked up to the glassless window where Dolores, aka Sour Face, was perched inside her wooden box of a desk, gaze focused on a computer screen Amber couldn't see. The clack of keys stopped when Amber approached, but Dolores's frizzy blonde head didn't turn.

Before she could come up with something to say, she heard, "Amber!"

A grinning Carl strode over. When he stopped a foot away, his mouth suddenly pinched and he scanned the area behind her. "Is your … *sister* here?"

He said "sister" as if were a swear word, one which his mother would box him on the ear for uttering in polite company.

Amber supposed he knew on some level that Willow had done something to make him abandon the strict orders given by the chief. She couldn't imagine how confused he must have been when the spell had worn off, and suddenly he'd found himself at the front door of the Manx Hotel's lobby, when he'd been on the stairs talking to Amber and Willow just a moment before.

"Just me," she said. "I wanted to talk to the chief. He's expecting me."

"Sure thing," Carl said, turning quickly on the ball of one foot, then motioning over his head. "Follow me!"

Dolores's clacking resumed.

Amber turned left, heading after Carl in the opposite direction from the tiny closet-sized interrogation room. She'd been ushered into said room a few weeks ago, shortly after she'd literally run into the chief as she attempted to flee the morgue where Melanie's body had been. The chief had been suspicious then that Amber had something to do with Melanie's demise, and her scurrying out of the morgue like her behind was on fire hadn't helped her case.

It had been a month and half since Melanie died; it still felt like it had just happened. Some part of Amber was still waiting for Melanie to call and invite Amber to play cards while they talked and laughed and drank wine.

But her friend was gone.

As Amber and Carl walked, the ringing of phones was a persistent sound in the background, paired with the murmur of voices. No other officers roamed the hall. Amber wondered how many were putting in long hours tonight, trying to track down leads relating to the maid's death.

Amber still didn't even know the woman's name.

They passed a handful of closed offices and interrogation rooms, then stopped at the end of the hall in front of a wooden door. At chest height rested a small black plaque with the chief's name etched in muted gold. However, it was more mid-stomach height for Carl, given his tall, lanky frame. He grinned at her, then rapped enthusiastically on the door in a familiar and easily recognizable pattern.

There was a slight pause before the chief said, in a mildly annoyed tone, "Come in, Carl."

Carl opened the door and gestured Amber in with a flourish. Once she'd stepped past him, one hand still on the knob, he said, "Hey, boss? How come you always know it's me?"

"You're the only one who knocks that way, Carl," he said, tone slipping past mildly annoyed territory and into "If you don't leave soon, I'm going to strangle you" territory. Amber had a sneaking suspicion that they'd had some version of this conversation many times over.

When Amber glanced back at Carl, he tipped his imaginary hat to her. "And *that's* why he's the chief, Amber. Excellent detective skills." He said it without an ounce of sarcasm.

The chief let out a gusty sigh.

"See ya, boss!" Carl closed the door behind him.

Amber took a seat in one of the chairs in front of the chief's desk, tamping down her amusement at the man, who was now rubbing the bridge of his nose with thumb and forefinger, as if hit with a sudden migraine.

While he pulled himself together, she surveyed the room, feeling oddly strange being in the chief's private office after all these years. It almost felt like being invited into his house; an intimate space belonging to a man who had once treated her with outright loathing.

She wondered if, after this meeting, that loathing would return tenfold.

The left and right walls were covered by floor-to-ceiling bookshelves. Most were crammed with what looked like thick textbooks and even thicker binders. Law books? Manuals? She assumed they were full of dull topics like citations, traffic tickets, city ordinances, and permits. A few of the top shelves were lined with plaques and trophies.

The back wall had a large window cut out of it, but the dark brown aluminum blinds covered up any hint of the world beyond it. A faint layer of dust coated them; Amber wondered when he'd last opened the window. Below that sat a short bank of filing cabinets, the top stacked with papers.

The chief continued to massage his face behind a modest-sized mahogany desk that ate up most of the available floor space. A computer monitor sat in one corner. The other side was piled with papers and folders. A keyboard rested atop a wide rectangle of plastic, business cards and photographs lined up in neat rows underneath it. A framed picture of him and his family faced out, the three Browns grinning at her. The chief had a nice smile when he decided to share it. He stood with an arm around his wife's waist, and a hand on his son's shoulder. The Space Needle in Seattle reached toward the blue, cloudless sky in the background. Jessica had a hand on her belly, though she wasn't showing yet in the photo.

"When is Jessica due?" Amber heard herself ask before she realized she was going to.

That snapped him out of his face massage, which had moved from the bridge of his nose to his temples. He glanced up at her, bleary-eyed, as if he'd just woken from a dream and couldn't recall how either of them had gotten here. "Four weeks."

"That's exciting," she said, plastering on a smile. "Sammy looking forward to it?"

"Sort of. He's getting a sister. He keeps asking if we can trade her in for a toy truck if he doesn't like her."

Amber laughed, easily imagining sweet little Sammy making his request with complete sincerity.

The chief smiled wistfully to himself for a moment before clearing his throat and sitting a little straighter. "So, what did you want to talk to me about, exactly?" He folded his arms on his desk. Though he was talking to her, he wasn't quite looking *at* her. He seemed to be focused on her nose, her forehead, a spot just to the right of her. "You say you have information about the attack on the maid that the department isn't privy to?"

Amber stared at him a moment. "Why can't you look at me?"

The accusation got him to finally make eye contact. His jaw clenched, and a vein in his forehead seemed to throb. Goodness. What did he think she would do, turn him into a toad? It took him a long time to finally say, "Based on what you said on the phone earlier, you know that I saw something … happen in your shop."

Her heart thrashed in her chest; he actually admitted it. "Yes. And … what do you think you saw?"

"A very clever magic trick?" His right eye gave a slight twitch. She wasn't sure if he'd blinked since he finally stopped avoiding her gaze. Then, in a rush, as if he'd been keeping this bottled up for weeks—which he probably had been—he said, "I had been across the street picking up a cake from Betty Harris and saw movement in your shop even though the majority of the lights were off. I peeked in, worried you might have a prowler, and then …"

Amber chewed on her bottom lip, hands grasping the armrests of her chair so tightly, she was sure her knuckles were white. She didn't dare tear her attention away from the chief to check.

The chief leaned forward a little, shooting a quick glance at the door behind her, as if he wanted to confirm that they were still alone, and goofy Carl wasn't loitering in the doorway, listening. "I saw you wave your hand over a dozen of those cat toys of yours and they all sprang to life. I told myself there had to be a remote control in your hand that I couldn't see. Some master switch that turned them all on at once. But they were all doing different things. I told myself it had to be very clever programming. But then one started hopping around like it had a mind of its own and launched off the table." Now that he'd started, his blue eyes wide and his blonde brows hiked toward his hairline, he seemed unable to stop, though his tone was still hushed. "Then you just ... reached out a hand and stopped the cat in mid-flight. I thought maybe it was some elaborate system of wires and string that I couldn't see since it was so dark. But then that look you gave me when you realized you'd been caught." He shook his head, a look of disbelief on his face. "That look is what sealed it for me."

Amber uncurled her hands from their death grip on the armrests, her fingers aching. The chief watched her hands closely, as if he thought they were loaded weapons. Perhaps that was how he saw them. "Sealed what, exactly?" She needed him to say it. Assuming he had the right word for it.

"After seeing the trick with the toy cats, how you saved Maddie from slipping into the pond at Balinese Park ..." He shook his head again. "The only word I have for what I've seen you do is ... magic."

Amber's eyes involuntarily closed, as if they wanted to shield her from whatever expression came with that admission from the chief. When she opened them again, his mouth was slightly agape. Clearly, some part of him had hoped she'd laugh in his face, tell him he was out of his mind. He knew her silence was as good as confirmation.

If this went south, she told herself, she had a memory-erase spell primed and ready to go. She'd gotten the idea from Aunt Gretchen when she admitted she'd used a memory wipe on Alice's mother a few days before the fateful night of the house fire. Amber could erase up to five minutes of his memory if it came down to it.

At the moment, he looked at her as if she were an exotic animal that had just wandered into his office. Fascinated, but not scared. Yet.

Just say it. See how he reacts. "That's right."

He visibly swallowed.

"It's a family trait," she said. "It's passed down from generation to generation, just like eye color or a cleft chin."

He snorted derisively. "I hardly think you can compare the use of … of magic with having a cleft *chin*, Amber."

Ah, the old tone was back. Amber somehow felt on surer footing now. This version of the chief she could handle. It was the version she knew best.

"Well, in my family, it's the rule, not the exception."

After a brief pause, which mostly involved him staring at her in slack-jawed confusion, he asked, "And what's the term for what you are?"

"I'm a witch." Saying it that openly was oddly freeing.

He scrubbed a hand down his face. "A … witch. What, like cauldrons and wands and broomsticks?" He stilled. "My God, can you fly?"

She fought a laugh. "No, I can't fly. And I don't know any witches who can."

He leaned back in his chair and crossed his arms, brow

creased. A faint, persistent jangle sounded then. She assumed his leg was bouncing nervously under the desk. Were there coins in his pocket? She couldn't tell if he was furious with her or terrified. "So what can you do then?" he finally asked, but it came out sharp, like an accusation. Almost defensive.

She understood his tone, even if his posture offered mixed signals. "*Tell me,*" his tone said, "*how dangerous you are.*"

"To be perfectly honest, I don't know the extent of my powers. I only just found out that my history is a bit more complicated than I was first told. But we don't turn people into animals or use eye of newt in our potions or whatever else you might think."

"I don't know *what* to think."

After a beat, she asked, "Are you scared of me?"

He visibly swallowed. "A little." Lips pursed, he said, "But this somehow makes much more sense than you being a *psychic*. Why on earth did you let me believe that? There I was, asking you about your otherworldly hunches and whatever nonsense. Were you just having a laugh at my expense?"

"First of all, I *am* sorry about that," she said, "but you barely tolerated me being a psychic—how would you have reacted if I'd told you I was a witch?"

The slight totter of his head told her that her assumption had been right.

"Second of all, I wanted to know what happened to Melanie. Having you believe I was a psychic helped get me there. And psychics *do* exist, by the way—that's not nonsense. I'm just not one of them."

He blinked several times. "Please don't tell me vampires, werewolves, and leprechauns exist too."

"I've never met any, but that doesn't mean they aren't out there."

He scrubbed a hand down his face again.

She chewed on her bottom lip some more while he processed all this. Though the furrow to his brow told her he wasn't having the easiest time with it, he hadn't gone screaming from the room or defenestrated himself from the neglected window behind him. That had to be a good sign.

"I have to assume this is a closely held secret, given the psychic cover-story and your look of sheer panic when I saw you use your … magic."

Amber nodded, aware that even saying the word made him uncomfortable.

"So why are you volunteering this to me now? What does this have to do with what happened to the maid? Was *she* a witch?"

And here came the part that truly could make him snap. It was ultimately what had broken her relationship with Max. When he'd started to realize there was a whole other world out there, one hidden just under the surface of the only one he'd ever known, he couldn't deal with it. It shook too many of his core beliefs to the ground. So Max had left.

Amber was almost positive he'd convinced himself that Amber was mentally unstable and that everything she'd told him was a figment of her imagination. That was easier for him to believe than the truth, she supposed.

If the truth about rival witch clans was what sent the chief over the edge, she'd yank the information back out of his head and replace it with something easier for him to handle. What that something was, she didn't know.

She blew out a breath. *Here goes nothing …*

"My aunt, who is also a witch, believes that a witch from a rival family—the Penhallow family—has come to Edgehill with the intent to harm me in some way. I believe the maid was in the wrong place at the wrong time, and a Penhallow killed her, not realizing it wasn't my aunt. That, or they were perfectly aware that it *wasn't* my aunt, and they're sending me a message that they're here."

The chief gripped his armrests now much like Amber had earlier, but his features had been schooled into indifference. Cop mode. "How do you know that's who was responsible? You didn't see the body."

"The Penhallows are cursed. Unlike my family, where magic is passed down from parents to children, the Penhallows' ability to perform magic was stripped from them. Centuries ago, the Penhallows had started dabbling in something you'd recognize from movies and TV shows as 'dark magic.' They found a way to take powers from other witches through siphoning-spells.

"A witch's powers are sacred and it's a cardinal sin to take them from another witch. After decades of this practice going unchecked by our council, several heads of prominent witch families banded together to strip the Penhallows of their ability to do magic.

"This infuriated them, of course, and they spent years trying to get their sentence reversed by appealing to the council.

The council denied them time and time again. Every denial made them angrier. One Penhallow, in his anger at the council, hunted one of the councilmembers down and killed him in cold blood. The councilmember's magic transferred to him through the knife the Penhallow had stabbed into his chest."

The chief's mouth was agape again. "Had a witch never killed another before? Wouldn't this transfer of power have already been a well-known possibility?"

"That's the thing—witches *had* turned on each other in the past. We're not unlike non-witches in that way. But the power transfer had never happened before. When a witch died, his or her power went with them."

He nodded slightly. "Did it have something to do with the Penhallow being stripped of power?"

"That's the theory," Amber said. "A witch is meant to have power; it's what makes us who we are. When the Penhallow killed the witch, the councilmember's powers filled the spaces left by his removed magic. But the power he received was twisted. Spells were heightened in strength, but would have the opposite intended effect. A spell meant to heal a wound, for example, became a spell that caused infection. A tincture meant to ease a troubled mind to allow for sleep, now caused horrific nightmares."

The chief mulled this over. "This fact didn't deter the Penhallows from stealing more powers? I would think this … curse, as you call it, would keep them from doing it anymore."

"You would think so, but the council didn't anticipate the intense instinct that would kick in for the Penhallows to restore their magic, no matter what it took," Amber said.

"The problem was, once they had some form of magic back, it poisoned their minds just as it poisoned their magic. This twisted, backward magic is what they pass on generation after generation now, along with an insatiable desire to acquire *more* magic. Yet, the more they get—"

"The madder they become."

"Yes," she said, nodding, relieved he seemed to be following along, even though he looked seconds from passing out and toppling out of his chair. "They're like parasites now. Like a sentient virus. They strategically track and hunt down witches who they think are the most powerful."

He cocked his head at this. "And … you're one of the most powerful?"

Amber couldn't even muster up the energy to be offended. The chief knew even less about her magic than she did, and even *he* seemed to doubt her skill.

"I don't know." She shook her head. "All I know is what my aunt told me, which was that a Penhallow was coming to Edgehill," she said. "You asked how I knew a Penhallow was involved in the murder of the maid? Penhallows, when they use their cursed magic, leave a trace of it behind. I felt it when I walked into the hotel room."

The chief sighed. "After what I saw tonight, it's hard to believe that woman's death was … normal." He rubbed his eyes for a moment, as if trying to scrub the memory from them. "Any idea what this Penhallow might look like?"

"No clue," she said. "Witches look just as human as anyone else. It could be anyone."

"They aren't surrounded by an ominous cloud of black?"

An unexpected laugh bubbled out of her. "Unfortunately not. But I want to help find who this is."

"Because you and your family are in danger now, too."

"Yes," she said. "I also have reason to believe a Penhallow killed my parents."

His head reeled back as if she'd struck him. "They didn't pass away in a house fire? Wasn't it ruled an accident—an electrical glitch?"

"I've always had my suspicions," Amber said. "If I find who did this to that poor maid, not only could it mean keeping the rest of my family alive, but I might be able to find justice for my parents, too."

The chief searched her face, remaining quiet for so long, Amber started to worry he was slowly cracking before her eyes as everything she'd told him started to sink in. "God help me, but I believe you."

Her shoulders sagged in relief.

"I promise to keep your secret as long as you promise not to bewitch me or my staff," he said, eyes narrowed.

One hand to her heart, the other raised in the air, she said, "I solemnly swear not to bewitch you or your staff."

He grunted. "I need a drink."

After a brief pause, she said, "Can you tell me what happened to the maid?"

"Honestly, we aren't sure," he said. "She looked ... almost like she'd been mummified. Like she'd been drained—"

"Of life?"

The chief swore under his breath. "For lack of a better phrase, yes. Drained of life. I've never seen anything like it.

The officer in charge of taking crime scene photos took one look at her body, then ran to the bathroom to throw up his dinner," he said. "I'm worried pictures or details will leak to the public somehow. How do I explain it? How do my officers fight something like this?"

Amber didn't know.

After another long pause, he said, "For what it's worth, in hindsight, everything odd I've associated with you has been tied to something positive. Little girls saved from ponds, kids saved from the path of speeding vehicles, little boys named Sammy being utterly enthralled by a plastic cat named Midnight …"

Amber felt her cheeks heat, oddly embarrassed by the chief's kind words. Perhaps they were just unexpected, given their rocky past. It was a welcome change. "Well, in that case, can I ask a favor?"

"You can ask anything you like," he said, "but it doesn't mean the favor will be granted."

"I need any information I can get about my cousin Edgar."

The chief quirked a blonde eyebrow. "Isn't he here in Edgehill?"

"He won't talk to me," she said. "I've tried."

"Amber, if the man doesn't want to speak to you, maybe you should respect that."

"He may be the only person who knows what happened the night of the house fire," she said. "I can't shake the feeling that the Penhallows had something to do with why he suddenly recanted his story."

That piqued his interest, even if he didn't say anything to

that effect. She could see it in the way his eyes squinted. His cop brain was working in overdrive. "I'll see what I can find. In the meantime, be alert. Call me the second you suspect anything or anyone, okay?"

She nodded. "Okay."

As she left his office, she realized she never once truly thought to use the memory-wipe spell. The chief now knew more than any non-witch should. And, not only had she *not* protected her secret, but she'd given up Aunt Gretchen's and Willow's secrets, too. She wasn't sure she could reverse that fact even if she wanted to now.

She hoped she hadn't just made the biggest mistake of her life.

CHAPTER 9

Things were tense in the Blackwood home for the next several days. Aunt Gretchen could hardly look at Amber. Willow could hardly look at Amber. Amber could hardly look at either one. Amber was desperate to tell Willow about her conversation with the chief, but Willow was scarcely around. And when she was, she steered clear of Amber altogether. Amber wondered if Willow was spending her time with Connor Declan when she wasn't holed up with them. Though, she supposed, she was likely soaking up free WiFi somewhere so she could stay connected to her office back in Portland and get as much work done remotely as possible.

Jack had called a day ago, but Amber hadn't picked up. And now, three days later, she still hadn't called him back. How long was too long to return a phone call before it was considered rude?

All this simmering tension made sleeping in the tiny studio apartment terribly unpleasant, but despite how upset they all were with each other, they knew they were safer together. Aunt Gretchen drank her foresight tincture every night, and every morning she informed her nieces that the Penhallow threat hadn't lifted. That the Penhallow was still in Edgehill, roaming the streets in plain sight.

There hadn't been any more attacks in town, and neither the sisters nor their aunt had run into the telltale signature of cursed magic. Amber worried this was all the calm before the storm.

Three days after her aunt's arrival, Amber found herself alone in the Quirky Whisker after hours, working once again on the lion toy that refused to be tamed. The boy's party was days away and Amber felt no closer to having a finished—and safe—product. Amber hated to cancel on a customer on such short notice, but her magic was as high-strung as she was, glitching constantly.

If she'd thought the incident with the lion and Tom had been bad, it was nothing compared to this. Just minutes before, she'd given the lion life—and mere moments after that, the little beast darted away, leaping off the counter and into the dark recesses of her shop.

"Ugh! Not again!"

She spent the better part of an hour chasing the thing. It would jump into drawers, wedge itself behind books, and hide behind corners of the pyramid-shaped shelves that dotted the store. It would slowly stalk her, its body low to the ground as it army-crawled after its prey. She'd sense it just before it attacked and it would dart away from her grasping hands, only to take up a hiding place somewhere new and this would start all over again. On more than one occasion, it nipped her. It bit her fingers, the fleshy pad of her thumb, and her wrist—twice. She was sure she'd be bruised by morning.

She was on hands and knees now, glancing around the side of a shelf. Nerves frayed, she contemplated leaving the thing down here to fend for itself overnight. But she wasn't sure she trusted it not to go berserk in its boredom and trash the shop.

She screamed.

The demonic little toy had clamped down on her ankle this time and hung on for all the world with its fangs. Shaking her leg, she dislodged it. Suddenly furious, she plucked a book off a nearby shelf and smashed the toy as if it were a scuttling cockroach.

"No!" she snapped at herself a moment later, plopping down on her backside right there in the middle of the floor.

That was it.

She'd have to call Vicky in the morning and tell her that her son wouldn't have the toy in time for his party. Amber couldn't keep doing this. Not until her magic was back under control. Her ankle throbbed.

She picked a shard of beige-painted plastic off the ground. The sensation to cry burned her eyes and the back of her throat.

"It attacked again?"

Amber startled, glancing up to see Willow standing at the base of the stairs. "Yeah. This used to be the one thing I was good at …" She hated how whiny she sounded.

After their parents died, Amber had become sulky and prickly. She'd been prone to bouts of such intense sadness, she wouldn't be able to function for days at a time. She'd sit on their bedroom floor, just like this, and stare off into space for hours. They'd started calling the instances "blackouts," because when she came to, not even Amber could remember when it had happened or how long it had lasted.

Willow had reacted outwardly. She'd found solace in

underage drinking, mic nights, and Connor Declan's artsy friends. Amber had envied her sister for that. Willow had found a way to purge her sadness and frustration and anger—and had come out on the other side a more well-adjusted person. Amber had bottled it up. Amber hadn't ever been able to move past it. Not really.

Willow walked over and sat on the ground across from her, slowly lifting the dream analysis tome off the plastic lion carcass. She winced. "I hardly think this little guy is worth a blackout."

Amber chewed on her bottom lip, gaze focused on the plastic shard, turning it end over end with her fingertips. "I'm sorry," she said softly, not looking at her sister. "I didn't mean to make this all about me. I know they were your parents just as much as mine. I just live with it hanging over my head all the time. I mean, my bedroom window looks out on the house, for crying out loud. I see it every day." She looked up then. "You have distance. *Literal* distance. I'm starting to see that was a healthier choice."

Willow scooted over until she was next to Amber, then wrapped an arm around her and pulled Amber in. Amber rested her head on her sister's shoulder. Willow wore black or navy blue pajama pants—it was hard to discern color in the low light of the shop—covered in little moons and stars. Her legs were stretched out in front of her and crossed at the ankles. Her nail polish was a dark color Amber couldn't identify.

"From what Aunt Gretchen has told me," Willow said, "it sounds like you've been right all along. It wasn't just a freak accident."

"I didn't want to be right," Amber admitted. "As much as I've wanted answers, deep down I've wanted to be wrong."

Willow rested her cheek on top of Amber's head and gave her a slight squeeze. "I know."

They sat like that for a while, not saying anything. They didn't need to. Amber knew Willow had forgiven her.

"If we stay cooped up in here too much longer, I'm going to lose it," Willow eventually said. "You know I love you, but you live in a shoebox."

Amber straightened at that, Willow's arm dropping away. "It's quaint!"

"I've seen postage stamps bigger!"

A slight smile tugged at the corners of Amber's mouth. It felt like the first time she'd smiled in days.

"I saw that!"

Amber shooed her away and finally got to her feet. Willow followed suit. They stared at each other for a moment before Amber pulled her into another tight hug.

They broke the embrace, then wordlessly cleaned up the mangled lion, dumping the parts onto the counter.

"I might have a couple ideas on how to fix this, if you'll let me fuss with it," Willow said.

"Yes, please!" Amber said. "My magic is glitching something awful lately."

Crossing her arms, Willow turned to Amber and rested her hip against the counter. "Any ideas on what we can do next? All joking aside, we really can't stay cooped up here for much longer. Gretchen has a life to get back to. I have a job. We have to figure out who the Penhallow is."

"And then what?"

"I don't know," Willow said, throwing her arms in the air, unable to keep her frustration in check. "Find out what they want?"

"Already know that," Amber said. "Me. Dead."

Willow's mouth bunched into a tight pucker. "Don't talk like that."

"Sorry," she said, frowning. A thought she'd had since Aunt Gretchen arrived started worming its way to the forefront of Amber's mind again. "When was the last time you saw Edgar?"

"Gosh," Willow said, head cocked. "Fourteen years?"

"How do you feel about a little family reunion?"

They waited another two days, both so Willow could complete the lion toy in time for the boy's party, and so Amber could get Lily and Daisy Bowen to help Gretchen man the store for a few hours on Saturday. Under normal circumstances, their aunt would have protested about them going to see Edgar without her, or being left to run the shop, but given the last conversation between Gretchen and Amber, a lot of her aunt's usual spunkiness had dried up.

Amber's anger at Gretchen had slowly turned from a boiling rage to a lingering sense of what she could only describe as betrayal. She knew it was only a matter of time before she cracked and forced another conversation with her aunt. But Saturday was not that day.

Amber and Willow called a goodbye to their aunt and the

two Bowen sisters in the morning, just before the shop was due to open. Willow stepped out into the thankfully mild February morning, but before Amber could follow her, someone lightly grabbed hold of her arm.

She turned to find her aunt staring up at her with wide, desperately sad eyes. "Tell Edgar I say hello."

"Okay," she said, offering her a tight-lipped smile before she turned to leave again.

But Gretchen grabbed at her arm once more. Keeping her voice low so the Bowen girls couldn't overhear, Gretchen said, "Before you leave, drink the tinctures I left in your purse. They should protect you both from a Penhallow attack—but likely only *one* blast of cursed magic each. It should give you enough time to flee, though, should you need to."

Amber stared at her, wondering not only when she'd made the tinctures, but when she'd slipped them into her bag. Gretchen had her bottom lip caught between her teeth now, giving Amber something akin to puppy dog eyes. The last time Amber had seen her aunt this sad, it had been the days after the death of Amber's parents.

A slight twinge in her chest caused Amber to pull her aunt into a hug. The woman gave a squeak of surprise before she wrapped her arms around Amber's waist, squeezing tight. Her aunt smelled like shampoo and mint. She smelled like home.

When they pulled away, Gretchen's eyes were a little glassy. She tentatively reached up and placed a cool hand on Amber's cheek. "I truly am sorry, little mouse. For everything."

"I know," she said. "We'll talk later, okay?" With that, Amber slipped out the door of the Quirky Whisker.

Amber could feel her aunt's eyes on her as she walked away.

"Everything okay?" Willow asked as Amber slid into the passenger seat of Willow's car. "I see no visible wounds."

Amber laughed weakly. "We're fine."

Willow pulled out onto Russian Blue Avenue, heading for the area of town not far from the Sippin' Siamese. Edgar lived beyond the little bar, though—out in the sticks. Amber often wondered how his family had managed to find the house in the first place.

"Have you been out here before?" Amber asked, her stomach in knots.

"Yeah, but never went in the house," Willow said. "Mom drove out here with me a couple times to bring Edgar stuff, but I always stayed in the car. Place has always given me the willies."

Amber had last seen Edgar nearly three years ago. He'd stopped answering her calls months before, so she'd resorted to swinging by his house occasionally. He only let her in once, and they hadn't gotten past the foyer before he got spooked and kicked her out. She tried bringing him pastries, groceries, and even gifts. The marble cat statue that had taken a tumble earlier and lost a tail and part of an ear had been something she'd bought for Edgar. It stayed on his porch for a week. On the seventh day of swinging by to see if he'd at least taken her offering into the house, the marble cat had a note tied around his neck that read, "Go away and take your unwanted gifts with you. The Blackwoods are dead to me."

She hadn't returned.

With an air of trepidation, only fifteen minutes from Edgar's house now, Amber told her about the marble cat incident.

Willow let out a long, gusty sigh. "Probably would have been a good thing to mention that *before* we left, Amber! What if he has a loaded shotgun by the door or something?"

Amber didn't reply to that.

The closer one got to the southern end of Edgehill, the more rural it became. They traveled up a two-lane road, flanked on both sides by quaking aspen, their trunks thin and white. The stark, bare branches were just starting to develop their furry, pussy-willow-like buds. The leaves would be a vibrant yellow in the fall, making their stark white trunks stand out in the landscape even more. Amber cranked her window down a fraction to let in the cool air. The sky was a bright, cloudless blue.

"The turn is coming up here in a few," Amber said. "It's easy to miss; there's no sign."

"It's hard to believe anyone lives out here," Willow said.

They hadn't seen another car for the past ten minutes.

The forest of quaking aspen started to give way to tall grasses on one side.

"Here it is on your left," Amber said, pointing.

The dirt road had waist-high grass growing on either side. With a muted whimper, Willow needlessly put on her blinker, then turned her little sedan onto the road, where it bumped along the uneven path. Willow slowed her car to a crawl, branches and leaves smacking the car like the hands of a protesting crowd.

Slap, slap, slap. "*We don't want you here. He told you to go away.*" Slap, slap, slap.

Amber chewed on her bottom lip.

Ahead, an old fence—so overgrown with ivy that it was

impossible now to see what was beneath it—stretched out to the left, marking the start of Edgar's property. The gate was forever stuck open, as the vines had claimed it on the other side of the opening, too. The twisting vines had also ensnared a tree just behind the fence, wrapped tightly around the trunk like a thick green blanket. The branches of the oak draped over the opening in the fence, creating an almost perfectly constructed archway. It would have looked like something out of a fairytale to anyone who didn't know better.

As they passed though the arch, Amber's hand firmly clutched the "Oh crap!" handle above the door to help counterbalance the excessive bouncing Willow's poor car had to endure.

The property was walled in on three sides by the vine-choked fence, pine trees stretching up behind it to help fully close him off from the world. They reached into the air like the long, plump fingers of a giant, ones that could hinge forward and crush them should Amber and Willow do something to upset the master of the house. Which, given Amber's history with the man, would likely happen sooner rather than later.

They continued down the path, the expansive area on either side of them overgrown with weeds. The grasses were as tall as the car's doors in some places. Amber could only imagine what manner of creature hid in all this.

After a slight curve in the road to the right, the house sprang into view. It was a two-story, modest-sized wooden monstrosity. Dying shrubs and tall weeds rose up around the structure, almost surrounding the wide porch. A couple of the windows on the top floor were boarded over. Amber sensed no movement from inside.

A truck sat out front, but it was just as old, dusty, and dilapidated as everything else here. Willow slowly pulled up next to the rundown vehicle, the crunch of tires over rocks and packed earth sounding too loud in Amber's ears. She rolled up her window. Edgar's only means of transportation, as far as Amber could tell, was a rusting, white pickup truck with a flat back tire. Luckily the tall grasses had been cut back around most of the house's front steps. Otherwise, they'd have needed a machete to get to the door.

Amber and Willow sat in silence, staring at the house for a long time.

"What if he's not home?" Willow asked, voice ticking up at the end in a hopeful tone.

"He's home," Amber said. "I called from a blocked number about an hour ago. He answered, sounding very tired and grumpy."

"Great," Willow deadpanned.

Pulling her purse onto her lap, Amber found Gretchen's protection tinctures in the same inner pocket as her rubber cat. She handed one to Willow.

With a delicate clink of the small glass vials, they uncorked them and knocked back the contents. Then both immediately coughed and gagged.

"Ugh! It tastes like gasoline!" Amber said, her eyes watering. She coughed, beating a fist against one knee, one eye squinted shut.

"Gasoline and despair," Willow said, heel of her palm

pressed between her eyes as if the pressure would dispel the horrible taste somehow.

It took a full minute for them to collect themselves. Willow noisily blew her nose.

After shuddering violently, Amber placed the empty vials back in her purse. "Ready?" Without waiting for a reply, she climbed out of the car, leaving her purse on the floorboard. The warm sun beat down on her face. The sound of birdsong was loud and raucous. She imagined it could be lovely to sit out on the porch here in the mornings to listen to the birds sing and scrabble in the brush.

But the house, much like cousin Edgar, didn't give off a friendly, welcoming vibe.

A grumpy-looking black-and-white cat was crouched on all fours on the pickup's hood. It fled the moment Amber made eye contact. Edgar's cat wasn't friendly either.

The wooden steps groaned underfoot as Amber cautiously ascended. Weeds poked through the slats of the porch. A lizard scurried across the wood and landed with a crunch in the tall brush ringing the patio.

Amber had just reached the front door when she glanced over at Willow. She had her arms folded tight across her chest, looking this way and that as if she were sure a mountain lion were lying in wait, ready to pounce. "Get over here, you! We need your charm."

Willow scoffed. "This is a terrible idea," she said, but moved to stand beside Amber, their arms flush. "How do you expect me to charm a guy who wants nothing to do with people? I mean, can he get any more obvious?" She gestured to the rug below their feet.

The mat was black with a red trim. In a cheery font, it said, "There Is No Reason For You To Be Here."

"Subtle," Amber said.

"I feel bad for the guy who had to deliver it," said Willow. "I bet all the drivers at Patch's Pizza draw straws to determine who *doesn't* come out here."

"I bet they make the new kid do it," said Amber. "Initiation ritual. If you can deliver the pizza to Old Man Henbane, then you're one of us. Like when kids dare each other to ring the doorbell at the scariest house on Halloween."

"That's probably this one, too!" Willow said with a laugh.

Just then, a sharp *click* startled them both. The rational part of Amber's brain told her it was a bolt sliding free on the inside of the door. The irrational part said it was half of the *schlock-schlock* of a shotgun being loaded. Aunt Gretchen would be *so* upset with them if they managed to get shot on Edgar's porch.

Amber grabbed her sister's arm, then slightly stepped behind her.

"Are you *really* trying to use me as a meat shield right now?" Willow hissed. "You're the older sister. You're supposed to protect *me*."

Click, click, click. Shlock, schlock. Click. Schlock.

Amber flinched with each one, her fingernails digging further and further into Willow's arm. Lord only knew how much more reclusive, grouchy, and hostile Edgar had grown in three years.

Then the door opened a crack and a sliver of man's profile came into view. It was unsettlingly dark in the house, but Amber still managed to make out Edgar's wild mop of black hair, his gray T-shirt and sweatpants, one slippered foot, and the bright white of one eye as the dark brown iris darted in Willow's direction, then Amber's, then back again.

"I thought I told you not to come back," came a gruff male voice.

Amber swallowed, but before she could get a word out, Willow piped up. "Hi, cousin. Do you remember me? I'm Willow. I must have been fourteen the last time you saw me."

Her voice was high and light, but Amber sensed how coiled tight she was, as Amber was still clutching her arm. Her very tense arm.

Edgar grunted in response.

"Can we come in and talk?" Amber ventured, prepared to have the door slammed in her face. It had happened enough times in the past; there was no reason to believe it wouldn't happen again.

"No," he said.

At the same time that he went to slam the door, Willow raised her hand, palm out. The screws holding the doorknob in place all unscrewed themselves. They fell to the wood below with a series of tiny clinks, like metallic rain. Moments later, the knobs on either side fell with a clatter.

Edgar growled like an angry bear, then flung the door open. Amber and Willow jumped back. Amber had yet to let go of Willow, the two now taking slow steps down the patio while Edgar, a disheveled mess, stalked toward them like a starved animal just released from his cage. His attention snapped to Amber. "I told you before, *Blackwood*, that your family was dead to me. That means *no* phone calls, *no* presents on my doorstep, and *no* destruction of my property."

Amber's back hit the railing behind her and she yelped, almost losing her footing and flipping over into the brush below with the hiding lizards.

"I didn't destroy anything," Willow squeaked out, her shoulders bunched up by her ears. "I can fix it."

He stopped a foot in front of them, his eyes wild. Sweat stains lined the area by his armpits and his beard and hair gave off the distinct impression that he'd been struck by lightning. Twice. The dark blue slippers on his feet were so worn, Amber could see a hint of his big toe poking through. "Can you two not read? I got that mat specifically for you, Amber. There is no reason for you—for anyone—to be here. Leave. I have nothing to say to you."

He turned and stalked back to his open front door, lifting a hand as he went. The screws and doorknobs were back in place before he crossed the threshold.

"A maid was killed," Amber blurted, then slightly shrunk behind her sister again.

Edgar stilled, hand on the newly fastened doorknob, his back to Amber and Willow. When he didn't move for several long seconds, Willow detached Amber from her arm and gave her a slight shove toward Edgar.

Amber stumbled forward a couple steps, then shot a wide-eyed look of horror at her sister. She held her hands out, as if to say, "*What am I supposed to say now?*"

Willow swept her fingers in Amber's direction, as if to say, "*Don't know! But hurry up and think of something before he slams the door in our faces!*"

"It happened at the Manx Hotel three days ago," Amber said, focusing her attention on her cousin's back. She didn't know what to do with her hands, so she clasped one over the other in hopes that would get them to stop shaking. "We think Aunt Gretchen was the target. The maid's body was found in her room."

He turned then, thick black brows pulled together. "Why do you think I care?"

"Because the door's still open?"

Somehow his brows pulled even closer together.

"She's your aunt too," Amber said. "I thought—"

"Thought what? That I'd want to get involved with all this simply because you want me to? How many times do I have to tell you to go away—that I'm not interested—before you get the hint? You have a knack for getting so caught up in what *you* want that you disregard everyone else's feelings. But like mother, like daughter, right?"

Amber pursed her lips, her fists clenching. Would it be in poor judgment to clock her cousin in the face? Yet, what he said hit home even harder than it would have otherwise, as it wasn't unlike what Willow had said to her earlier. Were they right? Was she too singularly focused? Had her mother been too? Her cheeks flamed.

Edgar's mom had passed away from diabetes complications when they were kids. There were few illnesses magic could truly heal. His father had been in Edgehill until Edgar turned twenty-one—a few years before Amber did—and then abruptly left after Amber's parents died, leaving Edgar behind. Amber had no idea where the guy was now, and given Edgar's current venomous expression, was too scared to ask about him. Edgar had been on his own out here in this falling-apart house ever since.

"Go away, Amber," he said, the edge in his voice gone now. "I'm not a Blackwood. I'm not a Caraway. I'm barely a Henbane. I'm no one, okay? I can't help you. I don't *want* to. I don't remember anything. Just leave me alone." He started to close the door.

"We think it was a Penhallow!" she blurted out, taking another step forward, hoping the words would slip in through the crack in the door before he slammed it and shut her out again. One of her eyes instinctively shut, wincing in preparation for the door closing and all those locks and bolts sliding home. But it didn't come.

Instead, he darted toward her, grabbed her by the wrist and yanked her into the house before she could react.

Oh, sweet Lord, this is it! I've finally pestered him too much and he's going to murder me.

"Get in here, Willow!" he snapped. "Now!"

Willow scurried in after them, Amber's wrist still firmly clenched in Edgar's grasp. When Willow was inside, Edgar unhanded her and quickly got to work locking the door. Amber watched as he did so, uttering spells under his breath, hands waving in the air like a conductor. Keys turned in locks of their own accord. Thick bolts slid along reinforced tracks.

Now it was Willow who clutched at Amber's arm. "Should we be worried?" she hissed in her ear.

Before she could answer, Edgar whirled to face them in the dark foyer. Amber swallowed a breath. Gretchen had told her that she had an affinity for the manipulation of matter and time, but at the moment, her mind was just a jumbled buzz of panic. Not like she could just craft a spell out of thin air anyway. Besides, he was part Henbane, too. And, if Amber had to guess, he was a far more powerful witch.

She had mace in her purse. But her purse was in the car. The foul protection tincture they'd drunk was meant to protect them from the twisted magic of a Penhallow. Would it work against the magic of a Henbane?

"Don't speak of the Penhallows in public," he said, then stalked past them.

Amber and Willow turned as a unit, watching his dark form travel further and further into the dark recesses of the house.

He turned in a doorway several feet away, the room beyond it even darker than the foyer. "Are you coming or what? If you want to talk, let's talk. I'll make coffee."

Amber and Willow looked at each other, shrugged, and then followed their cousin into the kitchen.

CHAPTER 10

The lights in the kitchen flicked on just as Amber and Willow stepped inside. All three of them squinted in the glare. Amber wondered why he kept the place so dark.

She'd half expected the kitchen to be a horrific disaster, the light revealing counters, walls, and floor caked in filth, dishes in the sink swarmed with flies, and stacks of pizza boxes towering precariously on every surface. While the sink and counter *were* stacked with dishes, there wasn't a fly in sight. The white tile could use a thorough mopping, but her shoes didn't stick to the floor, so she considered that a major plus. And only one box from Patch's Pizza lay on the center island. Patch—a smiling cartoon cat with a large patch of black splashed over one eye and sporting a chef's hat—graced the box's lid.

"Every pizza boy who delivers pizza here looks four seconds from soiling his pants," Edgar said from across the kitchen, his back turned to them as he fussed with the coffee pot.

Amber and Willow winced sheepishly at each other.

Once the coffee was brewing, Edgar turned and rested his backside against the counter, arms folded over his chest, and his ankles crossed. "So what's this about a …" He visibly swallowed. "What about the Penhallows? They went into hiding after your parents died."

A knot formed in Amber's stomach.

"That's what we heard too," Willow said. "But Aunt Gretchen unexpectedly showed up at Amber's place almost a week ago, claiming the Penhallows were resurfacing and they were after Amber."

Edgar's eyes cut to Amber. "Why you? Why now?"

"Million-dollar question," Amber said. "But their signature was all over the hotel room where the maid was killed. The Penhallow, whoever it is, is in Edgehill."

He jutted his chin at her. "And what do you want from me? As you're well aware, I don't get out much. So how would I know anything?"

Amber and Willow shared another look.

"Stop doing your weird sister-telepathy thing. Ask your questions so you get this out of your system once and for all—then you can get out of here and leave me alone."

"Why would the Penhallows want to kill our parents?"

Edgar pursed his thin lips. "He wanted Belle. Theo was collateral damage."

Blowing out a calming breath, she said, "Wanted her for what?"

Edgar cocked his head like a curious dog. "*That's* what you want to know? That's the most basic part of this whole thing. Penhallows want—need—magic, right? Well, as off their rockers as they are, they understand that they're cursed. They're constantly trying to find a way to *end* said curse. And we Henbanes have just the type of magic they think they need: the ability to manipulate time."

Amber blinked a few times. "So, what, they want to go back in time to before they were stripped of their powers to make sure they never get cursed in the first place?"

"Bingo."

"But Gretchen says our magic doesn't make us time travelers. A time spell wouldn't be able to take someone back that far, would it? Was she lying?" *Again?*

"Nope, she's right on that. There isn't a spell or magic affinity a cursed witch could steal to reverse this. The whole reason they were cursed was because they broke the cardinal rule of witchcraft: you don't steal power from another witch. So stealing power to reverse a curse *caused* by stealing power is, as the kids say, bass ackwards."

Amber arched a brow at him. If he thought that was the kind of thing kids were saying these days, he needed to get out of the house even more than she did.

"How *do* they reverse it?" Willow asked.

"The way I heard it," said Edgar, "is that a cursed witch has to willingly give up the search for magic. They have to *want* to resist the urge—but it's like an addict trying to go cold turkey. Not an easy task, especially now that the insatiable urge to siphon magic has been passed on for generations. It's instinctual now. It's been warping Penhallows for generations."

"So all a Penhallow has to do is resist the urge to steal magic and the curse is lifted?" Amber asked.

"Not quite. They also have to meet and fall in love with another Penhallow who's *also* made a similar choice, and then they have to create offspring who are pure of character. *Those* Penhallows will be the start of a reborn clan. It'll take generations to clean it up even if those first two resisters get the whole thing going."

Amber wondered if there was a dating site for magic-stealing-resistant Penhallows. *Swipe right if you're sick of that cursed life.* How were they supposed to find each other?

"Even when two of them meet, it's almost inevitable that one of them will crack. Plus, often when it's been revealed that there's a resister somewhere in their ranks, the cursed witches find a way to break their resolve. The majority of them are convinced there's a magical solution to all this, so resisters tick them off. Basically, they keep pursuing something impossible and are constantly digging the hole deeper."

"They really *are* like a virus. They even infect their own," said Amber.

"Yep," Edgar said.

"How do you know this much about them?" Amber asked, gaze sweeping over him.

He squirmed a bit under her scrutiny and uncrossed his arms, resting his hands on the counter behind him. "When Belle and Theo died, there were all these rumors about who did it ..." He crossed his arms again. "I was still connected to all this back then. Both the Henbane clan on my dad's side, and the Caraway clan on Mom's side. I heard a lot of them talking about the Penhallows. By then, I had enough spy-like spells up my sleeve that I could listen in on almost any conversation that went on in the house."

Amber wondered if one such spell was how he'd heard

herself and Willow discussing nervous pizza boys. "Have you ever met a Penhallow?"

"Not that I know of, but that's how they play it, right?" he asked with a laugh.

Amber hiked a brow at him.

"What?" he asked, gaze shifting from one Blackwood sister to the other, when his amused expression clearly didn't mirror theirs. "Their affinity is glamour."

"Like what Willow can do?" Amber asked.

"Wow," he said. "Belle really *did* keep you guys in the dark, didn't she?"

Amber crossed her arms tight over her chest.

He held up his hands. "Okay. Chill. Let's see how I can explain this. Each family, or clan, has an affinity. Just like how everyone in a family has, say, blonde hair. But just like you can have a kid with dark eyes show up in a family with mostly light ones, a witch doesn't always inherit affinities. Or one sibling can favor their father's clan's affinity, while another sibling picks up her affinities from her mother. I think that's what happened with you two." Edgar wagged a finger back and forth between Amber and Willow. "Or a kid can have *none* of the affinities of either parent, but has ones that their great grandparent had. Make sense?"

Amber and Willow nodded.

"All right," he said, "so Willow is a pretty classic example of a Blackwood, from what I can remember. You're good at changing what things look like, right?"

"Yeah. Better at changing objects though. Most every

change I do to people—like hairstyles or whatever—usually fades after an hour or two."

"Makes sense. Thing is, your ability is more about illusion, though a glamour spell on an object, like you said, depending on how complicated the change is, often holds up for a while on its own. You make someone *think* they saw the change, but you're usually not *actually* changing the makeup of the object or person in question. That's why the change never lasts long or why the supposed-glamour 'drops' when you lose your concentration. But what you're really doing is manipulating what someone sees. If you're maintaining the illusion for one person, you can hold the glamour longer than if you're maintaining the illusion for a crowd of fifty. Because in that case, you're manipulating the minds of fifty people at once. Much harder to keep going without depleting all your energy."

Willow was nodding at this, eyes wide, as if she'd just had an epiphany. Glamour spells had rarely worked well for Amber, period, so most of this went over her head.

"And that's different from what a Penhallow can do?" Amber asked.

"Yeah—" Edgar briefly closed his eyes, chin pressed to his shoulder. From the creases lining his forehead now, she wondered if he'd suddenly been stuck with a migraine.

"Are you okay?" she asked, starting to move toward him.

He held up a hand, eyes still closed, as if to ward her off. She settled back into place at the kitchen island, hands folded on the worn wood. After a long slow breath, he cracked open one eye, then the other. "I'm all right. I … uhh … what did you ask?"

Amber and Willow shared a sister-telepathy glance. Willow shrugged, frowning slightly.

"I asked if what a Penhallow can do is different from what a Blackwood can do," Amber said.

"Right," he said, nodding, resuming his semi-relaxed posture. "Penhallows can cast true glamour spells. They can change themselves—facial structures, gender, race, age. A twelve-year-old boy can become a thirty-year-old pregnant woman."

Amber blinked. "So they're like shapeshifters."

With a nod, he said, "In the past, a Penhallow couldn't hold the shape of another person for longer than twenty-four hours at most. But now that their magic is warped? They can become someone else indefinitely. And they can change shape at will."

So the Penhallow could be literally anyone—in a town slowly filling with tourists, with even more on the way thanks to the rumor about Olaf Betzen making an appearance at the junior fashion show. Soon the town would be a sea of unfamiliar faces. Great.

"Do they take on the personality and thoughts of the person they're glamouring?" Amber asked.

"No. They're stealing their appearance, not bodysnatching," he said. "So they're still themselves, just wearing a different skin. But their voice and mannerisms will match the person they've become. Muscle memory, I guess."

How were they supposed to find someone who could change shape constantly?

The coffee pot gave a click behind Edgar and he set about pulling three mugs from the cabinet above the pot. None of the cups matched. The trio spent a few minutes preparing their coffee to their specifications, then stood around the center island, idly sipping.

Over the top of her mug, Amber eyed her cousin. He stared off into the middle distance now, occasionally taking a drink from his "Cattitude" mug as if on autopilot. At least the wild look in his eye had diminished, and the sudden maybe-headache had left as soon as it had come. He was still a disheveled mess, though. How had he gotten like this? They hadn't been close as teenagers, per se, but they'd been friendly enough. He'd been a little quiet, a little closed off, but that hadn't seemed so strange for a young man grieving his mother.

His gaze suddenly fixed on her and she gave a start. "Why did you keep coming back here month after month even when I stopped answering the door? Everyone else gave up ages ago. But not you."

"I was worried about you way out here by yourself."

He shook his head. "Try again, Blackwood."

Well, he *did* say he didn't want her to waste his time. Might as well cut to the chase. She put down her mug. "Why did you recant your story about the fire? Were you lying then or now?"

Willow let out what Amber assumed was an involuntary groan.

Edgar worked his jaw. "Relentless."

"Wouldn't *you* want to know if things were reversed?" she asked. "Why claim something so specific and then say it didn't happen?"

"Because I was sick, okay?" he snapped, putting his mug down too. He tipped his head back, staring at the ceiling as if

131

the strength to get through this conversation could be found amongst the cobwebs clinging to the dark corners. He balled his fists on the kitchen island. They were mannerisms she recognized as her own. Was this another Henbane trait? Something she did instinctively when she was frustrated because it had been something her mother did? Something her uncle did and then passed on to his son?

Edgar focused on Amber. "I was troubled as a kid and that only got worse when Mom died. Belle and Theo were like parents to me in a lot of ways. I was jealous of you—both of you—for having such normal, loving parents. So when they died, making up an elaborate story about it helped me cope."

He'd slowly taken on a more poised tone the longer he talked, as if this was all something he'd said before. A well-worn explanation he could recite easily.

"How did a story about them being trapped—" Willow started, but Edgar cut her off.

"I had dreams about that night for weeks—before *and* after the fire. They felt so real, I'd convinced myself they'd actually happened. I blamed myself for their deaths, you see. Like the dreams had been a warning and I ignored them. Caraways often have prophetic dreams; my mom had them a lot when she was growing up. It was easier for me to make up some wild story than to deal with the guilt stemming from the fact that I'd had a chance to save them and didn't. I even saw the point of origin of the fire in my dreams. A charging battery pack that overheated and caused a spark. I could have gone to your house to unplug that thing so many times. I could have warned your parents. But I ignored the signs. That, paired with the issues I'd already been having?" He shrugged. "I cracked."

Amber stared at him for a long time, not sure if it was the words he spoke or his sudden calm that unnerved her more. The more he talked, the more his demeanor seemed to change. Something didn't feel right, but she couldn't put her finger on what. All those years ago, Gretchen had said Edgar was unhinged and had filled Amber's head with false hope, that the fire was a result of an electrical glitch. Now Gretchen said she believed Penhallows had killed Amber's parents, but Edgar was claiming it had been an unfortunate accident.

Amber worried she was in denial. She'd *needed* his original story to be true. That was the story she'd hung onto for years. The truth of what happened fourteen years ago was here in Edgehill, and Edgar's original claims had been a big part of what had fueled her doubts.

Yet now the person who was responsible, in part, for the path her life had taken, was telling her he'd made it up. Had Gretchen truly been right all this time? Edgar was simply "off his nut"?

"So you're saying the Penhallows *didn't* kill our parents?"

"I'm saying what happened was suspicious. There's no doubt about that. I'm saying I understand why a Penhallow *would* have wanted Belle dead. But I cannot say for certain that a Penhallow was responsible for that fire."

Why did Edgar suddenly have the countenance of a patient teacher entertaining the creative fancies of a child with a too-active imagination? What he said sounded too rehearsed. Alarm bells went off in her head.

"Are you scared of them, Edgar?"

His eyes darted back and forth, back and forth, like a spooked horse. Then, abruptly, the wild look vanished and Edgar shrugged his shoulders. He smiled slightly—the first one she'd seen from him in … years—and said, "But of course. Any witch worth his salt would be concerned. They're cursed and their magic is dangerous. I'm very sorry for that maid's family. I send them my regards."

The gruff version of her cousin, the one growling at them to get off his property, seemed to be retreating further and further, slowly replaced by someone much calmer and almost pleasant. Almost robotic. His posture was straighter, his tone more even. The scowl lines marring his forehead had smoothed out and a small smile touched his mouth. An expression that seemed stuck there. Her mental alarm bells grew shriller.

Somehow, Amber was more uncomfortable now than she'd been when she feared he was going to aim a shotgun at her. *Could* he *be a Penhallow? How do we know he's the real Edgar Henbane?*

Amber felt like she was losing whatever hold on him they might have had. "I don't suppose you could tell me about these time manipulation spells? Is that one of your affinities as a Henbane?"

"Sorry, no."

"Anyone I can contact from the Henbane or Caraway clans who might be able to help me? Do you have a Henbane grimoire I could look at?" she asked. "Willow and I lost all the family spell books in the fire."

Edgar's right eye notably twitched. "I don't know where it is. It's lost even to me. I'm not sure why I have to keep telling you that."

"Tell me what? You don't know where *what* is?"

"It's hidden even from me." He tapped his temple, hard, three times in quick succession. "Locked. No one knows where the key is. But at least it's safe."

Brow furrowed, Amber glanced over at Willow, who mirrored her confused expression.

"Edgar?" Amber ventured, when the seconds ticked by in silence.

"It's been lovely to see you, but I'm feeling a bit under the weather now." He then proceeded to rub his temples with his fingertips in slow methodical circles, eyes closed. "The lights are hurting my eyes. I need a nap. Perhaps … we can … maybe we can resume this another time?"

Willow tugged on Amber's arm when Amber did little more than stare at her cousin's bowed head. "Amber, c'mon, let's go. He doesn't look too great. We should let him rest."

Amber only allowed herself to be pulled away a couple of steps before she said, "Are you sure you don't have any grimoires here? Not even a personal one? We could take it with us and bring it back the next time we see you? Caraway, Henbane, Blackwood—I don't care which clan, really. I just need—"

Edgar slammed both hands onto the kitchen island, causing Amber to flinch back a step. Willow let out a yelp of surprise. "Get. Out."

"I—"

"Out, Blackwood! I have nothing for you! It's probably

not even here anymore. It's gone. Just like everything else." Then he squeezed his eyes shut and clutched at either side of his head, fingers grasping at his unkempt mess of black hair.

"But—"

"*Now!*"

Amber let herself be pulled then, and she hurriedly walked out of the kitchen, heart hammering. When Willow seemed confident Amber was actually following her now, she let go and hustled her way to the front door. Amber could hear the *click* and *shlock* of locks disengaging even though Willow hadn't made her way across the dark foyer yet. Moments after stepping over the threshold, Amber suddenly turned back, quickly locating the light switch on the kitchen wall.

One finger poised atop it, she gazed into the kitchen to see Edgar squatting with his back against the cabinets, knees pulled to his chest, fingers still clutching at his hair. His eyes were shut, brow scrunched. The lines marring his forehead were back with a vengeance.

"Feel better, cousin," she said softly, then shut off the light and rushed after her sister who'd managed to get the door open.

Edgar's plaintive wails followed them out of the house and haunted Amber's thoughts well after they'd driven away.

CHAPTER 11

A day after Amber and Willow's rather upsetting visit with their cousin, Amber had to attend one of the bi-weekly planning meetings for the Here and Meow Committee. In all the chaos as of late, her duties for the festival had started to fall by the wayside. At least she had Willow in town a bit earlier than planned; she could help Amber get some of her scheduled work done.

From what Amber had heard, the lion toy had been a roaring success. Literally. And given Vicky's excited chatter over the phone earlier that morning, Amber thought it was safe to assume this one hadn't bitten anyone. Amber wasn't sure what she would have done had Willow not stepped in to help her.

Now, as she sat at a traffic light a block away from Purrcolate, she tried to make herself focus on the upcoming meeting, not the fact that she was going to see Jack for the first time in almost a week. As her mind wandered, her tongue snaked out one side of her mouth and swept across her bottom lip. She immediately shuddered, the lingering taste of the protection tincture she downed before leaving hitting her with a fresh wave of revulsion. While Gretchen had known that the Penhallows were masters at glamour spells, she hadn't known about the extra wrinkle caused by the curse: they could become anyone at any time and could hold that shape for as long as they wanted.

Thanks for that extra dose of paranoia, Edgar.

The protection tinctures Gretchen whipped up lasted twelve hours at a maximum and started to become less effective with time. So, like clockwork, the three Blackwood women downed the horrible things at noon and midnight, constantly assuring they were safe from at least one blast of warped magic. Amber just wished they didn't taste like exhaust fumes.

Amber's apartment looked like the lab of a mad scientist. Her toy-making supplies had been swept into boxes and plastic containers soon after Gretchen's arrival. Dried herbs, fresh herbs, plant extracts, mortars and pestles, hot plates, jars, small vials—they covered nearly every surface in Amber's tiny studio.

Last night, they'd all been awoken and lurched into an immediate panic at the sound of glass shattering on the floor. It took several minutes of scrambling around in the dark, muttering curses, for the women to realize that, no, a Penhallow hadn't just shattered the windows of the shop below, but that a curious pair of cats had taken to late-night prowling around Gretchen's stash of glass jars full of foul-smelling leaves, and knocked them off the counter and onto the kitchen tile. If the sound hadn't rudely roused them from sleep, the stench of the fermenting bava leaves surely would have.

In order to get back to sleep, the three women had to use wind-shifting spells to shove the putrid air out a temporarily opened window.

After the ordeal, Gretchen sheepishly promised the next batch would taste better. Amber had shoved the remaining bava leaves in the garbage disposal when her aunt was in the shower that morning.

As far as Amber was concerned, the things got progressively worse with every batch.

Amber's stomach knotted further as she pulled into Purrcolate's lot. What was she supposed to do when she saw Jack? Pretend she'd never gotten his voicemail? Or his text message? Breeze in and give him the ice princess act so he'd get over his crush on her and moved onto someone more normal? Apologize profusely and claim she'd been caught up in family drama? That last one wasn't a lie, at least.

Ice princess was probably the best bet. If he thought she was an awful person, he'd give up once and for all. Yes. Dating non-witches was a truly horrible idea, no matter what Willow said. There was no sense in being this worked up over a guy who would take off as soon as he knew the truth about who she was, right? Might as well nip this in the bud now and save them both from the misery.

Steeling herself, she marched confidently across the parking lot and pulled open the door in her best approximation of a stone-cold witch.

Jack was behind the counter by the register, chatting with a male customer. Larry, Jack's brother, was rearranging pastries in the long, rectangular display case at the other end of the counter.

Larry looked up first. "Hey, Amber, long time no see, lovely." He abandoned his task so he could rest his arms on the counter and grin at her. "How are you? Can I get you anything before you head in? The usual suspects are already in the conference room—human and pastry alike—but can I get you something else?"

Her gaze involuntarily flicked to Jack then. He looked up and grinned, his pretty blue eyes twinkling. Amber's mouth inched up on one side before she could remind her face that they were going for ice princess. Ice princesses didn't smile. Ice princesses glared, assuming they could muster the energy to make eye contact with the lowly peons beneath her. But *no*, her face was doing whatever it wanted.

Larry groaned dramatically. "You two need to just go out already. Just the way you two are *looking* at each other right now is mildly obscene."

Face flaming, she glanced over at Larry. Was she really leering at Jack? If she was involuntarily leering now, she was going to hightail it out of here. But Larry was smiling at her.

"Don't embarrass her!" Jack said, throwing a wadded-up bar towel at his brother. "Can't you see you're embarrassing her?"

Larry deftly snatched the towel out of the air, then flung it over his shoulder as he resumed his work at the pastry case. "What's embarrassing is that you won't take this lovely woman out on a real date. Not an impromptu meeting at the Sippin'-*flippin*-Siamese of all places." He said all this without looking at them, engrossed as he was with positioning the scones *just so*.

Jack's face flushed, and he rubbed the back of his neck. After shooting Amber a cautious glance, he gestured with his head for her to move further down, presumably to get out of earshot of Larry, the man with superhero hearing. Jack pulled off his apron as he walked, then draped it over a stool. When he reached the end of the counter, he lifted a flap in the surface to let himself out. "Be back in ten!" he called to Larry.

Larry waved a hand in acknowledgement, but only had eyes for his pastries.

Amber followed Jack to the far corner, away from both Larry and the few patrons in the café. She sat across from him at one of the round black tables, the surface speckled with little flecks and swirls of gray and brown. Faux granite? It was very chic, she thought. Did they buy these in town? They certainly weren't from the Shabby Tabby.

Why was she even thinking about this?

She held her purse tightly in her lap. She felt like a kid who was in trouble and had just been sent to the principal's office to learn her punishment. How was she supposed to explain why she hadn't called?

It was then that she noticed the faint bruises on her hands and wrist from that dang lion toy nipping at her. They looked so much starker under the fluorescent lights. She wondered if Jack could see them.

"How's your aunt?"

The question snapped her out of her thoughts. "Oh, um … she's better. What happened to that maid was—is—a shock. We've all been staying at my place. The studio is a bit cramped with three people."

"She too spooked to stay at another hotel?" he asked. "I mean, I would be."

"Something like that." She scooted a little closer to the

table, folding her hands on top. Her purse felt heavy in her lap. Unable to look at him, she worried a peeling cuticle. "Look, Jack, I—"

He placed a hand over hers to still her nervous picking. One of his thumbs idly swept over the bruise marring the fleshy pad of her thumb. "You don't have to apologize, if that's what you were about to do. Don't feel pressured to do … anything. Aside from Larry's very embarrassing commentary, I don't think it's any secret that I like you. Been maintaining a middle-school-level crush for *quite* some time."

Amber managed a laugh, flattered and unsure of how to even address what he'd just said.

"And maybe the timing is off right now because of everything that happened with your aunt. And your sister is in town," he said, removing his hand, though keeping his arm on the table. "Maybe you're not interested—"

"It's not that," she said quickly, the words tumbling out before she realized she was thinking them, let alone saying them. "I'm just a bit of a mess, is all."

He shrugged a shoulder. "I'm okay with messes. But, honestly, call me if you want to. Or don't. I just wanted you to know *I'm* interested. If you want to go out sometime, I'd take you anywhere you want to go. Even somewhere in … *Marbleglen*."

"The scandal!" Amber whisper-hissed, bristling as was required whenever someone mentioned the name of Edgehill's rival town. "This middle-school-crush must be truly epic."

He blushed furiously. "I haven't made you a mixtape yet, but I'm thinking about it."

Amber laughed again, and despite her mind screaming

at her to not—absolutely not—get caught up with another non-witch, she said, "A real date sounds great."

"Excellent." He coughed, rubbing the back of his neck. "I'll call you this weekend?"

Amber nodded, standing up, strapping her purse back on to her shoulder. She fought the urge to reach out and shake his hand, as if they'd just completed a job interview. "Sounds good."

With an awkward smile, she hurried toward the conference room where the ladies and Nathan were likely already starting the bi-weekly Here and Meow Committee meeting. She assumed all the scones had been devoured by now.

As she walked past the counter, Larry, without looking up, held out his hand. "Bout freaking time!"

Amber offered him a high five, not slowing her pace.

"You're both horrible!" Jack called out from the other side of the café.

Amber found it difficult to keep the smile off her face for the entirety of the meeting.

A few days later, just after flipping her open sign to closed, ready to simply collapse behind the counter for a quick power nap instead of grabbing lunch with Willow at the Catty Melt, her cell started to ring. Problem was, she'd misplaced it. Again.

Unlike the last time she'd lost her phone—when Connor Declan had swung by the Quirky Whisker to lightly interrogate her in the days after Melanie's death—she was alone in the shop, which meant she could use magic this time. The Bowen sisters had left for lunch already, and Willow had run upstairs to get her purse. Aunt Gretchen was, presumably, still sleeping. Whatever illness she'd contracted before her arrival in Edgehill still had a hold on her. She slept often.

Briefly closing her eyes, Amber cast a quick locator spell. She'd had to use said spell so often, all she needed was to hold the image of her cell in her mind and flick her wrist. Her body lurched forward an inch, her magic pulling her toward the object in question. She walked toward the toy display, then abruptly came up short when she spotted a small basket filled with Christmas-themed toy cats. *What are these doing out?* She'd put them in storage back in early January. Seeing them made her frown with regret.

There were a dozen of them, all white with varying patches of black. All black paws for this one; black-tipped ears for that one. They all wore floppy Santa hats and had collars of holly or bells around their necks. Her grand plan had been to set them up on a table in the shop and have them meow Christmas carols like a tiny plastic *a cappella* choir.

Once she'd gotten them all set up, and they'd meowed a perfect rendition of "Jingle Bells," she'd been utterly delighted with herself. But then she'd immediately worried the magic was a bit too advanced to explain away. When she'd asked Willow's opinion, she'd agreed. So Amber had disabled their magic discs and sold them as plain, stationary Christmas décor. This dozen was all that remained.

Part of her was still sad no one had witnessed the feline choir—aside from Tom and Alley, that is. And only Alley had mildly appreciated it; Tom had growled his discontent from under the bed.

Her cell, somehow, was ringing from *inside* the basket. Amber plunged her hand into the pile of cats, bells on some of their collars tinkling.

"Chief Brown" was on her screen for all of a moment before the call ended. What on earth could he be calling *her* about?

Before she could call him back, a meow sounded. She glanced down into the basket that she still squatted in front of. She watched as a cat righted itself, shaking its head. The white ball at the end of its floppy hat knocked the cat in the nose. Bells tinkled and more meows vibrated out of tiny plastic throats. The basket was a sea of writhing black-and-white limbs and paws. Then they all started to meow, but not in any recognizable pattern.

She stood quickly, turning to look over her shoulder where she was sure Willow would be standing at the base of the steps, a smirk pulling up the corners of her mouth.

But Willow wasn't there.

"Hello, Blackwood."

Amber yelped, whirling to face the basket of cats. They all sat in neat rows now, peering up at her with golden glossy eyes. They blinked in unison.

Amber's breath was shallow. Not because of the display of magic itself, but because she could only assume the Penhallow was doing this. Her attention snapped to the glass windows of her shop. Tourists milled about outside, but she didn't see anyone with their hands cupped to the glass, peering in.

"It's rude not to say hello, Amber."

Lips pursed, she stared at the cats, her phone still clasped tightly in her hand. "What do you want, Penhallow?"

"Tsk, tsk," the cats said as one, their little pink tongues clicking against little white teeth. "I just want to talk. One witch to another. But these pesky wards won't let me in."

A literal mental warning bell went off, like a distant alarm clock in her mind. A sign that someone uninvited was trying to get past the protection spells Willow and Aunt Gretchen had encased the building in.

What seemed like moments later, Willow and Gretchen were pounding down the steps from the studio.

"Amber!" Gretchen called out. The panic in her voice caused a twinge in Amber's chest.

"I'm here," she said, gaze still focused on the cats. "I'm okay."

After they'd scanned the room, her aunt and sister took a spot on either side of her.

"Ah, the whole Blackwood clan together again," the cats said.

Willow gasped. Gretchen cursed.

"I ask again: what do you want, Penhallow? Why are you here?" Amber said, her own magic waking up. This cursed witch was after her family. She wouldn't stand for it, and neither would her magic.

"Give me the Henbane grimoire and I'll be on my merry way."

It wasn't what Amber had expected, and her brows pulled together. Willow grabbed her hand—out of fear or solidarity, Amber couldn't be sure.

Gretchen spoke before Amber could, her voice carrying

its usual steely edge. "We don't have Annabelle's grimoire. It was destroyed in the fire fourteen years ago."

"Do you think me a fool, Blackwood?" the cats asked. "Grimoires cannot be destroyed."

Amber's and Willow's gazes whipped to their aunt.

"Yes," the cats said. "She lies to you once again."

The cats tilted their heads back and sniffed the air in unison. The Santa hats on their heads somehow made it all the more creepy to Amber. "I can sense it. I've followed its scent here to Edgehill. But it's … hard to pinpoint the exact location now that I'm here." Their collective gaze moved to Amber and Willow. "Your mother was a Henbane. Surely you've seen her grimoire. If you've seen it, if you've touched it, then you can locate it. The spell you just used to find your phone, Amber, would be more than sufficient to locate the book. Just picture it in your mind's eye and your magic will take care of the rest."

"But we haven't," Amber said. "We were kept in the dark about our heritage. We're just as clueless about the grimoire's whereabouts as you are. So scurry back into the hole you crawled out of."

The cats hissed.

"Don't tick off the psychotic witch, Amber," Willow sing-songed out the corner of her mouth.

"I am not psychotic!" the cats snapped.

Using a basket of Christmas cats to state such a message was a poor choice, Amber thought. It was like being scolded by a piglet in a tutu. The cute factor sort of overpowered everything else.

The wards on the building rattled and the three Blackwoods

147

winced as one. Okay, so the witch could still be unsettling even if he chose to speak through cats.

"I'm watching you," the cats said, collective voice calm again. "Eventually one of you will lead me to the spell book. Unless I find it first. Then you'll regret not cooperating."

Then, rather abruptly, the cats froze. Half of them toppled over, limbs stiff and lifeless once more.

Amber bolted for the front door, unlocked it, and hurried out onto the sidewalk, despite the frantic protests from her aunt and sister. She shuddered when she slammed into a wall of sticky, web-like air. The Penhallow had been out here. There was no question of that. But where was he now? She looked up one side of Russian Blue Avenue and then the other. No one walking around the sidewalk struck her as suspicious, though several gave her a wide berth. She could only imagine how frantic she looked, hands balled into fists by her sides, eyes wide and scanning.

"Everything all right, sugar?"

Amber glanced across the street to see Betty Harris standing outside Purrfectly Scrumptious, one hand on her hip and the other shielding her eyes from the bright noonday sun. She wore a white apron over her clothes, the color a stark contrast to her warm brown skin. Savannah, her blue-eyed Maine coon, sat obediently by her feet, tail swishing.

Amber waited for a slow-moving car to pass by before she crossed the street. The second she stopped in front of Betty, Savannah gave a soft chirp, then flopped over on her back. Savannah always seemed to know when Amber was distressed. But before she could bend down to greet the cat, a giggling little boy—who had clearly pulled away from his father—ran over and fell onto his knees so he could rub Savannah's stomach.

Amber's attention shifted back to Betty. "Have you seen anyone … odd outside my shop today?"

Betty cocked her head. "Odd how?"

"I don't even know." Amber sighed. "Maybe someone who looked like they were casing the place?"

Her dark brows shot toward her hairline. "What do you—"

"Betty?"

Both women turned toward Purrfectly Scrumptious where Betty's husband, Bobby, stood in the doorway. He had a phone in his hand. "Hey, Amber! How you doing?"

"I'm okay. You?"

"Good, good. Sorry to interrupt, ladies, but Mr. Gillory's on the phone …"

"Oh, shoot," Betty said, turning back to Amber and giving her arm a squeeze. "I've got to take this, but I'll come check on you soon. You sure you're all right?"

Amber managed a faint smile. "Yeah, yeah. I'm fine."

With a nod, Betty took the phone from Bobby. He waved at Amber before following Betty back inside. Savannah stayed out on the sidewalk, allowing her stomach to be scratched by the little boy. Her eyes were squinted shut in pleasure.

The boy's father arrived a couple seconds later. "George!" he said. "What have I told you about running off?"

"Sorry, Dad." George stood, his head lowered. "I just wanted to say hi to the kitty."

The man was tall, dark, and handsome. He smiled at

Amber, shrugging sheepishly. "Sorry about that. Hope he wasn't bothering your cat."

"Oh, Savannah loves the attention," Amber said, trying to muster up false cheer. "In fact, she looks rather put out that the attention stopped."

The man chuckled. "I've had to apologize for George's enthusiasm half a dozen times today. Good thing everyone is so friendly here—even the cats."

"Part of Edgehill's charm," she said, smiling brightly as if she were a member of the Edgehill tourism committee.

"Indeed," he said, scooping George up and walking past her. He paused, then glanced over his shoulder. "Now be a helpful lamb and find that book, Amber."

She gaped at him, watching him walk away.

Only allowing the shock to affect her for a moment, she darted forward and grabbed the man by the elbow, hurrying around to face him. "What did you say?"

His brow furrowed. "Sorry ... do I know you?"

"It's the lady with the cat, Daddy," George said.

The man looked from Amber to George and back again. "What are you two talking about?" He shook his head. "I'm ... sorry, miss. I have to go meet my wife."

He held his son a little closer and then quickly walked away. Had the man been acting? Was that the Penhallow feigning ignorance? Or had the man been temporarily compelled to speak something against his will?

Stomach in knots, Amber headed back toward the Quirky Whisker, then immediately ran into another patch of the sticky air. Her breath whooshed out of her.

Not only was the Penhallow in Edgehill, but now he was toying with her. And Amber was not in the mood to play.

She flinched when her phone started to ring. It was still clutched in her hand. The chief was calling again.

"Hello?" she said, her voice sounding a little croaky. She cleared her throat.

"I need you to come down to the station," he said. "I have something you need to see. And I don't think anyone other than someone with your ... particular skillset can explain what it is."

"I'm on my way."

CHAPTER 12

After a very intense conversation with her aunt and sister, they finally agreed that it was likely safe for Amber to go talk to the chief. The Penhallow could be anyone, yes, but Amber also knew what he or she wanted now: the Henbane grimoire. Which neither Amber nor Willow had ever seen—they surely didn't have it.

What the Penhallow had said about the locator spell, though, kept replaying in her head. Since Amber had never seen the book, she didn't have the details needed to conduct a spell to find it. Had her mother kept the book from her and Willow because of that? Had she never let them see the book—not even as children—to ensure they'd never be able to give up the book's location?

But an even more nagging question plagued her. Why was the Penhallow harassing *them* for the grimoire? Edgar was the Henbane, not them. And Edgar was in Edgehill. He had been for years. Had the Penhallow's nose led him to Edgehill because of what Edgar potentially had squirreled away?

Given what the Penhallow said about grimoires being indestructible, and that Edgar said he didn't know where "it" was—that it likely wasn't "there" anymore—Amber figured the Henbane grimoire was still intact and in Edgehill. Somewhere.

She had no clue where to start looking. Up until an hour ago, she'd assumed it had been lost forever. Edgar apparently didn't know its location because it was "hidden even from him."

Whatever *that* meant.

Was it possible the Penhallow didn't know about Edgar? Perhaps the wards on his house were even stronger than the ones on the Quirky Whisker. If that was the case, and the Penhallow didn't know Edgar Henbane was out in the middle of nowhere with the hiding place of a highly coveted grimoire locked away in his mind, Amber wasn't about to lead the cursed witch to his doorstep. Visiting Edgar's again, even if the book *was* there, was out of the question—at least until she had a better plan.

What truly unnerved her was that the Penhallow had known about the Christmas cats. She was certain the box had been in storage. Had the witch been watching her as early as November or December, when Amber had been slaving over the intricate spells? When had the witch been in the Quirky Whisker to plant her phone in the box? It would have been in the past few hours, as Amber would have noticed the box last night when she did her quick tidying up of the shop after closing. Whose face had the Penhallow been wearing this morning while the witch went about the store, setting up their trick?

Yet, the sticky magic had been *outside* the store, not in.

This made her feel better, if only by a little. Now she imagined the Penhallow working during the dead of night, standing outside the Quirky Whisker while they used their magic to move items around the shop. Floating the basket out of a storage closet. Moving her oft-forgotten cell phone from one location to the inside of the basket.

The wards had held. They were still safe.

For now, anyway.

She wondered if the Penhallow was following her right this moment. Her gaze flicked to her rear-view mirror, then darted to her side mirrors, scanning for anything out of the ordinary.

By the time she pulled in front of the police station, she was a ball of nerves. She remembered her calming "turn it blue" spell too late.

When she walked into the station's lobby, she didn't bother trying to engage Dolores in conversation. Amber merely said, "I'm meeting with Chief Brown" as she passed by her wooden box-desk, then turned left, as she had with Carl only a few days ago. Dolores made no move to stop her. Amber was fairly sure the clack of her keyboard never faltered.

The station was relatively quiet. Were the officers out chasing down leads? Eating lunch?

When she raised a fist to knock on the chief's door, she was half tempted to use the familiar knocking pattern Carl kept trying to fool the chief with, just to see the look on his face. She resisted the urge and rapped twice on the door.

"Come on in, Miss Blackwood," he called.

"You *are* a clever detective," she said by way of greeting.

He managed a small smile. "I was both expecting you, and expecting Dolores not to escort you down the hall."

"Does she ever *not* scowl?" Amber asked.

"Wouldn't know," he said.

Taking a seat in one of the two chairs opposite his desk

and dropping her purse to the floor by her feet, she said, "So what did you want to show me?"

He huffed a breath out of his nose. He then stood and plucked up a folder from on top of the stack nearest him. "Dr. Bunson finished the autopsy on Wilma Bennett."

After a brief moment of confusion, she said, "The maid." She finally had a name.

"Yes. There was nothing in her system or her stomach that points to poisoning. She looks … shrunken, as I mentioned. Like all the moisture in her body evaporated at once. But from what Bunson can tell, he believes the cause of death was electrocution. As if a bolt of electricity hit her and stopped her heart."

How awful. Poor Wilma.

"Any of this sound familiar?"

"Not at all," she said. "If this shock to her system stopped her heart, does that mean the death was quick, at least?"

The chief, still standing behind his desk with the folder in hand, nodded. "Bunson thinks whatever happened to her was instant."

"Small blessings, I guess."

The chief nodded.

She stared at him, waiting for him to make the decision to round the desk and show her what was in that folder.

Several long, silent moments passed before he tapped it. "I have photos. I have no idea what this is. But I'm hoping you might."

Still, he didn't move. His gaze flicked up to her, then away. Twice.

"Chief, I'm still me. I don't bite. I don't carry a wand in my purse. I won't hex you or turn you into a frog," she said.

His shoulders relaxed a little.

"Besides, if I was going to turn you into anything, it would be a hamster. They're good pets. I had one a few years ago, but Alley ate him."

His mouth slightly dropped open, the color draining from his face.

"Chief! I'm kidding!"

He managed an awkward breathy laugh. "I know. Yeah. Yeah, I know." He rounded the desk. Tucking the folder under his arm, he shoved the papers and binders aside so he could make room. "Okay, so take a look at these ..."

Amber stood and closed the distance, watching as he laid the autopsy photos out for her in a row. She hadn't known Wilma—heck, until a minute ago, she hadn't even known the woman's name—but tears sprang to her eyes anyway. This poor, unsuspecting woman didn't deserve what happened to her. All because this cursed Penhallow wanted a book?

Due to Wilma's shrunken appearance, Amber couldn't tell how old she'd been before she died. But she also wasn't seeing anything in this series of four photos that struck her as particularly unique; her prone body and wrinkled skin were just as he'd described then. Amber was about to ask him if there was something she was missing, when he laid down another picture. He set the folder to the left of the laid-out photos.

This one was of the woman's bare stomach. In the center was a black circle, about the size of a dime, and tendrils of black radiated out from it. As if the blood in her veins had blackened. It looked vaguely like a scorch mark left on the sidewalk by a small firework. The tendrils, though, reminded her of what she'd seen in movies when someone's blood was poisoned by something supernatural. Actual blood poisoning left thick lines of red beneath the skin. This ... this was something else. Had he thought she'd have insight into this very nasty-looking wound because it screamed "not normal"?

"You said a witch did this to her, right?" he asked, voice soft, his gaze focused on the photos. "Can magic ... hit a person? Is it a physical thing?"

Amber shook her head. "No. That's not how magic works. Magic can move air, let's say. My energy can push against the air, but it's the *air* that hits the person. The magic is more like a catalyst for the movement, if that makes sense?" She glanced up at him, where he stood beside her with his arms crossed. He glared at the photographs as if they'd just insulted his mother.

"So this—" he said, tapping the impact site on Wilma's stomach, "isn't from a magical blast?"

"I've never seen anything like this," she said, staring at the black scorch-wound again, "but a Penhallow's magic doesn't behave like magic should. It's possible that his magic has been warped to the point that it can cause harm. It's not supposed to. Magic can be used to hurt someone, sure, but it's not the magic itself that's responsible."

"That sounds like a gun control argument," he muttered.

She wasn't getting into *that* debate, so she kept her mouth shut.

He reached over to flip open the folder, then pulled out a final picture and set it on top of the stack before Amber.

157

She gasped.

"This was taken today, whereas the one before this was taken the day Wilma was brought in," the chief said.

The picture was very similar to the first, except now, the area around the scorch mark was ringed in deep shades of purple and blue; a massive bruise that took up nearly her entire abdomen.

"I've seen postmortem bruising before," the chief said, "but nothing like this. It looks like she took a battering ram to the stomach, yet from all reports, no one heard a sound come from that room. Another maid had seen Wilma enter several minutes earlier to bring in the set of towels your aunt had requested before she went to pick up dinner. When Wilma wasn't back out after a couple minutes, the maid peeked her head in to make sure everything was okay, and then found Wilma in the position you saw her in: collapsed on the side of the bed."

Amber stared at Wilma's bruised stomach. Could that truly be an impact site created by magic?

"How did someone sustain injuries this extensive in only a matter of minutes and no one saw or heard anything?" he asked.

"I don't know," Amber said, finally looking up at the chief. She could see her own worry mirrored on his face. "But we need to figure it out before it happens again."

Because if Amber and her family couldn't locate this spell book, it was very possible that Wilma's fate would befall the Blackwoods too.

After calling Willow and telling her everything she'd learned from the chief, Amber asked if Willow and Gretchen would be able to man the store for a little while without her.

"Yeah, of course," Willow said. "But where are you going?"

"I don't know," Amber said. "I just need to think."

"I don't like you being out by yourself," she said. "We're safer together."

"I won't be gone long."

"I'm going to set the box of Christmas cats on fire, by the way. I feel like they're watching me."

"They might be. Who knows at this point?" Amber asked.

"I was joking," Willow said. "But now I'm not. Farewell, Christmas cats."

Amber could barely muster a smile. "Talk to you later, Will."

She disconnected before her sister could say anything else. Amber desperately wanted to see Edgar, to ask him if he'd ever heard of a witch causing wounds like the ones she'd seen on Wilma. But she couldn't risk revealing Edgar's location. They'd been lucky that the Penhallow hadn't followed them out there days before.

But the idea of going back to her tiny shop to deal with countless, unfamiliar faces was too much for her. She knew Willow and Gretchen were safe inside the store. The wards would keep the Penhallow out.

She was banking on her assumption that she was safe too— as long as the cursed witch believed Amber and her family were his best chance to find the grimoire, anyway.

After an hour of aimless driving, Amber found herself on the corner of Claws Way and Ocicat Lane. Ocicat was a short street with only a dozen houses on either side. The neighborhood was only half finished.

Amber's old house was at the end on the right. The street and sidewalk gave way to a field a few feet beyond Amber's old house, as if the construction team had given up halfway through the project. Amber wondered if her parents had chosen the house because of that fact.

Willow and Amber had spent hours of their childhood out in that field, running around like wild animals. Their cats would roam the wilderness with them, catching insects and mice. On long summer days, the sisters would fill their backpacks with snacks and make the half-hour trek to Chartreux Creek. The year Amber turned ten, their father had tied a tire swing to one of the sturdy branches of a huge oak. The girls spent hours out there reading and swimming and talking about boys.

The tree was gone now.

A lot was gone now.

Though Amber could see the house from her bedroom window, she hadn't been to the site of the fire in years.

A car honked and she jumped. Her gaze flicked to her rearview mirror. She was still idling at the stop sign. She waved apologetically and crept forward through the intersection, and soon parked at the curb in front of 543 Ocicat Lane. An empty lot sat to the right of the house. Her old neighbors had moved shortly after the fire. No one wanted to buy the house after the neighbors had vacated it, considering that the house next door was a blackened ruin. It eventually fell into such disrepair, it was torn down.

543 Ocicat Lane still stood, though. Waiting for someone to finish restoring her to her former glory. The house had been fixed up enough that it was no longer considered a danger.

Amber got out of the car and rested her arms on its roof, staring at the partially finished house. Gretchen had worked to get it repaired, so the inside was gutted. The roof had been replaced, but boards still covered a few of the windows. Somehow the porch had survived. She could still smell charred wood—or perhaps that was just her memory conjuring up the scent. To this day, actively burning fireplaces filled her with a mild sense of panic, solely because of the smell.

She could picture the red and blue lights flashing, silently cascading in swirling patterns over the neighbors' walls. She could see the ash in the air, falling like black snow.

She didn't know why she came today. It wasn't as if the grimoire could be here. There was nothing left inside the house and there hadn't been a secret basement, cellar, or attic.

Still, she closed her car door and walked around to the sidewalk. Weeds grew around the porch where Amber and Willow had played cards. Where Amber had sat with her mother, her arm around Amber's shoulders, as she sobbed over having her heart broken for the first time at fourteen. Where Amber and her father had painted the Adirondack chairs a bright orange that Willow and their mother hated.

Amber stood at the base of the steps now, hands in the pockets of her slacks, memories cycling through her head.

The front door had been replaced, since the firefighters had kicked in the old one.

A tiny mew pulled Amber's attention away from the door, and toward the brush surrounding the steps. She inched forward and pulled her hands from her pockets so she could rest them on her knees. She held her breath, waiting, not sure now if she'd heard the sound at all. Then the mew sounded again. Amber rounded the steps and peered under them as best as she could, but the weeds here put Edgar's to shame. These looked to be full of barbs and thorns, too.

Another mew and then another.

Standing to full height, Amber scanned Ocicat Lane and the houses across the street. She didn't see movement, but it didn't mean no one was watching her skulk about the yard of her old house.

The mewing was a tiny cacophony now.

Screw it, she thought, and cast a simple air spell, sending the air down toward her feet. A patch of the thorny weeds flattened as if someone had just stepped on them with a heavy boot. She flattened another patch, then glanced over her shoulder. No one was watching. She sent out another burst of air. She needed to clear a path for herself to get under the steps without tearing her hands apart in the process.

After a minute, she'd flattened the weeds enough that she was able to duck under the porch steps. And there, in a roiling mass of gray, white, and brown, were half a dozen newborn kittens. They cried and yowled, their eyes not yet open. Amber knew better than to touch them—hopefully their mother was nearby looking for food. But they looked rather sickly, despite being in possession of such powerful little lungs. She hoped they hadn't been abandoned.

After a minute or two of their tiny cries, she couldn't take it anymore and patted her pockets for her cell phone so she could call Nine Lives Cat Rescue. But then something shiny caught her eye.

It lay next to the wall of the porch, a few inches behind the kittens. In order to reach it, she would need to completely get underneath the steps. She used one more burst of air to flatten the brambles, careful not to further disturb the kittens. She gasped when she almost instantly recognized the object: her father's favorite watch. She crept forward, hunched over to avoid hitting her head on the steps, and plucked out the battered piece of jewelry. The watch face was almost completely blackened, and the clasp was missing entirely, but it was definitely his watch.

Crawling back out, she brushed herself off. As soon as she moved away from them, the kittens resumed their frantic mewing. Shoving the charred watch into her pocket, Amber returned to her car, finding her phone in her purse. She dialed Nine Lives.

After they told her they'd be there in fifteen to twenty minutes, she sat back to wait in the seclusion of her car. She hoped the mama cat would show up if Amber was out of sight—and then maybe Nine Lives could rescue her too.

She pulled the watch out of her pocket and flipped it over to read the inscription on the back. Most of the letters had been lost to wear, time, and the fire, but Amber didn't need to see the words to know what they said. "*To my beloved Theo. I cherish every second with you. Love, Belle.*"

Amber ran a thumb over the letters, a tightness building in her throat. She missed them both so much sometimes she thought it would drown her. She was beyond desperate to know what had truly happened to them. Amber didn't have many friends. She didn't date. She stayed home with her cats and stared out at this unfinished house hoping she'd remember something that would break the case wide open. When the house burned down, when her parents died, when this watch in her hands stopped ticking forward the seconds—Amber had stopped too.

Her thumb swept back and forth, back and forth over the worn inscription.

What happened, Mom? Dad? Who took you from me?

Then, abruptly, the world around her exploded in a burst of white light.

CHAPTER 13

When the light faded, Amber was somehow in her old house—but as it was fourteen years ago. The air here didn't hold a hint of charred wood. In fact, she couldn't smell anything.

She sat at the round table in the dining area where it was positioned in the little nook surrounded on three sides by windows. The walls were a cheery yellow here, the blinds and windows open. Bright, warm sunlight poured in. Her mother called it their "breakfast nook."

But Amber couldn't feel the chair beneath her, or the worn surface of the table under her arms. She couldn't feel the sunlight on her skin.

She could, however, see her mother sitting across from her. The sunlight streaming in behind her shone on her dark brown hair. Amber was torn between being awestruck that her mother was here in front of her—alive and healthy—and being floored by how similar she and her mother looked. Amber saw her own big, brown eyes, button nose, and heart-shaped face reflected back at her.

How was she here? How was her mother sitting in front of her as if the past fourteen years hadn't happened?

Had Aunt Gretchen been wrong? Was time travel actually possible?

But when Amber looked down, the arms resting on the table weren't hers. The watch she'd found—in perfect, shiny condition now—was wrapped around a wrist far more masculine than hers. They were her father's arms, she realized. His hands were clasped in front of him, and his gaze was focused across the table at Belle.

Her mother's lips, so much like Amber's own, turned up now, smiling at her.

No, not at her now. But at her father, back then.

"This is nothing to smile about, Annabelle," Theo said. Amber didn't feel her lips move. She wasn't possessing her father's body so much as she was a silent, undetectable passenger.

Amber could tell his words didn't have the bite he'd intended. Her father always had a hard time being upset with her mother for very long. "How did he find you?"

Belle sighed, her shoulders slumping and her smile slipping. She folded her arms on the table now, too, mirroring Theo's posture. "I don't know," she said. "We've been in Edgehill for years. I don't use my magic any more now than I have in the past, so it's not as if he could locate me based on my signature."

A witch's magic had a "signature"? And another witch could track it? That was news to Amber.

"What did he want?" Theo asked, and Amber could hear the bite in his tone now. Could tell the words struggled to make it past clenched teeth.

"Are you still angry with me?" she asked. "If you're going to yell at me again, I'll come back to finish this when you can talk to me without making half the kitchen explode. Again."

Theo huffed out a breath. "I fixed all the broken plates and glasses before the girls saw anything." He sounded like a little boy who'd just been scolded.

Belle stared at him for a beat.

"I promise to listen this time," he said. "So what did he want?"

"The same thing he's always wanted," Belle said, diverting her gaze.

"You?"

"Don't start, Theo."

"His obsession with you is why you've basically been a fugitive half your life."

Amber had never heard her father sound so … bitter.

"His obsession with the grimoire, you mean," she said. "He wants that more than he wants me."

"Don't be naïve, Belle," he said. "Why is he after it now? Isn't the book still cloaked?"

Belle pursed her lips and sat back slightly. "Of *course* it's still cloaked," she snapped, then leaned forward again. "I'm not an idiot."

"Okay, okay," Theo said, holding up a hand. "So he doesn't know it's here?" Some of the bitterness had faded and was replaced by a tone that had a classically hopeful Theo Black-wood note to it. Amber could tell where Willow had gotten that from. Amber and Belle had always been more cynical. "Was moving it here until we found another location for it a bad idea? Do you think he sensed it somehow? That he saw something?"

Belle shook her head. "No, he has no clue. He was wearing

the face of old Mrs. Wilton and ambushed me in Ma and Paw's. She was just asking casual questions while we're shopping, like any other week. But then she followed me out to the car and eventually started asking if you and I had done any traveling lately. I knew then something was off. Mrs. Wilton never gets very personal with her questions." She abruptly stopped talking.

"What?" Theo prompted.

"We move it, what, every five years? Do you think we've become predictable?" Belle asked, worrying at her bottom lip with her teeth. "*Did* we slip up somewhere?"

"I don't know," Theo said, sighing. "Maybe?"

"Everyone here is so friendly ... maybe over the years someone has been keeping track of our movements. Maybe someone asked about a family vacation and I inadvertently gave something away."

"It's possible he found us a long time ago and has been biding his time here, waiting for us to screw up."

Belle whimpered and dug her fingers into her hair, elbows resting on the table. "Is this all my fault?"

"Hey," Theo said, voice soft, and placed his outstretched arms on the table, his palms open and seeking hers.

Belle looked up, sighed, and took his hands. Amber wished she had more senses than sight at her disposal right now. She wished she could feel her mother's palms against hers.

"You said he didn't have a clue where it is, right?"

"Right," she said. "All he knows is that he can't find a trace of it. He dropped the glamour in the parking lot. I swear I almost fainted. I haven't seen that face in ... so long."

"You think he was just trying to scare you?"

"Maybe," she said, letting one of his hands go so she could chew on a thumbnail.

"I really wish there was a way to destroy a spell once it was written," Theo said. "Burying this thing in remote locations every time the cloaking spell wears off is getting old."

"I can work on crafting a spell that lasts longer," Belle offered.

"Band-Aid solution for a bullet wound."

"I know. I'm sorry. I don't know what else to do. We can't let anyone find it."

"I know, I know," he said, sighing. He rubbed his thumb back and forth across her knuckles. "But the girls will be of age before we know it. We have to tell them eventually. If something happens to us, Amber will have to be the one to keep it hidden."

Belle pulled her hand from Theo's and crossed her arms. "I know. I'm working on it. Kathleen and I are on to something. I can feel it."

Theo started to say something, but then stopped.

"What?" Belle asked.

"Do you think the surge in magic-use is what alerted him somehow?" he asked. "Even if it's Kathleen increasing her usage, maybe it could be tracked back here since she's doing all this *for* us?"

"You *do* think this is my fault."

"I don't," he said quickly. "I just … I'm out of my depth here, Belle. It's all starting to spiral. Can't you *sense* that?"

Belle wedged her thumbnail between her teeth again.

"Plus, I—"

169

She squinted at him. "I know that look. Out with it."

"Raph called the other day ..."

Belle's expression looked no less harassed. "You speak to my brother more than I do."

"He's worried, Belle," Theo said, voice soft. "All these spells Kathleen has been doing are starting to wear on her. Mentally, I mean. She's starting to develop insomnia; when she *does* sleep, she wakes up screaming."

Belle closed her eyes and massaged her forehead. "She hasn't told me that. She told me she's been a little tired since her magic hasn't been used this much in a while. I thought it was like muscle fatigue, not that she hasn't been sleeping."

"I understand why you're doing this," he said, tone still soft, "but there's only so much even a Caraway can see into the future. She can't see every possibility. There are too many variables."

"I *know*," Belle snapped, eyes still closed, fingers still massaging her temples. Then, softer, she said, "I know."

"We'll figure it out. His arrival in Edgehill doesn't change anything. Our plan has served us well for this long. He'll back off if we keep our heads down. Like you said, he's just fishing for information."

Belle's gaze flicked toward the stairs. Theo turned to look too. Amber knew he was looking at the small closet embedded into the side of the staircase.

When he turned his attention back to Belle, he said, "We'll keep you *and* the book safe. I won't let anything happen to my girls. *Any* of them," he said. "I promise."

Belle managed to aim a small smile in Theo's direction. "That might be a promise you can't keep, love."

Light flashed again, the relatively calm scene in the breakfast nook peeling away like paint stripped from a canvas. Then Amber found herself standing in the front entrance of the house, watching in bewilderment as a braces-wearing Willow and Amber's younger self came hurrying down the stairs and right past her on their way to the door. Her mother was hot on their heels.

"Bye, Dad!" Amber called out, but he stopped her with a, "Hang on! Give your dad a hug, pumpkin."

Amber had always acted like she hated the nickname, but deep down, she loved it. Only her dad called her that. She made a show of rolling her eyes, then doubled back to throw her arms around his middle. They were almost the same height now.

Though this memory was from her father's point of view, Amber started filling in things from her own memories. The way she'd felt that evening. How she'd been so carefree when she'd left.

"*Bye*, Dad," young Amber sing-songed, then tipped her head back to look up at him. He was still nearly half a foot taller. Her good nature immediately slipped when she saw the pained look on his face. "Dad? What's wrong?"

His bottom lip shook. "Nothing, pumpkin. I'm just going to miss you, is all."

"Oh, relax, Dad," Amber said, laughing now. "It's just a sleepover. I'll see you in the morning."

He nodded, though his eyes watered. "Yeah. In the morning."

A twinge in her chest at the sight of her father being near tears—he was an emotional guy, but he'd never cried over them going to a sleepover before—made her scramble for something to say that would lighten his mood. Was this some kind of midlife crisis? "We can try out that waffle iron Mom got forever ago. Think we could make blueberry waffles in that thing?"

He managed a smile then; he loved breakfast food. "That sounds great, pumpkin. Blueberry waffles it is."

Willow poked her head back into the house then. "Amber! Hurry up. Mrs. Carr is waiting."

"Hey, Will?" Amber said, letting her dad go. "Come give Dad a hug."

Willow shrugged and bounded over and gave her father a tight squeeze. He kissed Willow on the forehead.

It was then that Amber noticed her mom standing at the base of the steps, her arms folded and gripping her elbows. She looked just as pained as her father.

"Geez! What's *wrong* with you guys tonight?"

Her mom walked over and pulled Amber into a hug, too. "I love you so much," she whispered in Amber's ear as she smoothed down her hair with one hand. Then she pulled back, cupping Amber's face in her hands. "You know that, don't you?"

"Yeah, of course," Amber said, eyebrow cocked. "Is this because we haven't been to a sleepover in a long time?"

Her mom laughed, a tear slipping free before she quickly wiped it away. "Something like that."

Amber had wanted clarity—had craved it for fourteen years—but she suddenly knew that clarity was going to break her heart. Her parents' actions that night made so much more sense now. Had they known?

After her mother tearfully hugged Willow goodbye too, Amber and her little sister called one final goodbye and bolted out the door, slamming the door behind them.

By the time Theo—his vision blurry due to his tears—had turned around, Belle was on the ground on her knees, forehead pressed to the floor as she sobbed. He rushed to her side, wrapping an arm around her. "Come here, baby. Come here."

Belle threw her arms around him, the two now hugging each other while on their knees, both openly weeping.

Amber had never, in all her sixteen years of being around her parents, seen or heard either one cry as hard as she did now. It was hard to experience, this very private moment between two people who had now been gone almost as long as they'd been in her life. People who had a whole world of experiences and emotions that Amber and her sister had no clue about. People who had taken on a saint-like place in her mind for years, and who were now stripped down to two very human near-strangers.

The only good thing—if one could label *any* of this good—about being trapped in this memory was that she was still seeing the memory from her father's point of view; she didn't have to *see* them crying their eyes out. But hearing it undid her anyway.

What felt like centuries later, the two broke away from each other and stood. Theo cupped Belle's face with one hand and swiped his thumb under her eye, wiping away a remaining tear. "I love you more than I can ever possibly say, Annabelle."

Belle closed her eyes, leaning her face into his palm. When she opened them again, she said, "You and the girls are the best things that have ever happened to me. He was a dumb mistake I made when I was young. Once I met you?" She shrugged, smiling despite her red, puffy eyes. "He didn't stand a chance once I met you. I have no regrets. Every choice I've made, no matter how flawed, gave me you and the girls. I love you just as much now as I did the day we got married."

Theo let out a choked sound. "They'll be okay?"

Belle's bottom lip shook, and she trapped it between her teeth to stop it. "The visions point to this being the best option."

"That doesn't answer my question."

Belle let out a shaky sigh. "No, they won't be okay. Not really. But they'll adjust. What child would ever truly be okay after their parents disappeared without a trace?"

Amber couldn't react the way she would normally, since she was stuck in someone else's body, in a different time, but the realization that her parents had planned to abandon them was almost as shocking to her as the fact that whatever they'd planned, it hadn't worked. What had gone wrong?

"When is Edgar supposed to be here?" Theo finally asked.

"Any minute now," Belle said.

"And you're sure he'll show?" he asked, starting to pace. "This all hinges on him getting the—"

"He'll be here." Belle watched him as he walked the length of the foyer and back again. "He knows it's important."

Theo turned to her. "You didn't … I mean, he doesn't know …"

Belle shook her head. "He's got no idea about the spell in question, and the book is warded so he can't open it. Only Amber or Willow can. Though, given what Penhallows are capable of, they might be able to break the ward if they got their hands on it. The cloaking spell has been reinforced three times over. As long as he gets it out of here and does what he's supposed to do, the book *and* the girls will be safe."

Theo blew out a breath and started to pace again. Belle chewed on a thumbnail.

Within minutes, a knock on the door sounded. Theo rushed to answer it. An eighteen-year-old Edgar stood on the other side of the door, his hands shoved into the pockets of his jeans. His wild mop of black hair was no less wild now than it was in the present, but currently it flopped over one eye. He swiped it out of his face, then shoved his hand back in his pocket.

"Hey," he said. "Hope I'm not late."

Theo's gaze shifted over Edgar's shoulder and he eyed the shiny white pickup truck idling at the curb. A pickup that now sat rusting and abandoned in front of Edgar's house. "Right on time." He ushered Edgar in.

Theo led Edgar to the breakfast nook where Belle stood before two books lying on the round kitchen table. Both books were two inches thick and leather-bound, the covers a rich black. Stamped across the front of both was the name

HENBANE, the letters depressed into the leather as if they'd been burned there with a branding iron. The pages looked to be made of sturdy parchment. Amber was desperate to flip their covers open.

"Why do you have two?" Edgar asked. "Didn't you only want me to hold onto one?"

Belle nodded. "Can you tell the difference?"

Edgar took a step toward the books and placed a hand on either one. After a few seconds, he tapped the one on the right twice with an index finger and stepped back. "That one has a cloak on it? I can't feel the magic in it."

Belle grinned at him. "Your mother would be so proud." She placed a hand on the back of his neck and pulled him toward her so she could kiss his temple. He flushed. Edgar had always seemed a little uncomfortable with affection.

Theo slung an arm around Belle and pulled her to his side. Theo and Belle stared at Edgar. Amber wondered if they'd looked at him with the same tear-rimmed eyes as they had with herself and Willow.

"You guys in trouble or something?" he suddenly asked, eyeing them. He crossed his arms and leaned a hip on the table. "I mean, maybe you guys got into a fight before I got here or whatever, but it looks like you both have been crying. Anything I need to be worried about? I'll do whatever you guys need for whatever reason, you know that. But if you need help, you can be honest with me. I can handle it, whatever it is. Dad's a space case, but he's still your brother, Aunt B. He can help too."

Belle sighed, and she almost—*almost*—sounded like she

was going to confess something, but stopped herself. "You're a sweet boy. But we're okay. We just need help with this one thing. Can you take the cloaked one?"

Edgar frowned. Amber could tell he was hurt. Hurt that they'd shut him out when something was very clearly wrong. "Yeah, okay." He grabbed the book off the table and hugged it to his chest. "It's safe with me."

After a quick hug from both Belle and Theo, Edgar headed to the front door. He stepped over the threshold, glanced over his shoulder, looking at them both in turn, offered a sad smile, and closed the door.

Once they saw the sweep of his headlights as he made a three-point turn to get out of their makeshift cul-de-sac, Theo let out a long sigh. "That boy is never going to forgive us."

Belle hooked a hand around one of Theo's arms and rested her cheek on his shoulder. "If the spell works as it should, he won't remember enough to know he's upset with us in the first place."

The scene peeled away again, this time showing Theo and Belle in their bedroom. They each had an open suitcase on the bed and were frantically running from closet to dresser and back as they filled their bags.

"How much longer do we have?" Theo asked as he tossed a handful of folded socks into his suitcase.

Belle checked the clock on her nightstand. "The cloaking spell on the book downstairs faded about five minutes ago.

Neil, assuming he's still nearby, would have sensed it immediately. Just depends on how long it takes him to get here."

"Your uncertainty isn't helping my nerves, babe," Theo said.

"It's not an exact science," she said, throwing several pairs of folded jeans into her bag. "But he'll be here. I'd say a good ten—"

Something heavy thumped against the door several times in rapid succession. Theo and Belle froze, then looked at each other.

"Not an exact science, indeed," Theo said, then immediately headed out of the bedroom and down the stairs.

Thud, thud, thud.

Belle was right behind him. "Let him lead the conversation as much as possible. He likes the sound of his own voice. We need to get him out of here as fast as possible, so we have time to get the heck out of Dodge. We can do this."

"I know, I know," Theo said, but she knew he appreciated the pep talk. Theo Blackwood always loved a good pep talk.

Thud, thud, thud.

Just before Theo reached the door, it flew open with such force, it was knocked off its hinges and onto the floor. Theo stumbled back in time to avoid getting hit in the face.

A man stood in the doorway. He was handsome in an unnerving kind of way—close-cropped black hair, cunning hazel eyes, and a half-smile that was somewhere between dangerous and sexy. Amber recoiled mentally, knowing this was Neil Penhallow. Even without the knowledge these memories had given her, Amber had a feeling she'd have known he was a

Penhallow on sight. He sauntered into the house. Theo, with Belle behind him, took several steps back.

"I knew you still had it, Anna," Neil said, gaze scanning the foyer. He sniffed the air a few times, like a bloodhound scenting a fox. "I've been waiting and waiting in this little hellhole of a town. Waiting for you to give up the book. Waiting for you to leave your pathetic husband when you realized you made the wrong choice all those years ago."

Before Theo could reply, Belle said, "How long have you been in Edgehill?"

"Oh, I don't know," he said, stepping farther into the foyer. He had his hands clasped behind his back and surveyed the room without looking at either Blackwood. "Three years now? Sinfully boring place, this."

"How did you find me?"

"All those magical bursts from Kathleen Caraway tipped me off," he said. "It was luck, really. I had been nearby hunting down a lead on you, Anna, and stumbled upon Kathleen's signature all over her town. Her signature eventually led me to you."

Belle muttered a curse under her breath.

"But I would have found you eventually. I've always been drawn to you and your magic. One cannot simply run away from a bond like ours," Neil said, his tone almost a purr. Then his gaze finally settled on Belle and Theo. He gave Theo a disapproving glance from head to toe, then shifted to a spot behind him, presumably to where Belle stood.

"I knew I'd find you, and the book," Neil said. "You're too powerful to slum it with someone as lowly as a Blackwood,

Anna. You and I, we could have taken the world by storm. You could have been a Penhallow."

"*Never*," Belle snapped. "Theo is who I choose. It will always be him."

A vein in Neil's temple pulsed as he clenched his jaw. Then he sniffed the air again, letting out a low moan. "Where is it?"

"What makes you think—" Theo started to say, but Neil's snarl in his direction made the rest of the words die in his throat.

Neil's hand shot out, quick as a snake, and a hole opened up beneath Theo. He had enough of his wits about him to grab the edge of the opening on either side before he fell in. Then, just as quickly, he was yanked out and set back on his feet. He glanced over at Belle just as she lowered her hand; she'd moved him with her magic with ease, as if he hadn't weighed more than a feather.

"Leave him out of this, Neil! This is between you and me." Though her voice was strong, even Amber could recognize the incredulous look on her face.

"Oh, don't look so shocked, Anna," Neil said. "Your father should have buried my powers further. He should have killed me when he had the chance. You two made my thirst for power even stronger. If anyone is to blame for your current predicament, it's you."

Belle's brows pulled together. She allowed herself only a moment more of confusion, then straightened her posture and stalked up to the cursed witch, tipping her head back to look up at him. "I don't know how you found the book so fast. The cloaking spell wasn't down for long. But … I don't want trouble, Neil. I never have. I left Delin Springs to get *away* from trouble. I have a family now. That's where my priorities are. If we—"

Belle pressed a fist to her mouth. Amber wasn't sure if this show of emotion was real or staged for Neil's benefit. Then she turned to look at Theo, her eyes wide and pleading.

Theo nodded.

Focusing on Neil again, Belle lowered her fist and sniffed loudly. "If we … if we give the book … to you, will you leave? Will you promise never to contact us again?"

Neil waved a dismissive hand. "Yes, yes. The book is all I want. It's a good thing your little brats seem to have the magical prowess of rocks, otherwise I would have gone to *them* for the book."

Theo watched as Belle's jaw clenched, the tearful display of emotion having dried up almost instantly. "They have nearly no affinity to speak of."

Neil scoffed. "That doesn't surprise me. Even magic as powerful as yours would be diluted by a Blackwood as weak as *this* pathetic creature." He sneered at Theo as if he were a piece of gum stuck to his shoe.

Somehow, Amber could tell her father was holding back. She wondered if his magic pulsed and tingled beneath his skin in instances of high emotions, as it did with her.

"You and I would have created formidable heirs, Anna," Neil said, his tone sultry as he stepped forward and slowly circled Belle as if she were a shiny new car on the showroom floor. "But even you aren't perfect. It took three decades, but you finally slipped. That book of yours produced a beacon the moment the cloak dropped. We can sense it. We all want it. We can practically *taste* it." He stopped in front of her. "It's in better hands with me than with my brother, wouldn't you say? He wants the book even more than I do, after what you did to our father."

Belle recoiled.

"Give it to me, and I'll be on my merry way. Then the Penhallows will be after me, not you," he said. "It's safer for your *weak* little husband and your even *weaker* spawn. Wouldn't it be nice to no longer be in hiding?"

Belle stared at him for a long moment before she shot another quick glance at Theo. He nodded again.

After blowing out a slow breath, she stepped away from Neil and walked to a small closet built into the stairs—the same one she'd eyed during the first memory Amber witnessed. Belle opened the door, pulled out a small black suitcase, and brought it to Neil. She held it out to him by the handle.

Neil practically salivated at the sight and took the case from her. He gripped it in both hands and gave the seams a thorough sniff before he opened it. The shuddering sigh he unleashed was mildly obscene. Propping the case on one hand, he popped it open and pulled out the book. The case dropped to the ground with a thud that caused both Blackwoods to flinch.

"You'll … you'll be careful with it?" Belle asked. "There are very powerful spells in there, Neil. They require practice and careful—"

He waved her off. "You've made a wise choice, Anna." Clutching the book against his chest, he doffed his imaginary cap and headed for the door. With a flick of his wrist, the door refastened on its hinges. "My clan thanks you. We'll see you on the other side of history."

The moment the door slammed closed behind him, Belle and Theo bolted up the stairs. Their packing was more frantic now.

"What we have is enough!" Theo finally said, jerking the thick zipper along the edge of his suitcase, sealing it shut. "We've got to go. Who knows how long we have before he starts experimenting. We've got enough cash to last us a while."

"It should take him at least an hour to realize the book is fake," said Belle. "He'll try the smaller spells first to make sure they work."

"And we need at *least* an hour's head start."

Seconds later, they were pounding back down the steps, each with a suitcase in hand.

But they came up short just as they reached the base of the stairs, thanks to a crazed scream from outside. It was an animalistic scream. The scream from someone who had just received devastating news. Something slammed to the ground outside with a thunderous crash.

"Do you think me a *fool*, Anna?" Neil bellowed from outside. "I will not be fooled!"

Theo raised his hands, muttering the words Amber recognized now as a protection spell. Something similar had been used to ward the Quirky Whisker. But no sooner had he finished the spell, the house itself seemed to give a shudder. A great, groaning rumble. Amber wondered if the floorboards vibrated beneath their soles.

"Your wards won't work now, you traitorous mongrels!"

They dropped their suitcases and ran to the back of the house to the door that led to the garage, but the second Theo touched the knob, he was thrown backward and slammed into a wall.

"Theo!" Belle screamed, rushing to his side.

He shook his head, trying to unscramble his brain, then waved her off. "Try the kitchen door."

That one had been warded too. They tried windows, only to be zapped with an electrical current when they tried to open them. Every spell they tried fizzled out when it hit the wards, or bounced back. One particularly potent air spell bounced off a window and knocked both Belle and Theo off their feet.

They were trapped in their own house.

Soon, they were huddled together in the foyer.

Belle yelped when Neil peered in through one of the front windows, his face cupped to the glass. Neil's gaze flicked to the fallen suitcases on the ground. "What was the plan? You would give me the decoy and then run off with the real book? Were you going to leave your brats behind, or are they part of this asinine plan too?"

"They don't know anything about this!" Belle said. "They've never even *seen* the book."

"Oh, I know. I've watched them long enough to know how useless they both are. I should eliminate them just for being powerless abominations." Before either Blackwood could pro-test, Neil said, "Pity you decided to betray me, Anna."

"Stop calling me Anna!" she snapped.

Neil cackled. "I knew you couldn't sever the ties to your

grimoire and still keep it cloaked, so I've just been waiting for you to give up the location. I thought the most likely scenario was that you kept it well hidden somewhere with a powerful cloaking spell in place. Obscure locations that changed over the years—something like that. I never guessed you'd be stupid enough to keep it *in* your house, though. I do say, the Blackwood scum has ruined whatever good qualities you had left." He sniffed. "But I can still smell the dregs of it here. Perhaps it's in one of those bags."

Theo growled under his breath, glaring at the Penhallow's obscure form outside.

"What I *do* know about your grimoire, however, is that like *all* grimoires, it cannot be destroyed. Unfortunately, for you, *you* can be. Since you refuse to cooperate, I'll have to collect the book by force. I've run out of patience for you and this terrible little town. I will burn this house to the ground, and like a phoenix rising from the ashes, your precious grimoire will be reborn—as mine. We really could have been good together, you and I, Anna."

Moments later, the first burst of blue flames licked up the walls.

CHAPTER 14

Someone was yelling at her, though their voice was far away, like they were at the end of a distant hallway. Their hands were on her shoulders, though. They were close. Shaking her once, twice. Hard.

"Amber!"

She gasped for air, arms jerking up to protect her face. But she kept her eyes closed, scared of what she'd see if she opened them. What if she was still in the past? What if she was stuck there?

"Geez!" the man said. "Watch it with the elbows!"

He'd called her Amber. She could feel the weight of the watch *in* her hand, not on her wrist. She was herself again.

Slowly, she opened one eye, then the other.

Connor Declan's face, of all faces, swam into view. She was in her car; he was half-crouched by her open driver's side door. She was parked by the old, ruined house.

Then it came flooding back in. Her parents. Their plan to abandon her and Willow. Neil Penhallow. The fire.

"Oh God, Connor," Amber choked out, one hand to her mouth, the other, still clutching the watch, pressed to her stomach. "It was so horrible."

And then she was crying. Great, heaving sobs that shook her entire body and freaked Connor right the heck out.

"Oh crap. *Ooh* crap," Connor was muttering to himself. His hands fluttered from her shoulders, to her hands, to her face, but never touched any of them. As if she were a bomb about to explode and he couldn't figure out if he should cut the red wire or the blue.

Though some distant part of her knew she'd be horribly embarrassed by this later, Amber flung her arms around him, the back of his shirt bunched up in one of her fists, the other still holding tight to her father's favorite watch.

Connor fully squatted then, wrapping his arms around her. "Hey. Shh. Hey, it's okay." One hand cupped the back of her head.

She buried her face in his neck, crying all the tears she'd inadvertently kept in reserve for today. For the day she found out what had really happened to her parents.

How was she supposed to tell Willow any of this?

It took Amber a while to finally cry herself out, and when she did, that expected sense of embarrassment crept in. She pulled away, finally throwing the watch into her purse, and then used both hands to wipe at her face. A mirror wasn't needed to tell her that she was a snotty, puffy mess. She reached across the passenger seat to open her glovebox and pull out a small packet of tissues. Connor stood to full height and allowed her some semblance of privacy while she messily blew her nose a few times.

Once she felt at least a little calm, she climbed out of

her car and folded her arms tightly across her chest. "I'm sorry about—"

Connor raised a hand to stop her. "It's okay. Can I ask what happened, though? I love kittens as much as the next guy, but I'm guessing it's not because of them?" He pointed toward the house where a trio of people in bright green shirts were poking around under the porch.

Amber only then noticed that a white SUV—with large, green letters spelling out NINE LIVES CAT RESCUE on one of the doors—was parked across the street. "No, it's not about the kittens."

Connor frowned. "Can I do anything? Call anyone? Willow, maybe?"

An involuntary whimper made its way out of Amber's throat at the sound of her sister's name. Amber closed her eyes and pulled in a deep breath through her nose. She would *not* cry again. When she composed herself, she turned her attention back to him. She needed a distraction. "What are *you* doing over here?"

"I guess it's even weirder for me to be on this side of town than you," he said, laughing nervously. "I was at lunch with Greg over there discussing a story I'm doing for the *Gazette* about the rescue, and when he got the call about the kittens, I asked to tag along."

"I'd think most of your time was being eaten up by the junior fashion show," Amber said. "That was the story you volunteered to cover, right? And now the famous Olaf Betzen is coming to town."

Connor chuckled. "It's still my priority for sure, but I need to balance it out with some smaller stories here and there. Besides, I figured a couple pictures of kittens would be sure to sell more papers. Who can resist a cute kitten picture?"

Amber managed a faint, brief smile. "And when you got here, I was …?"

He winced. "Slumped over in your car. I was surprised—in a good way—to see you here, but then it looked like you were … like you might have been … I sort of panicked …"

"Ugh," she said, rubbing the spot between her eyes. "Sorry if I freaked you out."

After a beat, he asked, "What brought you over here in the middle of the day? Everything okay at the shop—I mean at home? Nothing weird going on?"

His last question gave her pause. But she *had* told him the place was crowded and tense with three people in such a tight space, hadn't she? Or had she told that to Jack?

She needed a long hot bath and a nap.

Her gaze flicked back to the house. Past the green-shirt-wearing rescue workers, and up to the porch. The porch Neil Penhallow had stood on as he peered into the house just before he called on flames to kill her parents. She wondered how furious he'd been when the book in question wasn't there in the rubble. When it didn't rise out of the ashes like a phoenix.

Questions buzzed around her head like a swarm of gnats. She wanted to swat them away, to think about something else. But she couldn't. How had none of her neighbors seen or heard anything that night? Had Neil done something to them—to their memories—as she suspected he'd done to Edgar?

Yet, the Penhallows were still looking for her mother's

grimoire. They'd never found it. They also didn't seem to know Edgar was in Edgehill. Edgar who had been given the Henbane grimoire for safekeeping. Edgar who was a Henbane himself. So where was the book now?

Then she recalled her parents' conversation as Edgar drove away.

"That boy is never going to forgive us," her father had said.

"If the spell works as it should, he won't remember enough to know he's upset with us in the first place."

If the spell worked. *What* spell?

"Amber?" Connor asked. "I asked what you were doing out here and then you disappeared into that head of yours."

She shook her head. "Sorry. I'm just chasing ghosts, that's all."

His brows rose. "Did you catch any?"

"Yes, actually," she said, still amazed at the magic that had hurled her back into time, at least in a memory. She had no idea how she'd managed to do it, or if she could do it again.

"That so?" he asked. "Did you find something out here? It looked like you were holding something when I first found you. It was gold, wasn't it? Was it a watch?"

Amber pursed her lips. "Is this journalist Connor talking?"

"Sorry." He managed a sheepish grin. "Being insufferably nosy is an occupational hazard, I guess. Can never have too many story ideas going at once. I've always been curious about what happened here. I know other longtime residents of Edgehill would be interested too. Especially if you found something that … survived the fire. Could I see what you found? I think I saw you put it in your purse."

A small, mental version of herself was dancing around in her head now, frantically waving a red flag. "I should get back to the shop."

"Yeah, of course," he said, holding up his hands. "Sorry if I was too forward."

"It's okay," she said, even though it wasn't. "I hope the kittens find good homes." She got back into her car and grabbed onto the handle to close the door, but Connor stopped it.

The red flag had morphed into a red banner flapping in a gale-force wind.

Connor bent over, hands on his knees. He cocked his head and smiled at her. "I hope you feel better soon. And if you want to talk about anything ..." His gaze flicked to her purse before returning to her eyes. "You know where to find me. You'll find that I truly enjoy talking about the discovery of lost items. Objects hold so many *memories*, don't they?"

How could he know?

"Have a good day, Amber," he said, then shut her door. She flinched. He slapped an open palm on the roof twice—making her flinch again—before he walked to his car.

The trio of rescue workers never once looked his way. Connor didn't have a notebook, phone, or camera out.

Doing her best to control her breathing and make a calm, three-point turn out of the cul-de-sac, Amber drove away from Ocicat Lane. While idling at the stop sign, her gaze shifted to her rear-view mirror. Connor stood outside his car, backside rested against the trunk and arms crossed, as he watched her drive away. He raised a single hand in farewell.

Once she made it back toward the heart of town, she could

no longer ignore the niggling thought in the back of her mind. She prompted her phone to call the *Edgehill Gazette*. A perky receptionist answered.

"Hi," Amber said. "Can I speak to Connor Declan, please?"

Say he's not there. Say he's out to lunch—that he's following up on a story about the Nine Lives Cat Rescue.

"Oh, sure, one sec," she said. "Luckily for you, he stayed in for lunch today. Though that's not weird for him lately."

Amber cursed.

"Miss? Are you okay?"

"Connor didn't leave for lunch today?"

The woman took a second to reply, the silence clearly saying, *Yeah, you weirdo. I just told you that.* "Nope. He's been swamped because of the upcoming junior fashion show. Olaf Betzen's coming to see it, as I'm sure you know. He's been glued to his computer for hours."

"Thanks," Amber said. "I'll just call him later. I don't want to bother him." She disconnected the call on the confused receptionist.

If Connor has been in the office all day, then who in the hell was I just talking to?

Amber was on high alert on her drive home, though she wasn't sure what she was looking for. The Penhallow could be anyone. She'd convinced herself that it was a witch working alone, if only to somewhat calm her nerves, but somewhere in the back of her mind, she knew there could be more.

She thought of what Neil Penhallow had said in the memory—that the moment the supposed cloaking spell had dropped, the book had become like a beacon to any Penhallows waiting for the signal. Was that why *this* particular witch was here now? He'd said he could "smell" the grimoire. Had the cloaking spell put on her mother's grimoire faded? Was the book like those floodlights outside the grand opening of a store or night club? Thick beams of white light sweeping back and forth across the sky and high into the air, summoning anyone in range to come see what all the fuss was about?

Long-lost Henbane grimoire up for grabs! First come, first served!

Was this Penhallow simply the first in an oncoming flood of cursed witches, all with Edgehill as their destination?

Amber desperately wished she could talk to her parents, if only so she could ask why they hadn't prepared her and Willow for this. Though, she supposed they hadn't planned for the fire. Perhaps they'd planned to stay in hiding until it was safe, then find them again when Amber turned eighteen.

But all that was in the past now. Time travel spells didn't exist. The past was the past. Fixed. Unchangeable. She had to focus on the present now—on her future. It wasn't something she'd ever been very good at.

It had only been two hours since the Quirky Whisker reopened after lunch, but the store was practically buzzing with people when she strolled in, the bell above the door announcing her arrival. The sound was lost in the din of chatter. Amber squeezed her way in, clutching her purse tight to her side as she made her way to the counter. Aunt

Gretchen and Lily Bowen—one of Amber's teenaged temp helpers—manned the cash register. Daisy and Willow were flitting about the store helping customers.

"Hi, Lily. I can help Gretchen," Amber said, raising her voice slightly to be heard. She threw her purse into a cubby under the counter.

"Phew!" Lily said, wasting no time with greetings, and hurried into the throng.

There was a stack of tea-order slips on the counter that no one had had time to get to yet, so Amber busied herself with pulling the requested items out of the drawers and jars behind the counter. Gretchen worked her way through the line.

The bonus of having *Ramp It Up* fans swarming Edgehill was that it kept Amber so busy, she didn't have time to dwell too long on what happened to her that afternoon. It didn't keep her from watching every new face with suspicion though, unsure who was an innocent tourist and who was a crafty Penhallow.

As the sun set on Edgehill, the streetlights lining Russian Blue Avenue flicked on, and the customers in the Quirky Whisker finally thinned out, Amber's urge to talk to her aunt and sister reared its head. After ushering out the last of the customers, Amber locked the door behind them and whirled to face Willow and Aunt Gretchen.

"We need to talk," she said. "But … upstairs. And are there … like … I don't know … sound-proofing protection spells either of you know?"

Thankfully her aunt and sister just nodded and followed her up the stairs without asking any questions.

Once in the studio, Amber quickly fed the cats. The nervous energy coming off the Blackwood women—Amber in particular—caused Tom to wolf his food down in record time, and then take refuge under the bed. Amber paced up and down the length of her apartment, wondering how much detail to give them. Though Amber knew Gretchen had always suspected a Penhallow was behind the death of Amber's and Willow's parents, Gretchen didn't know the gory details. Amber assumed few did.

"Amber? *Amber*," Willow said.

When Amber snapped out of her thoughts—coming to an abrupt halt in her pacing—she found her aunt and sister sitting shoulder to shoulder at the end of Amber's bed, watching her as warily as Alley was from the window bench seat. Tom's little pink nose poked out from behind the dust ruffle.

Amber steeled herself, then focused on Willow. "I know what happened to Mom and Dad."

"What?" Willow's brows pulled together. "How?"

Despite giving them a watered-down version of the memories she'd lived through, by the end—the blue flames flickering in the background of Amber's mind—Gretchen was white as a sheet, and Willow had tears tracking down her face.

Willow let out a shaky sigh, not bothering to wipe the tears away. "You didn't see what happened to Edgar after he left the house with the book?"

Amber shook her head.

"He was saying all that weird stuff just before we left. You think he still has it?" Willow immediately shook her head. "But if we go back, this lunatic Penhallow will follow us, won't he? We can't give up Edgar's—or the book's—location if the Penhallow somehow doesn't know they're out there."

"I agree," said Amber. "But what will he do the longer we refuse to give him the book? If it's the same witch who … who killed Mom and Dad, he had clearly already been well on his way to going mad *then*. Imagine what fourteen years could do. I'm also starting to think Wilma's death was a message to us. He picked off that innocent maid solely to let us know nowhere is safe. And to show us how powerful he is."

"And to possibly get us all into one place?" Willow asked. "Maybe he assumed if the hotel was unsafe for Gretchen, she'd come stay here with you."

"Maybe," Amber said, chewing on a thumbnail.

"Do you think he's been here in Edgehill all this time?" Willow asked. "Even after the fire? He waited for Mom and Dad to slip up. Maybe he's been waiting for us too."

"I don't think so. Seems like he got here recently because he suddenly sensed the book," Amber said. "And Aunt Gretchen being here this early in the year was a fluke. She wasn't feeling well. The Penhallow just got lucky that the book gave off a signal around the same time that Gretchen got sick."

Gretchen had gotten up and walked to the window while Amber spoke. Her arms were crossed, her back to her nieces. "Actually, I think my illness can be tied back to the Penhallow too."

"What?" Amber asked, quickly closing the distance between her and her aunt. Amber placed a hand on her elbow. "What do you mean?"

Gretchen turned to her, arms still crossed. "I was working

on another batch of tinctures the other day, and pulled out my container of gola blossom. It's hard to find, but it's one of the main ingredients for my foresight potions. Well, I'm getting near the end of my stash, and yesterday I found remnants of a very fine powder at the bottom. All this to say … someone put something into my supply that has been causing me to slowly get sick."

Amber's stomach knotted. She was reminded of Whitney Sadler's and Susie Paulson's slow poisoning of Melanie Cole with ethylene glycol. "Why didn't you say anything sooner?"

"I only just found it and I wanted to test it before I alarmed either of you."

Amber frowned. "Do you know what is it? Are you … is it—"

"I'll be fine," Gretchen said, taking Amber's hands in her own. "The powder is made up of two ingredients, one to induce vomiting and the other to aid in sleep. When combined, it left me feeling generally queasy and sleepy. No matter what I did, I never seemed to be getting better. But if this substance had been added to the supplies I use for my nightly tea, I've essentially been making myself ill for weeks."

Amber's magic thrashed beneath her skin like a moth slamming futilely against a bright light bulb.

"Calm yourself, little mouse," Gretchen said, giving Amber's hands a warning squeeze.

Willow spoke up from her spot at the end of the bed. "We have to either decide to give him the book and hope it doesn't horribly backfire on us, or live trapped in this tiny shoebox of an apartment forever and hope he gives up eventually."

"Belle and Theo wouldn't have planned to give you girls up unless something in that book was dangerous," Aunt Gretchen said. "They worshiped you both. We'd be dishonoring their memory if we gave up the grimoire."

Amber pulled her hands free from her aunt's light grasp. "What's the alternative, though? You just admitted that someone found some way to slip something into your supplies without you knowing. He could have killed you at any point between now and then, but he clearly *chose* not to. That could have been you instead of Wilma in the hotel room, but he chose to kill an innocent woman and ruin *her* family's life instead. He's toying with us. But he'll snap eventually. We have to figure out what to do before that happens." Amber's breath hitched. "I can't lose either one of you. I won't survive it."

Willow took one of Amber's and Gretchen's hands in either of hers. The trio formed a circle, hands clasped. "This Penhallow doesn't know who he's messing with. We're Blackwoods. We'll figure it out."

Amber angled a small smile at her optimistic sister, hope shining in Willow's eyes like it had always shone in their father's. But niggling doubt wormed its way through Amber's gut.

Amber worried her parents' life of secrets had sealed their own fate, dooming the remaining Blackwoods to something even worse.

CHAPTER 15

The following day, Amber, Willow, and Gretchen were no closer to figuring out what to do about their cursed-witch problem. Gretchen had concocted an even stronger—and more foul-tasting—protection tincture. Willow had perfected an airtight truth spell that could be used on anyone they suspected could be a Penhallow.

Amber, meanwhile, had worn a hole in the floor thanks to all her nervous pacing. Last night, her dreams had been so fraught with terrifying images, her magic reacted by lifting not only the dining room table and all the chairs off the ground, but the bed Willow and Gretchen had been sleeping in. When Willow awoke suddenly to find her nose practically touching the ceiling, she'd yelped, waking Amber and dispelling her magic.

Thankfully, Tom had been curled up with Amber on the couch; otherwise, he would have been crushed under the weight of the falling bed, whose frame cracked on impact. Amber was mildly surprised the whole thing hadn't fallen through the floor and crashed into the shop below.

So, at the end of the day, after the shop was closed and the three Blackwoods busied themselves with cleaning up after the tsunami of Olaf Betzen fans, Amber's already frayed nerves frayed further when her phone, miraculously wedged into her back pocket for once, started to ring. She immediately worried it was Chief Brown calling to report some new, awful piece of news, but the number that popped up actually brought a smile to her face.

"Ooh," said Willow from across the room. "I think a *boy* is calling her."

"Which one is it?" Gretchen asked absently, her attention focused on organizing a candle display. "The reporter or the baker?"

Amber and Willow exchanged a look. Before bed, Amber had told Willow that the last face the Penhallow had worn was Connor's. Amber had told her merely as a warning to stay alert—to remind her that it was impossible right now to know who was being impersonated by the witch. Her sister's expression had shuttered a bit after that. Amber truly wasn't sure if Willow was jealous or merely worried. After all, the Penhallow would have chosen Connor's face for a reason. Was it because the witch knew the two were acquaintances? Or had the witch sensed a deeper connection between Amber and Connor and tried to use that to his advantage?

"The baker," Amber said now, before accepting the call. "Hi, Jack."

"Hey," he said. "Is now okay? I figured the shop would be closed by now, but the town's so overrun, I know several people are staying open later to soak up as much extra business as possible, so I wasn't—"

Amber interrupted his rambling with a laugh. "Now is perfect."

Then, before she let guilt convince her not to, she mentally uttered Willow's new truth spell, and sent a tendril of her magic toward Jack.

"Why are you calling me, Jack Terrence?" she asked, wincing a little at the formality of the question, but her magic needed a clear direction, otherwise it would circle aimlessly.

She could hear the smile in his voice when he said, "I, Jack Terrence, am calling you, Amber Blackwood, to ask if you'd be my date to the junior fashion show on Saturday." He paused. "Wow, that was weird. I'd planned to ease into that a little more."

Amber's magic quickly retreated. He was very much Jack, and he very much was asking her out. Her cheeks heated slightly. "I'd love to."

"Yeah?" he asked. "I know it's not the most glamorous of first dates, but Purrcolate is providing refreshments that night. Sort of a trial run for the Here and Meow. Would be nice to have distractingly lovely company while I'm mentally having a meltdown."

Amber laughed. "I would be happy to be your distraction."

"Excellent," he said. "Maybe we can grab a bite to eat after? The show is from four to six since the stars of the show are all minors."

Amber was oddly flattered by how nervous he sounded. "Can't wait."

"Cool," he said. "So … yeah. Cool. I'll come pick you up around two? I assume the Whisker—why did I just call it the Whisker?—will be closed early since most of the town will be at the show. I have to set up the refreshments and whatnot, so I need to be there early. Or, I mean, I could start and then leave to come get you and then Larry can set up without me for a while. He's a grown man. Or—"

"Jack!" Amber said, laughing. "Breathe. Not only will I be your distraction, you can put me to work. I'll be ready as soon as you need me. You'll just owe me dessert."

She was almost positive he was grinning now.

"Sorry," he said. "Middle-school-level crush, remember? You said yes and my brain short-circuited." Releasing a slow breath, he said, "I will pick you up at two on Saturday."

When she finally hung up, still smiling, she looked up to see Willow and Gretchen watching her, equally goofy smiles on their faces. "What?"

"It's good to see you making an effort to get out of the house more," Gretchen said.

"And with a *boy*," Willow offered in her best little girl voice, fluttering her eyelashes dramatically.

Amber rolled her eyes, shoving her phone back into her pocket.

"I would say to leave a sock on the doorknob if you and the baker need some alone time Saturday night, but there aren't any doors to speak of in that shoebox of yours," Gretchen said.

Amber stifled a gasp. Willow clapped her hands over her mouth.

Gretchen turned to face them, hands on her hips. "Oh, don't look so surprised! And don't let this calm outward demeanor fool you. I've been around the block a time or two. In fact, I've had a man I know back in Portland 'blowing up my phone,' as you say, because he's itching for me to get back." Then she waggled her eyebrows at them.

Amber and Willow shared a long, horrified look, then burst out laughing.

The next couple days, since Amber seemed to be useless at all things magic—though she hadn't made the bed levitate in her sleep again, so she called that a win—she was tasked with trying to get a hold of Edgar on the phone. She only had a landline number for him; she had no idea if he owned a cell. He'd answered the first time she tried yesterday, but no sooner had she gotten the words "Hi, Edgar, please don't hang up" out of her mouth, he'd hung up. Every couple of hours, she'd call and leave a message on his answering machine.

It was her lunch break now and she was trying him again, except this time it just rang incessantly. After the twentieth ring, she hung up and tried again. This time, she got a busy signal. Had he taken the phone off the hook? She imagined him waiting for the ringing to stop, then plucking it from its cradle, leaving the receiver lying on a table, then trudging up the steps of his house, letting the discarded phone blare its persistent, weary cry into the dark.

Sighing, Amber ended the call, then dropped her cell onto the counter. She propped her elbows on the worn wood, fingers thrust into the hair at her temples. Why did Edgar have to make this even harder than it already was? Then she chastised herself for blaming a mentally ill man for any of this. It wasn't *his* fault his mind had cracked.

She nearly toppled off her stool when her phone started to ring. But it wasn't Edgar. Her stomach lurched.

"Hi, chief," she said, phone pressed to her ear and a thumbnail wedged between her teeth.

"Hi, Amber. Is this an okay time to talk?"

She wasn't sure if it was a good or bad sign that he was calling her "Amber" rather than "Miss Blackwood." Swallowing, she gave the chief the same treatment she'd given Jack a couple days ago. Once the spell had been uttered, she said, "What is the reason you're calling me, Chief Owen Brown?"

Almost robotically, he said, "I'm calling you, Amber Blackwood, to inform you that I have recently had a telephone conversation with an acquaintance of mine in which we discussed one Edgar Henbane and his time at the Belhaven Psychiatric Hospital."

Truth.

Her magic retreated.

"What in the—" Then in a hushed tone he said, "Did you just do your ... *hocus pocus* thing on me? *Through* the phone?"

If Chief Brown were the kind of man to clutch his pearls, Amber figured he would be doing that right now. The image made her smile, despite how frazzled she was.

"It's a spell for truth," she said. "The Penhallow is losing control of his sanity—or maybe just his patience. The spell is very short-lived and merely proves you are who you claim to be."

After a long pause, he asked, "Do I want to know?"

"Probably not."

"Fair enough," he said. "So, like I *forcefully* said earlier, I talked to my guy at the hospital. Clients' records are sealed for privacy reasons, so I can't get direct access to his files unless I get a warrant—and I currently have no reason to do so."

Amber sagged.

"But, in the process of talking to him, he let slip that the arrival of Edgar had always stuck with him because he came in with an unusual wound."

Amber perked back up. "What kind of wound?"

"Rumors about what happened to Wilma are already making the rounds within law enforcement fields in the surrounding areas, and since my buddy occasionally is in contact with the police for various reasons, he heard about Wilma too. And said the starburst mark on her stomach sounds a lot like the starburst mark that Edgar came in with. He said the black lines covered nearly his entire back."

"No way," Amber hissed. "But … how did it not kill him?" She asked herself more than she asked the chief, but he replied anyway.

"Possible he was affected differently because he's, you know, *magical* and Wilma wasn't?"

"I … guess so? I really don't know. Penhallow magic behaves very strangely. No one really knows what the extent of the curse is."

Amber wondered now if being hit with this cursed magic is what caused the drastic change in her cousin. If being hit with this magic didn't kill a person, did it slowly drive him mad, just as it did with the Penhallows?

"You have any clue who this witch is?" the chief asked. "We've got … nothing. Virtually no evidence left at the scene. We're chasing tips but they aren't leading anywhere."

Amber sighed. "You aren't going to like this …" Then she explained the witch's ability to change faces.

He was silent a long time before he said, "You're right. I don't like this." Grunting, he added, "I want him *out* of my town."

"We're working on it."

He chuckled darkly. "The tables seemed to have turned on this one. It's not often that I'm calling up a civilian hoping *they* have information."

"For what it's worth, I prefer when the crimes are run-of-the-mill and I have no idea they've even happened."

"Same here," he said.

Silence descended on the conversation. Was she supposed to hang up now? Ask him how he was doing? How his wife was feeling? They weren't friends, not really. "You going to the fashion show?"

"Strictly in a professional capacity," he said. "These Olaf Betzen fans are something else. Need to be there to keep an eye on things. Jessica will be there with Sammy, though. He's a fan of the show. Said he wants to be on it when he's older. He made me a vest out of felt."

Amber snorted. "I'll be sure to say hi if I see them. I'll be going with Jack Terrence."

"So you *do* date," he said, then immediately seemed to catch himself. "Oh, I mean … uhh … you keep to yourself quite a bit. Wasn't sure if maybe that wasn't a thing you did …"

Amber might have been offended, but she could easily picture how embarrassed he was, and it only amused her. "I admit it's been a while."

"Well ... glad to hear you're getting out there," he said. "Does Jack know about the ... how you ... that you're a—"

"Definitely not," she said. "You're the only one in town who knows. Well, aside from my aunt and sister."

"And the cursed, face-changing psychopath," he added.

"Yeah, and him," she said. "Thanks for the information about Edgar."

"You bet," he said, sounding a bit more like himself, and also relieved she'd given him a way out of the conversation. "I'll be in touch."

Amber only had enough time to run upstairs to grab a bite to eat before she had to open the shop again.

The street outside was swarmed with people. She saw quite a few women with shirts that said, "Ramp it up and sew some chaos!" She could only assume it was a catchphrase from the show.

She tried to imagine what her cousin's starburst mark must have looked like. Was it still there? Was it still a stark black on his skin, or had it faded over time?

What happened to you, Edgar? she wondered as she unlocked the door. *And how do I keep it from happening again?*

On Saturday morning, Amber, Willow, and Gretchen worked in the shop until noon. The Bowen sisters had the day off, especially since their niece was one of the junior designers competing in the show today. After flipping the lock on the door, Amber took down her chalkboard sign and headed behind the counter with it in order to shield it and herself from any possible prying eyes outside.

Sweeping a hand over the board, the word "Open!" changed to "At the fashion show. Good luck, Edgehill designers!" The bespectacled cat logo now had a yellow fabric tape measure draped around his neck like a scarf, and he wore a black band around one wrist, a round pin cushion resting in the middle. A trio of red-tipped pins stuck out of it. The other paw held onto the brim of his top hat, and he winked one eye.

After placing the sign back on its peg, she dashed upstairs to get ready for her date.

Amber refused to wear anything more elaborate than jeans and a nice sweater, but she allowed Willow to style her hair into a cascading wave of curls. Willow smudged on eye shadow, swept mascara onto Amber's eyelashes, dusted her cheeks with a faint pink blush, and applied a soft, shiny gloss to her lips. Then she cast a no-smudge spell to assure every curl and lash stayed in place for the majority of the evening.

"I've had to do enough work events to warrant the perfection of such a spell," Willow explained as she finished, taking a step back from where Amber sat on the closed toilet lid, to examine her handiwork. "You'll never have to run to the bathroom to freshen up. Unless of course you hate your date and are planning an escape."

"I don't know why I'm so nervous," she said. "It's just Jack."

"It's because you actually like Just Jack," Willow said.

"You also said that about Connor."

Willow ignored that. "You haven't really let yourself like *anyone* since Max. Things are looking up!"

Amber pursed her no-smudge shiny-pink lips. "Have you talked to Connor? He must be totally stressed out today."

"No," she said quickly, busying herself with putting her makeup supplies away. Abruptly abandoning the task, she left the bathroom.

"Will?" Amber said, following her sister into the main part of the studio. "What's wrong?"

"Nothing," she said, riffling through her purse on the bed. Amber could tell she wasn't actually looking for anything—just trying to keep her hands busy.

"Will," Amber said again, walking over and putting a hand on her sister's elbow.

Willow stopped and turned to Amber, arms crossed. She shrugged. "It's stupid."

"Try me."

With a huff, Willow said, "We talked a couple days ago. He called me out of nowhere and was really flirty and said we should go out sometime and that he regretted not asking me out in high school."

Amber grinned, but when she saw Willow was still frowning, her smile slipped. "That's good, isn't it?"

"Seventeen-year-old me was ecstatic. I had it so bad for him in high school. Like vision-board bad. But he was kind of pushy in the conversation a couple days ago. Asking a lot of questions about you and Mom and Dad. I tried to convince myself it was because he's a journalist now, but …"

Frowning, Amber said, "You think it was the Penhallow."

"I knew something was up, but I didn't know what. He

called this morning, asking if I wanted a special press pass since he knows I was really into *Ramp It Up* in high school."

Amber cocked a brow. "Really?"

"*Amber!*" Willow said, laughing. "I had a poster of Olaf on the back of my bedroom door!"

Amber winced. "*That* was Olaf? I thought he was in one of those emo bands you were obsessed with."

Willow thunked herself in the forehead with the heel of her palm. "Anyway, after he asked about the press passes, he asked how I was since he hadn't had a chance to catch up with me since the night of his birthday, since he's been so busy with fashion show stuff."

Amber nodded slowly. "Which means it wasn't him who called you a couple days ago."

"Right," said Willow. "So … I'm just feeling like an idiot right now. He wasn't flirtatious at all this morning. I think I'm still his buddy Willow. Just like high school. And I don't know what's going on with *you* and Connor so—"

"Nothing," Amber said quickly. "Absolutely nothing. I promise."

Willow absently scratched at her ear. "I live in Portland anyway. It doesn't matter. Long distance is hard even in the best of circumstances." Groaning, she added, "I was so happy when he called two days ago, Amber. Like … *pathetically* happy."

Amber couldn't help but smile at that.

"I feel like such a moron for turning into teenage me again just because Connor Declan flirted with me for half a second," Willow said. "And then it wasn't even real."

Amber took both of Willow's hands in hers, the two

standing toe to toe. They were both barefoot and sported bright red toenails. "Not that you need my permission for anything, but if you still get all hot and bothered for Connor, I say go for it even if you live in different cities. And if he shoots you down, it's his loss."

"Thanks," Willow managed, still looking at her toes.

Gretchen cleared her throat and they looked over at her. Their aunt wrung her hands. She'd never been the best at dealing with "feelings." She was the rock you could rely on when you were falling apart. She was practical and levelheaded and could solve big problems like a champ. But she wasn't necessarily the person you'd choose to cry to when you struggled with something less dire, like being confused about a guy. In high school, Amber and Willow had relied on each other for the small things.

Wincing slightly, Gretchen said, "Would it make you feel any better if I let you doll me up like you did for Amber?"

Willow's mouth dropped open. "You better not be teasing me, woman! You know this is my dream."

Aunt Gretchen offered the least convincing smile Amber had ever seen. "I'm not teasing you."

Willow squealed, let go of Amber, grabbed Gretchen's hand, and pulled her across the apartment. "Let me at them eyebrows!"

Gretchen shot a pleading look over her shoulder at Amber.

She could only offer her a sympathetic wave before her aunt was yanked into the bathroom, the door slamming shut behind her.

CHAPTER 16

Jack arrived at two on the dot. Amber had been pacing the empty shop for the better part of ten minutes, so she saw him as he walked up to the front door, waving at her.

"I'm leaving!" she called out.

"Tell Jack we say hi!" Willow called back from somewhere upstairs.

Ten minutes ago, Gretchen had still been complaining about how thin and sore her eyebrows were. Willow and Gretchen were going to meet her at the Edgehill Community Center closer to three. Amber wasn't sure if Willow had decided to accept the press passes from Connor or not.

Amber let herself out onto Russian Blue Avenue and took in Jack's dark blue jeans, black button-up shirt, and navy blazer. He was somehow effortlessly casual and professional at the same time.

"You look amazing," he said, holding out an arm for her.

She hooked a hand around his elbow. "You're not looking too shabby yourself."

Between getting into his car and heading west on Russian Blue Avenue, Jack hadn't uttered another word. The radio wasn't even on. After several more minutes of absolute silence, Amber couldn't take it anymore.

"Are you breathing?" she asked his profile.

"Nope," he said. "I don't think I've blinked in four hours."

Amber laughed. His shoulders seemed to relax a bit at the sound.

"So what are the Terrence brothers offering as refreshments?" Amber asked.

That got him talking. He rambled on about blueberry, lemon seed, and raspberry scones. He listed half a dozen other pastries. Larry was in charge of coffee and his raspberry iced sweet tea that people seemed to purchase by the gallon. Then Jack went on a very long tangent about the second oven he had installed a few days ago and what a difference the larger model had made for him. She knew he'd slipped well into panic-rambling mode, but the excessive talking seemed to calm his nerves, so she didn't interrupt him.

When he pulled up to the light just outside the community center, he abruptly stopped talking. He seemed to have just spotted the news van they idled behind. It was a giant white thing with a satellite dish on top, and a ladder running up the length of one of the back doors. A splash of the van's blue logo wrapped around one of the doors, the majority of it plastered on the side and out of view.

"Oh good," Jack said, sounding vaguely nauseated. "The media is here. They'll be able to report my meltdown live. Olaf-flipping-Betzen is here. What was I *thinking*?"

Amber placed a hand on his arm. "During that very impressive and informative rambling session I just experienced, you said you hired a couple people to help out, right? Baking round the clock?"

He nodded.

"You'll be fine. I promise. Your pastries are amazing and everyone will love them. Larry's tea is like crack." When he didn't say anything, Amber asked, "Okay, why are you really this freaked out?"

The light turned green and he followed behind the Channel 4 news van as it turned left into the busy parking lot of the community center. They were early enough, though, that they found a spot close to the back of the lot with relative ease.

He parked, then turned slightly in his seat to face her. "I'm prefacing this with the fact that I absolutely love my brother …"

"But?"

"But Purrcolate was more Larry's dream than mine. I told you I've always wanted to start my own bakery, right?"

Amber nodded.

"But I've had that dream for *years*. I'm too scared to follow through. I'm very good at coming up with excuses not to do it. But if this goes well and the Here and Meow goes well … I might actually consider it. I don't know what that would look like yet or if it's something I could do to expand on what Purrcolate already offers, but I'm thinking of trying something on a much bigger scale."

Amber grinned at him. "You'd be great at it."

He heaved a breath. "I made a ton of new recipes. I got business cards made. I even have clotted cream!"

Laughing, Amber said, "Well, put me to work. Let's impress the pants off everyone."

They climbed out of the SUV and Jack stood behind the car. "Be warned. There's … a lot."

When the back door swung open, Amber's eyes doubled in diameter. There were white pastry boxes with "Purrcolate" written in black on the sides—the "o" sporting a pair of cat ears—stacked six high. There were three rows, and the rows were two deep.

"And this is just my batch. Larry has just as many."

"I'm impressed," Amber said.

They each grabbed three boxes and then hustled toward the redbrick building. The front door had a peaked white awning supported by four columns. A small lawn stretched out on either side of the front entrance, dotted at intervals by tall oval-shaped hedges. Since it was still winter in Edgehill, the grass had seen better days, but she knew it would be a bright sea of green come spring.

Instead of heading for the front door, Amber followed Jack down the sidewalk and around the left side of the building. Grass ran between the building and a chain-link fence. Someone's house lay beyond it. A bouncing, barking golden retriever ran along the fence, tongue lolling.

Amber walked over and the dog pressed his body against the fence, looking at her with a pleading expression. She squeezed her fingers through diamond-shaped holes so she could give the side of his face a scratch. When she stepped away, the dog flopped down on his haunches and whimpered pathetically in their general direction.

"Sorry, no time right now, boy," Amber told the dog.

Jack smiled at her as they reached a gray metal door. He balanced the boxes with one hand, then rapped on the door with the other. "I would have pegged you as a cat person. And not just because you live in Edgehill."

"I've always wanted a dog," she said. "But my dad was allergic so we couldn't have one growing up. There were hints that I'd get one for my seventeenth birthday, but ... well, that didn't happen."

Jack's face took on an "Oh no! I've indirectly brought up a dead parent—abort mission! Abort mission!" expression.

"If I had a place with a yard," Amber said, trying to save him from uttering an obligatory platitude, "I would love to have a dog. Though Tom Cat might never forgive me."

The gray door swung open before Jack could reply, and he hopped out of the way just in time to avoid a dropped-pastry disaster. A very tall, lanky man with thinning hair stood at the door. He sagged with great relief. "Oh, thank the heavens! The natives were getting restless in here without snacks. Hurry, hurry!" A large rock sat just inside the hallway, and the man picked it up and used it to prop the door open. "It only has a lock on the inside," he said, then hurried away.

Amber and Jack shared a look, shrugged, then followed after him.

After a very short trip, the man opened a door to their left and held it open for them. "This room is for the models and the designers."

Amber followed Jack into the spacious room. There was no one inside, certainly no one "restless for snacks." The back wall was lined with tables, and given the carafes of coffee and water, someone had already started setting up.

"We'll have a spread in here and one out in the main lobby

for the guests and the media. Extras can be stored in the kitchen." The man still stood at the door, holding it open. Then he peered out into the hall and said, "Sally! Paul! Come help carry in pastries! We're dreadfully behind."

The room was filled with clothing racks lined with hanging black garment bags. There were duffel bags and suitcases stacked around them. Amber assumed they were filled with makeup, shoes, and accessories. It was eerily quiet inside, the hanging bags quietly waiting for the excitement to start.

"Your brother said you have a special batch set aside for the guest of honor?" the uppity man at the door asked.

Jack turned to him after placing his boxes on the table. "Yes, I have them in the car."

The man's nostrils flared. "Well, do be a lamb and fetch those?" he asked, suddenly assuming a rather pronounced English accent he certainly didn't have just moments before. "Then you can let Sally and Paul know which things go where. Mr. Betzen and his people are scheduled to arrive at any moment and it's *imperative* that everything is perfect for him."

"Yes, of course," Jack said, grabbing Amber's hand. "We'll be right back."

They scuttled past the man, who had his nose hiked so far in the air, Amber could practically see his nose hairs.

Sally and Paul, it turned out, were a pair of teenagers who looked two seconds from fainting dead away in the hallway. They both stood behind the uppity man, pressed against the wall as if they hoped it would do them a favor and swallow them whole. Sally wrung her hands. Paul had his hands buried under his armpits, eyes the size of saucers.

217

"My car is near the back of the lot," Jack said in a tone usually reserved for scared cats one is trying to coax out from underneath the bed.

Wordlessly, the teenagers peeled themselves off the wall to follow them. They both shot looks at the man still loitering in the doorway.

Once they'd made it back outside, Jack said, "*Do* be a lamb …" in the same affected English accent.

Sally snorted, then clapped a hand over her mouth. "He's not usually like this," she added. "He's our drama teacher at school, so they got him to help run the fashion show. He was totally normal until we found out Olaf Betzen is going to be here. Now he's—"

"A complete nightmare," Paul offered.

"The whole town has gone a little nutty," Amber said.

Jack and Amber loaded the teens with boxes and instructions on where to take them, then off they went again. Amber grabbed another three boxes, while Jack pulled a small fabric cooler out of the back seat. He slung it over his shoulder and patted the top gently when he caught Amber looking at it. "These are the special ones made for the king himself."

Amber laughed. She wished she knew what all the fuss was about, but then again, she'd never been one to get starstruck. And she didn't know the first thing about fashion.

Once they were back inside—and Paul and Sally were on their way back to the car to grab another stack of boxes—Captain Nightmare led Jack and Amber past the room full of hanging garment bags and a set of bathrooms before coming to a small door with a printed sign taped to the wood. "Mr. Olaf Betzen" the slightly askew sign read.

"This," Captain Nightmare said, placing an open palm on the wooden door, "is where Mr. Betzen will be lounging during his stay here until it's time for the show."

Amber wondered if, when Olaf left town, Captain Nightmare would emerge from his celebrity-induced haze and regret his actions come morning—like a hangover.

"Can I trust you two to set up the necessary accoutrements while I make sure Paul isn't stuffing all the pastries in his pockets? Positively dreadful, that boy."

"We'll be fine," Jack said.

"Splendid," Captain Nightmare said, clapping his hands once. "Take care to get in and get out so you're not mucking about in his room when he arrives."

And then the man was taking long strides across the hallway.

"That poor man needs a sedative," Jack said.

He then let Amber into the room, closing the door behind them. The space was shabby at best. There were two country-plaid sofas, the fabric crisscrossed with forest green, navy blue, and a muted yellow. Each had a pair of matching pillows resting on the couches' backs. Amber wondered if the sofas were always in here, or if someone's mother was currently without couches until the great Olaf Betzen breezed back out of town.

A low stand sat against the back wall, a small flat-screen TV sitting on top. A fake tree, its pot filled with fake Spanish moss, stood to the right of the TV. Thick dust coated some of the leaves.

In the middle of the room was a round table topped with a forest-green tablecloth, a vase of bright yellow sunflowers—also fake—in the center. A small stack of platters waited beside the vase. Without a word, they started plating the pastries. There was a box filled with fluffy pumpkin muffins, spiced shortbread cut into perfect triangles, and cranberry scones topped with a light drizzle of icing.

It took everything in Amber's power to not be *dreadful* like Paul and shovel all the pastries into her mouth. She imagined being covered in crumbs and sugar, only to have Captain Nightmare come in, see the destruction, then collapse in the doorway, hand to forehead. She chuckled to herself.

"What?" Jack asked, smiling at her.

Before she could answer, the door to the room opened and in walked the most *beautiful* man Amber had ever seen. She, being the classy lady she was, dropped the pastry box she'd been holding. Thankfully, it was empty. She flushed and hurriedly went to pick the box up off the floor—and while she was down there, she grabbed her jaw, too.

He was around five-eight, purposefully bald, had piercing blue eyes, high cheekbones, and his button-down blue shirt was tucked into well-tailored black slacks. The shirt had two buttons undone, showing off a hint of well-muscled chest underneath. His shoes were shiny and black.

The man strode for her, hand out. He didn't seem remotely fazed by her reaction. Amber blinked at the perfectly sculpted hand before her, then realized she was supposed to shake it. "Oh! I … uh …" She giggled. Amber Blackwood was *not* a giggler.

Amber wedged the pastry box under her arm, then shook the man's offered hand. His tanned skin felt as if it were made of silk. His skin was free of blemishes, save for a tiny white scar above his right eyebrow. The small imperfection somehow made his face even more stunning.

He smiled at her, revealing two rows of perfectly white teeth. Amber nearly melted into a puddle.

"I'm Olaf Betzen," he said, voice carrying a slight accent, though Amber didn't have the faintest clue where it was from. "And you, my lovely, are …?"

Amber swallowed. "Blamber Ackwood." She giggled again. This was becoming a problem. "No! Amber. Amber Blackwood."

He was still smiling at her. "It's lovely to meet you, Amber."

It occurred to her then that she should use her truth spell on him. One could never be too sure. Even if he was so impossibly attractive it was hard to imagine him capable of anything sinister. The worst thing he could possibly do was have a smile so dazzling, it made the sun jealous.

Gracious. What was happening to her?

Forcing herself to take a slow, calming breath, she mentally uttered the incantation, then asked, "What is the purpose of your time here in Edgehill, Olaf Betzen?"

A vein twitched in his temple. Was he annoyed by her question? It was the only sign she'd seen that he was anything but perfectly agreeable. But with these famous types, she had to assume a large part of their outward demeanor when addressing the public had to be fabricated. It took him a few moments to formulate a reply. "I'm here to sow a little chaos." He laughed.

Then Amber remembered that "Let's sew some chaos" had been the phrase on several of the *Ramp It Up* fan shirts. It wasn't a lie as far as her magic was concerned. Amber wasn't sure what "sewing chaos" meant on the show, but she assumed it had something to do with extra challenges for the contestants to keep them on their A-game. Was he planning something special for the Edgehill designers?

His gaze cut to someone behind her. "And you are?"

Someone else was here?

Jack! Jack was here.

"I'm Jack Terrence," he said, coming around the table to shake Olaf's hand now.

"Ah, yes, the baker of the treats I was promised," Olaf said, eying the table of goodies. "This is quite the spread."

"Edgehill wanted to give you a warm welcome," Jack said, talking like a normal human who remembered his name. "Is there anything else we can get you?"

Just then, several people laden down with bags appeared in the doorway, looking nothing short of harassed. They practically pushed their way into the room without a glance at either Jack or Amber.

Olaf sucked in a quick breath through his nose, eyebrows going up. "Well, it was lovely meeting you both. And I'll be sure to let you know what I think of your pastries, Mr. Terrence. Your reputation precedes you, I must say."

And then suddenly she and Jack were out in the hallway and the door was closed. She stared at the askew sign on the door. No wonder the entire town had lost its collective mind. It had only taken her all of ten seconds to fall under his spell.

Taking a calming breath, she turned to Jack, not sure how to address the fact that the mere presence of Olaf Betzen had turned her into a ninny.

Jack was barely holding back a laugh. "Shall we go find our seats, Blamber?"

"I hate you," she said, turning on her heel and marching away from him, not entirely sure where she was going.

It took Jack a while to stop laughing.

The auditorium had been transformed into something Amber had only seen on TV—though admittedly not on *Ramp It Up*. The stage stood at the back, its black curtains pulled shut. Down the middle of the room, until about halfway, ran a stretch of thin, light-colored wood; a darker brown strip ran down the center of it. Amber guessed the makeshift runway was about three feet wide, and rows of chairs had been set up to face it. The rows were each three deep, with a space behind them for people to stand if they weren't lucky enough to snag chairs. Front row was reserved for families of the designers and models, as well as press. A man with a massive camera on a tripod was getting set up at the end of the runway in the dead center.

Larry had already set up the refreshments here, the table by the entrance piled high with treats. It was the most popular location in the room.

A news anchor stood near the entrance of the auditorium, talking animatedly to her cameraman.

Amber and Jack stood just beyond the rows of chairs, but away from the news anchor and the swarm of people sampling Jack's pastries. Their own little patch of no man's land. "This whole thing is a bigger deal than I realized. No wonder you've been panicking."

"Not helping," Jack sing-songed as he took in their surroundings.

"Where's Larry?" she asked, scanning the room now too.

"Who knows," Jack said. "He's not big on crowds. I'm guessing he's observing things from afar and will slip in to watch the show once it starts and everyone is focused on the runway." He let out a gusting sigh. "I should probably help at the table over there, right? Sally and Paul are passing out plates and napkins. Poor kids look like they need a vacation."

For the next half hour, Amber helped dish out pastries. Jack answered all manner of questions and passed out a handful of Purrcolate business cards. A woman was having an English tea as part of her sister's birthday celebration next month and wanted Jack's scones on the menu. Another woman was having a Mad Hatter wedding and wanted Jack's help. A man wanted several dozen pastries for an upcoming family reunion. Amber had to dash off to the kitchen to grab more boxes to help replenish the stock. Twice.

The nearer it got to 4:00, the more crowded the auditorium became. People—many in *Ramp It Up* fan shirts—streamed into the room, pointing and whispering to one another. The news anchor interviewed person after person in hopes of snagging that perfect soundbite to play on the air later.

With a half hour until the show, Jack ran clean out of pastries. The table was littered only with empty platters and crumbs now. He couldn't seem to wipe the smile off his face. He left a stack of his business cards on the table.

They found some seats in the middle of the second row.

Amber bumped him with her shoulder. "What was that—five orders?"

He grinned at her. "Seven."

"Told you," she said.

He draped an arm around the back of her chair and slipped down in his seat a little, finally relaxing. "Thanks for hanging with me today."

"Of course," she said, smiling at him. "Thanks for inviting me."

"Ugh!" someone said.

Amber glanced up to see Larry standing in front of them. "You two are always making with the goo-goo eyes. It's really quite gross."

"And where have you been?" Jack asked, ignoring his brother's previous comment.

"Working the crowd," he said. "I think I got us three orders."

"I got seven."

Larry wrinkled his nose. "Such a show-off."

"You an Olaf Betzen fan?" Amber asked him.

"I'm human, aren't I?" Then Larry got a goofy smile on his face.

"We met him earlier."

Larry dramatically plopped into the chair in front of them. "No! What happened? Tell me everything."

"Amber here was so completely besotted—"

"Besotted is a stretch …"

"Like I said," Jack said. "She was so besotted, she mispronounced her own name."

Larry winced. "That's rough. But he's also the most beautiful man on the planet, so …"

"I had no idea," Amber admitted. "The poster on Willow's door back in high school didn't do the man *any* justice."

Larry tsked. "I'm glad Jack here is getting your butt out of the house more. You've been folded into the Terrence brothers' inner circle now. You can't be Edgehill's recluse anymore."

Amber frowned. Edgehill's recluse? Had she really gotten that bad?

When music—some pop song she didn't know—started pumping through the speakers spaced out all over the room, Larry moved from his row into theirs, taking a seat on Jack's other side. Others scrambled to their seats too. The press people in the front row whipped out small notepads, and the man at the end of the runway checked his camera's viewfinder and adjusted a few things on his equipment.

A few minutes later, the music got a bit louder and the lighting got a bit dimmer. Cheers and applause rang throughout the room and Amber had to remind herself that this was a fashion show, and not a concert. A pair of women behind Amber squealed.

Mayor Deidrick stepped out onto the stage, much to the disappointment of the crowd. Amber hadn't seen him since the town hall meeting a month or so ago when he'd named Kimberly Jones the new committee head in the wake of Melanie's death.

He was in his early fifties and had one of those disarmingly charming smiles despite being a rather plain-looking man. Amber supposed most people in office had some charm factor. Someone who was good at talking to random people with ease.

"I'm very pleased to welcome you all to Edgehill's first junior fashion show!" the mayor said into his microphone.

The crowd cheered. Someone started chanting "Olaf! Olaf!" in the back but was quickly shushed.

Mayor Deidrick just smiled. "As you all know, we have a very special guest here tonight. Before I welcome him to the stage, don't forget the real reason we're all here: to showcase the talent of Edgehill's young people. They have been working tirelessly for weeks to put together their best collections for you all to see. We are very proud of our young designers."

The crowd cheered again, though it was a bit more muted.

The mayor knew he was merely an opening act for a big name. "Without further ado, please give a round of applause to our guest of honor: Olaf Betzen!"

He walked offstage.

If she hadn't met the very alluring Olaf earlier, Amber would have continued to think all the fuss over the man had been over the top. Now she got it, even though she couldn't completely explain it.

A light shone down on the now-empty stage; the seating area nearly pitch black. The tension in the crowd was palpable. When the curtains finally parted and revealed a dapper

Olaf in all white, the reaction was nearly deafening. Amber found herself clapping enthusiastically and had to remind herself to calm down.

"Hello and welcome, everyone," Olaf said, his voice like a purr. A woman behind Amber swooned. "I am Olaf Betzen."

Half the crowd jumped to their feet to applaud him further.

He grinned, doing his best to look abashed. His teeth were another flash of white to match his outfit. "Please, please," he said. "You're all too kind."

Amber noticed then that there was a cameraman on either side of the stage, both focused on Olaf. She wondered if this footage would be used in one of his shows.

"As you all know, today we're here for a fashion show in Edgehill, Oregon. It wasn't a place I'd ever heard of before, but the Instagram feed of one Letty Rodriguez—"

The crowd cheered again.

"—and her infinitely talented son Diego, put this little cat-loving town on the map for me. When I saw what some of the young designers were working on here, I knew I had to come see it for myself." He paused dramatically. "I don't often make appearances at events such as this, so I'm sure you've all guessed that I have a little surprise up my sleeve. You know how I love surprises."

The audience chuckled knowingly.

Without preamble, he said, "The winner of today's fashion show is guaranteed a spot on *Ramp It Up: Junior Edition*, season 3!"

The crowd was on its feet again. A distant chorus of screams and cheers sounded beyond the auditorium and

Amber pictured the young designers jumping up and down at this news. She hoped the smile on Sydney Sadler's face was so wide that it hurt.

Olaf beamed. "So, dear hearts, let's get this thing started! Ramp it up—"

"And let's sew some chaos!" the audience called back.

"What on earth is happening?" Jack whispered in her ear.

She laughed, turning back to look at him. The room was dark, so she could barely make out his features in the half light. "You're not an avid *Ramp It Up* viewer?"

"I think I've seen ... two episodes? Three years ago?"

"*Travesty*," Larry trilled from his other side, his superhero hearing still in tip-top shape.

When the crowd started to cheer again, Amber turned back to the stage. A young boy stood there with a microphone. He looked so tiny standing up there by himself. And downright terrified.

"Hi, everyone." He waved awkwardly. "My collection today is mostly menswear and stuff for boys." Then he abruptly walked off the stage.

The crowd chuckled politely.

Music started seconds later, and the first male model made his way onto the stage from the dark recesses that lay beyond the curtains. Amber had no idea if the models came with Olaf, or were professionals acquired from outside of Edgehill, or Edgehill residents—perhaps some combination of all three. Each collection had six looks, but from what snatches of conversation she'd heard today, the designers would feature ten looks for the Here and Meow.

Amber knew very little about fashion, but she found herself truly amazed at what these kids were able to create with just fabric and thread. Amber considered it a small miracle when she could refasten a button, and she usually had her magic to help her.

The third designer to take the stage was a young girl Amber knew: Sydney Sadler. Amber had met her briefly last month when she and Connor had visited Letty Rodriquez's Angora Threads. It was during her conversation with Sydney that Amber realized the person responsible for the death of her friend was Sydney's mother. What was young Sydney's life like now that her mother had been arrested for murder?

Guilt clouded her mind every time she saw or thought about Sydney.

"Hi," the blonde said into the microphone. "My collection today was inspired by the 1950s. It's an era my mom really loved and she and I watched old movies from that time together a lot. I love the fashion of that time and thought it would be fun to create some designs of my own. Hope you like them!"

She smiled slightly, then speed-walked off the stage.

By the third design, Amber had fallen in love with Sydney's collection. The flowing skirts, the collared shirts, the abundant use of polka dots—all the pieces were things Amber would love to wear herself. Given the oohs and ahhs from several people around Amber, she knew she wasn't the only one impressed with the twelve-year-old prodigy.

It was around design five though, that there was a shift in the crowd. From across the runway, a slight commotion broke out amongst the viewers. Chairs creaked, people turned in their seats, fingers went to mouths to shush the suddenly rowdy guests behind them.

But then a chair toppled over. Someone screamed. Then another, and another.

On Amber's side of the runway, someone groaned and pitched back in their chair, which hit the ground with a sickening crunch. Amber hoped it was the chair that had made that sound, and not a skull hitting a hard, unyielding surface. Someone behind her cried out. Then the man directly in front of her pitched backward. Had Jack not pulled her out of the way, the man would have landed right in her lap.

But her thank-you to Jack died on her tongue when she saw what looked like tendrils of black crawling up the fallen man's neck, onto his chin, and then snaking across his face. The lines scuttled over the man's skin like spider legs. Amber knew if she pulled down the collar of his shirt, she'd see the starburst mark the spindly lines radiated out of.

She jumped to her feet, eyes scanning the crowd that was quickly starting to panic, some already running for the door.

Then she spotted Olaf Betzen on his feet near the stage at the start of the runway. Despite the chaos erupting around them, Olaf somehow only had eyes for her. He hadn't been lying when he said he was here to sow chaos. Unfortunately, he hadn't simply been repeating a catchphrase—he'd meant it literally.

Then he finger-waved at Amber. A playful gesture. Taunting.

She didn't know if Olaf himself was a cursed witch, or if a

cursed witch was currently wearing his face. Either way, one thing was certain: the Penhallow had struck again.

CHAPTER 17

All around her, people cried out and screamed and made for the exits. Yet, Olaf and Amber hadn't torn their eyes from each other.

Suddenly, he turned his attention to one of his shoulders, clad in pristine white. He flicked an invisible wayward thread off the material. The moment his finger shot forward, a woman in front of Amber, who was trying to climb over one of the folding chairs, let out a sickening groan, back arched. She collapsed onto one of the chairs, sitting awkwardly on her hip while she scrabbled with the hem of her shirt. Pulling it up, she revealed snaking black lines creeping around her side. The woman shrieked, rubbing frantically at the lines as if that would make them retreat. Amber knew there would be a starburst mark on her back where the Penhallow's magic had hit her.

Jaw clenched, Amber started toward the witch, something akin to anger blurring her vision at the edges. She had no idea what she'd do when she got to him—she wasn't sure she *could* do anything—but she wanted him to stop.

As she hurried down the thin aisle made by the chairs, she was vaguely aware of Jack and Larry calling after her. She stepped over discarded jackets, plates covered in crumbs, and even the occasional prone form.

A wall of blue rose up on her peripheral vision and she glanced to her left to see Chief Owen Brown fighting his way through the crowd streaming in the other direction. "Amber! Where is he?"

Carl was a few people back, helping a woozy man toward the doors. It was of little surprise that the news anchor and her cameraman were still documenting the event.

Amber swiveled her attention back to the chief, then said "Olaf" to him as loud as she dared. The chief's expression hardened and he started pushing past people with more force now, not bothering to apologize.

When Olaf, who hadn't moved since he started all this, caught sight of the chief heading his way, he smiled at Amber. "Oh, how quaint!" he said, clapping his hands together and then resting his chin on his steepled fingers. "You've befriended a member of law enforcement. Do you think he's better equipped to handle this than the others here?" Olaf suddenly held out a hand before him and turned it this way and that, as if he'd never seen it before. "This one has the softest hands. Clearly hasn't worked a day in his life."

Well, that confirmed this wasn't actually Olaf.

Where on earth were Willow and Aunt Gretchen?

Closer now, but still a dozen chairs away, her gaze flicked to the slumped form of a man sitting in the chair beside where the Penhallow stood. He wore all white. The *real* Olaf.

"Shall we see? All these fine people have only gotten a half dose. Imagine if I used the same dose on your little cop friend as I did on that maid …"

Then the Penhallow's expression turned serious, brows furrowed, as he focused his attention on the chief. Chief Brown was still behind her, pushing his way through the crowd. Amber moved faster, nearly losing her footing as a shoe clipped a chair leg. Her heart thumped wildly.

The Penhallow raised his hand, fingers splayed; his palm faced the chief.

Amber thought of the pictures she'd seen of Wilma. Of the withered flesh. She thought of Jessica and little Sammy and the baby on the way whose lives would all be irrevocably wrecked if the chief were killed here today.

Six chairs away.

The Penhallow's lips began to move. He was uttering an incantation. Amber's own magic thrashed beneath her skin even more wildly than her heart in her chest.

Three chairs away.

The frustration of the past week overwhelmed her. Her aunt's illness, the maid's death, the secrets her parents kept, that her aunt kept, and the fact that this Penhallow—or someone he knew—more than likely had been the one to trap her parents in their own home and then set it on fire. She felt like a volcano primed for explosion. Her vision tunneled further. "*STOP!*"

And the Penhallow did. His outstretched hand and features froze. But, so did everything else. The screams and cries and pounding feet were abruptly silenced. Amber came up short and looked around the auditorium. It was like being in a room full of mannequins. People were frozen with mouths open, with one foot off the ground as they ran, and one man was even frozen mid-fall, his stuck-open eyes staring at the floor that had, just moments before, been rising up to meet him.

What the …

Amber found the chief just a few feet behind her, his serious, determined expression focused on the Penhallow.

The Penhallow! She had him now. Frozen in place. But what was she supposed to do with him? She couldn't very well mortally wound him while he was stuck in time.

Could she?

She closed the distance between them, then forced his hand down so his open palm now faced the floor. Should she turn his hand to face him, so that when time unfroze, the magic erupting out of his palm would blast him with a "full dose" of his own magic? Surely that would end him. Then both Edgehill and her parents' secrets would be safe.

She had just grabbed his wrist again when—

"Tsk, tsk, Miss Blackwood."

Amber yelped and stumbled back, almost toppling over a chair as she did so.

The man pretending to be Olaf flashed her a grin full of white teeth that didn't belong to him. "So the rumors *are* true."

Amber swallowed. "What rumors?"

"That Theodore and Annabelle Blackwood's children were far more powerful than anyone was led to believe."

"I'm not—"

"Come now," Fake Olaf said, walking from his spot in the front row, past Amber, and into the area just beyond the three rows of chairs, where late-arrival guests had been standing.

Fake Olaf spread his arms wide. "You froze nearly a hundred people! And with only a single word. Annabelle had been a prodigy with time magic, and it seems she passed it on to you. It took three decades to unleash it, but here it is. I figured you'd need a highly emotional situation to wake it up."

"You … you set this up?"

"Well," he said, peering into the face of a frozen woman, practically touching his nose to hers, "I honestly didn't know what I was going to do to shake your magic free, but then *this* ridiculous creature—" he gestured at himself, "showed up with all his sycophants, and an idea was born."

Amber scanned the frozen crowd, spotting Willow and Aunt Gretchen in the doorway in the middle of the room. They both clearly had been looking for her. Jack was caught in a mid-lunge in her direction, Larry close on his heels. She didn't see Connor anywhere.

Her gaze skated over the still-safe chief before landing on Fake Olaf again. "Why go through all this trouble?"

"For the *book*!" he snapped. "Haven't you been paying attention? I. Want. The. Book."

Amber glared at him. "And I already told you that I don't have it. I've never *seen* it."

"Tut. Lying won't help anyone," he said, resting an arm on the head of a little boy frozen in place, as if he were furniture. Fake Olaf crossed one foot over the other, the tip of his shiny black shoe resting on the floor. "I've given you all the pieces. You didn't really think you found that watch on accident, did you? I knew you couldn't resist the cry of weak creatures in torment, so I left those kittens where you would find them.

Then it was just a matter of placing your father's old watch *just so*. I saw how you were hurtled into a memory. What did it show you?"

Amber's skin crawled.

How long had he been watching her?

He took several steps toward her. Though a row of folding chairs and a few people-statues were between them, he still felt too close.

"What did you see?" he asked, eyes gleaming.

She was consoled by the fact that he only knew she'd been shown a memory, not which memory specifically. She had, of course, seen the book. But Fake Olaf didn't need to know that.

She clenched her fists by her sides. "I know the fire was no accident. I know Neil Penhallow trapped them inside their own house and then set it on fire. Was that *you*?"

He laughed. "No, that was my brother."

The same brother who, when mentioned even in general terms, had made Amber's mother recoil.

"What happened to Neil?" Amber asked.

Fake Olaf's jaw clenched. "Neil was institutionalized not too long after the fire. He's nearly sixty now and all he's seen for decades are the gray walls of the institution *your* mother's actions forced him into. She really did a number on him."

Then, before Amber's eyes, Olaf Betzen's gorgeous features melted off the Penhallow's face, like turpentine thrown on a canvas, the paint slipping off. Amber half expected to see a silicon suit of Olaf lying at the Penhallow's feet as Olaf's features, clothing, and skin sloughed away. Beneath was a man who Amber initially would have thought was Neil, but the longer she looked at him, the more she saw the differences. A longer nose, wider-set brown eyes—rather than hazel—a rounder chin. But undeniably related to the man who killed her parents.

"Pleasure to make your acquaintance, Miss Blackwood," he said, bowing deeply. "I'm Kieran Penhallow."

By the time he stood to full height again, Amber had willed her breathing back under control. "Why are you so desperate for this book? Why did you hurt all these people and kill Wilma?"

"Who the devil is Wilma?"

"The *maid*."

Kieran waved this off. "Your mother perfected a time travel spell. Don't tell me the spell doesn't exist or that travel isn't possible. It is. And your mother selfishly locked it away in her grimoire."

Both Aunt Gretchen and Edgar said time travel wasn't possible. Had her mother lied to them, or was the Penhallow currently lying to Amber? It was very possible he was deluded and believed wholeheartedly in a myth.

"You want to reverse the curse?" Amber asked.

"To be determined," he said. "I have a much more pressing matter. You see, your family killed my father and drove my brother to madness. I want to save them from that fate. Wouldn't *you* go back in time to save your family if you could?"

"You mean the family *your* brother killed?" Amber snapped.

Kieran waved away this comment too.

Deep down, Amber knew she'd use the spell. That if she'd known about it, she'd have been desperate to find it, and for the same reason Kieran wanted it: to bring back loved ones. But her parents had gone to great lengths to keep the spell out of the Penhallows' hands, hadn't they? There had to be a good reason for that. Assuming it existed at all.

But then the rest of what he said caught up to her. "What do you mean my family killed your father?"

"Oh, they left that part out of your family's history books?" Kieran asked. "Let's see. Did you know your mother and my brother were desperately in love when they were twenty-somethings?"

Amber shook her head.

"It's true. Neil planned to marry her—had the ring picked out and everything.

"Your mother had always been a prodigy with time spells and the two worked together to figure out how to turn back time. It was *your* mother who wanted to end the curse. She knew any future children of theirs would inherit the curse, and she wanted to find a way to make sure she and Neil could live a happy, fulfilled life together."

He paused for so long, Amber wondered if he was doing it merely to torture her.

"*And*?" She hated the desperate note to her voice. She didn't believe any of this, did she?

Grinning, he continued. "Well, your grandfather Miles caught wind of their plan and decided to put a stop to it. Even though Penhallows have been treated horribly for generations, your mother saw past the curse and fell for the man underneath. Miles, however, didn't approve.

"The night the two planned to conduct the time-travel

spell out in a secluded field, they had only just gotten started when Miles happened upon them. They got into a screaming match and started hurling magic around.

"My own father had heard rumors about what Neil and Anna were planning, so when he heard the commotion, he came running. Miles was prepared to not only kill Neil to stop him from using the spell, but his own daughter. Miles hurled a felled tree at them, planning to crush them both. But my father jumped in the way and pushed them to safety. He took the full brunt of the strike and died instantly.

"Miles then bested Neil and tried to sever his magic from him, but botched the job. It left Neil mad. In fear of retaliation, Miles made the entire Henbane family flee that very night. Scattered to three parts of the country. Anna one way, Raphael another, and Miles and his wife went a third."

Amber merely stared at him. Could that truly be what happened? Was *that* why her mother had been on the run?

"So," Kieran said, "your family owes it to mine to right this very egregious wrong. My father would still be here, my brother wouldn't have lost his grip on reality, and the Penhallow curse would be no more. Find me the grimoire and all will be forgiven."

"And if I don't?"

He shrugged, then motioned to the room at large. "Then this happens on a larger scale. What I did to the maid will look like a mercy. You have one week."

Without warning, he thrust his hands toward her, a gust of wind knocking her off her feet. It was enough to stun her, releasing her hold on her magic. Her head smacked into something. The room erupted in a clamor of voices. Luckily no one seemed to realize they'd just been frozen in time—they merely resumed their panicked escape.

The chief reached her, his expression pained. "How did you manage to land on the floor when you were just—you know what? Never mind. Don't tell me." He helped her to her feet.

Amber touched a tender spot on her temple. She scanned the room, looking for Kieran Penhallow. But she knew it was no use. He would have assumed another face and slipped out among the wave of people spilling out into the lobby and the parking lot beyond.

One week.

She had one week to find this grimoire.

She knew deep down that her parents wouldn't have done all this to keep the book out of the Penhallows' possession if they hadn't thought it was vitally important, but Amber wondered how much of what Kieran had told her was true.

Jack reached her next, fingertips gently probing the spot around the bump on her head. "Are you part cheetah? How'd you get over here so fast? Who were you chasing?"

"No one. I'm okay."

He scanned her face. "I keep thinking you have this secret life you're not telling me about … but that's crazy, right?"

Her semi-hysterical laugh didn't help matters, because his brow furrowed.

She placed a hand on her forehead, shut her eyes, and swayed a little. "I think I hit my head harder than I thought."

The chief was saying something about a possible concussion. Aunt Gretchen and Willow were there now too, offering

242

to drive Amber home. Connor, who seemed to have materialized out of thin air, hovered nearby, asking what happened.

The sudden flood of voices and shouting *had* triggered a headache. She needed to lie down.

"Rain check on the dinner and dessert?" she asked Jack, wincing slightly.

"Yeah, of course," he said, but his tone was a little flat.

Willow took Amber by the arm and started to lead her away. "We'll patch her up and she'll be good as new in a day or two."

"Yeah, yeah, of course," Jack said again.

As Amber let herself be led to the front door, she noticed that the mood in the room had slowly started to shift toward confusion, rather than panic, now that the threat, whatever it had been, was gone. How on earth were the chief and the mayor going to explain this one? Insects? Rabid bats?

Every person who looked her way could be Kieran. Would he be watching her closely for the entire week? He clearly had been watching her for a while now.

She silently sent a preemptive apology to the 99.9% of Edgehill residents who currently were *not* Kieran Penhallow, because if she couldn't find the grimoire in time, they were all in danger.

And it would be her fault.

CHAPTER 18

The Blackwood women argued well into the night in Amber's soundproofed studio about the best course of action. To turn the grimoire over to the cursed witch hell-bent on rewriting history, or *not* to turn the grimoire over to the cursed witch hell-bent on rewriting history …

All Amber knew was that the more they argued, the more she started to lean toward giving it up, if only to protect Edge-hill from this monster.

It was just after midnight now, and Aunt Gretchen was fast asleep on the bed, Tom draped over her stomach and Alley curled up next to her. Amber and Willow were downstairs in the dark shop. While Willow reinforced the protection spells on the doors and windows, Amber made them some hot chocolate. Willow added a couple soundproofing spells too, just in case.

Shortly after they'd left the fashion show fiasco earlier, the dark sky had opened up and drenched the town. The rain had been reduced to a light smattering now, streaks of water slowly running down the glass.

Once Amber was done, she and Willow sat shoulder to shoulder behind the counter, steaming mugs of hot chocolate before them. Willow's had several plump marshmallows bobbing on the surface.

While Aunt Gretchen was fully in the "we are, under no circumstances, giving up the grimoire" camp, and Amber was in the "giving it up might be the lesser of two evils" camp, Willow was squarely in the middle. It was hard for perpetual optimists to make a choice when both options were terrible from all angles.

"I was thinking …" Amber said.

"Congratulations." Willow immediately laughed, somehow finding that joke to be evergreen. "Sorry. What about?"

"Kieran basically forced that memory of Mom and Dad on me, but just like with the freeze spell, I didn't use an incantation. It just sort of … happened."

"Like when we were kids," she said. "It was harder to control our magic back then."

"Exactly." Amber rocked halfway off her stool so she could fish something out of her pocket. Then she placed the white rubber cat on the counter.

Willow gasped softly, placing her mug back on the counter. "I haven't seen this in ages. I have no idea where mine is. I think I lost it when I moved. I tried dozens of locator spells and could never find the thing." She carefully picked it up, laying it in her flattened palm, then shot a look at Amber. "Does it still work the same way?"

"Yep."

Focus returned to the cat, Willow said, *"One by one, let's have some fun. Two by two, let's turn it blue."*

The cat's white fur flipped to blue. Willow grinned. Seconds later, it turned white again. Then she frowned, placing it on the counter. She wrapped her hands around her mug.

With a sigh, she said, "I miss them so much sometimes."

"Me too," Amber said.

"But these past couple weeks? I'm a little pissed off."

Amber laughed softly at that. It took a lot to make Willow angry, and Amber could hear it clearly in her sister's voice. "I know the feeling."

"*Anyway* … you were thinking?"

"Yes," Amber said, picking up the cat and turning it over in her fingers. "Objects from sites where highly emotional and traumatic events took place hold energies and memories, right? That's why Kieran left the watch for me. Dad either had been …" Amber blew out a breath. "Dad either had been wearing it at the time of the fire or had it packed in his suitcase. The watch picked up that energy and stored it until I touched it. Before I ended up in that memory, I was kind of pleading with Mom and Dad to show me what happened to them, and I was rubbing my finger along the back of the watch when I did it. I think a combination of all of that is what woke up my magic."

Willow nodded. "That makes sense," she said. "I hate the idea of Neil picking through the rubble after the fire looking for the book, by the way. *Hate* it. Do you think Neil had been holding onto the watch all this time and then gave it to his brother?"

"Maybe," Amber said. "I don't know where Neil is now, exactly. Kieran only said he had been institutionalized."

"I can tell you where I *hope* he is. There's fire *there*, too."

Amber snorted. "Well, this cat is the last thing I have of

Mom's. What if I try to get pulled into another memory? But maybe a specific one. I had no idea what was going on the first time, but maybe I can be strategic now."

"What memory would you try to see?" Willow asked, keeping her dubious expression focused on the rubber cat in Amber's hands.

"What really happened between Mom and Neil. Knowing if she really *did* figure out a working time-travel spell might help us decide if we want to give something like that over to the Penhallows."

"Are we willing to deny him the book at the risk of what he'd do to the town and maybe even the ones beyond it?" Willow asked. "For all we know, more of his Penhallow buddies are on their way."

"Depending on what Mom has in her grimoire …" Amber shrugged. "Maybe giving Kieran the book would be the worst scenario."

It was the same back and forth argument they'd had all night.

"Do it," Willow said. "If knowing what Mom and Dad knew helps us figure out how to make a decision, then do it. I'm here for whatever you need."

Amber set the rubber cat on its four paws on the counter, draped an arm around Willow, then rested her cheek on her shoulder. Together they whispered, *"One by one, let's have some fun. Two by two, let's turn it blue."*

Though most of the Olaf Betzen fans had fled Edgehill in droves as soon as Olaf had, it was still busy enough in the store every day that Amber had to practically drag herself up the stairs into her studio in the evenings. She'd felt bad for Sydney Sadler, along with the other fashion show contestants, who didn't get a chance to re-show their designs—and some who didn't get to showcase their work at all. Olaf was a busy man and had obligations elsewhere, but he swore to uphold his promise to allow one of the Angora Threads' interns to join the next season of *Ramp It Up*. The designers were to send video diaries of their collections to Olaf's team, and he would make the selection remotely. Amber hoped Sydney got it.

At night, the three Blackwood women pored over their personal grimoires and crafted their own spells in hopes of creating something Amber could use to gain entrance into another memory.

So far, the only memory she'd been able to tap into had been of the rubber cat's, which featured long, dark days inside Amber's purse more often than not. How an inanimate object had memories was beyond her, so she tried not to think about it too hard because it creeped her out. Though she was considering giving the cat a better location to spend its days after they figured out the spell.

She'd tried working specific dates and locations into the spells. Willow suggested using specific names. Aunt Gretchen thought infusing memory-aiding tinctures into the paper they wrote the spells on might help. None of them had experience with memory magic, and it proved to be more fickle than Amber anticipated.

Then, two days after the fashion show, as Amber stared at the rubber cat, she wondered if there was a way to come at the spell in a much simpler way.

"*One by one, let's have some fun. Two by two, let's turn it blue.*" She idly swiped a hand over the cat, watching as white flipped to blue and then back again.

"Three by three," she said, not giving what she said much thought, "please let me see. Four by four, if what Kieran said was truth or lore."

"Amber?" It was Willow's voice.

"Uhh … something's happening …"

A blinding white light tore through her vision, and she only had a moment to yelp in surprise before she was transported somewhere—some*when*—else.

When the light faded this time, Amber was sitting in the front passenger seat of a moving car. A pair of legs were propped up on the dashboard. The girl's feet were bare, the toenails painted a bright red. From what Amber could see, the girl wore cutoff jean shorts. Resting precariously on one bent knee was the same rubber cat Amber now held. It was a much more pristine white now, both ears and the tail intact. The girl swiped a hand over the cat, half-singing as she did. "*One by one, let's have some fun. Two by two, let's turn it blue.*"

"Why are you always carrying that thing around?" a male voice next to her asked playfully. It was a younger man, Amber guessed.

"Oh, I don't know." She swiped her hand over the cat again. The fur flipped to blue. "My mom gave it to me a couple of months ago. She's not really the gift-giving type, so it feels special somehow."

The guy laughed softly. "You can get those things in pretty much any novelty store. It's the kind of thing little kids pull off shelves when they're bored in line with their moms at the grocery store."

The girl turned to look at him, gazing at his profile. Then he glanced over at her, grinning. He was boy-next-door handsome. He had slightly shaggy sandy-brown hair, deep brown eyes, and an easy smile. That one grinning look told Amber he loved her.

But, if Amber had truly succeeded in jumping back in time to a memory where her mother and Neil had been in love, Amber had no idea who *this* boy was.

"Even if it's just a novelty, I hope I can pass it down to my own kids someday," she said. "But I'd have to get a second one. Sara Caraway assures me I'm destined to have two daughters."

"Don't you mean *we're* destined to have two daughters?" he asked, attention shifting to her briefly again before turning his gaze back to the road.

Given the quick disruption of the girl's vision, Amber guessed she'd just rolled her eyes. Then she laughed. "Yes, silly boy. You know you're the only boy for me, Neil Winters."

"And you're the only girl for me Annabelle Henbane. Annabelle Winters has quite the ring to it though, if I do say so myself."

Amber's mother laughed again. "You know I can't think about any of that until I'm done with school."

"I know, I know," he said. "I just like reminding you that I'm crazy about you."

Neil *Winters*. Not Penhallow?

But before she could get an answer to that, the scene peeled away. This time Amber's mother sat at a desk littered with open books, the thick grimoire Amber had seen in the other series of memories, scribbled-on sheets of paper, and several empty mugs. The boy from before sat next to her, the two hunched over a sheet of paper with line after line of handwritten notes.

"Just one more line," Belle said. "This one better work. My hand is cramping up again."

She had just finished the last line at the bottom of the page when all the words on it suddenly burned yellow before fading back to black.

Both Belle and Neil jumped back in surprise, almost toppling out of their chairs.

"Is that it?" Neil asked, voice soft. "Did we really do it?"

Belle had her hands in her hair. After letting out a series of colorful curses, she said, "I think so?"

Neil picked up the sheet of paper and then held it at the top between thumb and forefinger with both hands. Then quickly jerked his hands in either direction, clearly intending to shred it. The paper reacted as if it were made of solid steel.

Amber remembered then how Neil said a grimoire couldn't be destroyed. She supposed that was true for individual spells too. Amber had never been compelled to tear up a perfectly good spell, so she'd never had reason to test this.

With shaking hands, Belle took the sheet from Neil, though it looked like the boy had released it with some reluctance. Reaching for her grimoire with her free hand, she flipped the cover open.

"What are you doing?" Neil asked, his voice going up in pitch just slightly.

Belle glanced over at him. "What do you think I'm doing? I can't just leave something like this lying around. I can't believe you even talked me into creating something this dangerous …"

Neil scoffed, then slipped his arm around her waist. "You didn't fight the idea that hard, babe. You're so much more powerful and talented than you know. You just don't see it. You're a *prodigy*."

It was Belle's turn to scoff. She gently leaned into his side, where the side of his torso rested against hers. "I admit I was intrigued by the challenge."

"I knew it," he whispered in her ear. "Delin Springs isn't big enough for witches like us. It only took you four months to crack *time travel*, baby. Imagine what else we could do."

When she turned her head, their noses almost touched. Amber wasn't sure she had the proper word for the expression on Neil's face, but it instantly put Amber on edge. The Neil she'd seen in the first set of memories, the predatory, mildly dangerous version of him, was there in that look now.

And then it clicked for Amber. *Whose face are you wearing, Neil?*

It had been true that Belle had been in love with Neil, but she'd loved the brown-haired, boy-next-door Neil Winters. Not Neil Penhallow in a mask.

With her nose still close to his, she scanned his face. Focusing on the smattering of light freckles on his cheeks, then, briefly, to his lips, before traveling up to those deep brown eyes, the predatory gleam in them gone. "But that's all this was, Neil. A challenge. We can't *use* this." She moved away from him and gently shook the sheet of paper covered from top to bottom in Belle's condensed, neat handwriting. "Can you imagine what could happen if a Penhallow got a hold of this?"

Neil's voice was flat when he said, "Would that really be so bad?"

Belle reared back from him as if he'd just struck her, scooting her chair several inches away. "Are you *kidding*? They're cursed, Neil. They're ... they're hardly human anymore. All they care about is stealing powers from other witches. They kill dozens of innocent witches *every* year. And those are just the ones we hear about."

He turned in his seat, then grabbed her free hand. "You love me, don't you?"

"Of course," Belle said without hesitation. "But ... what does that have to do with anything?"

"You and me forever?"

"You're scaring me, Neil."

He brought her hand to his lips and kissed it. "You and me forever?" His tone was pleading.

"Yes. You know that," she said, voice a bit softer. "Forever."

"Good," he said. "Good." He kissed her hand again, then let go. He pushed his chair back a few inches. "Just ... hear me out, okay? What if *that* spell—" he pointed at the paper still in her hand, "could actually reverse the curse?"

"We can't know what kind of a ripple effect that would have, though. That's reversing something that happened, what, five generations ago now? You and I might not even exist in this new future."

"Our love would find a way to bring us together again. Maybe we'd be in different bodies, but our hearts would be the same. I truly believe that." He paused for a long time. "And, at least in the new future, we could be together. No one would let us in this one."

"Neil," Belle said slowly, lightly wringing her hands. "*What* are you talking about?"

"Remember, you said forever …"

Before Belle could react, Neil Winters's face melted away, revealing the black-haired, hazel-eyed Neil Penhallow beneath.

Belle stumbled out of her chair so quickly, she nearly hit the floor. She kept stumbling away from him until her back hit the wall by her bedroom door. "Who … who the hell *are* you?"

Neil got to his feet, hands out. "Listen, Anna—"

"No!" Belle snapped, hands out. "Stay there. Don't come any closer until you explain who you are and what you did to Neil. Did you steal his face as some ploy to force me into coming up with that spell? Where is he? What did you *do* to him?"

"Anna. Anna! Listen to me! I'm Neil. The same Neil you fell in love with." He motioned to his face. "This doesn't matter. Neil Winters was a mask. But you've seen my true heart. I swear it. I've always been honest with you."

Belle's laugh bordered on hysteria. "Honest with me? *Honest* with me? I didn't know your real name or your face! You've lied to me from the beginning."

Neil, with his hands still out, approached her slowly, as one would a terrified, wounded animal. "Baby, please—"

"Don't call me baby!" she snapped. "Stay where you are."

He halted. "It's always been about you, Anna. I knew I loved you from the first moment I saw you. But I knew you'd never accept that I was a Penhallow—"

Belle let out a sound somewhere between a whimper and a sob.

"So I presented you with a neater outer package that you could accept. Remember, you love *me*. Not the mask I wear. You've seen what's underneath. *That's* who I am."

Her voice was flat when she asked, "If it's always been about me, why did you convince me to write the one spell all Penhallows want? Hmm? Did someone send you here? Are you a spy for the Penhallow clan?"

When he didn't say anything right away, she threw her hands up in dismay. "Oh my God. You are! I'm such an idiot." She thunked her forehead over and over with the heel of her palm. "Idiot, idiot, idiot."

"Anna, no," Neil said, pulling her hand away from her face. But the moment he touched her, her magic lashed out, flinging him away from her as if she were a live wire.

Belle opened the door to her bedroom. "Get out, Neil."

He struggled to his feet. "Anna, I—"

"Out!"

Neil took a final parting look at the table where the holy grail of spells still lay, then headed for the door, shoulders slumped. When he reached her, he softly said, "I'm still me, Anna."

She refused to make eye contact now. "Goodbye, Neil."

His dejected sigh was filled with anguish. Belle slammed the door behind him, then locked it for good measure.

Rushing to her desk, she grabbed the newly crafted spell with one hand, and pulled her grimoire closer with the other. She frantically flipped through the book until she came to the first blank page, roughly halfway in. She placed the new spell on top of the blank page. The book's inner spine flashed a golden yellow as the loose page fused itself to the grimoire, accepting it into the book.

Belle slammed the cover closed, then held the book tight to her chest.

Though Amber couldn't feel anything her mother had, Amber knew her mother was crying now. She dropped to her knees, hunched over the book in her arms, and wept.

Amber wished she could crouch beside her mother and drape an arm around her shoulders. She wished she could console her mother about her first major heartbreak, just as Belle had done for Amber on the front steps of 543 Ocicat Lane.

Soon the scene peeled away to show a middle-aged couple—perhaps mid-to-late fifties—standing in a kitchen. Amber was struck by how similar this kitchen was to the one on Ocicat Lane. Had Belle tried to bring a piece of home with her to Edgehill?

Though Amber had never met these people, she knew in an instant that these were her maternal grandparents. Miles and Ivy Henbane. Belle had Ivy's wavy brown hair, though it was liberally streaked with gray. Miles and Belle had the same nose and mouth.

At the moment, her grandparents wore matching worried expressions.

"Are you two *sure* this is the only way?" Ivy asked. "There's got to be something less … risky."

"Sara Caraway has cast dozens upon dozens of foresight spells at this point," Miles said. "This is the only scenario that minimizes how many people get hurt. Neil will be … changed, but it's for the best. He's a con man, and a cursed one at that. He needs to be stopped. And *if* he's stopped, he no longer will be obsessed with the time-travel spell. We don't need Penhallows sniffing around Delin Springs. I'm still not even sure how he got in."

"Does the council know?" Ivy asked.

"Not yet," said Belle.

"And if we can stop him, they won't have to," Miles added. "This ends with Neil."

"How can we be certain he hasn't told other Penhallows about the spell?" Ivy asked.

"Because he told me he hasn't," Belle said.

Ivy laughed. "Sorry, Anna, but haven't we already established no one can trust a word that comes out of that boy's mouth?"

"Yes," said Miles. "But he wants to reconcile with her."

"I told him I need time to think about everything, but the truth about the spell has to remain a secret if he wants any chance with me. I said keeping this to himself will help prove that the boy I fell in love with is still in there."

Miles wrinkled his nose at this. Ivy still looked unconvinced but didn't comment.

"I'm supposed to meet him at seven," Belle said.

Miles looked at his watch. "You've got twenty minutes. You better get going. Keep him talking as long as possible so I have time to get into position."

Ivy crossed the length of the small kitchen to take Belle's face in her hands. "Be safe, heart, okay?" She kissed Belle on the forehead. As she left the room, she said, "If either of you doesn't come back, I will be *furious.*"

Miles watched her go, then turned his gaze to his daughter. He half-winced, half-smiled. Amber could only hope Belle's expression matched his. A playful moment before the event that presumably broke up Belle's immediate family, scattering them to the four winds, and turned Belle into a paranoid nomad. At least until Amber and Willow were born.

After yet another scenery jump, Amber stood just past a well-worn dirt path. It stretched out in either direction, the right side snaking off into the growing darkness, the ground covered in a wispy fog. Trees were to her back. The left of the path curved around the side of the trees. Where Belle stood now was a perfect hiding place from anyone coming up the path. A full moon shone overhead, illuminating patches of the low, drifting fog. Hundreds upon hundreds of stars littered the sky like a dusting of sugar. Amber experienced her mother briefly closing her eyes, making the world go black. Had she been giving herself a pep talk? She opened them again when she heard Neil's voice.

"I honestly wasn't sure if you'd show," he said, as he rounded the curve in the path.

He wore his true face now, and Amber knew her mother

was thrown by the sight, given how she took a tiny step back and hunched her shoulders closer to her ears. Just as quickly, she stood straighter.

"I'm a woman of my word," Belle said.

Neil winced slightly at that, clearly recognizing a dig at his character when he heard one. He approached her slowly, gaze roving her face. Searching, Amber guessed, for any sign that Belle still loved him. That she'd give him a chance despite the lies and deceit.

"I was a little surprised you wanted to meet at our spot," he said, then walked past her.

She turned to see him approach a heart carved into the bark. NW/♥$ AH.

Neil ran a fingertip along the grooves of the heart, then the letters. He swiped a hand across the front of the heart and the W changed into a P. He turned to Belle then, the hopefulness in his expression almost enough to break even Amber's heart. When he was half a foot from her, he carefully reached out to take her hands, which had been hanging by her sides. Belle stared down at their clasped hands for a long time before she looked back up.

The clearing was rapidly growing darker.

"Have you made a decision?" he asked.

"Can you tell me why you had me create that spell?" she asked. "The truth this time."

Neil sighed and dropped her hands. He ran his fingers though his black hair, then rested his palm on the back of his neck. "Rumors about the Henbane girl who can manipulate time have been going around the Penhallow clan for years. I can't tell you how many of them have been trying to find you."

"Delin Springs is warded to high heaven," Belle said. "How did *you* get in? The wards sense Penhallow blood. You shouldn't have been able to get past our defenses."

Amber wondered why the wards hadn't reacted once he reverted to his real self. She supposed there weren't any contingencies for what to do about a Penhallow *inside* their protective spells, as they hadn't anticipated anyone being able to get through in the first place.

Neil managed a soft smile. "My glamour spells are so strong, I can truly become someone else, even down to what runs in my veins. Perk of the curse."

Belle folded her arms. "Who was the real Neil Winters?"

"A guy I met on one of those ridiculous magic retreats in the mountains," Neil said. "He was a Fellway or a Grinnell or something. He didn't have any living family and was trying to find people he could connect with at the retreat. I needed someone no one would miss."

Amber's blood ran cold and she wondered if her mother's had too.

"What?" Belle asked, voice barely above a whisper. "You only glamoured yourself to *look* like him, right? You didn't … you didn't actually …"

"I had to *become* him, Anna," Neil said. "I needed more than his magic. I needed his life—as sad and lonely as it might have been. I needed to live as him for a while for the glamour to really take hold."

"So you … you killed him and assumed his identity just to get into Delin Springs? You did all this for *me*?"

Neil's grin was a bright flash of white in the dark. Amber knew he thought she sounded awe-struck, but Amber had heard incredulity. "Yes, baby. I did this all for you. I admit I had a one-track mind when I got here. I had a mission to complete. I'm a dedicated man. But then I saw you and … I was head over heels immediately."

Something in the forest beyond them cracked, like someone had just stepped on a thick stick. Neil's head whipped in that direction.

Belle reached out and placed a hand on his face to bring his attention back to her. "Did you expect me to create the spell, and then run away with you?"

"Yes," he said simply. "The world will be made better by your spell. The clan will be ecstatic. You, a Henbane, bringing the spell to the clan would be the first step in bringing *all* the clans back together. It would be a way to ensure you and *I* can be together."

Amber saw the massive shape of her grandfather materialize out of the shadows just behind Neil. Amber wondered if her mother had kept her expression neutral. Amber would have fainted dead away.

In seconds, Miles had hold of Neil on either side of his head, his massive hands clapped over the boy's ears. Belle jumped back, pulling her grasp from Neil's. Neil howled, thrashing in Miles' grasp as Miles began an incantation. Amber could hardly make out the words, thanks to Neil's screaming fit.

The boy scratched at the older man's hands, kicked backward with his heels.

He sunk to a knee, still screaming while Miles held fast to his skull. Belle stood back, tears blurring her vision, hand pressed over her mouth.

Just as some of the fight seemed to go out of Neil, Miles was hurled off his feet. He hit the dirt path, rolling across it like a vehicle flipped in an accident.

"Dad!" Belle cried out, rushing over to him. She crouched beside his body and gave him a shake. She clearly sagged with relief when he groaned. Still alive.

Belle glanced up to see a man emerge from the darkness of the trees. "Mr. Gregory?"

The man checked on Neil. Satisfied the boy was still breathing, he stepped over his prone form and moved toward Belle, who was still crouched by her father.

Then, just as it had happened with Neil, Mr. Gregory's face melted away to reveal a black-haired man around her father's age underneath.

Belle stood. "You're his father."

He grinned. "Working at the Gas & Stop was a good cover, wasn't it?"

Before Belle could reply, Neil shrieked in pain, back arched as he writhed on the ground, hands clutching his head.

"What have you done to him?" the man snapped, pointing behind him without tearing his gaze away from Belle. "*Reverse it*, Henbane."

Miles got to his hands and knees, shaking his head like a dog, then unsteadily got to his feet. "He'll be fine, Penhallow.

Collect him and get out of Delin Springs and we'll pretend none of this happened." He stood beside Belle now.

Neil still screamed and thrashed in the tall weeds behind them.

The man tsked. "Not without the girl and her book."

"Absolutely not," Miles said, taking a step forward and placing a protective arm in front of Belle. She peered around him.

"There are more Penhallows here in Delin Springs, you know. You really think we trusted this mission to a twenty-year-old boy? And a lovesick one at that." He laughed. "Allow the girl to come willingly with us, and I can promise you that every Penhallow will leave with me. Neil will take good care of her. Once they know about the spell and that I have it—and its creator—with me, they'll follow me to the ends of the earth."

"So they don't know about the spell yet?" Belle asked.

Miles pushed her a little further behind him.

Neil howled in pain. The man hardly reacted.

"I'll be the first to admit that we're a volatile bunch," the man said. "It's not news to toss around lightly. But if you refuse to cooperate, well, I'll be forced to let all the little spies know, and then your life will be shredded to pieces. And then your bodies will follow. No stone will be left unturned until the book is in Penhallow hands."

"No," Belle snapped.

The older Penhallow's eyes narrowed to slits. "You want to do this the hard way, I see. I wonder what poor Ivy Henbane will think when a weeping Mr. Gregory comes to her door with the news that her daughter and husband suffered a horrible wild animal attack in the woods."

Without warning, he thrust his hands toward them. Amber saw the magic shoot from his hands like black tendrils. The polar opposite of the aimlessly wafting fog on the ground; this mist had a purpose.

Belle thrust out her own hand half a moment later and the entire scene froze, save for Belle and her father. The black mist, which almost looked like a clawed hand, had stopped mere inches from Miles' chest. He gasped and stumbled out of the path of it.

"Dad! Are you okay?" She scanned his face, and patted his chest, checking for anything bleeding or broken.

"I'm fine."

Whimpering, she threw her arms around his middle. "What are we going to do? They can't find the book." Without letting him go, she peered up at him. "Sara says it would be disastrous. Every foresight spell she's cast to show her what happens if they get the spell—"

Miles sighed, rubbing a hand up and down her back. "I know." He paused, then said, "What if we make *sure* he can't tell anyone?"

Slowly, Belle pulled away. "Dad, we can't. We'd be no better than them ..." she said, but her gaze was focused on the frozen Penhallow.

"He threatened your mother," he said. "Raphael would be on their list too. Your friends. Your friends' friends."

Belle blew out a long, audible breath. "How would we even do this?"

He stepped away from her to examine the thick thread of black mist. "If we place a protective shield at the right angle, we could make the magic ricochet and hit him. This," he said, motioning to the magic, "was meant to be a killing blow."

"We have to hurry," she said. "The spell won't hold long, and his fingers are starting to move." Amber watched as the pinky of one outstretched hand and the thumb of another gave a couple of faint twitches.

Belle and Miles worked quickly, determining the best place to erect the shield. They spoke as if they were planning the best way to make a creative shot in billiards, not the most effective way to kill a man.

At the same moment Miles cast the protection spell, Belle dropped the time freeze. The black mist slammed into the shield so hard, Miles was shoved back a few feet, the heels of his boots leaving gouges across the dirt path. The Penhallow's own magic careened into his body, his eyes going wide a mere millisecond before impact—registering what was about to happen before it actually did.

He gasped, then pitched backward into the tall weeds.

Neil's cry now was that of a wounded animal.

"What about Neil?" Belle asked, her voice shaky.

"Can you hold him still while I complete the job?"

Belle nodded.

When her father joined her, Belle dropped to her knees by Neil's side and pressed her hands to his shoulders. Miles took the spot by Neil's head, then quickly grabbed the boy's skull as he'd done earlier. Neil gave a few violent jerks, like a fish tossed onto the bottom of a boat, and then relaxed. By the time Miles had finished the spell, beads of sweat had formed on his forehead. He swiped his sleeve across his skin.

Seconds after Miles sat back, Neil began to stir. He sat up, looking nothing short of disoriented. "I feel ... very strange."

"This isn't something we decided to do on a whim, son," Miles said.

Neil scrambled onto his feet, moving away from the older man. He was several feet away before he spoke. "I'm not your *son*. I'm no one's son now, thanks to you."

Neil thrust out a hand. Nothing happened. He tried again and again. He brought his hand before his face, staring at it as if it had betrayed him.

"Those powers you had weren't yours," Miles said. "You stole them from Neil Winters just like you stole his identity. I know the void you feel must—"

"That's just *it*," Neil snapped. "There's no void. The desire for more power is gone."

Belle's attention whipped to her father. "Did you somehow break the curse?"

Miles looked bewildered. Shaking his head, he said, "I only severed his connection to the stolen magic."

"I think you did more than that, old man," Neil said, almost sounding wistful. "I think you cut me off from magic altogether. I can't even feel it anymore."

"Dad ..." Belle said slowly. "What did you do?"

Miles visibly swallowed.

Neil lunged for him, a battle cry tearing from his lips.

Belle threw a sleep spell at him, sending him crashing to the ground at Miles's feet. A cloud of dust rose in his wake. Moments later, he was snoring softly.

"Dad, this is bad," Belle said. "This is really, really bad.

We completely stripped one Penhallow of his magic, and oh by the way, we also *murdered* his father." She paced back and forth in a tight line as she ranted.

"Anna!" Miles snapped. "We don't have time for a meltdown. Plus, I didn't actually sever his connection to magic. I just needed him to believe that."

Belle abruptly stopped pacing. "What?"

"Halfway through, he was still fighting it too hard and I was wrung out," he said. "Instead, I buried his powers so far down, he *thinks* they're gone. And it sounds like it buried his obsessive drive, too. Best of both worlds. Now, come on. When he wakes up, we need to be gone. And by gone, I mean out of Delin Springs. We leave tonight."

Belle didn't respond right away, her attention shifting between Neil's sleeping form and his father's deceased one.

"Anna, let's go, hon. We don't have long before someone realizes what happened out here." He paused. "Anna?"

Belle turned to him. "I don't think I want to be called Anna anymore. A new life. A new name."

He thought about that for a moment. "What about Belle?"

Belle's vision swam with tears. "Perfect."

Then she hurried after her father, leaving the Penhallows abandoned in the dark.

CHAPTER 19

When the bright light faded, Amber was momentarily disoriented. Mostly because when the memory had started, she'd been sitting upright on a stool next to Willow. Now, she was flat on her back behind the counter of her shop.

Willow's face popped into view and Amber let out a strangled gasp. "Oh you're back! You scared the bejesus out of me!"

Amber pushed herself into a sitting position. "How'd I end up on the floor?"

"It was like you were talking in your sleep. Your eyes were closed but you kept saying really weird things, like you were reacting to a show only you could see?" Willow shrugged. "I guess maybe that's accurate."

Heat flooded her cheeks. "What did I say?"

"Hmm. One time you said, 'Neil *Winters*, not Neil Penhallow?' Another time you said, 'Look behind you!' You were silent and still for most of it, though sometimes you flailed your arms around. That was one of the longest fifteen minutes of my life. I kept wondering what would happen if you got stuck in the past or something. I am *not* equipped to handle that."

Amber smiled briefly.

"Did you see something helpful?"

She huffed a humorless laugh. "Let's go talk to Aunt Gretchen."

Ten minutes later, the three Blackwoods were in the same positions they were in the last time Amber recounted what she experienced during a relived memory. Willow and Aunt Gretchen sat at the end of Amber's bed, Tom hid underneath, and Alley watched from the window bench seat, where she was currently fastidiously cleaning the spaces between her back toes. Amber paced.

"I knew Belle had been involved with a Penhallow," Gretchen said. "I had no idea that she'd been duped into falling in love with one, though. Goodness. No wonder she never wanted to talk about it."

"Poor Mom," Willow said, hugging her arms close to her body.

"Even though I know what he did was wrong—not even counting the fire … I can't think about the fire," Amber said now, measuring her words carefully. "I somehow still felt bad for him in the moment. He really *did* love Mom. He really thought somehow it would work out. Then he lost his father *and* his powers that night. Anyone would crack under those circumstances. He just *really* went off the deep end."

"But … wait," Willow said. "So does that mean Neil found a way to unearth his powers again? Grandpa buried them, didn't he?"

Amber nodded. "Yep. So burying powers is only a temporary fix."

"If you want an old lady's opinion …" Aunt Gretchen said. "We need to get the grimoire from Edgar. The time travel spell is real, yes, but who knows what else is in there. It could help us with Kieran. Knowing Belle, a spell for severing powers from a witch would be in that book. Either one she'd learned from her father well before all this Neil business happened, or one she crafted after the fact as a backup plan, should Neil's powers ever return."

Amber knew, since her magic seemed to take after her mother's more than her father's, that if they were to get hold of such a spell, she'd have to be the one to do it. Her stomach gave a lurch. "How are we supposed to get the book from him? Not even *he* knows where it is. We have five days before Kieran starts targeting innocent people."

"We can assume the witch who attempted to poison me was also Kieran, yes?" Aunt Gretchen said. "I've only just started to feel better, but I haven't left the building that much. What if I were to have a relapse and we all really play up how sickly I am. I won't come down to help in the shop in the morning, so if Kieran is wandering outside the store, he won't see me. Then sometime during the day, one of you can take me to see a doctor. We can make him think I'm truly ill."

"You're not really going to take more of that stuff, are you?" Willow asked.

"No, dear, it'll all be for show," said Gretchen, seeming to warm more and more to her own idea. "The following day, before we come down to the shop in the morning, Willow can glamour me to look like Amber, and then Amber can find a way to sneak out and get to Edgar's."

"Should I be worried about how fast you came up with that?" Amber asked.

270

"It's been cooking for a while," Gretchen said with a laugh. "That'll teach him to mess with a woman's bava leaves …"

Amber snorted.

"How is Amber going to get out, though?" Willow asked. "She can't sneak out a second-story window. How will we know he's watching us and not tailing Amber?"

Aunt Gretchen deflated a little. "I hadn't gotten that far …"

But Amber's mind had taken off at a gallop. "Wait. I have an idea. Okay, remember how I said Neil claimed he was able to track down Aunt Kathleen, and then Mom, because Kathleen had been using more magic than ideal? He tracked her using her signature."

They nodded.

"Okay, at the end of shift, Willow can glamour me to look like a customer and I can stroll on out of here with the others. Then, once the Quirky Whisker is closed for the night, what if you two use your magic to lure him to the shop. Maybe a ton of healing spells? You two can talk to him while keeping the wards up—maybe using that box of cats again? Oh, what if we magic them to look like Valentine's cats rather than Christmas ones so he's not suspicious about why they're out again? Once he's here, Willow can text me that he's preoccupied, and I'll book it to Edgar's house."

"I tried calling him all day and the phone just rings and rings …" Willow said. "I even sent him a really cryptic letter! I bought stamps and everything."

"I've tried quite a few times on my cell too," Aunt Gretchen said. "Nothing."

Amber hoped he was just ignoring them and not that

Kieran had already paid the poor man a visit. "Any objections to the plan?"

"I would just like to state for the record," Willow said, "that I think it's *highly* suspicious Aunt Gretchen's plan looks a lot like a ploy to get herself out of dealing with the exhausting tourists."

"It's a sacrifice I'm willing to make." Aunt Gretchen grinned. "And now I can catch up on my soaps."

Amber laughed.

The following day, during her lunch break—which was sorely needed without Aunt Gretchen helping them in the shop— Amber called Jack.

He answered almost immediately. "Hey, Amber! How are you doing? Any better? Was it a concussion?"

A concussion? Then she remembered the fashion show and Fake Olaf and her tumble over a set of chairs.

"A minor one, yeah," she said. "But I feel a lot better. Trying to rest as much as I can."

"Good, good," he said. "Cool, cool."

"So … about that rain check. How do you feel about an early dinner tomorrow?"

"I would love that," Jack said.

Amber felt a little guilty that she was using Jack as a way to be out of the studio tomorrow night, but she really *did* want to see him. She felt awful for running out on him the night of the fashion show without saying much. But it had been a … very weird night. The last she'd heard, the chief and the mayor were calling it a freak insect attack. Within hours of Kieran's assault, the starburst marks on people had gone from a black scorch with tendrils of black snaking out of them, to large red welts surrounded by fairly significant bruising.

Amber wondered if Kieran was behind that, or if that had been a natural progression of the marks' healing when only a "half dose" of magic was used. The starburst marks would have been much harder to explain away. No video—not even from cell phones—from the chaotic night had been aired or shown up online, though the Channel 4 news team had brought up the fashion show often. Amber wondered if Kieran had something to do with the lack of footage too.

The Edgehill Community Center had been closed since the evening of the "infestation" and an intense round of fumigation had started yesterday.

Amber was sure it was only a matter of time before the question of "Where were you the night of the exotic insect attack?" became part of Edgehill's commonly discussed history.

Amber and Jack settled on Mews and Brews. Knocking back a couple of Cat Scratch beers before her attempt to get the Henbane grimoire from Edgar sounded not only enjoyable, but vital. After she, her sister, and her aunt had come up with their plan, Amber had been unable to sleep.

When she got off the phone with a very jazzed-sounding Jack, she yawned deeply, then made herself yet another cup of green tea.

Amber was lucky Willow was as skilled with illusion spells as she was, because she was able to stroll out of the shop at six without anyone being the wiser. The number of things that could go wrong with their overall plan seemed too numerous to count, so Amber did her best not to think about them. She needed to focus on her part of it: wait for Willow's text, then haul tail to her cousin's house and hope he let her in.

In the meantime, she would enjoy her time with Jack.

Mews and Brews was a ten-minute walk from the Quirky Whisker. She tried to enjoy the stroll.

Last night, Amber had rushed an "ill" Aunt Gretchen to the doctor. Willow had met them there a couple of hours later. When they left, Willow had helped both her aunt and a tearful Amber into her car, leaving Amber's in the hospital's parking lot overnight. Amber had been impressed with her own acting skills and hoped Kieran had been watching in smug satisfaction that he'd indirectly made Aunt Gretchen so ill, and not in suspicion that the Blackwood women were up to something.

The restaurant was half cozy sit-down, and half bar—the two separated by a glass wall. They had both the best burgers and best beer in town. Amber walked into the sit-down section, then asked the girl at the maître d' podium if she could use the restroom. The front entrance was so crowded with people, the waitress hardly glanced her way as she pointed out the direction of the bathroom.

Amber slipped inside, grateful only one of the two stalls was currently occupied. She pretended to take care of business, then stood in front of one of the sinks, pretending to look for something in her purse. She'd caught a brief glimpse of herself in the mirror and had been fully creeped out that the face looking back at her wasn't her own, so she kept her gaze averted. She'd seen enough, though, to know the illusion Willow had put on her was fading. The false face had blue eyes when Amber left the Quirky Whisker, but now they were back to her usual brown. The ends of her falsely blond hair were turning brown too.

The woman in the stall finally came out and washed her hands. Then she touched up her lipstick. And fluffed her hair.

Meanwhile, the beauty spot on Amber's right cheekbone had just vanished.

Get out, lady! Get out!

The woman must have sensed Amber staring at her, because she glanced over then. Amber tried to smile at her, but it was more like a grimace.

The woman offered her own fake smile, threw the paper towel she'd been holding into the trash and said, "Have a nice night" before sauntering out.

When the door finally closed, Amber flipped the lock on the inside of the door. No sooner had she done so, someone tried to get in.

Hurrying back to the sink, Amber turned on the tap. Willow had told her that the best way to knock an illusion loose was a shock to the system. Amber let water pool in her cupped hands, then cast a quick incantation to turn the water ice cold. Aside from sleep spells, the ability to drastically alter the temperature of water had been a favorite pastime when Amber and Willow were kids. Especially when one sister was taking a shower and the other was annoyed that her favorite shoes were missing.

Amber splashed two handfuls of freezing cold water on her face now, wincing and cursing as she did. Goosebumps broke out on her arms. When she glanced in the mirror, her face was back. How had Neil spent *years* wearing someone else's face?

A fist pounded on the door.

Amber hurried over to unlock it. "I'm so sorry! I must have locked it on instinct."

It was the same lady who had been in the bathroom with her a minute ago. She did a double take. "I ... uh ... think I left my phone in here."

Amber stepped aside as if she were granting someone entrance to her home. This lady must have thought she was more than a little screwy.

As the woman crept past her and into the stall she'd been in earlier, Amber dabbed her face with paper towels. Thanks to another of Willow's no-smudge spells, Amber's makeup hadn't been affected by the ice bath.

Phone in hand, the woman came back into view behind Amber. "I heard you lock the door the second I left. There was another woman in here, wasn't there?"

Amber shrugged. "Nope, just me."

The woman's brow furrowed. "Hmm." Then she left without another word.

Shaking the encounter off, she fished her phone out of her bag. Jack had sent her text a minute ago, and said he was on the restaurant side at a table.

Amber found him poring over the menu when she slipped into the chair across from him.

He started. "Oh, hey."

"Hey." She pulled her cell out of her purse and placed it on the table. She tapped the screen so she could quickly see if she'd received any text notifications between leaving the restroom and arriving at the table. An unobstructed picture of a sleeping Tom and Alley filled the screen.

When she looked up and he smiled at her like she was the greatest thing he'd ever seen—and not like a witch who confused innocent people in bathrooms—her stomach gave a little flip. She had no time for stomach flips tonight, so she quickly snatched up her menu to give herself something else to focus on.

Nearly everything on the Mews and Brews' menu was both cat and movie-themed. Much of the artwork on the walls were posters from classic movies but starring cats. They were all hand drawn by the owner's son.

Amber ordered the Catsablanca burger, which was smothered in white cheddar cheese, and Jack decided on the Merry Pawpins. His could also be called "everything but the kitchen sink," because nearly every burger fixing one could think of was on that thing.

"Ambitious," Amber said.

He grinned at her.

She really wanted a Cat Scratch beer or seven, but if she was going to have to bolt out of here in a hurry, she supposed she'd need all her faculties in order.

While they discussed the various odds and ends of their

day—mostly seeing who could top who in Today's Most Annoying Customer category—Amber knew it was only a matter of time before he asked her about her head injury and what she thought had happened during the fashion show. It found its way into most people's conversations one way or another.

It took him until they were halfway through their dinner for him to broach the subject. "So how are you feeling? You know ... with the whole ..." He gestured vaguely at his skull.

"Better. I think most of it was the shock of the fall. It happened so quickly."

He paused for a moment, then took a long sip of water. "Were you ... did you see someone there you knew? I mean—" He chewed his lip. "It seemed like everyone was trying to run out of the auditorium, yet you were running *toward* something. Or some*one*. And then I could have sworn I heard the chief ask 'Where is he?'"

Crap. Jack was more observant than she gave him credit for. Stalling for an answer, she quickly tapped her phone screen. Still no messages.

He must have taken her phone-check as a sign that she was uncomfortable with his line of questioning, because he said, "I'm not trying to be nosy or anything." He scratched the back of his neck, then leaned toward her a bit, looking more conspiratorial than suspicious. "It's just that the insect story is a little weird, isn't it? No one heard buzzing. No one saw anything flying around. I hear a lot of gossip at Purrcolate and no one is really buying the crap the chief and the mayor are dishing out."

Amber's heart rate ticked up from a slow stroll to a light jog. Was he merely curious or was he accusing her of something?

"Connor Declan said he's been interviewing a lot of the staff about that night and none of them buy the insect story either."

"I didn't know you and Connor were friends."

"We're not. Not really … he just stopped by Purrcolate to ask me some questions since we provided the refreshments. Wanted to know if I'd noticed anything weird that day."

She tapped her phone again. It felt like a nervous tic now. A tic that likely made her look both rude and potentially flighty.

But then her paranoid mind started to whir. What if Willow hadn't texted yet because they'd been unable to get Kieran to show up? What if the man sitting in front of her asking all these questions *was* Kieran?

After mentally uttering the truth spell, she asked, "What do you think happened during the attack at the fashion show, Jack Terrence?"

Robotically, he said, "I don't know. But I think you and the chief know more than you're letting on."

Amber's magic retreated.

Jack's face flushed bright red. "Oh man. I didn't mean to actually say that. I don't think you're guilty of anything. The whole thing just seems strange and I could have sworn the chief hated you a month ago and then this incredibly strange thing happens and you both seem to know what's going on when no one else does and—"

"Jack," she said, and he quickly shut his mouth. She could work with this. She just needed to soothe his anxiety. She realized she truly *did* like Jack; she wasn't ready to scare him off yet. "You know how that maid, Wilma, was killed at the Manx?"

He nodded, brows creased, clearly unsure of why the conversation was now headed in *this* direction.

"The chief and I both think whoever did it had meant to harm my aunt, but Wilma was in the wrong place at the wrong time. My aunt mentioned an odd man loitering in the hallways at the Manx, so we've been keeping an eye out for him based on my aunt's description of him. I thought I saw him at the fashion show. It was totally unrelated to the attack there; an unfortunate coincidence that I spotted him during the chaos. I saw the guy and just took off running. I wasn't really thinking it through."

Jack winced, frowning slightly. It looked like he was currently mentally kicking himself in the butt. "I'm such a jerk."

"No, not at all," she said. "I totally get why you thought it was all related. And it was such a weird night."

"I shouldn't have jumped to conclusions." His face flamed again. "Was it the guy, by the way? The one who attacked Wilma?"

Amber shook her head. "Wasn't him."

She wondered where Kieran was now. She tapped her phone.

"Does the chief really think the guy is still in town?"

"Hard to say." She focused on Jack again, willing herself to keep her hands away from her phone screen. "But as long as my aunt is in town, there's reason to believe he might still come after her. The chief says we can't be too careful."

Jack nodded absently at that. "Any idea why someone would want to hurt her?"

"Nope. Which makes it even scarier."

Their food arrived and Amber was grateful for the momentary distraction. Mostly because she felt terrible about lying to Jack, but it was better this way, wasn't it? If she kept him in the dark, the truth couldn't hurt either one of them.

But she wasn't sure she even believed herself anymore.

Jack had somehow managed to plow through his Merry Pawpins without covering the front of his shirt in sauce. Once the waitress had cleared their plates and brought them a dessert menu, Jack reached a hand across the table, palm up. She placed a hand in his. "I'm sorry this turned into an interrogation. I was just worried."

"I know," she said. "I appreciate it. You're very sweet."

He smiled at that. "Speaking of sweet. I believe you still owe me a raincheck on dessert. Have you ever had the Sundae Meowtain?"

"I have not."

"There's an option to add a tuxedo or brindle brownie. I suggest the brindle—chocolate and caramel."

"Sold!"

After finishing the decidedly delicious Brindle Brownie Sundae Meowtain, they left the restaurant. Amber's nerves were starting to get to her, worried something had gone wrong back at the shop.

Be patient.

"Where are you parked?" he asked as they slowly walked

down the sidewalk, each with their hands stuffed into the pockets of their zipped-up jackets.

"My car's actually still in the lot at the hospital."

He quirked a brow at her.

"My aunt got sick last night, so I had to rush her over there. She's fine," she added quickly when she noticed Jack's stricken expression. "Turned out just to be a bad stomach bug."

"It's too cold for you to walk back to your place," he said. "I'll drive you over to get your car."

"That would be great."

The smile he angled at her made her stomach twist even further with guilt.

The car ride from Mews and Brews to Edgehill General took about fifteen minutes. She'd only checked her phone twice in that time span, which she thought was commendable.

That was, until Jack said as they idled at a light a block away from the hospital, "Is everything okay? You expecting an important call? From the doctor, maybe?"

Amber realized then it had actually been *three* times in fifteen minutes and she dropped her phone into her purse as she mentally chastised herself for being the world's rudest date. "The chief said he might have a lead on Wilma's attacker. He said he'd call if he heard anything."

Lies upon lies upon lies.

Making things up on the spot was growing easier for her. This was why she stayed locked away in her shop and studio. It was easier to have secrets when you didn't have anyone to keep them from.

Amber directed him to where her car still sat. He put the

car in park, and turned slightly to face her. "So I was wondering if—"

Amber's phone buzzed loudly twice in rapid succession. She flinched. "Sorry!" Fumbling in her purse, she pulled out her cell.

He's here.

Go.

"Oh crap."

"You okay?"

"I … uhh …" Amber swallowed. "Yeah. Yes, I'm good. Sorry, but I need to go. It's my … it's my aunt again."

Amber's hands shook as she scrambled for the door handle to let herself out.

Jack was there seconds later, staring at her with confusion and worry lining his forehead.

"I had a great time," she told him. "Sorry I've been so distracted. Just family stuff, you know?"

"Yeah," he said, nodding. "Of course. I hope she's all right."

She gave him a quick hug goodbye, then unlocked her car. "I'm sure she will be."

Her phone buzzed again and she winced. Her heart hammered in her chest. "Have a good night, Jack."

Seconds later, she zipped out of the parking lot.

CHAPTER 20

At the stop light, Amber glanced at her phone to check her last text. It was from Willow.

Have you left yet?

Amber quickly fired back: On my way.

She wanted to call Willow and get details on what was happening back at the shop, but she figured Willow was sending texts as discreetly as possible. They had to keep Kieran distracted.

Just then, the mental alarm connected to the wards on the Quirky Whisker went off in her head. Kieran was getting restless already. Amber pressed down harder on the accelerator.

The long stretches of back roads heading to Edgar's place were deserted. With no street lights, Amber was sure she was going to miss Edgar's road in the waning light, as it was hard to locate even in the middle of the day. But a lone rectangle of light appeared in her peripheral vision near the area where she thought his street might have been, guiding her like a beacon to where she needed to go.

She made a slow turn onto the dirt path, the slap of branches and leaves against her car even creepier in the growing dark. Thankfully she could still see well enough. Driving this in total darkness would have completely done in her nerves.

Her car bounced and the beams of her headlights jerked wildly as she did her best to get to Edgar's house without the wheels falling off. The one small rectangle of light on the top floor was the only sign of life. She'd called him a couple more times, but he still wasn't answering.

Climbing out of the car, she eyed his old, rusted pickup truck, and remembered the memory she'd seen of it idling at the curb outside 543 Ocicat Lane. It, like its owner, had seen better days.

Before she could convince herself not to, she hustled up the creaky front steps, across the weather-worn patio, and slammed a fist repeatedly against the door. "Edgar! It's Amber. Let me in!"

She waited for him to call out obscenities from an open window upstairs, to hear the pounding of footsteps down steps, or the sharp *shlock* of bolts sliding free. But it was silent.

She pounded on the door again. "I'm not going away, Edgar! I know what my parents gave you fourteen years ago to keep safe. We have to find it. The whole town is in danger otherwise."

Nothing.

She let out a groan of frustration, head tipped back toward the spiderwebs clinging to the wooden porch's ceiling. Then she remembered what had gotten him to open the door last time.

"There's a Penhallow in town and he's already killed someone. He's going to kill others, Edgar! He's going to do the same thing to them as Neil Penhallow did to you. The starburst mark on your back? The same mark was found on Wilma. That's what killed her."

Amber bit her bottom lip. Her next plan was to hurl rocks through the windows, so she really hoped he didn't make her resort to that. Her throwing arm wasn't great, and who knew what would happen if she threw a rock at one of Edgar's heavily warded windows. She imagined the rock bouncing back as if hitting rubber, then knocking out all her teeth.

Schlock, schlock, schlock.

Amber flinched.

Seconds later, a disheveled Edgar peered out at her. He didn't look much different than the last time she'd seen him. She hoped he was at least taking regular showers.

"You Blackwoods are persistent witches …"

"Hello to you too, cousin," she said in her most cheerful tone.

His gaze flicked over her shoulder and he scowled. "Is that your sister? I'm not sure I can deal with two of you right now."

Amber whirled around and made her way across the porch, the boards protesting loudly. Sure enough, a car with its headlights cutting through the dark was bouncing its way up the drive. She'd been so busy yelling at Edgar, she hadn't heard the car approach. Nor had she seen anyone following her. Her heart thundered; if Willow was here, something had gone very wrong.

But as the car moved up the drive, the surer she became that it *wasn't* Willow. Could Kieran have found them? She could feel Edgar standing right behind her now. Whether he planned to shove her in Kieran's direction as a distraction so he could bolt inside to safety, or he planned to be a united front with her against the cursed witch, Amber couldn't be sure.

Her hands tingled as she funneled her agitated magic toward her fingertips, ready to blast Kieran with a sleep spell if he was the one who got out of the car.

It was to her great surprise, relief, and general annoyance that the person who emerged from the car now parked beside hers was Jack.

The wards on her shop gave another sharp rattle. Amber winced. But at least that meant Kieran was at the shop and this Jack was the real one.

Her magic needed an outlet. Her nerves couldn't take much more of this. She should blast Jack with the cued-up sleep spell if only to make sure nothing happened to him.

"Jack Terrence! What are you doing here?" A truth spell hadn't come with the question this time, but she hoped he'd answer truthfully anyway.

Jack stomped up the steps and halfway across the porch, hardly looking her way. He jammed a finger toward Edgar's face. "Why are you harassing her? She was anxious all night. I don't know if this is connected to her aunt, but you need to back off, buddy!"

"Jack, I—"

"And *you*!" He whirled to face her and she came up short. "I had a box of pastries in my car I forgot to give you, so I followed you back to your place so you could give them to your *sick aunt*. Well imagine my surprise when you didn't even head in the direction of your place! You ended up in the middle of nowhere. Is this who you saw during the fashion show? Is he the supposed lead the chief told you about? Is *he* the reason why you ended up with a concussion? Is this some abusive ex you're scared to say no to? Is this where you got those bruises all over your arms and hands?"

Good gracious. She'd somehow broken the mild-mannered guy.

"Jack—"

"I don't even know what to think anymore. I really don't. There have always been wild rumors about you, but I just figured you were shy. I don't know. Maybe this crush has clouded my mind," he said, now seeming to talk to himself more than her. "Maybe this is your bad boy boyfriend who's all rugged and dangerous and you're bored with 'sweet' Jack Terrence."

It was pitch-black out in Edgar's yard now. Amber stared out at it, wondering what she could possibly tell Jack to calm him down. It wasn't like the truth was any better.

"Can you take your domestic squabble off my porch?" Edgar asked, turning on his heel and heading back inside.

She'd almost forgotten. "Edgar, no. I need the grimoire." Then she winced.

"Grimoire?" Jack asked from behind her. "Like … a spell book?" He laughed incredulously. "Are you a witch, Amber Blackwood? Is that the story you're going to go with next? It's a new one at least. I'll give you that."

Amber was just about to say something else when her phone buzzed in her purse. She fished it out.

"What is it with you and that phone!" Jack snapped.

She ignored him. He was in full meltdown mode now and she wasn't sure how to get him out.

It was a text from Willow. He's getting antsy. Don't know how much longer we can keep him here.

Crap.

"Oh, now I see," said Edgar, resting a shoulder against the doorjamb of his open door, arms crossed. "Lover boy here doesn't know your little secret and he's trying to figure out why so many weird things happen around you—and now he's losing his cookies. I've seen it happen before."

Amber turned to glare at him.

"Lose your cookies somewhere else!" Edgar said, pushing away from the jamb and grabbing the door as if to close it.

Without thinking, Amber thrust out her hands. Her magic had been boiling under her skin like a volcano about to blow. She'd just reacted. High emotion and magic were rarely a good combination—especially for her. A gust of wind knocked Edgar clear off his feet and sent him skidding into the dark entryway of his house and out of sight. She heard his cursing well enough, though.

But now Jack was cursing too. "Oh. Oh my God. You *are* a witch? That wasn't a joke?"

Amber squeezed her eyes shut for a moment, then turned around. She stared at him.

The longer the stare lasted, the more he began to wilt under her gaze, as if he were worried she was using her magic to liquify all his organs.

"Amber?" he asked, somewhat shakily.

Something in her snapped. "*Yes!* Okay? That's the big secret. Happy now? I'm a witch, my sister's a witch, my aunt is a witch. Even the foul-mouthed man in the house who is *in desperate need of a shower* is a witch. A rogue witch killed the maid at the Manx. The rogue witch is related to the man who killed my parents—who were also witches—and now wants my mother's grimoire, which has a very powerful spell in it that could rewrite history as we know it if the witch gets a hold of it. Edgar, my very stubborn *cousin*, has been keeping the book hidden for fourteen years even though it's *mine and my sister's*. He claims he doesn't know where it is even though my parents *gave* it to him. It's very possible the rogue witch is on his way here now. We won't have the first clue how to stop him from killing us the same way his brother killed my parents because Edgar. Won't. Cooperate!"

Her chest rose and fell. But just as quickly as her anger and frustration had fueled her rant, it was retreating now, and embarrassment was taking its place.

Edgar had gotten back to his feet during her tirade and was in the doorway again. "Fine," he snapped. "Get in here. You too, lover boy. Unless you want to get incinerated on my porch when the cursed witch shows up."

Amber watched Jack and waited for him to make a decision. She expected him to scream bloody murder and bolt for his car. Instead, he huffed out a breath and stalked into the house.

Once they were inside and the door was closed, Edgar turned into a conductor of lock and protection spells again. Jack watched in slack-jawed amazement as bolts and keys slid into place and turned on their own. Then Edgar conducted a few more elaborate hand motions and the house gave a shudder. Then another.

Jack rocked on his feet a bit, hands out, as if he were on a surfboard and the water had just gotten choppy. "What the hell was that?"

"I just reactivated the cloaking spell on the house," he said. "No one finds me unless I want them to." Then he glanced at Amber. "Almost. Can't seem to keep family out, no matter what I do."

"Love you too, cousin."

With a flick of his wrist, three wall sconces in the front entryway came to life. Jack flinched. Edgar wore ratty sweatpants and a stained gray shirt again. His hair was a wild mess of black curls and he was well past the stage of keeping his facial hair in any sort of order.

"Don't look at me like that," Edgar said to Amber. "I'm fine. And, for the record, this isn't me not cooperating or being stubborn. I really don't have any damn clue where the damn thing is. I don't. All I know is that they gave it to me. I have this … compulsion to stay here. My gut tells me that I can't leave the house for very long because if I do, someone will find the book. I'm stuck here."

Amber's brow furrowed. "My parents *trapped* you here?"

He shook his head. "No, not them. Best I can figure out, they put a spell on me to forget the location of the book. To forget about it completely. But when I was attacked, things got all scrambled up here." He tapped his temple. "His name was Neil?"

Amber nodded. "At least I assume it was him."

"I can't even remember the attack," he said, the edge to his tone gone. "I just know it happened."

"Do you still have the mark?"

"Yeah," he said, idly scratching at his side with one hand.

Amber wondered why, after fourteen years, his mark still lingered. Wondered why being hit with the magic had killed Wilma and not Edgar. "Can I see it?" she asked cautiously.

He dropped his hand. He crossed his arms, uncrossed them, crossed them again. Then, without a word, he turned around.

Amber shot a quick look at Jack, more or less to make sure he hadn't fainted yet. He stood wide-eyed a few feet from her. She wasn't sure he'd moved much in the last five minutes. Or blinked.

Amber turned back to Edgar and carefully lifted up the hem of his shirt until his shoulder blades were exposed. She let out a soft gasp.

Suddenly Jack was beside her. "Geez! Is that … that's what those supposed bites looked like from the attack at the fashion show."

Except this appeared to be infected. The black snaking lines looked like the thick branches of an elaborate tree tattoo that covered nearly his entire back. But instead of a trunk as a base from which the branches originated, it was a two-inch-wide scorch mark in the center of his back, right over his spine.

Amber reached out tentatively with the hand that wasn't grasping the hem of his shirt. She touched a finger to one of the thick lines closer to the middle of the mark. He slightly jerked away from her touch, but she figured it was due more to surprise than pain. The skin wasn't at all upraised like a welt or brand. "Does it hurt?" she asked softly.

"No," came the choked reply.

What happened to you?

Her fingertips drifted to the starburst mark, and she touched the eye of it. She imagined the tendrils of black hitting his spine. It must have hurt then. Had he writhed in agony on the ground as Neil had in the grass while his father was more concerned about the whereabouts of the grimoire?

Who did this to you, Edgar?

And then a burst of bright white tore through her vision.

When the light faded, Amber was standing on the sidewalk outside 543 Ocicat Lane. The front door was closed, her parents inside. Were they already running up the stairs to pack? A few seconds later, Edgar was behind the wheel of his still-idling pickup truck.

Some alternative rock song she hadn't heard since high school played softly on the radio as he made a U-turn in the cul-de-sac and then drove away.

The grimoire sat on the passenger seat, sliding a little here and there on the faded blue fabric when he turned. He cut glances at it periodically, the word HENBANE staring up at him from the thick leather cover.

Once he got home, he grabbed the book and got out of the truck. But almost immediately, he froze in place, his gaze focused straight ahead. Amber wished she could hear the thoughts of her hosts as she watched their memories, but she was learning she was merely a passenger along for the ride.

"Yes, I understand," he suddenly said to no one. "Yes, I understand."

Then, for what seemed like several hours, Edgar was hard at work. He got a large trunk out of the house, put the grimoire inside, dug a huge hole on the side of the house, dropped the trunk into the hole, and then dragged debris to sit on top of it. Old farm equipment, broken tools, and other rundown items were added to the pile. As soon as he was done, a bright burst of yellow light pulsed from the spot under the debris and then faded.

Edgar swayed a bit and put a hand to his head. "How did I get … where … when did I …"

Amber knew then that Belle had layered a memory-wipe spell on top of everything else. To ensure, Amber supposed, that then even Edgar would forget where the book was hidden. Just as he suspected.

He truly hadn't been lying when he said he had no clue where the book was.

Edgar paced back and forth along the wooden porch that wasn't nearly so creaky then as it was now. "Something is wrong. Something is wrong."

Then he gasped and dropped to one knee, grabbing a fistful of his own shirt, near his heart. "Aunt Belle," he groaned. "Uncle Theo."

And then he was running so fast he almost hit the ground again, scrambling as he was to get his feet underneath him. He started the pickup once more and peeled out into the night, racing back, Amber knew, to Ocicat Lane.

But the house was already on fire by the time Edgar came to a screeching stop out front. He flung himself out of the car, leaving the driver's side door open in his haste, and thrust his fingers into his hair, staring in horror at the jumping blue flames. He called his aunt and uncle's names, but there was no sound save for the crackle of fire and the splitting of wood and the bending of metal that got too hot and then collapsed in on itself. The one time he tried running up the front porch steps, the fire had reared up like a wild horse, nudging him back.

Tears blurred his vision.

"Tragedy, isn't it?" someone asked from behind him.

Edgar whirled around to find Neil Penhallow—though Edgar didn't know his name yet—leaned against the passenger-side door of Edgar's truck, feet crossed at the ankles, and hands in his pockets. Edgar frantically looked up and down the street.

Had any of the neighbors called the fire department? Amber didn't hear the scream of sirens in the distance. Not yet.

"Where is everyone?" Edgar asked, his voice hitching. "Oh God. Poor Amber and Willow." Edgar sunk to his knees on the sidewalk, clutching at his chest.

Neil appeared in Edgar's view again, shoes first. Edgar pulled himself together enough to start a slow scan of the man, but Neil soon dropped into a squat before him. The man leaned in and gave Edgar's shirt an intense sniff—on a spot by his right shoulder. Edgar appeared to be too shocked to even react to this.

Neil sat back on his haunches. "She gave *you* the real one. Why you, I wonder. I can smell it all over you, boy."

"Wh-what?"

"Where is the grimoire, little witch? It's your fault I had to resort to arson, you know. If you had told me you had the book, I wouldn't have had to kill them." Anger and grief flashed across Neil's face.

Edgar scuttled backward like a crab until his back hit one of his tires. He yelped. "*You* did this?"

"Yes, I've already told you as much," he said. "Where is the book? Her hold on it was supposed to be severed when she died, but I can't sense it now. It's not *here*."

"Who cares about the book!" Edgar said, voice shrill. "Where are all the neighbors? Did anyone call the fire department?"

"Oh, I cast a sleeping spell on the whole street," Neil said. "Had to be sure no one intervened. That no one saw what they shouldn't. I'll plant a few memories in their heads later so they *think* they saw the fire. And I promise to take care of all that once I get what I came here for."

"I don't know where the book is," Edgar choked out, knees pulled to his chest now. He rocked slowly back and forth.

Neil sighed. "Oh, do stop your sniveling. They really don't make witches like they used to. Just tell me where it is, and I'll be out of your hair."

"I don't *know!*" Edgar snapped, his tears drying in an instant. "Annabelle made sure I wouldn't remember. If it's anywhere, it's up here." He angrily jabbed at his temple. "But not even I have the key."

Neil reached out, quick as a snake, and grabbed Edgar's skull, just as Miles had done to Neil decades before. Edgar cried out and thrashed while Neil's forehead scrunched in concentration.

Then Neil snarled, shoving Edgar so forcefully that he

tipped over, and then stood to full height. He turned around to glare at the burning house. "Leave it to Anna to screw me over even in death."

Another choked sound came out of Edgar as he pushed himself back to a seated position.

"Get out of here, you useless wretch," Neil said. "Call the fire department too if it'll make you feel better. They're gone, though. Nothing anyone can do about it now." When Edgar had yet to move, Neil whirled to face him; Edgar's back was pressed against one of his truck's tires again. "Go before I change my mind, Henbane!"

Edgar scrambled to his feet. He had just rounded the front of the truck when he was shoved. He yelped, arms thrown up to break his fall as he crashed to the asphalt. Amber saw snatches of things then. The grill of his truck, the unscathed houses across the street, the dancing flames. She realized then that this was the moment Neil had hit Edgar with his magic—when Edgar had his back turned.

His thrashing stopped abruptly when Neil's face swam into view. The cursed witch had Edgar's jaw clasped in his hand. "I could have hit you with a force strong enough to kill you, but I showed restraint. Why? Because a dose of cursed magic will slowly eat away at your mind. It will open you up, will reveal secrets you keep even from yourself. And when my magic unlocks the place where the book is hidden, you and I will find it together."

Edgar could only whimper in response.

"Run on home now," he said, focus returned to the house. Edgar watched as Neil dug his hands into his hair. He tore at it. Then Neil started to scream. A sorrowful, angry, pained scream. He shouted Anna's name over and over. He pleaded with her to forgive him, then in the next breath, said she brought this on herself.

Edgar drove away as fast as he could, but the unhinged Penhallow didn't seem to notice. Even after Edgar was blocks away, he could still hear the witch howling his grief at the night sky.

CHAPTER 21

When Amber came to, she was, unfortunately, flat on her back again, looking up at a ceiling. Had she fainted?

Once the two men on either side of her noticed she was awake, they talked at the same time.

"Oh my God. Amber? Are you okay?" from a worried-sounding Jack, and "What did you see?" in a clipped, flat tone from Edgar.

Perhaps he was annoyed she knew pieces of his past that were hidden from him, or perhaps he was upset that her magic had weaseled its way into his mind without permission.

Amber pushed herself to sitting, trying not to think about how utterly disgusting Edgar's floors likely were. "I know where the book is."

Edgar immediately squatted in front of her, his brown eyes wide. "Really?"

"It's not actually *in* the house."

Edgar's slightly bushy brows pulled together. "I've been warding the house all this time for no reason? Is it safe? Did I—"

"It's still on the property. Right next to the house," she said quickly. "Your wards have worked. Kieran doesn't even know *you're* here, let alone the book. He followed the traces of the grimoire to Edgehill, but he can't tell where they're coming from."

He nodded slowly at that. "I think the cloak on the book is fading. That's why he's here. I don't know how long your parents wanted it to be hidden, but that thing has been cloaked for over a decade and the Penhallows are only recently crawling out of the woodwork. Your parents were really, really powerful to be able to craft a spell that held even after they died."

Amber knew they'd wanted her to have it by the time she turned eighteen—a dozen years ago—but she didn't want to tell him that now and make him feel even worse. As it was, even if she'd known at that age about the grimoire, she wouldn't have had the first clue how to go about finding it.

"So you know where it is?" Edgar asked, redirecting her attention. "What do we need?"

"A shovel and lanterns."

A few minutes later, Edgar let them out of the house. They each held a battery-powered lantern, and Edgar had the shovel. Amber led them to the place she'd seen in Edgar's memory. When they reached it, Edgar cast a spell to keep the three lanterns floating in midair so they had better light and free hands.

Jack's mouth had hung open as the lantern he'd held rose on its own out of his hand and then hovered above his head. Somehow *that* was the display of magic that got to him. "I think I liked it better when I had no idea what was going on," he muttered, staring at the lantern.

Amber involuntarily slumped a little at that. Jack wouldn't be able to handle this any better than Max had. She wasn't sure why she was surprised.

She'd have to deal with that later. She just needed him to keep it together until they got rid of Kieran. Assuming they could even figure out how to do that.

The spot in question was piled even higher with debris and odds and ends now than it had been in the memory. Among the flotsam was a rusty bike, a pair of broken lawn chairs, piles of rotted wood, and a literal kitchen sink. The shovel now rested patiently against the side of the house.

"This ended up being the place I threw all the stuff over the years that I needed to haul to the dump," Edgar said, staring at the rather daunting mound on the side of his house. "Guess I never got around to it."

"Can't you just … magically move all of it?" Jack's skin looked pale in the bluish glow from the lanterns.

"We can do that for the heavier stuff, but the more we use our magic, the more chance we run of Kieran sensing it," Amber said. "And if he can sense it, he can track it."

"And Kieran is the one who wants to rewrite history and incinerate people?" asked Jack.

"That's the one," Edgar said.

"Fantastic," Jack muttered.

His stricken expression almost made Amber want to tell him he didn't have to stay, that she would understand why he'd want to hightail it in the other direction, but then he bent down to grab a few planks of rotted wood and tossed them out of the way. Amber and Edgar joined him, using their magic to lift the bigger items when necessary.

Amber kept waiting for a buzz or trill from her phone alerting her that Willow had sent a message. But she hadn't heard anything since the text from half an hour ago, sending her—and, indirectly, Jack—to Edgar's house. Amber hoped no news was good news.

When the spot was cleared, sweat beaded on Amber's upper lip and trickled down her back despite the chilly air. She was sure she had half a dozen splinters embedded in her fingers.

Wordlessly, Amber grabbed the shovel and started to dig. When the hole was half a foot deep, she hit something hard. She thunked the spade in the same spot a couple more times, then looked up. Both men were grinning.

Amber dug faster. When the shape of something rectangular was clearly visible, Edgar and Jack dropped to their knees, wiping away dirt from the top of the object, and scooping handfuls of damp earth from around the sides until they found handles they could grab hold of. They counted to three and heaved the trunk out of the hole, dropping it just in front of Amber's now-dirty boots.

Her magic thrummed.

When Amber had just stared at the trunk for several long seconds, Edgar stood to full height and asked, "Well, are you going to open it?"

She nodded, wiping her sweaty palms down her pant legs. "If I open this, is he going to know?"

"Probably," he said.

But their only hope for stopping Kieran lay within the book. Either in handing it over or using its contents against him.

With the aid of her magic, she lowered one of the lanterns so it hung a foot above the trunk, then she squatted before it. It was padlocked, but the moment her fingers touched the rusted metal, the lock sprang free.

"*Only Amber or Willow can open it*," her mother had said.

The trunk's hinges groaned loudly as Amber flipped the lid open. And there, lying inside the black-velvet-lined trunk, was her mother's grimoire. She tentatively ran her fingertip over the slightly sunken letters spelling HENBANE across the cover. The book was wide enough that when she grabbed onto either side, her fingers didn't touch in the middle. To her surprise, just beneath her mother's book lay a similar grimoire, this one with a deep maroon cover stamped with BLACKWOOD.

"Did you know this one was here too?" she asked Edgar.

He was smiling. "Nope. Your parents were crafty."

Some small part of her felt like she had them back now. And she supposed she did, at least in part. Every spell book held a little of their owners within its pages.

A muted yellow light pulsed from both books, then went out.

Seconds later, Amber's phone beeped. With one arm wrapped around the grimoire, she grabbed her phone out of her back pocket with her free hand. She had a text from Willow. Just two simple words.

He's coming.

"All right, boys, back inside!" Amber said, scrambling to her feet. "Cursed witch incoming!"

"I really don't want to be incinerated," Jack half-whined, wide gaze focused out onto Edgar's dark property.

"Then you better get your butt inside, lover boy," Edgar said, using his magic to make the three lanterns float into a single-file line and then follow him inside like obedient ducklings.

Jack grabbed the shovel and hightailed it after them.

Amber plucked the Blackwood grimoire out of the trunk and dropped it on top of the Henbane one she already held—which was a feat in itself given how thick they were. It was like hefting two phonebooks or extensive encyclopedia volumes. She hurried after the guys.

Edgar was ready to lock the door and re-ward the house the second she got inside. Once done, and the house gave three magnificently loud shudders, he turned to her. "What now?"

"You take the Blackwood book and see what you can find that might help us," Amber said. "I'll go through my mom's. There's gotta be something in here about severing powers. Aunt Gretchen is sure Mom would have had spells like that as a failsafe should Neil ever get his powers back."

"Wouldn't she have used said spells when Neil showed up fourteen years ago?" Edgar asked.

"I'm pretty sure spells like that need physical contact," Amber said, remembering Miles placing his hands on Neil's skull, and Neil placing them on Edgar's. The thought made her vaguely nauseated. "Which means we need spells that will help me get close enough to touch him."

Edgar recoiled. "I don't envy you, cousin."

"What about me?" Jack asked.

She'd almost forgotten about him. Why, oh why, had he followed her tonight?

Because you're a liar, her mind informed her. *And not a very good one.*

She needed to give him a task that would keep him safe. She thought of Wilma's shrunken body, of the starburst marks on people's skin, and another brief wave of nausea rolled through her stomach.

"You can help me keep an eye on my phone and be our lookout," she said. "We need to know when Kieran shows up."

He still looked deathly pale. "I think I can handle that."

Edgar took Jack upstairs to a bedroom overlooking the property. It was the window Amber had seen light shining out of earlier, and had the best vantage point to see someone coming even before they turned onto Edgar's tiny road. Before he'd headed up there, Amber had handed him her cell phone, which he clutched tightly in his hand as if it were a life raft that would keep him from drowning.

"If Willow texts, come get me," she said. "If she calls, answer it."

He'd nodded numbly and followed Edgar without a word.

When her cousin joined her downstairs again, she was standing at the kitchen island, the closed Henbane book in front of her. The Blackwood book was turned the other way, waiting for Edgar across from her.

Edgar really didn't look much better than Jack did. His skin had paled and sweat beaded at his hairline.

"You up for this?" Amber asked. "I can search them myself if—"

"I'm good," he said, taking the spot opposite her. "This is just a lot of excitement for me." He paused. "But, I figure, if I'm not supposed to protect the book anymore, then I'll protect you and Willow. Your parents would have wanted that."

She managed a smile at him. He quickly broke eye contact and focused it instead on the Blackwood book.

After a mini mental pep talk her father would have loved, Amber flipped open the cover of her mother's grimoire. The spine gave a muted creak, but fell open easily enough.

The first handful of pages were dedicated to herbs, listed in alphabetical order. Amber had never seen her mother draw much, but these pages were filled with intricately detailed sketches of plants. Herb names were written in a calligraphy style, the letters swooping and curling. Her handwriting was neat and legible. Amber knew where Willow's artistic side had come from now. Amber felt a pang that her mother had kept her talent, along with so much else, sequestered between these leather covers.

Next came tincture recipes. A tablespoon of this, a pinch of that. Amber knew from Aunt Gretchen that her mother hadn't been any better at tinctures than Amber was, but Amber liked that she catalogued some of them anyway.

The majority of the grimoire was filled with spells, organized by type. Spells for sleep, good dreams, banishing nightmares, and cures for sleeplessness were all clustered together. But Amber wasn't sure how the spells as a whole were organized. They weren't in alphabetical order—that much she could tell, at least.

She glanced up at Edgar half-slouching across from her, one elbow on the counter, his dark brows knitted together, as he carefully flipped through the Blackwood grimoire. "How you doing over there?"

He didn't move his head, merely shifted his gaze from the book to her face. "Fine."

Amber pursed her lips. She couldn't help but remember how he'd been the last time she'd seen him: back pressed against the cabinets, hands clutching at the hair on either side of his head, and groaning in pain.

"Your pitying looks are worse than your persistence," he said.

"I just don't want you to push it, you know?" Amber said, sure she was already saying the wrong thing. "I know none of this has been easy on you either and I'm sorry I kept harassing you when you clearly wanted to be left alone."

His furrowed brow relaxed a fraction, as did the tension in his shoulders. "At least you cared enough to harass me," he said. "Even if it was relentless and very annoying."

She cracked a smile. "I'll take it."

They'd only been silently flipping through their spell books for another few minutes before he spoke again. "I hear voices. Well, *a* voice."

Amber looked up, tucking her lips between her teeth so she wouldn't say something and make him stop talking. Edgar Henbane wasn't one who shared information freely.

"It's a male voice, but it's not mine," he said, gaze focused on the book again, though he clearly wasn't reading it. His thumb idly flicked back and forth against a corner of one of the grimoire's thick pages. "It's been there ever since I was attacked the night of the fire. When I talk about that night or the Pen-hallows, the voice gets louder. Yells at me to not share 'our' secrets. It says I can only talk to *him* about the book. That the book belongs to us and only us. If I stay by myself, I don't hear the voice as much."

Amber frowned. "Is he saying anything to you now that the book is here?"

"He hasn't shut up." Edgar wiped the back of his hand across his sweaty brow.

"And he was yelling at you the last time we were here?"

He nodded. "He started telling me what to say to get you guys to leave. Told me to talk slower and more controlled. If I went off script, he started screaming at me again. I don't know how he can see me. I don't know if he *is* me." He chewed the inside of his cheek. "But ever since you started back up with being your annoying self, I've started to wonder if the voice is him. Neil. Or his magic. You heard him say that it would poison me like it poisons him, right? So I think it *is* me—the voice I hear, I mean. But it's also his magic at the same time. I don't really know where it ends and I begin anymore."

As if Amber needed any more reason to hate Neil Penhallow.

"Once we figure out what to do about his brother, we'll see what we can do to help you, too," she said.

Maybe Aunt Gretchen could come up with a tincture to slowly cure the infection caused by the cursed magic in his system.

But it had been infecting him for fourteen years. Amber hoped it wasn't too late—assuming it was possible to purge him of the foreign magic to begin with.

Edgar nodded awkwardly, then went back to the Blackwood book.

Unable to avoid it any longer, Amber started flipping more

quickly through her mother's grimoire until she found the infamous spell. It was a long, complicated one somewhere in the middle of the book; it was built of several smaller spells, though they got progressively more complex. Amber thought of it like leveling up on a video game: you had to master level one before you could get to level two. This one had nine "levels." Intent with spells like this was crucial. Any falter in one's resolve could result in the spell failing and the witch needing to start over.

But with such a spell, Amber wondered what would happen if it wasn't executed perfectly. Willow had been half joking when she'd said that she worried Amber could get stuck in the past—but what if something like that were really possible?

In her gut, she knew it wasn't a spell to play with. It could cause irreparable damage if it was cast perfectly. But who knew what would happen if it wasn't?

Amber kept flipping, looking for spells about severing powers from a witch. The practice was what resulted in the Penhallow line being cursed, so she wasn't totally convinced that her mother would have dangerous spells in her grimoire—let alone illegal ones.

Gretchen, however, had seemed convinced there'd be something they could use against Kieran Penhallow.

Edgar moved from his spot across from her to grab a pad of paper out of a kitchen drawer—which he closed with a rattling clang that made Amber jump—and then he stood in front of the Blackwood grimoire again. He tore a strip off the pad and stuffed it between two pages before flipping forward a few more places and placing another strip into the book. She hoped that was a good sign.

Amber found a whole slate of spells that dealt with people's minds. They were the kind of spells Amber had gravitated toward naturally. Spells to reveal guilty pleasures. Spells for truth. But while Amber's often were simple—a spell that revealed the truth in a sentence or even in just a yes or no—these had much more depth. Truth about a lie once told. Truth in the face of unyielding denial. Truth when memories fail.

They all, like Amber had known instinctually, needed physical contact with a subject to be the most effective.

There were spells associated with dreams and nightmares and secrets. With happiness, loss, and grief. Spells to enhance emotions and to dampen them.

With a rising sense of disappointment that what she needed wouldn't be here, she turned to the last page and she found something different. She gasped softly when she saw her name in her mother's neat handwriting.

Amber and Willow,

If you have this book, I hope that means our plan has worked and you've made it this far into my grimoire because you're reading it cover-to-cover out of curiosity and not necessity.

If it's the latter, and a Penhallow is still after the book, I'm sorry. Truly, truly sorry. Your father and I tried so hard to protect you. Please believe that.

This is not the last page, but you must read this in its entirety for this last spell to appear. It will only appear for you two should you need a severing spell.

Do not tread lightly with this decision, girls. There are rumors that if one truly severs a witch from her powers, it's not reversible. The witch will be forever changed, though no one is truly sure how.

I'll let you in on a little secret that my father told me: the council didn't actually sever power from the Penhallows—not completely. They scooped magic out of them, like gutting a melon, but they didn't remove the drive for magic. That's the trick, I believe. To truly sever magic from a witch, you don't remove their abilities. That's treating a symptom. You must sever their desire to do magic in the first place. You must take away a fundamental part of their being.

This is no easy feat. These rumors may simply be old wives' tales. Myths. It may be impossible to ever really take magic away from a witch.

It's never been done before, at least not as of my writing of this. All recorded attempts have resulted in madness and an even stronger desire for acquiring magic. The most notable attempt is the Penhallow curse which has now lasted for generations.

You must enter the mind of the witch and find their drive. Find what fuels their soul. And then snip that away and cauterize the wound so nothing worse grows back in its place.

I hope you never need it.

All my love,

Mom

Amber wasn't sure when she'd started crying, but when the book gave a pulse of yellow behind her mother's note, it sobered her up some. Her eyes widened as several pages materialized under the one she currently stared at. She wiped the tears from her face.

When she looked up, Edgar's eyes were wide too.

Then, from upstairs, she heard, "Someone's coming!"

Amber swallowed, then jutted her chin at Edgar. "Got anything?"

"Not going to tell me what you found?" he asked, brow raised.

"Not yet."

"Did you hear me?" Jack called from upstairs. "Is it the incinerating guy?"

They both ignored him. Her magic hummed. She was so full of nervous energy, she was starting to fidget. Her foot tap, tap, tapped on the floor in a soft, frantic rhythm.

"I found some of the most powerful sleep spells I've ever seen," Edgar said. "There's one in here that essentially can put someone in a coma. But like a cryogenic-freeze kind of coma. They won't age. They'll just be sleeping ... indefinitely."

"Yikes." She chewed on her bottom lip. Scratched at her ear. "Out with it, Blackwood."

"I found the sever spell," she blurted.

He softened his tone when he asked, "We gonna use it?"

"If we do this wrong, it could backfire even worse than the Penhallow curse. I'm ... I'm worried I'm too green. What if it's too complex for me? I didn't even know I had powers like this a week ago."

"I get that," Edgar said. "No one can make that call but you."

Jack's heavy footfalls sounded as he pounded down the

steps, across the foyer, and darted into the kitchen. He thrust the phone toward Amber. "It's Willow."

Amber met him halfway and plucked the still-ringing phone from his hand. She almost didn't hit accept in time. "Hi, Will?"

"Oh thank God," Willow said, heaving out a breath. "Kieran has a head start on us so I didn't know if he'd made it to you yet."

The house gave a great shudder then, the windows rattling and the floor vibrating. Edgar and Jack took turns cursing up a storm.

"I think he just beat you here," Amber said, a little breathless.

From outside, Kieran screamed, "Give me the book!"

The house lurched again.

Edgar bolted out of the kitchen and into the foyer, words of an incantation already leaving his lips. He was reinforcing the wards Kieran was currently trying to tear down.

Jack stood in the middle of the kitchen, hands clasping his elbows, eyes as wide as saucers. He nearly jumped out of his skin every time the house rumbled.

"Is there any way I can convince you to go back to the shop, Will?" Amber asked, walking to the doorway of the kitchen, watching Edgar work. "We're in a warded house. You're not."

"Not a chance, big sis," Willow said. "Aunt Gretchen and I took a hit of her protection tincture before we left."

A sickening groan sounded, reminding Amber of a ship at sea.

"That's only good against *one* strike. You know what a full dose of his power can do to you," Amber said, aware of the

313

rising panic in her own voice. "You'll be like sitting ducks out there."

Kieran screamed outside again, demanding the book. Something exploded, followed by cackling.

Jack hit the floor like a bomb had just gone off, his clasped hands protecting the back of his neck. He was muttering to himself. Maybe he was praying.

"Did you find the spell?" Willow asked. "Tell me what you need us to do. We'll be there in two minutes. Gretchen is currently driving at speeds I didn't know were possible in a car this old."

Amber pretended she hadn't heard that last part. Walking back into the kitchen, she took in Jack's crouched form on the floor and the two open grimoires on the counter. Glass shattered outside. She winced.

Then a lightbulb went off in her brain.

"I'm sending you pictures and instructions, Will," Amber said, her heart and her magic pulsing in unison. "I have an idea."

CHAPTER 22

After sending everything to Willow's cell, Amber shoved her phone in her back pocket and then rushed to Jack's side, placing a hand on his shoulder. He jumped at the touch, but he unfurled from his crouched position on the floor.

"How are you so calm?" he asked, then immediately winced as that horrible groaning-metal noise sounded again. He rested his back against the island.

It truly sounded as if a giant had a crowbar wedged under the house and was trying to pry it loose from its foundation.

"I'm not," she said, squatting beside him. "I'm just good at compartmentalizing."

He didn't reply to that.

"In a couple minutes, I'm going to go outside."

"What?" he asked, perking up and turning to her. "You can't. You said *incinerate*. Your cousin's keeping him out, right? We just have to wait till he goes away."

"Jack—"

"No, Amber," he said. "You have to—"

Then something exploded in the front room. Edgar cried out. Amber was on her feet and running in an instant. She darted into the foyer to find the front door had been blown off its hinges. Edgar was on the ground, grunting and cursing and trying to get back up.

Kieran appeared in the open doorway. His face lit up with a grin when he spotted her.

Before he could lift a finger or start an incantation, she sent a burst of air at him that had so much rage behind it, it knocked the startled Penhallow clear off his feet, over the patio's railing, and into the bushes.

"Up, Edgar!" Amber called out, using sheer adrenaline to pick up the heavy wooden door. "We have to re-secure the house."

The weight of the door vanished. Edgar was upright again, his magic not only refastening the door back into place, but layering on another protection spell. Kieran's growl from outside was punctuated with a rattle from the reattached door. Kieran was tearing the defenses down almost as fast as Edgar was putting them up.

"You got a plan, cousin?" Edgar asked, even paler now than he had been earlier. "I'm gonna run out of juice eventually. He's stronger than I am."

If Neil's magic was still speaking to him, Edgar must have been both physically *and* mentally wrung out.

"Yes," she said. "Keep him occupied."

"Keep him occupied," he repeated sarcastically. "What do you *think* I've been doing?"

"I'm going out the back."

"The yard is a jungle," he said. "Be safe."

"You too."

The house gave another shudder.

316

She bolted back into the kitchen, then to the back door. There was a shelf stacked with cooking staples—flour, sugar, oil—that clearly hadn't been used in a while, given the coating of grime on their containers, bottles, and caps.

"I need your help, Jack!"

"This can't be a good idea, Amber," he said, though he still joined her to assist in clearing a way to the door.

Once it was unobstructed, she grabbed the knob, only to find it locked.

A great gust of air sailed between Amber and Jack, slamming into the door and blowing the now slightly splintered wood clear out into the dark beyond it. Jack yelped. Amber whirled around, hand outstretched and magic buzzing. But it was only a wild-eyed Edgar in the doorway to the kitchen.

"Sorry! I just remembered the door was locked and I have no clue where the key is," he said, shrugged, and then ran back to the foyer.

Which was helpful, but also meant Jack was considerably less safe in the house now. If another Penhallow was around, Jack didn't stand a chance.

"Come with me!" she said, grabbing the Henbane grimoire and tucking it under her arm, then jogging into the foyer and up the stairs from where Edgar was still battling it out with Kieran, the door between them. Jack was hot on her heels. They ran down the dark second-floor hallway and into the bedroom that still had light pouring out of it.

"So you decided to wait it out?" Jack asked, tone hopeful and a little breathless. "We could probably shove a dresser or something in front of the door. Is the chief on his way? He can stop him, right?"

"Maybe," Amber said.

The bedroom was tiny. Its only furniture was a three-drawer dresser, twin bed, and a single nightstand adorned with a lamp—a dusty, slightly askew shade resting on the bulb. Its muted orange glow was the only light in the room. Amber peered out the small window. She could hear Kieran out there—screaming and generally causing mayhem—but she couldn't see him. It was a sea of black down below. Out in the distance, though, she could see part of the rutted road that led out of here, the ground lit only by moonlight.

Where were Willow and Aunt Gretchen? Gretchen's speeding hadn't resulted in some horrible end for them both, had it?

No. She couldn't let herself think that way.

Jack plopped down on the twin bed, the mattress' springs issuing a creaky reply. He winced slightly, then angled a small smile at her. He clearly felt safer up here, especially with her here with him.

So she felt no small amount of guilt when she made eye contact, focused her magic, and said, "Sleep."

Jack's eyes rolled back in his head and he tipped over sideways, feet still on the ground, the bed creaking even louder now as he collapsed onto it. His face and body relaxed completely. She placed his feet on the bed, while keeping the grimoire under her arm. Then she moved to the door.

"Sorry, Jack," she said softly, then closed the door behind her.

Across the dark hallway, down the steps, through the foyer,

and into the kitchen she went. The hole where the door had stood—a black, forbidding rectangle of night—reminded Amber of a missing tooth. Steeling herself, she dashed out into the dark, the late-February air cold on her face.

She waited a couple moments for her eyes to adjust, for the pitch-black yard to morph into a landscape of dark gray and midnight blue shapes. She could make out the tops of the tall grasses behind Edgar's house, which were nearly waist-high. A swath of them were flattened, thanks to the door Edgar had hurled out here. Tall smudges of soft black marked the spots where trees stood several feet away. A jungle indeed.

Problem was, she was sure to make a racket tromping through all this brush that rose up not far from Edgar's back door. But a light would give away her position. And she still had no idea where Willow and Aunt Gretchen were.

A rattling clang sounded from the front of the house. Amber would just have to hope Kieran and Edgar were making enough noise that he wouldn't hear her coming.

She started off, using her hands to swat away the weeds that slapped at her and tore at her clothes as she crunched her way through the overgrowth, the grimoire clutched to her chest.

She'd just rounded the back corner of the house and was creeping along the side toward the front porch, the sound of Kieran's battle with Edgar growing louder, when her back pocket vibrated. She couldn't hear it, but she felt it. Then again. And again.

Amber halted and pulled her phone from her pocket. Twenty-three missed texts from Willow. Amber cursed under her breath. She quickly lowered the brightness level of her

319

phone screen, then read the messages. The first had come in two minutes before, and they'd grown increasingly frantic since then. Had Amber briefly lost reception out here?

Another one popped up. I can see you on the side of the house. Aunt G and I parked in the woods and hiked in. We're ready when you are.

Without replying, Amber stuck her phone back into her pocket and then picked up the pace, remaining in a semi-crouched position so she could stay out of sight as much as possible when she made her dash past the porch where Kieran was losing his ever-loving mind.

She was able to make it to the front of the house without Kieran seeing her, but he'd clearly sensed her, because he suddenly stopped hurling magic at Edgar's front door and whirled around.

Amber was partially hidden behind the old pickup truck. Between that and the pitch black, she knew he couldn't see her. But he was sniffing the air again, scenting the book she clutched.

He didn't seem nearly as worn out as Edgar. Did Penhallows not tire from excessive use of magic the way non-cursed witches did? Amber had hoped that he'd be at least a *little* drained by now.

"I know you're out there, Blackwood!" Kieran called, facing the dark yard. The lights from the porch lit up his back, casting his face into shadow. "You've brought me the book like a good little girl, haven't you? Come out, come out, wherever you are."

Amber remained quiet, knowing her lack of response would infuriate the already unhinged witch even further.

"Come ouuuut," he called, drawing out the words. He rested his hands on the railing surrounding the porch as his gaze skated over the vague shapes in the dark. "Come out!" His hands tightened harder on the railing and then started to yank and pull. He growled in frustration, then lashed out with his feet at the lattice work below the railing. "Come! Out!"

While he melted down, Amber sent a burst of air directed at the foot not currently whaling on Edgar's porch. The gust was enough to put him off balance and he crashed to the porch. She needed him out here with her. Closer to Willow and Gretchen and further from Edgar and Jack.

Kieran roared, then scrambled to his feet. He called out an incantation that Amber recognized a moment too late—one she hadn't heard before, but knew what it would do once it was complete.

A blindingly bright burst of blue light erupted out of Kieran's hands, spider webbing off his fingertips like small fireworks. It was brief, and likely expelled a ton of energy, but it had been enough. It illuminated Edgar's dark property like lightning on a stormy night. His gaze locked on where she still stood near the back of Edgar's truck. She hadn't ducked out of the way in time.

"There you are," he said, grinning, and then the light went out.

Amber turned and bolted, knowing he was in pursuit from the pounding of feet on Edgar's creaky porch, down the steps, and across the ground. As he ran after her, wild puffs of air from his nostrils made her feel like she was being chased down by a bull.

She ran down the rutted dirt path, clutching the grimoire to her chest. The farther she got from the house now, the more the moon lit her way, everything taking on a bluish-silver glow. She could make out the odds and ends that littered the property here, the wild shrubbery, and the rows of tall pines lining either side.

Her feet and lungs burned but she continued to run. His wild breaths told her he was exhausted—finally. She hoped it wasn't due to the burst of cardio, but from how much magic he'd been using. She was banking on that.

Just as she passed the first tree in the line of pines, she shouted, "Now!"

Something almost instantly hit the ground behind her. Something that grazed the back of her ankles. She yelped but kept moving. Willow and Gretchen emerged from behind a pair of trees on either side of the path, hands out and words pouring from their mouths. It was the incantation she'd sent Willow earlier. The sleep spell Edgar had found that could essentially put someone into a coma.

Amber ran a few more steps, then turned around. Kieran was on the ground, struggling to get back up. It was a complicated spell with four "levels." Each one compounding the last until the person succumbed to sleep. Kieran had a gash in his forehead, blood tricking into his eye. He stood, shakily, and grinned at Amber despite being covered in dirt. Blood smeared his teeth.

"Give me the book, Blackwood," he ground out, taking slow, shuffling steps toward her.

For every step he took forward, Amber took one back.

Willow and Gretchen still advanced from behind, hands out as they worked their way through the spell. Kieran was caught in the middle of a triangle made by the Blackwood women, and the spell was considerably slowing him down, but he still only had eyes for the book.

"The. Book." He had a dirt-streaked hand out toward her, just feet from her now.

A faint pulse of blue ignited on both palms of Willow and Gretchen, and Kieran groaned, hands clutching his skull as he listed to one side. He sagged, dropping to one knee. They'd passed the second level of the spell. Two more and he'd be out cold—indefinitely—until they figured out what to do with him.

Just lie down, Kieran. Give up.

With another groan, he stumbled to his feet.

He was like a wild animal who'd been struck by a tranquilizer dart but refused to go down. He shuffled toward Amber again. She and this book were the carrot on the end of a string for him, a distraction for his singularly focused mind, while Willow and Gretchen completed the spell. Amber had hoped that both of them would be enough to knock him out faster.

Another pulse of blue from their palms—the triangle they made was smaller now; they were only six feet away from him—and his knees gave way. He hit the ground, sending up a puff of dust in his wake.

Yet, no sooner had the tension in Amber's shoulders loosened, Kieran curled in on himself, then flexed, his limbs pointing in four directions, back arched. A burst of his magic pulsed out like a wave. The spell on Willow's and Gretchen's lips was abruptly cut off as the blast knocked them clean off their feet. Amber was launched too, though she managed to hold fast to the book, protecting it like a newborn. She hit the rutted road, was rolled a few times—elbows, knees, shoulders hitting rocks and barbed weeds—before skidding a few feet on her side and slamming into what remained of an old tractor. Thankfully her back hit one of the giant tires. It knocked the breath from her lungs, but if her skull had hit the tractor's metal side, at the very least she would have been knocked unconscious.

Her entire body hurt. She was almost positive there were dirt and bits of rock embedded in the cuts on her arms and legs. Her black slacks were torn at the knees. But she didn't have time to do a wellness check on herself because Kieran was back on his feet and prowling toward her.

And he looked well and truly ticked off.

Oh crap.

She struggled to stand, but her knees throbbed and her head swam and the book was oh so heavy in her arms. "Willow! Aunt Gretchen!"

No reply.

Amber's throat tightened. They were fine. They had to be fine.

She had just stood to full height, the tractor against her back and keeping her upright, when Kieran's hand shot out toward her, palm out.

Amber was too disoriented and off-kilter and in pain to react in time. She watched, as if in slow motion, as that swirling tendril-like magic of his flew toward her. She slammed her eyes shut, bracing for impact.

Sorry, Mom. Sorry, Dad. Willow. Gretchen. Edgar. Jack. Sorry, everyone in Edgehill. And probably beyond. Because this cursed witch was going to kill her and take her mother's book and rewrite history.

But instead of hitting her, like she'd seen the magic do to others, something unseen grabbed hold of her neck. She choked out a gasp and her eyes flew open.

She kicked her feet, which were hovering several inches above the ground now. She clawed at what felt like fingers squeezing her throat, trying to crush her windpipe. But her fingers only met air. Kieran stood just feet from her. Swirling black poured from his outstretched hand and slowly choked the life out of her.

Her vision blurred at the edges. She kicked and clawed for air.

"If you had just given the book to me," Kieran said, and then thrust out his other hand.

The grimoire was ripped away from her and her choked cry only further robbed her of air. Her limbs felt heavy, her eyelids slipping closed.

An odd, uneven noise played at the back of her mind, but she was so deprived of oxygen, she couldn't place it.

CLANG!

Air rushed back into her lungs and she hit the ground.

Thud.

On all fours, one hand clutched at her neck, she tried to pull in more air through her bruised throat. Her nose ran and her eyes watered. Her vision was still a bit blurry.

She managed to look up and see Edgar standing over

Kieran's prone form. Edgar tossed the object he'd been holding aside.

"Did you ... really just hit him over the head ... with a shovel?" Amber asked.

Edgar shrugged. "When your magic is depleted, sometimes you have to go old school."

Amber laughed despite herself, then instantly regretted it. She got to her feet. "Thanks, cousin. I was pretty sure I was a goner." Then she started limping past him. "Willow! Aunt Gretchen!"

"We're okay!" Willow called back from several feet away. "That protection tincture really helped, I think. But Gretchen was knocked into some brambles and is pretty banged up. We should probably *actually* go to the hospital this time."

Relief that everyone fared okay almost brought Amber to her knees, especially now that whatever adrenaline had been coursing through her veins was fading. Turning back to Edgar, she saw that he had the Henbane grimoire in his hands.

"I think this is yours," he said.

She took it from him, running a gentle had over the smooth cover. "You think you can teach me how to cloak it again? And soon? Who knows how many Penhallows are aware of it now."

"Of course," he said. "But, speaking of ..." He jerked his head toward the rumpled, dirty, and bleeding Kieran at their feet. "What are we going to do about this guy?"

She sighed, gently touching the tender skin at her throat. This was only one Penhallow, and who knew how many others there were. How powerful the others were. She needed to know if she had the skills to protect people—her loved ones especially—from their cursed magic.

"Let's get him inside," she said. "I have a spell to do."

CHAPTER 23

Amber, Willow, and Edgar all placed sleep spells on Kieran before they attempted to move him. Aunt Gretchen had gathered her wits about her by then, and even though she had a split lip, scratches all over one side of her body, and a significant limp, she refused to be escorted to the hospital until the "Penhallow problem" had been taken care of.

Once they were sure Kieran was out cold, Edgar and Willow used levitation spells to float the cursed witch across the property and into the house. Amber would have helped—this particular spell seemed to be depleting what energy Willow had left—but Edgar told her to save everything she had for the next spell. Magic could only be replenished by rest, so she took it as easy as she could.

Amber had always known that using one's magic was like flexing a muscle, but neither she nor Willow had used their magic as much in a month as they'd used it tonight. It was like training for a 5k and then deciding at the last minute to run a marathon. They were both exhausted.

After placing Kieran on the kitchen island, Gretchen hobbled up the stairs to check on Jack. Amber hoped he'd slept through it all.

Amber stood in front of Kieran's head, then set up the

grimoire beside it. She eyed him warily, worried he'd wake up at any moment and try to choke her again. Her neck still ached horribly, and she knew it would be even worse tomorrow.

"You can do this," Willow said from across the island where she stood at his feet. "We're here for whatever you need."

"I just need you two to make sure he stays asleep. The spell you and Aunt Gretchen were doing before was ten times as powerful as the ones on him now and he still fought it. I'm worried once I start, it'll wake him up."

"We've got you covered," Edgar said, standing to Kieran's right, the Blackwood grimoire opened to one of the pages he'd bookmarked. "I've got a couple Willow and I can do after you get in there."

In there. Kieran's mind.

Taking a calming breath, she went to the last page of the Henbane grimoire, scanned her mother's warning one more time, and then flipped past it.

Oddly, the spell itself was short. What was depicted here were mostly suggestions. Things to look for. Things to avoid. There were also notes scribbled in the margins.

A complete severing of power has yet to be done, remember that—what is shown here is what I think will work. But I'm not sure. I've never had a Penhallow to test it out on, nor a non-cursed witch who was willing to run the risk of losing their powers.

Be sure this is what you want, girls. And then go in with pure intention. Do not waver.

Edgar and Willow waited patiently for Amber to decide

if she was willing to go through with this. But at this point, what was the alternative? Keep him in a coma forever?

She looked up at them. "Ready?"

They nodded.

Amber gave the spell another quick glance, memorized the words, then closed her eyes. She placed her hands on either side of Kieran's skull. Just the touch alone ignited her magic. She said the incantation, stated her intention, and then … she was somewhere else.

She didn't have a physical form—not like she did when she was in someone's memories. There was no host to inhabit here. There was no light, no sound. There was just a *pull*.

So she followed it.

She imagined it was like being in a maze with her eyes closed. Her destination could only be reached if she utilized the rest of her remaining senses.

The pull was similar to what she felt when her magic itched to be used. A tingling, an urge, a compulsion. *That* was what she was following.

She let it pull her this way and that, not resisting when she was suddenly yanked in a new direction.

A sound reached her. More a sensation of noise, though. A vibration.

Something told her Kieran was fighting this now. Resisting.

She needed to move quicker.

The more Kieran fought, the more objects started to pop up in this not-place. Blurred images. Nothing she could label concretely. Bursts of color that faded as quickly as they appeared. A picture desperately trying to form.

And then suddenly, she was surrounded by the sensation she'd been following. It was like being caught in a tornado. There was an ache in her chest that nearly brought her to her knees. It swirled around her. Round and round and round it went. A mind-numbing desire. A need so great, she felt vaguely nauseous with it. She craved it so badly she wanted to scream—and yet she wasn't even sure what "it" was. Just that she needed it now or it would surely kill her.

Was this how Kieran felt all the time? How all the Penhallows felt?

Amber hated it. She needed out. This wasn't drive or passion—this was obsession. An all-consuming one that felt so impossibly wrong to Amber that she could hardly stand it and she'd only been here for a matter of minutes.

Focus, she told herself. *Find the source.*

She willed herself to sift through this jumble of feelings, this bone-deep ache for something she didn't even have a name for. She dove deeper, pushed further.

And then she sensed it. She pictured it like the scorch mark that marred Edgar's back. A fixed point before her from which the chaos emanated. A twisted, gnarled tree whose roots had rotted. She needed to yank it out. Not pluck off the leaves, or trim back the branches—the whole thing needed to go.

The swirl of panicked colors, of the thing that was trying to take shape, was moving in closer now. Kieran was fighting with everything he had. His magic didn't want this. His magic had taken root decades before and had turned him into a dedicated, unflinching follower. A brainwashed, powerful witch who had lost his free will and was now at the twisted magic's beck and call. She wondered if this magic—the magic that had turned Kieran into this twisted version of himself—would simply cease to exist if she did this right.

Was it fighting for its own survival?

She focused on the eye of this magical storm.

And she *pulled*.

The colors burst around her like a fireworks show at close range, minus the sound. Explosion after explosion of color. It was disorienting. An overload of the senses. But she willed herself to focus. This was for Kieran. To give him a chance to live his life without this festering thing warping him into something he wasn't. Some horrible essence that had become an insult to magic.

And *pulled*.

Light and sound and upraised voices assaulted her ears.

Her ears!

She stumbled back, hitting the bank of cabinets behind her. Losing her footing, she slipped and fell to the ground. Willow's face swam into view. Amber's eyes couldn't seem to focus on anything.

"Did it work?" she croaked out. That just-ran-a-marathon feeling hit her like a ton of bricks. Her head lolled forward, but she forced it back up. Her throat throbbed in time with her heart.

Willow had Amber's face in her hands, tipping her head back. "It worked."

Amber managed a faint smile, then slipped into unconsciousness.

When Amber woke up, it was in an unfamiliar bed. It took a moment for that initial panic to subside, and then recognition started to kick in. She lay on a twin bed in a tiny room with only a three-drawer dresser and nightstand for furniture.

She was still in Edgar's house.

The bed creaked something awful as she attempted to sit up.

Willow was in the open doorway in an instant. "Oh thank God!" she said, then hurried to Amber's side, pushing some of Amber's sweaty hair out of her face. "How are you feeling?"

"Horrible," she said groggily, scooting back until her back touched the wall. "What time is it?"

"A little after two in the morning," Willow said sitting on the foot of the bed. "You've been passed out for three hours."

Memories of her time in Kieran's mind came rushing back in. She gently pressed a hand to her throat and willed herself to stop sounding like a seasoned smoker. "You said it worked? That wasn't a dream?"

Willow grinned. "You were amazing! Kieran woke up about the same time that you passed out. He almost immediately started sobbing. He remembers all of it, but said it was like he'd been trapped in his own body for his whole life. The magic ruled him. You freed him from that."

"Is his magic gone?" She wondered how bruised her neck was—could non-corporal hands still cause bruises? It certainly felt bruised.

Willow offered a small nod. "We think so. We're pretty sure he's fully human now."

Amber blinked at that. Somehow some part of her still felt guilty for taking something away from a person that made them who they were.

"Want to come talk to him?" Willow asked softly.

Amber hesitated, then nodded, mostly curious how his transformation could be so complete that the others felt comfortable having him in the house after everything he'd done.

It took a while to get down the stairs, as every part of Amber's body hurt. Someone had tended to the gashes on her knees, but she was still a grimy mess and her other scrapes and bruises would need to be tended to.

"How's Aunt Gretchen?" Amber asked just as they reached the base of the stairs.

"Hopped-up on pain killers—Edgar had some left over from some dental work a few months ago, apparently," Willow said. "She said she wouldn't go to the hospital until she knew you were okay. Stubborn old bat."

Amber managed a laugh, though it hurt.

"Jack is still here, too," Willow added in a whisper.

Amber's stomach flipped. "How's he taking it?" she rasped.

"Uhh … why don't you deal with Kieran first."

Great.

They all—Kieran, Aunt Gretchen, and Jack—were in a room just off the foyer. A room Amber hadn't known was there, since this front area was usually kept so dark. The door for it had completely blended into the wooden wall.

Even though the door stood open, and likely had been for

a couple of hours, the room still smelled musty when Amber followed Willow inside. It looked like an old Victorian woman's sitting room—maroon, old-fashioned, wing-backed sofas and chairs dotted the space; a giant gaudy rug designed with swirling patterns in burgundy, dark blue, and cream covered most of the floor; and heavy, dark curtains covered windows that were already boarded up on the outside. The crackling fire in the fireplace was a nice touch, though.

The vibe in the room was somber. Edgar sat on one of the couches, Aunt Gretchen sleeping soundly with her head on his shoulder. Jack paced in the far corner of the room.

And Kieran stood before the fireplace, gazing into the flames. He turned when she walked in, then immediately straightened.

He strode over to her and held out a hand. The memory of him staring at her with unadulterated rage while magic clutched at her neck came back to her. She placed a hand to her sore throat. This man, even if he was changed now, had tried to kill her. He'd almost succeeded. His face would be burned into her memory for a long time, if not forever.

Frowning, he dropped his hand to his side. "I know there's nothing I can say to fix anything I did. I don't expect forgiveness. I don't deserve it. But please know I will be forever grateful to you for releasing me from that. I've been a prisoner in my own mind and body since birth."

She stared at him for a long time, searching his face for some sign of malice or deceit. Finding none, she said, "You're welcome."

"And I wanted to be the one to tell you that I will be turning myself over to Chief Brown for the murder of Wilma Bennett," Kieran said, lightly wringing his hands. "I realize I'm setting myself up to go from one prison to another, but at least in this new one, my mind will be my own."

Movement on the couch caught Amber's eye. Edgar had moved Gretchen off his shoulder and propped her up against the couch's back.

He approached the group and said to Amber, "Chief Brown is expecting us. I called him a couple hours ago. We're taking everybody back to town. You and Gretchen need to see a doctor, and Kieran here needs to go to the station. We've only got one working car—Gretchen's—which is still parked out near the woods. Kieran here destroyed yours and Old Blue Eyes."

Amber cocked a brow at him.

"My old truck. Blew them both to smithereens."

Well, that was going to be a problem.

Edgar glanced behind him at Jack who was still pacing on the other side of the room. "I think you need to talk to lover boy, cousin."

Amber sighed, glancing that way, too.

"We'll give you some privacy," Willow said. "I'll keep an eye on Kieran while Edgar fetches the car."

And then suddenly Amber was alone with her snoring aunt, and a man she really hadn't wanted to scare away so soon. Steeling herself, she walked over.

He had been so lost in his own head that he truly seemed startled to see her when he finally heard her approach. His bottom lip shook and he pulled her into a sudden, fierce hug.

Amber bit back a yelp of pain.

He quickly released her. "Crap. Sorry. I forgot. Well, no, I didn't. I … I'm glad you're okay. I mean, mostly okay."

"I just need some rest," she said, trying to muster up a reassuring smile for him.

"I saw it, you know," he said, after a brief beat of awkward silence. "I woke up in that room and I looked out the window and I saw it. I saw what he did to you. That Kieran guy," Jack said, his voice shaky and words coming out in a rush as if they'd all been lined up and waiting patiently in his mouth so he could set them loose the moment he saw her. "I can't unsee that. I know they said he's different now. Changed from whatever you did to him. But he almost killed you, Amber, and I can't stop *seeing* it."

Her eyes welled with tears. She didn't know what to tell him. Didn't know how to make him feel better because she would be reliving this for a while, too. But at least she'd known magic and witches were real before tonight. Jack hadn't.

His voice was low and biting and desperate when he softly said, "Can you take it away?"

Brow furrowed, she shook her head. "What do you mean? Take what away?"

"What I saw. Can you make me forget?"

"How *much* of it do you want to forget?"

"All the …" He waved his hand vaguely in the air. "All the magic. I don't want to know this kind of thing exists. I want to go back to flirting with you at Purrcolate—back when this was simpler."

Amber's shoulders slumped. She didn't know why she was

so heartbroken over this. Perhaps because he looked completely wrecked and she was the one who'd broken him.

"I can do it," came a voice from behind.

Amber turned to find her aunt watching them from the couch. Amber wondered how long she'd had been listening in.

Jack immediately headed for Gretchen, her words a magnet, but then backed up a couple steps so he could face Amber. He took in her disheveled appearance, her bruised neck, her undoubtedly sad eyes. "I'm sorry."

The way his voice broke on the last word was almost enough to break her, too.

Amber watched as Jack walked to her aunt and sat beside her. Once he confirmed this is what he wanted, Gretchen's gaze found Amber's.

"And are *you* okay with this, little mouse?" she asked, frowning.

Amber took in Jack's disheveled appearance and his sunken, haunted eyes. "It's his choice, not mine."

She started across the room, tears running down her face; she knew this was likely the best choice for Jack. This was the reason she didn't get involved with non-witches. Jack proved she had been right about that, no matter what Willow tried to say to convince her otherwise. As she stepped over the threshold, the first spoken words of a memory-erase spell rang in her ears.

EPILOGUE

Connor Declan spun lazily in his desk chair. Every few seconds, the bright glow of his laptop—the cursor blinking incessantly on a blank page—would appear in his vision before he rotated away again.

"Bro!" Wesley said. "Can we *please* go out tonight? This is my last night in town and you've paid more attention to your laptop than you have to me. I cannot—can not—go hang out with my sister and her goofy husband again, bro. I will *lose* my mind. Let's go stare at some foxy ladies instead of you staring at your computer and me staring at the side of your head."

Connor stopped spinning so he could focus on his friend. His friend who was now sprawled out in the middle of Connor's living room floor, arms and legs spread wide as he did his best impression of a starfish.

"Isn't that fashion show thing over already?" Wesley asked the ceiling. "What are you even working on now?"

It took Connor a bit of internal debate before he spoke. He hadn't voiced much of this out loud. "You hear about what happened out at Edgar Henbane's place?"

"Duh," said Wesley, who had yet to move from his splayed-out position. "Everyone's heard about it. Not every day a pack of kids from this boring little town ransack and vandalize a dude's house. They set his *and* Amber's car on fire, bro. You know I love a good arson story."

Connor rolled his eyes. "Doesn't that story seem a little odd to you? Why would kids go way out there to do that? It's not like the house is easy to get to; you have to know it's there to find it. No witnesses. No kids in town talking about it. And then the same night *that* happens, some guy comes out of the woodwork to confess to the murder of that maid? Did you hear someone saw Edgar Henbane drop the murderer off at the station?"

That made Wesley sit up. "Wait, really? They knew each other?"

Connor shrugged. "I don't know. And then that 'insect attack' at the fashion show? More BS. Something weird is happening around here, Wes. And I hate to say it, but Amber Blackwood is tied to this stuff one way or another most of the time."

"Willow's foxy sister?" Wesley asked, then blew a raspberry at Connor. "What are you even saying? What do you think she's up to?"

"I don't know yet," Connor said. "But I was talking to Heather Miller yesterday about what she saw during the supposed insect incident, and somehow we got on the topic of the Blackwoods. She said she had this really weird experience over at Mews and Brews where she was in the bathroom at the same time as this blonde woman she'd never seen before. She leaves, and the second—I mean the very second—she leaves the bathroom, the woman locks the door. Heather had forgotten her cell in there, so she kind of loitered around outside

340

for a while, thinking maybe the woman needed privacy. The door unlocks, Heather goes to open it, and bam—who does she see? Amber Blackwood."

Wesley blinked at him.

"Different hair, eye color, clothing …" Connor said. "The blonde had been the only other person in there."

"Wig? Contacts?" Wesley asked.

Connor shook his head. "Heather said it was like it was two different people. Even their voices were different."

Wesley stared at Connor for a long moment, then laughed. "Bro. What are you even saying? You think Amber is a shape-shifter or something?"

Well, it sounded ludicrous when put that way. Connor sighed.

Maybe Wesley was right. Maybe Connor had been working too hard; the fashion show had ended up being his most involved Edgehill story to date. A break wasn't a terrible idea. He reached forward and slapped his laptop closed.

"Sippin' Siamese?" Connor asked.

Wesley hopped to his feet, clapped twice, and then pointed finger guns at Connor. "*That* is what I'm talking about!" Then he darted off toward the back of the apartment, presumably to change.

Still, even as Wesley's incredulous laugh echoed in Connor's head, he couldn't shake the feeling that he was onto something here—something big.

Resolve solidified in his chest. Something about Amber Blackwood was off—it always had been. He'd chalked it up in the past to her being the older, mysterious sister of the girl he'd had a thing for since freshman year. But he'd had little niggling thoughts about her lurking in the back of his mind for as long as he'd known her. After the last two months, those thoughts and whispered rumors he'd heard for years were becoming harder to ignore.

As he pulled on his jacket and cowboy boots and followed a cheerful Wesley out of his apartment, Connor smiled to himself.

He had his next story.

And her name was Amber Blackwood.

About the Author

Melissa has had a love of stories for as long as she can remember, but only started penning her own during her freshman year of college. She majored in Wildlife, Fish, and Conservation Biology at UC Davis. Yet, while she was neck-deep in organic chemistry and physics, she kept finding herself writing stories in the back of the classroom about fairies and trolls and magic. She finished her degree, but it never captured her heart the way writing did.

Now she owns her own dog walking business (that's sort of wildlife related, right?) by day … and afternoon and night … and writes whenever she gets a spare moment. The Microsoft Word app is a gift from the gods!

She alternates mostly between fantasy and mystery (often with a paranormal twist). All her books have some element of "other" to them … witches, ghosts, UFOs. There's no better way to escape the real world than getting lost in a fictional one.

She lives in Northern California with her very patient boyfriend and way too many pets.

Her debut novel, *The Forgotten Child*, released in October of 2018. She is currently fast at work writing both the Riley Thomas mystery series, and the Witch of Edgehill series.

You can find out more about her upcoming books at: https://melissajacksonbooks.com

AcknowlEdgEmEntS

As always, I have to thank my growing beta-reader army. Love you guys! Thank you, Mom, Krista Hall, Margarita Martinez, Brandon Moore, Christiane Loeffler, Jennifer Laam, Lauren Sprang, Garrett Lemons, Lindsey Duga, Tristin Milazzo, Julianna Taylor, Jacynthia West, Jasmine Warren, Kara Klemcke, April Newton, Sophia Arnold, Bobby Lewis, Mary Studebaker, Samantha Lierer, Kimberly Ann Shepard, Kirsty Lawson, Jesika Olson, and Stefan Anders. And thanks again to Courtney Hanson for your epic cheerleader skills. SSDGM forevah.

Thank you, Maggie Hall, for these colorful, witchy covers. I want to come up with a new series idea ASAP if only so you can design more covers for me.

Thanks to Michelle Raymond for the cat-filled formatting. And for dealing with my neuroses. You're a saint.

Thank you to Justin Cohen for being such a great nitpicky proofreader. You're so lightning quick and fun to work with.

Thank you to Drew Clark for the lovely family tree. It was great fun working with you and I hope we can do so again.

Brittany. Girl. Thank you. One day we'll figure it out, right? Ha. Chad, you're a cat-pun master. Keep 'em coming!

Thank you again to Victoria for bringing Amber and all the kooky residents of Edgehill to life. It's been great working with you!

Thank you to Sam for putting up with my crazy writing (and editing) hours. Thank you for taking care of the domestic stuff and helping me hold down the business. Thank you for the *Overcooked!* breaks even though it fills us both with rage. You're still my favorite, I like your face, and I love you to bits.

Finally, thank you to my readers! Whether this is your first book of mine or your third, I'm so glad I get the opportunity to share my stories with you.

Thank you for reading *Pawsitively Cursed*! If you enjoyed this story, please consider leaving a review. Reviews mean the world to authors. Reviews often mean more sales, and more sales means more freedom to write more books.

Continue the series with:

Pawsitively Secretive – December 2019

Pawsitively Swindled – March 2020

Pawsitively Betrayed – June 2020

Other books by Melissa Erin Jackson:

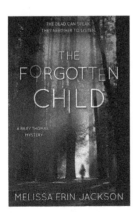

If you're looking for a slightly darker tale, consider *The Forgotten Child*, a haunting paranormal mystery starring a reluctant medium.

The dead can speak. They need her to listen.

Ever since Riley Thomas, reluctant medium extraordinaire, accidentally released a malevolent spirit from a Ouija board when she was thirteen, she's taken a hard pass on scary movies, haunted houses, and cemeteries. Twelve years later, when her best friend pressures her into spending a paranormal investigation weekend at the infamous Jordanville Ranch—former home of deceased serial killer Orin Jacobs—Riley's *still* not ready to accept the fact that she can communicate with ghosts.

Shortly after their arrival at the ranch, the spirit of a little boy contacts Riley; a child who went missing—and was never found—in 1973.

In order to put the young boy's spirit to rest, she has to come to grips with her ability. But how can she solve a mystery that happened a decade before she was born? Especially when someone who knows Orin's secrets wants to keep the truth buried—no matter the cost.

Available at Amazon, Kobo, Barnes & Noble, and iBooks. Now available as an audiobook, too!

CPSIA information can be obtained
at www.ICGtesting.com
Printed in the USA
BVHW031227061220
595044BV00027B/183

9 781732 413474